FAMILY
CRYSTALS

Amber Vorda

FAMILY CRYSTALS

~ BOOK ONE ~

AMBER VONDA

atmosphere press

PROLOGUE

McCleary, Washington was one of those token "small towns" that America boasted. With a population of barely one thousand people, not one stoplight could be found to halt traffic on the tree-lined roads, crime was nonexistent, and in town, one grocery store that wasn't even half the size of a typical Walmart was the only shopping option for McCleary citizens. Much like a location that was surrounded by high walls and a moat on the outside, all was quiet. They remained unencumbered, unaffected by the rest of the world...until a pandemic erupted that invaded even McCleary's steadfast silence.

Spreading across the lush, green scenery, the sickness blazed like an out-of-control forest fire. An illness that brought death and pain...turning an area of beauty into one of confusion and terror.

But, oddly enough, while the world was in fear of this

virus—for one family in McCleary, it would end up being the least of their worries.

CHAPTER I

What a shame. Angela gazed longingly out the window. Here it was, Christmas morning, and there was no snow in sight.

As her entire family gathered to celebrate yet another holiday, she remained in her own familiar world, wishing there was more to life than her hometown. Being thirty-two and not once ever traveling outside McCleary was as depressing as always. She wanted a little excitement in her life. It pulled her down like an invisible anchor wrapped around her neck. Having one failed marriage on her resume, and currently in a successful one—although it had its problems—everyone would say, "Angela, just enjoy what you have already accomplished. Don't long for more."

Well, she couldn't help it. It's not like her life was miserable. After all, she had a beautiful home, a reliable car that was able to comfortably fit all of her incredible children, and an adoring, somewhat needy husband. She should feel blessed...right?

"Mommy, Mommy," her son Liam tugged on her red and green Christmas pajamas.

Looking down at his cherubic face, Angela thought how lovely his blond hair was, even though it was badly in need of a cut.

"Yes, dear?"

"Can we open presents now?" he pleaded, hopping up and down in front of her, thoroughly excited.

Even though she wanted to cave, they couldn't open presents yet. She, Liam, and Angela's mother, Julia, were the only ones awake. She smiled down at him. "No, we have to wait for everyone else to join us so they can enjoy opening their gifts, too," she said in her sweetest tone of voice, hoping to avoid the tantrum he was sure to throw because he was told, "No."

Angela's daughter Bella was the next to wake up and straggle out of bed, along with Angela's niece, Sylvia. Bella was exquisite. Tall and thin, she possessed light brown hair that fell past her shoulders, bright brown eyes, and olive toned skin. She was also getting very close to passing Angela in height; however, seeing as Angela was around five feet, that wasn't a difficult goal to achieve. Her beauty was memorable, but poor Bella had already gone through so much in her twelve years of life by having to deal with her beloved parents' divorce. And now—Angela shuddered just thinking about it— she'd soon be hitting those teen years that involved nothing but angst for young women.

Sylvia, on the other hand, took after her own mother, Neveah. Gorgeous, she had jet black hair, her body was completely toned and in shape, and was already over the five-feet tall mark. Being two years older than Bella made Sylvia already a teenager and full of sass. She, too, had to deal with a father who was not very nice. He was a man who had made it clear that no one could ever measure up to his expectations. When he had decided to abandon Sylvia and Neveah, it was not a depressive time; in fact, since he had been gone, the entire family was able to enjoy life because they knew they wouldn't be constantly chastised by the maniac anymore.

"Good morning, gals," Angela said, smiling at the tired, yawning young ladies.

"Good morning." Sylvia smiled back.

"Morning, Mom," Bella grumbled. She walked towards the couch, hunched over like an old woman who'd lost her cane and was going to drop at any moment.

Without another word both girls flopped down on the couch, cellphones already in hand, completely prepared to wait until the rest of the family woke up to join them.

Angela sat there looking at the girls, shaking her head. *I wonder what they'd do if electronics ceased to exist and they no longer had a way to let the world pass them by.* She laughed a little thinking about it.

Neveah, Angela's sister, was the next to rise along with her son, Zackery. Standing a bit taller than Angela at five-foot-four, Neveah possessed lovely, caramel-toned skin and long, wavy black hair. Being thirty-seven and an exceptionally talented woman, she fought with her own self-doubts on a daily basis. She acted guarded most of the time, and when it came to getting a good night's sleep, for Neveah it was like asking the gods for a million dollars. Not ever getting enough of it was leaving dark circles under her eyes. Although, she did have every right to be that way, with an ex-husband who'd treated her terribly, it was going to take something big to make Neveah come out of hiding and leave the nightmares behind.

Sylvia, Zackery and Bella had moved on to sorting the Christmas presents and making piles dedicated to every beloved family member. All the kids certainly thought it was going to be just like every year, excited when a holiday tag appeared on a gift just for them. Liam, of course, was giddy, helping his elders every step of the way.

Sylvia picked up a present addressed to Bella and handed it to her. "This one's yours; it feels heavy," she giggled, lifting it with both hands and putting it in Bella's lap.

"Thanks," Bella said, taking the beautifully wrapped package and placing it with the rest of her gifts that were already piling up.

As Angela continued watching the children, with Neveah beside her already enjoying her phone, a noise came from her bedroom and out walked Arik, with Leah in his arms. Angela's heart filled with joy as she stared at Arik, her adoring husband, and Leah—their first beautiful child together. Six-years-old, she sported long, silky blonde hair that was impossible to cut. When Leah was only three, she'd been officially diagnosed with nonverbal-autism, and, to this day, did not tolerate anyone touching her hair.

"Good morning, dear," Arik said, walking over to his beautiful wife and kissing her on the lips. Placing Leah in her arms, he proceeded to walk to the recliner, sit down, and start sending out Christmas wishes to everyone on Facebook.

Angela remained silent. After all, she couldn't chastise the man seeing as that everyone else was addicted to their phones, too. Even Leah had the urge; although autistic, she was a true genius with technology.

Angela handed Leah her own phone, set her in the chair, walked to the kitchen and looked for the much-needed coffee beans kept in the top cupboard above the pot. To her dismay, they were out.

The adults got up from their seats at Angela's heartfelt groan and walked into the kitchen; Arik was already getting the pen and pad off the refrigerator to make out the list he'd have to get as he ran down to the local coffee shop.

"Can we open presents *now*?" the kids yelled in unison from the living room. Oblivious to the need for caffeine, they were focused on the only important thing in their unified world.

"Hold on," Angela called back, trying to keep the grumpiness from her voice.

Izak, Angela and Neveah's brother, was the last family member to wake up, apparently rising because his sister's voice had annoyed him just enough. The epitome of what most would call "a ladies' man," every friend they'd had when they were growing up had always chased after him, commenting that he was nothing short of "mouthwateringly gorgeous" every time they saw him. With his thick, jet black hair and caramel toned skin, even though he only reached around five-feet-eight and possessed a medium build, Izak's brilliant smile and amazingly alluring voice were among the gifts that caused women to go crazy.

Izak was also a wonderful brother. Highly supportive, it was hard to imagine him having a temper that could shake you from the inside-out and make your brain want to run for cover. It was heartbreaking that he had to struggle with his own internal demons that the world labeled as "addiction." The family continued to hope that one day he would come out of his subconscious completely, leave the drugs behind, and see the light of life once again shine in his beautiful eyes.

As the kids' fervor grew, the adults tried to clear their heads. They were exhausted from wrapping gifts all night and desperately needed that coffee. With a busy morning ahead, they required caffeine energy to conquer the day.

"Could you grab me some smokes when you go coffee hunting?" Angela asked.

"I suppose," he said, rolling his eyes, teasing his wife. He knew the line would be incredibly long and was not entirely thrilled about it, but Arik always wanted to make the family happy.

Angela smiled at him. Arik was a truly kind man. Of course, for those who didn't know him, they would be very intimidated by his physical appearance. At over six-feet, Arik was built like a Viking. Add in bright blond hair, a short, well-manicured beard, and a face decorated with a set of charming dimples that allowed him to produce a smile that could knock a woman off her feet, and it wasn't a surprise that Angela felt envy from those around her.

"Hey, everyone. Whatcha doin?" Izak said, making his way into the kitchen.

"We're ordering coffees, do you want one?" answered Neveah. By just looking at her brother, she knew he was high.

"Why do we have to wait for you guys to get coffee?" Bella interrupted, her voice bordering on rude.

"Shh, just a second," hushed Angela, as everyone shouted out their order.

As every instruction from 'triple shot' to 'frap' to espresso' to 'mocha' came at him, Arik wrote it all down, gave his wife a kiss, and headed for the door. "I'll be back."

Watching him drive away, Julia and Izak sat on the porch, playing with the dogs. Izak, instead of being a father to children, had four canines and was interested in breeding them. He looked at his mom, asking for advice on when the best time would be.

"I think you should wait until the females are over a year, past their first heat," Julia responded, trying not to look him in his bloodshot eyes.

"I agree."

* * *

The kids remained inside with Angela and Neveah. Playing on their phones, they fought the overwhelming urge to start tearing the wrapping paper off the boxes. Leah remained quiet, as Liam looked over Sylvia's shoulder watching her play a game.

"Sis, come look at some new jewelry I made," Neveah said

excitedly, walking out of the kitchen towards the living room table, and sitting down. Angela followed behind and slid down the bench seat to sit beside her.

"Sales have been nice, what with the holidays and all," said Neveah, pulling a black leather case out from the drawer of the table, and presenting the charming display of rings, neckless charms, and earrings of all different colors and shapes to her sister.

"Wow...these are all so beautiful," exclaimed Angela. "You're really talented. I'm glad you started this business."

"You really think so? Thank you," Neveah beamed with joy. "Oh...I also got some new crystals from that little street fair we went to in Seattle a week ago." Neveah proceeded to tell Angela about the intriguing stand, and the odd woman named Arianna who ran the place that sold gems, stones, and crystals.

When Neveah finished telling Angela the story of the gypsy and the crazy experience she had there, Angela noted that her eyes seemed to glaze over and her voice grew deep. "Ever since I got these though, my dreams have become even more... vivid."

"What does that mean?" Angela asked.

"It's...I'm in a different realm, with all sorts of unknown creatures. The land is beautiful, Angela, with a huge castle right in the middle of it." Neveah shook her head, "I know it sounds crazy, but there are new things I see that are completely unrealistic."

Angela waited a moment, taking it all in. Finally, she smiled. "I think that's cool. Who knows, maybe the chick was a gypsy after all," Angela said teasingly. Although she didn't really believe in that kind of stuff, she was happy her sister had finally found *something* to be excited about.

"I wish we could live there," Neveah said, using the same dreamy voice. "It seems so peaceful...so much better than the world here."

"So tell me about these crystals," Angela said, feeling a bit awkward.

Taking them out of the black box, Neveah handed them to Angela one by one, letting her study the amethyst and Tiger's eye before handing her the stunning Dragon's Heart crystal that the gypsy had raved about.

"I absolutely *love* this one," Angela remarked as the final, unique stone met her flesh.

As soon as Angela placed the glistening family of crystals back in Neveah's hand, the air grew still. Looking at the small decoration in the center of the table Angela could swear she saw the legendary reindeer's token smile contort into an evil sneer. As Santa's sleigh upended, the ground began trembling as if an earthquake was stirring beneath her feet.

Racing in from the porch, Julia screamed. "Quick, under the table! Take cover," Julia called out as she ran in with Izak, who was pulling Zackery behind him.

Angela jumped up and ran to Bella and Leah, pulling them both and pushing them under the table.

"What's going on, Mom?" Bella panicked, gripping Angela tightly.

"It's an earthquake, honey. It's okay...I've got you," she reassured the kids, using her strength to hold Bella and Leah firmly against her.

Sylvia followed the family's lead. After picking up Liam, she dove under the table to join her own mother.

Neveah, still grasping the crystals in her right hand, whispered, "Please protect my family. Please...please, protect my family."

The children had never experienced an earthquake before, and none of the adults had felt anything so powerful. Scared, huddling under the table, each offered up silent prayers to any god who was listening.

When the bright, blinding flash burst into the room, they shut their eyes tightly. Angela found herself wondering what god had shot the lightning bolt and who, *exactly*, they were trying to hit.

CHAPTER 2

Once the earth had quit shaking, Angela and her family looked at each other in wonder. As images raced through her mind...Arik on the road going to the coffee shop...the dogs outside...the house, itself, and what was still standing—the not knowing was the scariest thing Angela had ever felt.

"There's got to be some serious damage from that quake," she said, her voice cracking with the fear and anxiety she felt.

"I'll go look." Izak was the first one to climb out from under the table. "Wait here; I'll let you know if it's safe."

The group nodded their heads in agreement as Izak climbed out and began his scan of the house. After looking out the window, he announced: "Everything actually looks good, guys. You can come out now."

Slowly following his lead, Angela left the cover of the table and browsed the room...completely confused by the sight of it all. From what she could see, there was no damage done whatsoever. No windowpanes had been cracked. The dishes in the kitchen had not moved an inch. Even Santa's sleigh was back in its original place as the centerpiece of the table, and Rudolph looked as happy as ever. The family witnessed no aftereffects at all from the earthquake.

Neveah, joining her sister, looked down at her now empty hand, noticing for the first time that the crystals were gone. She suddenly shook her head as if thinking this had something to do with her dreams, but remained silent. It seemed she had no interest in her family looking at her like she was more than a bit odd.

The children, still trembling under the table, left the cover when they heard Neveah tell them everything was fine.

"Mom, that was *really* scary," Zackery cried, running towards her. She knew he'd be traumatized the most out of all the children because he was such a sensitive little boy.

Neveah held her ten-year-old close. Although the rest of the world saw Zackery as very athletic, which was only because his father wouldn't have it any other way, he was actually the shy, quiet type who just wanted to keep to himself. Zack was far more interested in video games and computers than football and wrestling.

"It's going to be okay, honey," Neveah said, continuing to comfort her beloved son. "It's all over now, I promise. You don't have to be afraid anymore."

"Okay," Zack replied, resting his head on her shoulder.

"Why don't you go sit at the table with Sylvia and Bella while we figure out what's going on."

"Fine."

Neveah watched her son sulk back to the table. In her mind, she pleaded with the gods listening that everything *was* really okay.

"Oh, no! Where's Maui?" exclaimed Julia, running outside to look for him.

Julia's pit-bull, a short-legged, grey and white, round dog had been playing outside with Duke, Angela's chocolate heeler pup, when the quake had begun. Hoping both dogs were unharmed, Angela raced after Julia, calling out for them.

"Duke," yelled Angela. Sounding devastated, already thinking the worst, she screamed again. "Where are you?"

"Maui, Maui," Julia hollered.

In seconds, the canines ran out from behind the barn in distress. Whining, with their tails tucked between their legs, Maui and Duke raced past the women and straight through the open door of the house.

"Well, I guess the earthquake just scared them," Angela said as a wave of relief shot through her body. As they stared at the barn and the property before heading back into the house, the feeling of amazement was shared by them both: All appeared completely fine. The barn was upright, no trees had fallen over, no branches had even snapped, and the cars were in the same condition as they were before Mother Nature released her wrath on McCleary.

Walking back into the house, they remained completely bewildered. "All of it looks the same," Angela announced in a voice that was barely a whisper.

"This is *so* strange," Julia agreed, peeking in her bedroom for both dogs and finding them hiding under the bed. She closed the door to let them sleep.

Angela watched Bella, Sylvia, and Zack talk about the tremors at the table, while Leah and Liam ran around playing with their toys. Leah stopped every once in a while to turn the light switches on and off, a particular routine she always did when she was bored. Only this time, there was no electricity when she switched them on.

Julia noticed right away. "The lights aren't turning on. I'll hit the breaker," she said, walking to the box in the laundry room, opening the door, and flipping the lever up and down. "Nothing's happening."

"Must be a side effect from the earthquake," Neveah said logically.

"Weird," Izak mumbled under his breath. "We just had the biggest one ever, there's nothing out of place or knocked off the counters, but we don't have electricity?"

Angela snorted. "Maybe the aliens were sick of the New Mexico desert and wanted some rain," she said, causing the kids to laugh.

Izak turned and glared at her. "I happen to believe in aliens, and if we were in fact abducted by them, I doubt you'd be poking fun at the situation." He turned back to peer out the window, not saying another word.

Angela stood there. "Sorry," she mumbled. "I shouldn't have joked in a situation like this." She hated apologizing for her personality. It was a fact she tried to keep a sense of humor in any situation; it was the one thing that could be relied upon to relieve the actual stress and fear she and the kids were feeling right now. She couldn't shake the anxiety, knowing that it wasn't possible to have an earthquake of that magnitude and not incur any damage at all. Something very mysterious was going on.

"The water still works," Bella announced, as she filled a glass at the sink and walked back to the table. Her smile faded. "But our phones aren't working," she added, "They're completely dead."

Julia pulled her phone from her pocket; hitting the buttons, the screen remained solid black. She stared at Angela and Neveah in distress, "I'm going to drive over to Daniel's and make sure they're okay, too," Julia said with fear in her voice. "Dan and Kat should have been here by now."

Daniel, Julia's ex-boyfriend, was taking care of their granddaughter on his side of the family. A shorter, muscular man, Dan suffered from severe selfishness and an egotistical personality disorder, two reasons why he'd been left by Julia.

Unfortunately, Katherine had to stay with him, only

getting to see Julia a couple of times a week. Dan had promised to bring her over this Christmas morning, however, for Julia to enjoy.

"Mom, could you go through town and see if Arik's okay, too? He should have been back by now."

"Of course, honey," Julia reassured her before grabbing her truck keys off the counter.

"Thanks, Mom."

Just as Julia was about to walk out the door, Izak came out of his room; the token cigarette hung from his mouth. "Going into town, Mom?"

"Yeah. Did you wanna come?"

"Yeah," he replied, tightening the belt on his pants.

Opening the door, Julia and Izak heard what sounded like a huge cat fight playing out inside the barn.

* * *

"Quiet, you filthy felines," whispered Arianna, annoyed with them for making so much noise that they could easily bring people running into the barn and expose her.

The three barn mousers lived on the property, and they were obviously not enjoying this recent visitor at all. It was as if they could feel the gypsy's dangerous energy; it emanated from her and they clearly were letting her know she was not welcome on their turf.

Doing her best to hide from Neveah and her family, Arianna grasped the charm around her neck and began to chant, "Metamorfónomai ailouroeidís!" Before the mousers could blink, their female visitor quickly turned into a cat as black as midnight right before their eyes.

Arianna now stood on four paws, her back raising in anger as she hissed at the others, frightening them away so they wouldn't blow her cover. The powerful chant had quickly exhausted the magical energy of the sapphire, sapping

Arianna's own energy and causing her to fall down on the cold, concrete floor of the barn.

The cats offered one loud hiss as they departed.

Julia stuck her head in the doorway and screamed out, "Hey, knock it off in there," before walking to the truck and joining Izak.

* * *

"I swear, Mom...something doesn't feel right," he said. "That was no ordinary earthquake."

"I know," was the only response Julia could come up with.

Julia also felt a little depressed as she climbed in the driver's side of the nice, new pickup truck. She'd been so excited to drive it, yet when putting the key in the ignition and turning it, the motor remained silent. "Great. It's dead."

"What do you mean, it's dead? You just got this truck," Izak said with annoyance. "Did you leave a light on or something?"

"No, I left nothing on."

He offered a dramatic sigh. "Well...let's see if we can take Neveah's car."

Izak and Julia opened their doors to head back to the house.

"You go ahead. I'm going to have a smoke." Izak told his mother before walking over to Neveah's car and leaning up against the door. "It's not aliens. It cannot be aliens," Izak said nervously to himself, trying not to lose his cool.

Julia went back inside. "My truck won't start. Can we take your car?"

"Sure, Mom," Neveah said, handing her the keys.

Julia walked back outside. "Ready?"

"Yep," Izak replied. Flicking his cigarette, he opened the door and got in.

When Julia sat down beside him, she somehow knew the

end result would be the same. Something was wrong; the interior light didn't flash on inside the car when the door opened. But, just to check, Julia turned the key and found out that the car had suffered the same unexplainable fate as the pickup.

Going back into the house, her voice filled with worry, she told Neveah, "Yours won't start either."

"This is bullshit," Izak followed his mother in, yelling. Looking highly panicked, he stormed into his bedroom and slammed the door shut behind him. Acting like a child, he ended up frightening the real children, sending them running over to their parents.

"Scary," Liam cried, running up to Angela and hugging her leg.

"What's wrong with Uncle Izak?" Sylvia and Zack asked their mother.

"Why is he so mad?" Bella added.

Angela and Neveah stared into each other's eyes, trying to figure out what they were going to say. In the end, of course, they knew that they couldn't say anything about Izak that the kids didn't already know.

"Uncle Izak is mad because the cars are dead and he can't go to town," Angela said first, thinking he had every right to be upset now. Things were getting overly weird, and she knew he didn't like it.

Neveah interrupted her thoughts. "He will cool down soon and come join us in a little bit," she said to the kids. "Can you guys play with Liam and Leah while we talk to Grandma?"

"Yeah, okay," Bella and Zack replied, shuffling over to the living area to play with the younger ones.

Leah handed her tablet to Zack.

He shook his head. "I'm sorry, Leah, it's not working. See? It's dead," he said, holding it up to her so she could see the screen remained black.

Leah let out a cry of temper and stuck her thumb in her

mouth, running over to the couch and burying her head in its cushions.

"What's going on, Mom?" Sylvia whispered. Being older and more mature than Bella and Zack, she noticed that her family was once again wearing their overly concerned faces.

"We don't know...but we're going to figure it out," Neveah told her daughter in all honesty. "Please go join the others; the adults need to talk."

Sylvia walked out of the kitchen and laid down on the floor with the other kids.

Angela, Neveah and Julia sat at the table, discussing the next steps they should take.

"We should walk down the driveway and see if we can find help," Angela suggested.

"We could at least ask the neighbors if they're having issues with their electricity, phones, etcetera," said Neveah.

"That's a good idea," Julia agreed. "But we should tell Izak before we go."

Deciding to take the kids along, wanting to make sure they were away from Izak until he calmed down, Angela walked outside and got the little Radio Flyer wagon set up for Leah and Liam to sit in. She let out a sigh. Whereas most people were happy to take a stroll, Angela knew it would be a trial. Kids were always difficult to maintain, and Leah, being autistic, brought a further challenge because she definitely did not like to "stay close" to her mother. She loved wandering around far more. On the other hand, Liam—being just too little to keep up with the rest of the family—was a bit easier. Thankfully, he loved the wagon.

"Everyone ready?" Julia asked.

"Yeah, let's go."

As if the question had been asked to the world, a choir of birds suddenly burst into song from every direction. Looking up, they stared at two beautiful bald eagles perched atop the barn roof. They were joined by a murder of crows cawing from the branches of the alder tree, and two ravens sitting on the electrical pole above. The unusual trait the birds shared was that they all seemed to have their eyes focused on the family.

"That is so cool," Bella said.

"Is it just me, or does it look like they're all staring at us?" Sylvia asked.

"Look at that gorgeous bald eagle," Neveah said, pointing one out.

"Wow," Julia spoke. "Look at those ravens. We have some serious luck coming our way."

Neveah smiled. She knew what her mother referred to. In the spiritual world a belief that ran rampant was that if a raven stood upright on a pole, it was a good omen; if it hung upside down, it was bad luck.

As the rest of the family remained staring at the congregation of birds outside, Angela walked to her brother's room and knocked.

"What?" Izak yelled, as he swung open the door.

Angela took a deep breath. "We're taking a walk to get help, or ask the neighbors if they're having issues, too."

"Fine." Turning and grabbing a smoke, he followed Angela outside before lighting it.

Although upset that he felt the need to come along, Angela stayed quiet and followed him out to the porch. When they stepped outside, the birds scattered, flying away in different directions.

"That's awesome," Izak said, watching it all play out.

"Beautiful," Angela agreed.

After watching the birds soar, the family started walking from the steps to the end of the driveway.

Being the first to reach their destination, Izak yelled, "What the fuck? No...no...no!" Visibly frightened, he wrapped his arms around his head and turned back towards them.

"What is it this time?" Neveah asked, already trying her best to curb the annoyance she had with her brother. Running ahead of them at bit, Neveah saw the scene Izak witnessed and felt her heart catch in her throat. There was no road past Julia's driveway. In fact, there was nothing but grass as far as the eye could see. Even the familiar houses of her neighbors had disappeared.

"Mom, what's going on?" Angela asked anxiously. She stood beside her, holding up her hand to the older kids behind her so they would halt in place. She didn't want them to see this.

"I don't know. This isn't...right. This isn't...it can't be real," answered Julia, fighting her own distress.

Neveah said nothing. Turning the kids around before they could take in the landscape, she rushed them back to the house as quickly as possible. She tried her best to show no fear, even though she was quite literally scared to death.

"I thought we were going for a walk," Zack complained.

Not replying, completely lost in her own thoughts, Neveah pulled the wagon even faster. All she wanted was to get the children back in the house, lock the doors, and hope that they would all be okay.

Izak paced back and forth. Throwing a new tantrum, he shot his swear words left and right, refusing to turn back around.

Angela and Julia simply stared at each other in shock, both wondering where the hell they were; or, even worse, where the hell everyone else had gone. Their jaws dropped for what seemed like forever, until a strange noise met their eardrums and a burning wave of hot air struck them from behind.

Upon whipping their bodies around to see what the source was, time stopped. Completely paralyzed with terror, they came face-to-face with a creature found only in legend.

CHAPTER 3

Before the trembling had begun, Arianna had been keeping a close eye on Neveah. Ever since the woman had left her stand in Seattle, all Arianna had been able to concentrate on was the last words she'd heard Neveah speak: "I can't wait to show these crystals off to my family on Christmas."

Once she'd announced her plans, Arianna had made sure to be near at all times; she had to be for her plot to work. Gathering up all the ingredients for the potion, including Neveah's own blood that she'd gathered at the stand when the woman had pricked her finger by mistake, she proceeded to pour the combination over her large sapphire crystal. Staring at the charm, she watched Neveah come into focus.

Arianna watched every turn she was taking, until she'd pulled into her mother's driveway. The witch had then known her destination, and after witnessing the scene, Arianna packed up necessities for the trip, walked to her car, and headed to McCleary with an evil smile of joy on her face. She'd been waiting a long time for her journey to begin.

Driving through the small town, Arianna had pulled into the small drive-thru of a coffee shop. Parking in line and waiting for her turn, she took note of the van pulling up behind her. Looking in her rearview mirror, eyeballing the driver, Arianna couldn't help but stare at the attractive, large man inside. Appearing to be on his phone and smiling, she took in the strong man's beautiful smile offset by dimples, the thick, blond hair, and lovely white skin he possessed.

"Goodness," she whispered. "That man could actually make me want to stay in this awful world." Continuing to daydream, not realizing she'd made it to the window, Arianna jumped when the lady inside started talking to her.

"Sorry...what did you say?" asked Arianna. "I was... distracted."

The lady kept her completely fake customer service smile in place. "I just asked what I could get for you this wonderful Christmas morning, Ma'am."

"Oh...yes. Could I get a sixteen-ounce, white chocolate with caramel, triple shot hot, please?" Arianna asked. "I have a busy morning ahead of me and need the energy."

"Well, I won't keep you waiting then. That will be five fifty, please."

Arianna handed her six dollars and eventually drove off with her drink.

At her next destination, Arianna had pulled into Julia's driveway and quickly headed into the field, attempting to stay away from any prying eyes inside the house. Heading to the barn on foot, through the swamp, Arianna had only been on the property for five minutes when the earth began to tremble.

Startled, a pair of canines came running straight at her, frightened by the sudden movement. Deciding to comfort them while it continued, she kept her eyes wide open to witness the blinding flash of light she'd been waiting an eternity to see.

* * *

"Merry Christmas. What can I get for you today?" the coffee specialist asked the next customer in line.

"Good morning," Arik replied, handing the barista a piece of paper with all the coffee orders on it so he didn't mess anything up.

"Oh, that's so strange."

"What's strange?" asked Arik with a smile.

"The lady in front of you asked for the same order as this one," The woman read one of the requests on the paper out loud.

"Oh, yes, that's my wife's favorite. The lady who left must have good taste, too," laughed Arik.

She smiled, turning around to work on the drinks. "Any fun plans today?" The girl asked, as if finally happy to see a handsome man at her window.

"Yeah, just picking up coffees and heading to my mother-in-law's house to open presents with the family."

"Well, that does sound like fun," she responded, a little depressed at the news of a wife. She sent a shot of espresso into the drinks that required them.

It didn't take long before the barista was finished and ready to hand Arik the order. "That will be twenty-five-fifty, please."

Arik handed her his debit card while taking the drink carrier in return. Signing the receipt with a five-dollar tip, he said, "Merry Christmas," before driving off.

When he turned down Main and then took the road Julia

lived on, the van suddenly wobbled beneath him.

"What the...hell?" Arik kept his eyes on the road at the bridge up ahead. As his shaking swerved from the tar to the gravel, a bright flash of light burst through the windshield of the van.

"Ahh!" Arik yelled, covering his face with his arm.

Losing control of the vehicle, the van banked to the right and went over the side of the bridge, landing in the creek below. The front end crashed into the dirt bank, pinning Arik's right leg between the seat and the dashboard. His head connected with the driver's side window, knocking him unconscious.

* * *

Earlier, Papa Daniel watched Kat wake up and eat her Christmas breakfast quickly, eager to sit in front of the Christmas tree and open the colorful gifts waiting just for her.

"Papa, can I open my presents now?" Kat asked.

"Let's get Uncle Jonathan first," replied Dan before yelling down the staircase. Below sat another living room adjacent to his son's bedroom. "Jonathan! Come open presents with me and Kat."

"Okay, be up in a second," Jon yelled up the stairs.

At almost forty-two years of age, Jonathan had still never left the nest. Not many could blame him for that, of course. After all, who in their right mind would leave a mansion you lived in for free, had no responsibilities whatsoever, and whose life was focused on smoking pot all day, every day?

Jon was loud coming up the stairs, jumping every other step. Looking up at his father waiting at the top, he stopped when Dan raised his finger to his face.

"Your eyes are blazing and you smell like a skunk," Dan fumed. "I do not want Kat to see you like this. Go back downstairs, put in some eyedrops, and go spray yourself with something."

Instead of breaking into another argument that they both wanted to have, the men just glared at each other.

"Fine," Jonathan said, stomping back down the stairs.

Dan stood there, watching him until he was out of sight, then went back into the living room to sit with Kat.

"Is Uncle Jon coming?" Kat asked in an excited voice.

"Yeah, he'll be up in a couple minutes," Dan answered irritably.

It wasn't long until Jon arrived and walked directly to the living room, ready to celebrate Christmas with his father and Kat.

"Good morning, Jonathan," Kat said with a smile. Everyone who knew Kat, knew she loved her uncle. In fact, she spent a great deal of time wishing Papa and Jon wouldn't fight so much.

"Good morning, Kat," Jon replied.

"You can open presents now," Dan interrupted, slightly sickened by the respect Kat showed his son, considering what he did...and didn't do.

As Kat reached for the first present, the ornaments on the tree began to clink and clang on the branches. Everything was suddenly shaking. As the colored Christmas lights blinked on and off, Kat screamed and threw herself into Papa's arms.

Reacting instantly, Dan picked up Kat and took cover under the large oak table with Uncle Jon. Both men wrapped Kat under them and waited for the earth to stop moving. Suddenly, what looked like a flash of lightning erupted, and the earthquake came to a halt.

Dan looked down at Kat's frightened face. Pale as a new snowfall, her eyes were as wide as golf balls and full of tears.

"It's okay now, honey," Dan said reassuringly. "The earthquake is all done."

"What's a...an earthquake, Papa?" Kat stammered.

Jon thought fast. "An earthquake is when the earth gets so

excited, it starts laughing." Dan shot a warning look at Jon. "The earth just laughed so hard that it made the entire world shake. It's probably excited over Christmas."

Jon had tried his best to take the fear from Kat with his lie, even though Dan despised telling tales. Thankfully, it worked.

"Maybe someone told a joke and the earth thought it was funny," Kat said.

Both Dan and Jon started laughing as Kat's innocent voice turned the stressful situation into fun.

"What do you say we get out from under this table and open those presents?" Dan said.

"Yeah!" Kat said excitedly, jumping up and running to the tree. Stopping short, she stared at the tree now laying on its side on top of the gifts. "Uh, oh."

"It's okay, Papa and I can pick it up," Jon reassured her.

The men righted the tree with no problem and Kat proceeded to tear through the wrapping paper, opening presents one by one. Toy after toy, clothes for dress-up, make-up, Play-Doh, and so much more gave her thrills. After the treasures were all opened, Kat turned her focus to heading out and going to celebrate with all the other kids at Julia's house.

"Can we go to Grandma's now?" Kat asked pleadingly.

"Yes, of course," Dan replied. "Let's get you dressed first."

"Yay," screamed Kat. "I want to wear a pretty Christmas dress."

Doing just that, Kat picked out a lovely red and white dress and put it on. Grabbing her shoes and coat, she ran up to Papa. "I'm ready to go now," she said, standing in front of the hand-carved doors that led outside to the fancy set of steps.

"Okay, let's go," Dan agreed, grabbing his coat and heading out the door. Carrying Kat down the steps, he strapped her in the back in her car seat, and headed to Julia's.

He knew they were running late, seeing as they'd slept in and opened presents at the house first. Thankfully, he lived in a huge log house in the next town over from McCleary, and the entire trip would only take about ten minutes to complete.

Driving over the familiar bridge, not noticing the strange skid marks that seemed to disappear off the edge, Dan drove around the corner, slamming hard on the brakes. "Oh, my god," he whispered. Julia's land had completely disappeared. Slowly pulling closer to where her driveway should have been, he stared into a huge, black pit.

Spotting Maria and Thomas standing on their own front porch, staring in disbelief at where Julia's property should have been, Dan pulled into their driveway and parked in a spot where Kat wouldn't be able to see anything from her viewpoint.

"Stay in the car and play on your tablet. I need to talk to the neighbors really quick," he told Kat.

"But what about Grandma?" Kat whined.

"Just stay in the car; we'll be at Grandma's in just a little bit."

Dan got out of the car and walked over to them. "Do you know what...what happened here?" Dan stared at the pit and tried to keep his voice calm.

"Oh, my gosh...there was a big earthquake...then a tremendous flash of light coming through our windows," Thomas replied. "When it was over, we walked outside and saw...*that*."

"I think it might have been an asteroid," Maria said with sadness in her voice, allowing a couple of tears to escape.

Getting a bit nervous, wondering if he'd parked far enough away to keep Kat from seeing any of this, Dan pointed behind the house. "Do you mind if I park my car over there? Kat is in the back seat and I don't want her to see...or ask questions I can't answer."

"Yes, of course."

Dan started walking back to the car with his phone in hand. Dialing Julia's number, it went straight to voicemail. After repeating the process five times with the same results, Dan started crying.

Being a strong, masculine man, Dan wasn't someone people would ever catch shedding tears. But even with all the problems he did have that made it impossible to be with Julia, he still loved her as much as possible...in his own way.

* * *

The strange squeal of brakes and the thumping of wood above his head had brought Arik awake. Reaching up slowly to touch his head, he felt the wetness and stared down at the blood that now adorned his fingers. In an attempt to wipe off the blood onto his pants, he suddenly realized his leg was stuck. It didn't feel broken, but it was definitely bruised. Placing a hand on each side of his right thigh, he tried to pull his leg free. Once successful, he started searching for a way out of the van.

"Fuck," Arik mumbled to himself when he tried the driver's side door, and found it wouldn't open.

He could maneuver himself over the center console to the passenger side door, but that one wouldn't open either. Lifting his non-injured leg, he kicked against the windshield, causing it to fall over in one enormous chunk.

Scrambling over the dash as carefully as possible, he freed himself from the confines of the vehicle. Struggling to climb up the bank of dirt and make it to the road, he finally started limping toward Julia's house. As the pain grew with each step, he became sure that he'd had to be driven to the hospital as soon as he got back to the family.

Making it around the corner, he suddenly noticed that Julia's always familiar line of trees was absent. As his pulse began to race, anxiety replaced the pain and Arik took off running. Making it to the end of Julia's driveway, a wave of panic enveloped him and he fell to his knees.

"What? No," Arik sobbed as he shouted. Retching, he suddenly heard a familiar voice.

"Arik? Is that you?"

Feeling a moment of relief, believing they'd survived whatever this was and had run across the street to safety, Arik turned. Like an object had once again hit his head, he faced the tear-filled eyes of Dan.

"Please tell me they're with you?" Arik and Dan asked each other simultaneously.

"We have to call the police," said Arik quickly.

Dan tried to think fast. "I have to take Kat home and then I'll come right back," he replied. "Can you get the police here?"

"I don't have my phone. I was in a car accident...from that flash. I ended up under the bridge; I think the phone's still under there," Arik said.

"I won't be gone long." Dan handed him his own phone, walked back to his car and started driving Kat home, hoping she witnessed nothing along the way.

"Why are you so sad, Papa? Are we going to Grandma's now?"

Dan had already figured out what he was going to say to Kat. Right now, being that he had no idea what had occurred, he couldn't tell her the truth. "Grandma is in the hospital with the virus, so we won't be able to see her for a couple of weeks." Dan believed telling her that was best. Considering what he'd seen, it would also make her less sad until the day he had to lie once again and tell her that her grandma had died from the virus.

"Can we call her and tell her we love her?" Kat begged.

Dan stared at the little girl's face in his mirror and his heart sank. All he could remember were those same stunning eyes looking up at him in pain when she'd lost her parents in a tragic car accident just two years ago. "No, she's sleeping right now, honey. We'll call her tomorrow," he replied.

* * *

Arik dialed 9-1-1 from Dan's phone and a dispatcher answered immediately.

"9-1-1, what's your emergency?"

"My entire family is...gone. There's nothing but a big, black...pit where the house used to be," Arik sobbed, knowing he sounded like a person suffering from lunacy with the words he spoke.

"Sir...where are you? Do you know where you are?" the dispatcher asked.

"5683 Elmer Hickerson Road in McCleary, Washington. They're all gone...everything's gone," Arik repeated.

Feeling more than a little disoriented, Arik started repeating the same things over and over again. He reached up to put his hand on his head, feeling a small amount of fresh blood still seeping from the wound.

"Sir, what's your name? What do you mean by, 'they're all gone'?" the dispatcher asked, typing in the address and notifying the nearest McCleary police officer of the location.

"There's nothing but a *huge, black pit.*" Arik uttered these last words in a weak voice before fainting. As he fell to the ground, the phone cracked on the asphalt beside him.

CHAPTER 4

Angela and Julia remained frozen in fear, unable to do anything but stare at the enormous dragon. Sitting on the property before their very eyes was the animal that was seen only in fairytales. As it stared back at them with a pair of huge, flaming eyes, they could feel the anger and disgust that radiated from the glossy scales that covered its body like a blanket.

Gorgeous and frightening at the same time, it possessed a wide, extended green chest, and long neck that reached the tip of the treetops. Its angular head was adorned with a green snout that changed to a turquoise color, before ending in royal purple at the tips of the spikes sticking out. The image was crowned in colors that flowed like hair, making it scary enough to face Medusa's own gaggle of snakes. The wings had a span easily measuring a car length each. Four huge legs with sharp, curved claws, and a long, spiky tail ending with a spear that could plunge through a human body like a gigantic stingray rounded out the package.

Izak had quit pacing and now gaped at the fire-breathing beast. "What are you doing? Run!" Izak screamed, as he ran back towards the women.

Finding their voices, Angela and Julia screamed and turned to run back to the house. Before Angela could get a few steps, the dragon lifted its wings to fly above them. Swooping down, extending his sharp claws, he snatched her up by her legs. She screamed while hanging upside down in the air.

Julia attempted to grasp onto her arms before the dragon could fly away, but Angela's body, coated with the cold sweat of fear, slipped right out of her mother's grip.

"Mom! Help me!" Those were her final words as she was carried out of sight.

"I'll find you, honey. I promise!" Julia yelled back, her voice fading in the wind.

Taking hands, Julia and Izak raced back to the house.

"Neveah!" Izak yelled in distress as he made it to the porch.

Neveah flung open the door, shutting it solidly behind them. "What's wrong?" She watched her mother and brother, holding their stomachs, sobbing with pain and fear. "What the hell happened?" Neveah instantly felt the tears come before she even received an answer. The fear was already overwhelming her body and soul.

"Angela's gone..." Julia said gasping for air.

"A *dragon*," Izak chimed in, attempting to complete his mother's explanation, "*a fucking dragon came out of nowhere and grabbed her! It just...flew off with her!*"

"What?" Neveah's brain was scrambled as she wrapped her arms around her mother and held on tight.

"I'm going to get her back," Izak said immediately. Opening the door, he ran toward his room, apparently ready to pack for the journey he had just vowed to take.

Julia and Neveah followed him. Neveah continued to grip her mother, walking Julia into her own bedroom to lie down beside Maui.

"It's going to be okay, Mom. I'll tell the kids...something." Neveah had no idea what her plans were, but she tried to reassure her mother as she shut the door behind her.

She turned to the children standing in the doorway with questioning eyes. Leah and Liam were absent from the group, sitting in their highchairs now while they ate the peanut butter and jelly sandwiches that she'd given to them as a treat for suddenly canceling their "walk" outside.

The questions came fast.

"Where's my mom?" asked Bella.

"Why is Grandma so upset?" Zack asked.

"Something *else* happened, didn't it?" Sylvia shouted.

Neveah wasn't entirely sure how to answer any of them. Deciding the truth would be best, she encouraged the kids to follow her into one of the empty rooms so she could explain.

"Well..." Neveah couldn't even think about it without her eyes filling with tears.

"A dragon came, swooped down and flew away with her," Izak interrupted, stomping out of his bedroom and joining them, with only one mission on his mind. "I'm going to get her back."

"A *dragon*? Like a...a *live* dragon?" Zack gasped, pale as a ghost.

"No! What's going to happen to my mother?" Bella wept.

"Oh, my gosh! Is it going to eat her?" asked Sylvia, looking like she was going to throw up.

Sylvia's question sent Bella into a waterfall of tears.

"Shut up, Sylvia," bellowed Izak. "No, Bella, it will *not* eat her! If it were going to, it would have done it right in front of us!"

Neveah watched her brother. She knew that Izak honestly believed his words and she hoped they were all true. Besides, if it turned out that thing's intention was to have her sister for lunch, she knew Izak would spend the rest of his life hunting it down.

Ready to go, backpack on, Izak grabbed enough food for his travels and walked to Julia's bedroom. When Izak opened her door, the poor, crying, grieving mom was not the sight that met his eyes.

Throwing things into her bag, completely angry at the world and holding a long rifle in her hand, Julia shouted, "Let's kill this mother fucker!"

"You got another one of those?" asked Izak.

Julia nodded and grabbed another rifle from the cabinet, handing it to Izak.

"Ready then?" asked Izak, anxiously waiting.

"I'm ready. Let's go," Julia replied.

Heading to the door after telling Neveah the plan, Izak reached out for the knob. Suddenly, a knock came from the outside.

"Who could that be?" Julia whispered. Carefully raising her gun, she aimed at the door and whatever stood behind it.

* * *

Angela moved further and further away from the ground, as the dragon gained height, escaping over the trees and into the clouds. It certainly had no feeling for the woman screaming within its grasp, or for the humans crying and screaming to bring her back.

Angela finally stopped screaming. She spoke, as if somehow believing the mystical creature could understand her words and feel some kind of sympathy for her. "I don't want to die, *please*! I have children, I have a husband, I have a family that needs me!"

Letting his claws open in midair, the dragon sent her falling to meet her death. But when her noises ceased, it swooped down and reclaimed her with its claws. The dragon was more than happy that the human had fainted and fallen silent on her way down.

"At least *that* shut you up," the words came from the dragon's mouth as he continued on his way home.

The enormous castle, attached to a cave that served as a dungeon, sat atop the highest peak of the mountain range.

Landing in the huge yard in front of the monstrosity, the dragon set Angela in a bed of grass. Transforming into a man, he picked up the female and carried her to the dungeon. Dropping her on the cot that sat behind a wall of bars, the man slammed the steel door, transformed once again, and flew away.

* * *

Julia and Izak continued to stare at the front door, wondering who or what stood outside.

"Open it," Julia told her son.

Taking in a deep breath, Izak whipped open the door to set eyes on a trio of muscular men standing on the threshold. Each adorned with long, black hair that was braided to their knees, their skin was as dark as coffee beans. Clearly all related, their handsome faces stared back at him with ebony eyes.

"Who the hell are you?" demanded Julia, pointing her gun directly at their forms. "What are you doing on my property?"

"Hello. My name is Atticus," the biggest of the men spoke slowly; calmly. "These are my brother's, Declan and Leo."

"Okay...what do you want?" asked Izak defensively.

"We have come here because you are new to our realm," explained Atticus. "The ground shook and now this house... your land...you are all here."

Julia's eyes widened as she slowly aimed her gun back at the floor. Thinking quickly, she suddenly knew that if they wanted to get Angela back, they would have to listen and learn everything they could about their mysterious location before dismissing the three men.

"Wait here," Julia ordered. "Let me speak to my family before we hear anything else."

They nodded their heads in agreement as Julia shut the door.

She and Izak returned to the dining room where Neveah was sitting.

"We need to talk to you." said Julia.

"Who was at the door?" asked Neveah.

"Let's go in my room."

Instructing the older kids to watch the little ones, the adults headed into Julia's room and shut the door behind them.

"What's going on? Who was at the door?" repeated Neveah. She already felt completely in the dark; she had no idea what else she could possibly handle. One of the darkest thoughts running through her head was the fact that she had experienced dreams that were remarkably familiar to what they were going through now, but she was still too scared to mention it. Worried her family would be mad at her, blame her, or simply not believe her, Neveah kept the information to herself.

"Three big men are at the door saying that we're in their 'realm.'" Izak said oddly.

Julia told Neveah everything that they'd said, and that they were still outside waiting. "After everything that's happened today, I think we should listen to the strangers in order to try and figure out what the hell is happening."

Neveah agreed. "Okay...let's go outside and hear what they have to say."

Opening the door, they watched the kids step back from their attempt to overhear what the adults were saying. Leah and Liam remained on the floor, oblivious to the strangeness happening all around them.

"We're in a different *realm*?" Sylvia spoke first.

"Where there are *dragons*?" asked Zack.

"Are they going to tell you how you're going to get Mom back?" Bella's words were filled with sadness.

Julia answered all their questions by stating that she would ask the men outside. And that finding Angela and getting her back was the first question they needed to address. Walking to the door, they opened it, stepped out, and closed it behind them. They would tell the children everything once the answers were attained.

The older children ran to the door and pressed their ears to the wood.

* * *

Angela woke up slowly, sitting up very carefully on the strange cot beneath her. Her thoughts were scrambled inside her mind, as the vision of the recent past suddenly exploded in her memory. Realizing the last thing she saw was the ground rising towards her as she fell to her death, released from a dragon's talons, the scream rose inside her throat. Looking around, scanning her location, she stared at a dimly lit dungeon; her body was surrounded by bars and walls of rock. Standing up, she grasped the bars and attempted to pull. Shaking them with all her might, her fear grew as the bars refused to yield.

"HELP! HELP ME!" Angela yelled at the top of her lungs. "Is anyone there? I don't belong here!"

The tantrum continued...minutes seemed like hours within the dungeon's walls. Losing her energy, she sat back down on the bed and hung her head in her hands. Nothing but horrible thoughts attacked her from within. Her children... were they okay? Was she ever going to see her adoring husband again? Was her family coming for her, or did they think she was already dead? Was it really a *dragon* before her very eyes? Before getting completely lost in her thoughts, Angela heard a loud door from somewhere up above her clang shut, followed by loud footsteps stomping down the wooden staircase she could barely make out in the corner.

Rising from the bed, Angela walked closer to the bars. As the intruder stepped closer, she could make out the face of a man. Eyes widening, she observed his stunning features. Tall, medium build, the stranger appeared very strong. His dark brown hair fell perfectly; his hazel eyes were adorned with gold specks that surrounded the pupils. Short, scruffy facial hair grew randomly around his chin, above his mouth, and along the sides of his high cheeks.

Angela, not able to stop herself, kept studying the man. When finally realizing this, she sent her gaze to the floor in embarrassment. Taking a deep breath, needing to get some answers, she looked back up and practically jumped at the look of anger and disgust on his face. Straightening her shoulders, Angela stepped forward again, feeling braver as she tried to channel her own mother's amazing strength. "What do you want from me?"

"I want to know how you got back here and who, exactly, helped you do it?" His voice was strong and firm, demanding an answer.

Angela focused on what the man said, yet she was completely dumbfounded by his question. Knowing that it was she who deserved some answers, Angela altered her attitude. Turning to the kind approach, she attempted to be nothing but a frightened lady. "What do you mean, 'back here'? Where am I?" she asked, completely clueless to the scene that was playing out before her.

"You can play dumb, Arianna, but you know I'm not stupid," he shot back, clearly irritated.

Her mind raced. "Why are you calling me Arianna? My name is Angela," she replied. The truth dawned on her immediately. "Oh, my gosh...That's it. You have the wrong person," Angela stated, her body feeling lighter with relief.

* * *

He stood there quietly, examining the woman before him, wondering if her words could even be possible. Never in his life had he forgotten a face. In fact, he considered his perfect memory to be a power that he possessed. This woman had the same face as Arianna, yet...her innocence and strangely kind energy made no sense to him. Unnatural empathy, another power he possessed, hit him ten-fold. *It's not possible*, he thought. *There is no way two people with the same face would cross my path.*

Ignoring her words that seemed to be true, and his own senses, he spoke: "Well, if you're just going to lie, you can stay in here and rot!"

"Please believe me, sir," her words were pleading. "I have three children back home. I...I was taken by a dragon and brought here!" He watched the tears race down her lovely cheeks, as she continued. "I don't know who this Arianna is, sir, and I don't know where I am. I just want to go home!"

He despised being an Empath; he had no need or want to feel this woman's pain the way he was now. Every tear that fell down her face brought pain to him, as well. Needing to think, knowing that the day was fading outside and he hadn't eaten, he made her a promise. "I'll bring you some food."

He left this...Angela...in tears. This stranger, lying on a bed, tears falling...a woman who said with all honesty that she wanted nothing more than to be with her children.

That's all he wanted, too. Storming up the staircase, he disappeared from her sight.

* * *

Julia and her children faced the strange trio, wanting nothing more than to know where Angela was, and the name of the hell they'd been sent to.

Julia spoke, trying not to sound as strange as she felt while making her statement. "A dragon came and grabbed my daughter; it flew off with her. Do you know *anything* about this beast?"

The supposed brothers, Atticus, Declan, and Leo, stared at one another in silence. It felt to Julia as if they were reading each other's minds. Looking back at her as if they were trying to judge how much she already knew, Atticus spoke. "The *drakon* is a very important leader in our realm. I don't know why he took your daughter, but I'm sure he has no intention of hurting her."

"Then why would he take my sister, if he had no intention of hurting her?" asked Izak.

"Alister is a great drakon and highly respected. He must not know about you and took her to ask questions," Atticus replied with a smile this time, an attempt to let the family know this missing woman would be unharmed. His voice and manner worked a little, as a bit of anxiety and fear left the faces of Julia and her children.

"Alister is the dragon's name? Why do you call it a 'drakon'? And how is it possible that a dragon is a leader of men?" Neveah asked.

Julia watched Atticus observe her daughter, and immediately knew he was admiring the beauty and intelligence standing before him.

"The drakon can speak, just like you and I. Drakon is our language; we can speak many. I apologize that he took your sister without saying why," Atticus stated.

"What? That thing could speak and it said nothing?" Izak shouted angrily.

In tandem, the men's faces fell, turning from kind to angry at Izak's belligerent words. "I would advise you to hold your tongue, sir. Alister will not be spoken about as a thing!" The younger brother Leo reacted to Izak's statement, but Atticus stopped him from saying another word.

"That's enough," Julia interrupted the adrenaline-charged atmosphere. "We have questions that need to be answered. Are you going to answer them?"

"I will answer your questions," Atticus said. "I will also be the only one who speaks from here on," he added, glaring at his feisty brother.

"Where are we?" Julia asked.

"You are in our realm; it is called Drakous. The king and queen requested us to come here and see what's going on; they wish us to bring back answers, as well. Queen Tiana has also ordered us to bring back anyone we find. Would you mind?" Atticus' voice held a slightly pleading tone. "The king and queen can explain much more to you; things we are bound not to share."

"A king and queen," Neveah repeated, a bit nervously. "Do they live in a beautiful castle surrounded by a gorgeous blue ocean and golden sand?"

The face of Atticus grew a bit troubled. "Yes. Have you been here before?" The confused tone now ran through his words, as well. "Where, exactly, do you all hail from?"

"Earth. Why?" Izak asked.

* * *

Atticus and his brothers felt a shot of excitement run through them. Hearing someone speak of the realm called Earth was amazing. Up until now, they believed that all the stories about such a place were spun from nothing but myth...no more than a legend. They had grown up hearing about how the evil sorceress from their own realm had been banished there as punishment for the awful curse she'd cast that killed many people, while injuring many more.

Knowing what awaited these strangers, and now knowing why their daughter may have been taken, Atticus knew that they needed to get them to the palace as soon as possible.

"We know of Earth," he finally spoke, clearing his throat. "And we are sure the king and queen can help, as well as answer your questions far better than we can." Atticus stared at the sky. "It is getting dark. Will your family come back with us tomorrow to the palace?"

"Yes," Julia answered quickly, not bothering to bounce it off her son and daughter.

"Wonderful. Pack for the journey and we will return with a carriage in the morning for your family and belongings. It may be...some time before you return here, so I would bring all that you require. Fair well," Atticus said. Turning away from the family, the brothers walked down the porch steps, and disappeared into the trees.

Julia, Neveah, and Izak simply stood there, going over all that they'd learned. Sitting on the porch bench, they joined hands and each sent out a huge breath of air they'd felt like they'd been holding the entire time.

* * *

Angela woke to the sound of the steel door creaking under its own weight as it opened. She watched the man enter with a plate of food and a large cup of milk. Glancing at her, he set the items down and proceeded to place a bucket filled with white cloths on the ground. Angela watched him in silence as he set everything up.

Walking out of the cage, he locked the door, pulled up a chair that was resting against the dungeon wall and sat down in front of her, and stared.

"You don't really expect me to use that, do you?" Angela asked, pointing at the bucket.

He shrugged. "Yes, I do. Unless you want to just use the

floor."

She gasped. About to offer a snide remark, Angela opened her mouth but then decided to stay silent. Instead, she peered down at the food, listening to her stomach grumbling. Concluding she would eat the familiar food that certainly looked and gave off the delicious scent of barbeque ribs and potatoes, she took a bite and closed her eyes, letting the flavors fill her mouth. She released a small, blissful moan.

The man shifted uncomfortably in his seat as he continued to watch Angela enjoy the meal. She knew from the look on his face that she'd caught him off-guard, making him even more angry. Apparently, having the slightest attraction to her was appalling to him.

"So...I have decided. If you truly aren't who I think you are, you will tell me everything about yourself," he stated. "If you convince me, I will let you go in seven days' time."

"What? *Seven days!*" Angela almost choked on the food. "My family could be back home by then. They could leave me behind."

"Seven days!" The man repeated. "I will check and make sure what you are telling me is the truth, and monitor the others I find that are like you."

No one ever had the nerve to speak to him the way this woman did. He could not get over the kind, brave, stubborn personality she exuded; it was driving him crazy. Defying him, having the nerve to talk back—all of it was wrong. Then again, he was holding her captive, and no matter what feelings she brought forth, she *still* wore the face of his enemy.

"What about them knowing that I'm okay?" Angela asked, looking down at the floor with sadness in her voice.

"I will send word to the land queen, because that is where they will be," the man replied with words that were obviously odd to her.

Finishing her food, taking a drink of the milk, she brought the cup to her lips in an attempt to swallow it. But as he watched, the fluid came spraying back through her nose and out of her mouth in a rush.

"Oh, my gosh," Angela shouted. "That's warm. It's disgusting!"

Watching the milk fly, he could not stop his reaction. Bursting with laughter, he proceeded to laugh so hard that he began coughing. Catching his breath, he held his sides as they began to ache with humor.

As she watched him and listened to him, he looked up as a chuckle came from her throat and she joined in the fun.

Stopping to listen to the woman's laughter, he felt the warmth inside of him spread, admiring her instantly. With a smile so lovely, reaching all the way to her eyes, the feeling and emotion that swept him was suddenly too much to handle. He caught himself and soon replaced the face of an angry man.

"Why are you so mad at me?" she asked, once again returning to sadness.

He raised his chin. "You may not be Arianna, but you still wear her face. That one trait makes it impossible not to hate you with every nerve in my body."

"I'm sorry you feel that way," Angela said. "But I am not her. Whatever this Arianna did to you, it was not *me* who did it!"

Noticing his struggle as he sat before her, still dealing with the doubts in his mind, Angela rose from the bed, walked over to the bars and reached her hand between them.

"Let's start over," Angela said, smiling. She hoped that he would take her offering of peace. "My name is Angela McLean. What's your name?"

After what seemed like an eternity, he chose to ignore her extended hand, standing up and walking towards the staircase instead. Turning around before taking the first step, he addressed her. "You can call me, Your Majesty...of this entire realm."

With that, he walked up the stairs and disappeared from

Angela's sight. Stunned, her mouth hung open at his royal proclamation.

CHAPTER 5

"I need an ambulance," the police officer announced on his cell as he knelt beside the man lying on the asphalt. Putting his fingers on the victim's neck, he checked his pulse, noting signs of life. "I have a man who definitely needs a doctor here," he added, offering the address once again to the dispatcher.

Just as he heard the wail of the sirens and witnessed the flashing lights, the police officer spied the car following close behind the ambulance. He moved quickly as he watched the large man jump from the driver's seat and come running towards the scene.

The two emergency technicians worked fast, quickly securing the harmed man to a gurney, and carefully lifting him into their vehicle.

"What happened?" The stranger slowed down, shouting his question at the emergency personnel.

"Sir, you can't be here," the officer's voice was commanding as he raised his hand in the air.

"Wait, that's my...he's a member of my family."

"Sir," the officer continued, "What is your name? What is this man's name?"

"My name is Daniel Wilkerson. His name is Arik McLean."

"How did you know this man was here?"

"I was with him. I had to leave...I had a child with me...I didn't want her to see..." Dan struggled to explain.

"Calm down, sir," the officer interrupted, placing his hand on the obviously frightened man's shoulder. "When you left here, was this," he looked down at his notes, "Arik McLean awake?"

Dan nodded quickly, watching the EMTs inside the ambulance hook Arik up to a bag dripping some sort of substance into his arm. "Yes. I left him with my phone. I told him to call you...bring officers out here...because of that," he didn't exactly need to point at the gaping hole that opened only a few feet away of them, but he did.

He also pointed to Thomas and Maria who stood close by. "These are the neighbors. They were here."

Thomas stepped forward, explaining the quake they'd felt, the flash of light, and the black hole that once was the setting for their neighbor, Julia Carrier's home. They continued to quickly relate what they'd seen with Arik on the phone and then fainting on the asphalt. "His head was bleeding," Maria concluded the conversation. "It looked like he'd been in an accident."

The officer nodded, as if not quite knowing what to say about the tale he'd just been told. He stared over at the man named Daniel; he was basically hopping up and down in panic as he watched the ambulance doors close.

"Sir, I will need to ask more questions." He pointed to the vehicle. "But if you wish to head to the hospital with him, I can meet you there."

Daniel stared at him, realizing that the officer was giving him leeway to leave the scene. Not a surprise, considering the small town of McCleary rarely had any violence to mention. "Where is he going?"

"It's going to the ER at Pluto General Hospital," the officer replied, as another black car pulled in. When the doors opened, releasing more badges, they quickly went to work setting up a gate at the edge of the asphalt and posting caution tape all around.

"I'll follow."

He nodded. "I'll know where you are," the officer said, as if in warning. "I will be talking to you again soon, but Mr. McLean shouldn't be alone."

Shaking hands, Dan quickly jumped in his car to follow the flashing lights of the ambulance to the hospital in the next town. He prayed that somehow Arik would be okay.

* * *

Rushing into the ER, the doctors and nurses on call took over instantly from the hardworking techs. The scene was a mad one, to say the least. Completing an EKG on Arik's head to test all activity within, upon discovering the swollen state of his brain, they concluded it would most likely be at least forty-eight hours before Arik would be opening his eyes.

The topnotch crew proceeded to patch up his forehead, with stitches and bandages, and wrap his leg, doing their absolute best to heal the wounds the man's accident had granted him. After securing a room for their new patient, all that was left was to wait and see how the next step would go.

* * *

Dan ran straight into traffic on his way to meet Arik at the hospital. Finally arriving, frustrated that his own fancy car couldn't keep up with the ambulance, he burst through the doors of the ER, halting at the front desk.

"Excuse me, ma'am, I'm looking for my son-in-law," he stated quickly, knowing that only a family member would probably be able to see him. "He was brought in here with a head injury," he explained further.

"Yes, sir. And what is his name?" she asked.

"Arik McLean."

"He's being placed in room twenty," she replied, handing him a clipboard. "While you wait, if you could fill out as much information as possible about Mr. McLean, it would help. I will also need some identification in order to print you out a visitor's badge."

Dan reached in his back pocket and pulled out his wallet, handing her his license.

Placing it on her scanner, the lady produced a badge that would allow him access to the room. Pointing to the waiting area, Dan sat restlessly trying to fill out data he really didn't know. Watching the clock move slowly, he finally heard the front desk lady speak: "Walk down this hallway, sir," the lady pointed to the right. "Go seven doors down; the first door after the restroom on the right-hand side is Mr. McLean's room."

"Thank you," said Dan. "Could you please notify the doctor that I'm here? I would like to speak to him."

"Of course, sir."

Following directions, Dan stopped at room twenty and opened the door. Walking in, he quickly observed the fact that Arik had already been well taken care of. Laying there in the hospital bed, completely unconscious, the clean bandages were apparent on his forehead, as were the odd-colored wires adhered to his skull, monitoring his brain on the beeping screen of the machine placed beside Arik's bed.

"Can I help you?" Dan jumped as a doctor in a white coat walked through the open door.

"Yes," Dan sighed, trying to calm his own pulse. "I'm Dan

Wilkerson, Arik's father-in-law." He reached out and shook the doctor's hand. "I followed the ambulance here when they picked him up; I've been waiting out front. Is he okay?"

The doctor shook Dan's hand and then proceeded to tell him what they'd found. "He's okay, at the moment. He has suffered a head injury and is currently in a comatose state. We will know more in a couple of days, once the swelling goes down," explained the doctor. "Do you know what happened?"

"I had arrived at my..." he stopped, struggling to find the right term to explain Julia and the situation he'd found. He suddenly felt ill admitting the woman he loved, who'd now disappeared, had been an "ex" in his life. The beeping of the monitor brought him back. Swallowing his grief, Dan looked back at Arik's lifeless form on the bed. "He was talking to me a few hours ago and said he had gotten in a car accident."

Dan proceeded to tell the doctor the tale of everything his family had experienced this Christmas morning. He also told him how they had no idea what had actually happened to their family.

Apologizing for their loss, looking at him with a very odd expression, the incredulous doctor wished him well. Telling Dan that he would be notified when Arik woke up, the next trauma call rang out over the PA system, calling Doctor James back to the ER.

After a moment of silence, Dan's shoulders dropped. He walked out of Arik's room, back down the hall, and out of the hospital to his car. Sitting in the driver's seat, he let the tears come. The feeling of hopelessness and loss was too much to bear. There was still so much to do, people to contact, and family members that would have to be told the unknown, unbelievable story of what the hell happened to Julia and her family.

Taking a deep breath, Dan put his key in the ignition and started the car. Halfway home to his town of Elmer, his phone started ringing. Peering down at the screen, he saw the name

"Paula." His heart sank a bit. Paula was one of Julia's older sisters, and they were very close. Considering she was calling him, Dan figured she must have heard something on the news or had been calling her sister to wish her a Merry Christmas. When her sister hadn't answered, it was logical that she'd try him as a last resort. Taking a deep breath and releasing a sigh, he hit the green button to answer.

"Hello."

"It's...it's all over the news. Tell me it isn't true; tell me my sister is okay! *Please* tell me that there was no one at her house," Paula sobbed, pleading with Dan for any good news he could offer.

"Unfortunately, it's true," stated Dan. "I really don't know what they're saying on the TV, but there was an earthquake here and—"

"They were showing pictures of the property...it wasn't there."

"Paula...that's true, too. I don't know how it happened. I just know they're gone."

Dan could hear her talking to others, most likely her daughter and son-in-law, telling them what he'd said. The sounds of even more cries wafted through the phone.

"Have...have you called anyone else?" wept Paula. "I'll call...everyone on our family's side, anyway."

"Thank you," Dan began, but stopped when he heard the click. Paula had already hung up on him.

Dan continued to his house. Arriving, he pulled into the driveway and stepped exhaustedly up the wood staircase. Opening the door, he went straight into the living room, where he passed out cold on the couch.

Struggling to wake up the next morning, he found himself with a stiff neck and what felt like an empty heart. His brain kicked into gear and Dan immediately dialed Arik's mother, Kaitlyn. She lived in Illinois, so he knew she was three hours ahead.

"Hello," answered Kate.

"Hi, Kate. It's Dan, Julia's...boyfriend," he said. "Arik's in the hospital, he's been in a car accident and fell into a coma."

Dan went straight through the story, telling Kate everything he knew about the earthquake, all the way up to the ambulance and how he pursued it to Pluto General Hospital. He concluded by letting her know her son's room number.

"My baby boy," Kate wept. "I'm on my way!"

"I'll see you here. Safe trip," he added, absent of any other words.

Next on Dan's list was to contact Bella and Zackery's father. Getting up and walking to the front door, he stepped out onto the large front porch and lit up a cigarette, desperate to find some kind of calm as he dialed Jason's number.

"Hi, Dan. How's it going? Everything alright?" asked Jason

The concern in his voice didn't escape Dan, but he wasn't surprised. Seeing as that he hadn't called Jason in a while, it made sense that the man would be worried to suddenly hear from him now.

"No, Jason, nothing's alright," Dan answered. "There was an earthquake. Angela, Bella, Liam, everybody is gone."

"What? What do you mean, 'gone'?"

Dan started relating the same tale to Jason that he'd told both Paula and Kate. All he could do was apologize, continuously, when he heard Jason crying uncontrollably on the other end of the line.

Dan waited, then said, "I would like to have a memorial... for all of them at some point..."

"Just let me know. I'm sorry, Dan, I have to go," Jason's voice was small and vacant, coughing and choking on tears before hanging up the call.

Dan took deep breaths. Delivering this news...not even knowing the whole story himself, was unbearable. He felt as if he was living through his own personal nightmare by breaking the hearts of others with only one phone call. He knew, lastly, he would have to call Neveah's ex. He knew Ricky was most likely working, but he had to try.

Dan knew this would be the most difficult one, not because he was worried in any way about Ricky's feelings, but because Dan had no desire to hear the man's voice. He, like most, simply didn't get along with Ricky, but as far as Dan was concerned, that didn't make Ricky the "victim" of the family. Ricky was more than guilty of mentally abusing his wife and kids for many years, and currently that information was coming out through a very expensive divorce process.

Taking a minute, Dan walked back into the house and poured himself a cup of coffee in the kitchen. Taking a seat at the big oak table in the dining room, he dialed Ricky's number. Dan felt more than a bit of happiness when it went straight to voicemail and all he had to do was leave a message.

When the beep resounded, Dan spoke: "Ricky, it's Dan, you need to call the McCleary Police Station; it's an emergency. It's about Neveah and the kids," Dan added to the answering machine message and hung up.

Sitting there, Dan listened to the slight ticking of the grandfather clock in the corner. He thought about all the times he'd mistreated Julia...all the things he had put her through during their relationship. He knew, considering his own background, that hating Ricky for doing the same type of thing to Neveah was something he had no right to feel. Watching the images fill his brain, reminding him of all the stupid shit he had said and done, Dan regretted every moment. He wished with everything he had for another chance to go back and change it all. Deciding right then and there, Dan vowed to at least be a better man in honor of the woman he still loved. After all, even though Julia was gone, he could still turn over a new leaf and become what his precious Kat needed him to be.

* * *

Finding the nearest nurse's station, Kate met up with Arik's doctor on his rounds. "Sir, I'm Kate, Arik McLean's mother," she said. "In room twenty."

Doctor James immediately offered a comforting smile. "Yes, ma'am. I haven't gotten to see him quite yet this morning. How is he doing today?"

"I wanted to let you know that he did wake up, but then fell back to sleep," Kate explained. "He said he can't remember anything since moving here from Illinois. That would roughly be the last seven years."

"Really? Well, it's not a surprise. Considering the swelling he had to deal with from the accident, it was highly possible for him to awaken with some form of amnesia. I'll put the nurses on alert and I will check on him when he wakes up again."

"Thank you so much, Doctor."

Turning to walk back to Arik's room, Kate stopped and decided to call Dan and ask him to come to the hospital.

Sitting on the chair just outside the door to Arik's room, she pulled out her phone.

Dan immediately picked up. "Hi, Kate. How's Arik?"

"He's good, Dan. He actually woke up for a few minutes and spoke," replied Kate.

"Thank god," Dan sent his relief over the line.

Kate continued, "I was wondering if you could come to the hospital later to talk for a bit. It's important."

"Yes, I could do that. When are the others coming?"

"They should be here soon."

"Okay. Give me an hour or so, and I'll get there."

"Wonderful. Thank you," she said appreciatively. "Bye, Dan."

"Bye, Kate."

Entering Arik's room, she walked to the couch and fell asleep.

The time for peace was short. Only a half-hour later, Kate was stirred by the pack of familiar voices.

David, Arik's sweet, wonderful father had arrived with Arik's sisters, Jennifer and Mary, in tow. After reuniting with Kate, they were just about to sit down when Arik began to stir. This time, Arik thankfully seemed to know exactly where he was, and began looking for his mother. Scanning the room, his smile grew wide as he was greeted by the entire family.

"Hey, everybody," Arik said happily, trying to deal with the eyes looking back at him, filled with tears.

One by one, not wanting to overwhelm him, they walked up to the bed and gave Arik a hug.

"You don't have to treat me like porcelain," laughed Arik. "I'm alright; I won't break." He gave a small snort and looked down at the brace and bandages wrapped around his leg. "Well...I suppose I can break if I really try."

"We know you're tough, son," David said with a wink.

"Stubborn is more like it," Jennifer teased.

It didn't take long before the happy family was laughing and catching up, even bringing up some wonderful memories that Arik had seemingly lost somewhere in his mind.

When Dan walked into the room, the faces literally fell. It was as if everyone knew that the time had come to tell Arik...everything.

"Who are you?" asked Arik, looking at Daniel.

Dan, uninformed that Arik had suffered memory loss, took a visible step back in response to the odd question. Wondering what to say, Dan took the most careful route and turned to Kate. "Can I speak with you?" asked Dan. "In the hall?"

Kate pasted her smile back in place and turned to Arik. "We'll be back in a second, sweetheart," she told her son. "I'll ask a nurse to put an order in to get you some food."

"Thanks, Mom," he replied. "I am hungry."

As the family marched behind Kate and Dan into the hallway, they closed the door behind them.

"Why doesn't Arik know who I am?"

"He just came out of a coma and the doctor believes he has amnesia," Kate answered, feeling a little guilty that she'd decided not to prepare him with the information over the phone.

"Why didn't you tell me?" asked Dan.

"I just wanted to talk about it when you got here," she replied, now feeling even more guilt at Dan's pained expression. "I don't know what to tell him."

"Okay, but do we really *need* to tell him? I mean if he doesn't remember anyway?" asked Dan. "I have to say, I wish *I* didn't remember, then I wouldn't feel like...this."

Grasping for straws, Dan looked at Arik's family to see their mouths now open in shock. They couldn't believe he would even suggest that.

"Alright, we'll tell him," Dan said, feeling completely defeated.

"We better," David said.

"Hold on. I have to get a nurse and ask for that meal order I promised," Kate said, walking towards the nurse's station.

"Hi," she addressed the first person she saw. "May I order some food for room twenty?"

"Yes, of course, ma'am. What does he want to eat?"

Not knowing the answer, Kate just ordered something normal. "How about a ham and cheese sandwich? If you have that? A tall glass of milk, fruit, with a piece of chocolate cake for dessert. Please," Kate added.

"Not a problem at all," the nurse replied with a smile.

"Thank you so much," Kate said, turning around to rejoin the rest of the nervous humans gathered in Arik's room, hating the fact they had to tell him about this horrible tragedy.

With the family circled around Arik in his bed, Dan began to speak.

"I'm Daniel Wilkerson. I was your...sort of your father-in-law."

Arik tilted his head, looking completely dumbfounded, as Dan continued with the help of Arik's family members who chimed in with extra information. They told him all about his wife and children, even remarking on how lovely the wedding was. They pulled out their phones and showed him pictures on their online accounts that he and Angela, his wife, had posted. They continued on, hoping for that moment when the fire of remembrance would erupt in the depths of his eyes. They told him about everything—from his beautiful new home to the job he loved, and everything in between.

When a nurse came into the room, they found a stopping point and stepped away, allowing her into the room to set down Arik's food on the extended tray table she moved across his bed.

"Hello, how are you feeling?" the nurse asked him.

"I really don't know." Arik replied in a ghostly tone of voice, while she checked his vitals.

"Well, I'm Nurse Betty and I will be taking care of you today," she said, smiling, placing at button beside him on the bed. "If you need anything, just push this and I'll be here in a jiffy."

Walking out the door, Arik felt a rush through his body. A loud ringing began in his ears and he had to blink his eyes hard to stop it.

"What's wrong, honey?" asked Kate anxiously, noticing the strange reaction playing out on his face.

"Nothing...I think. Something about 'jiffy,'" Arik said strangely. "Mom...I could smell coffee. My ears started to ring, but...it sounded more like steam releasing than bells ringing."

The family remained silent at his sudden announcement. Finally, Kate reached out and pat his hand. "Were going outside for a bit, honey. You've learned a lot in a short time...we'll get some fresh air and you need to eat," she said. "We'll be right back; I promise."

"Okay," Arik said, shaking his head. "I'll be here."

She smiled at the slight joke, then herded the family out the door.

* * *

Arik sat up in his hospital bed and ate his food. He was trying to make sense of what he'd learned, heard, and the emotions that were messed up inside him. He also worked to figure out what he'd just told his family...try to understand what memory had been triggered by the nurse's choice of words. He wondered if it was somehow related to this family of his. He had children, a wife, a home...everything he had ever wanted. He smiled just thinking about such a reality. Finishing the ordinary, but much-needed food, Arik sat back and began to daydream about what he had attained in his life.

Mary's voice broke through his thoughts. "Feeling better?"

Arik stared up at his favorite sister and smiled. He liked being able to speak with her alone, seeing as that Mary always had little to say around their mother because they didn't get along very well.

"Yeah," he said. "Well...you know me, as long as I feed this belly, I'm always good." He followed with a laugh, hoping he could erase the worry that shone on her sweet face.

The rest of the family returned to the room, quickly interrupting their conversation.

"Did you get enough to eat? How are you feeling? Does your head still heart?" His mother's questions shot out one after the other.

"Everything's fine, Mom," said Arik with affection. "But I want to hear the rest of the story. Please."

Arik turned to Dan and looked at him with pleading eyes. He wanted to know; of that, Dan was certain.

Dan stepped forward and explained how Arik was in an accident. He apologized, feeling bad now that he hadn't asked how Arik came to be in the car accident when he'd first seen him. Moving on, he told him about the black pit now replacing Julia's home and land. Dan's eyes filled with tears when he told Arik that the police had called and said, after their search, there was so far no sign of Julia's home or loved ones in the pit.

Arik's face went from pale to a burning, angry red color at his words.

"Do you want me to keep going?" asked Daniel.

"Yes," Arik responded through gritted teeth. "I need to know. I need to...get this over with."

Dan continued to tell Arik about everything that'd occurred, covering all the things Dan knew before and after the most powerful earthquake that'd ever been felt in this area hit. Dan spoke of the tremendous flash of light that apparently, from all the stories told by neighbors, had come from Julia's home. "Then, it was gone. They were all gone," Dan ended, completely exhausted.

"Everyone thinks it was an asteroid," Jennifer told her brother. "But there's no proof yet."

A stunned Arik, his eyes wide, registered everything his family had told him. Without another thought, he looked at his family and cried out in pain. Ironically, his tears came not because he could actually 'feel' the loss of the beautiful wife and children he adored, but because he couldn't feel it...any of it. In the blink of an eye, he'd lost everything he had ever wanted, and didn't even have memories to carry him through the darkness.

Arik just wanted to be left alone. He was tired. His brain was completely exhausted, and he just wanted to be able to go over everything in his own head.

"I'm sorry...can all of you please leave?" Arik asked, trying not to offend anyone. "You could stay at this house of mine if you want. Get cleaned up and come back tomorrow. Okay?"

Completely understanding, no family member was offended at all. Saying their goodbyes, Arik's family walked out of the room.

Arik laid in his bed, going over every word Dan had told him, recalling every picture and image his family had shown to him. He searched for the smallest memory he could find locked up in his head. He wanted to know his family; he wanted to know, feel, and mourn the ones he'd lost. And, above all, he wanted them back.

As Arik closed his eyes in an attempt to sleep, his doctor walked through the door and up to his bed.

"Hello, Arik. I'm Doctor James," he introduced himself. "Your mother tells me you have memory loss."

Arik felt his pulse begin to race, hoping that this medical man could somehow retrieve what he lost. "Yes. I can't seem to remember what my mother says is the last seven years of my life."

"She informed me of that, too."

"My mother can be very persistent," Arik said.

"That's a good thing, in this case. I would like to get you prepped for an MRI, to see if there is still swelling in your brain that's causing the memory loss."

"Will my life come back?" asked Arik.

"Odds are high it will, once the swelling goes down," replied Doctor James.

"I need it to."

The doctor nodded. "The nurse will come get you ready and bring you to the imaging room." He wrote notes on his clipboard, gave Arik a pat on the shoulder, and exited the room.

Arik slowly began to rise, needing to visit the restroom. Moving his legs slowly to a sitting position, he stood up, putting pressure on his limbs and using his left hand to brace himself on the bed railing in order to lift himself up. Halfway into his stance, Nurse Betty walked into the room.

"What are you doing?" her voice rose. "You can't get out of bed all by yourself."

"I need to use the restroom," he explained.

"That's what your button is for," Betty reminded him, speaking to Arik as if he was a disobedient child. "You need to call me."

Helping him up, Betty's well-toned muscles, gotten from years of working with patients who needed her, led him into the restroom. Once inside, Arik handled things on his own, but Nurse Betty, like the dedicated woman she was, waited right outside to help him back to the bed once his chore was complete.

Washing his hands, Arik finished and used the walls to get back to the dutiful nurse.

Stepping into the hallway, Betty grabbed the wheelchair she'd left there, and helped Arik into it. Wheeling him down the hall and into the imaging room, she helped Arik up onto the gurney that slid into the tunnel where the pictures of his brain would be taken.

The voice of a faceless technician entered Arik's ears through the small speaker inside the tunnel. "You doing okay?"

"Yeah," replied Arik, his body twitching from the claustrophobic space. "It's just hard for me to relax, so let me know when you're ready to take those pictures."

"I'll say 'now' when I need you to stay still," the tech instructed.

"Okay."

The distant sound of buttons being pushed on a computer met his ears, as Arik imagined the technician looking through the large glass window that separated them. When the computer had apparently connected and focused on Arik's brain, he heard the tech's order loud and clear. "Now."

Arik tried to stay still, but his body seemed to twitch and tremble no matter what he tried to stay calm. The differences he saw and experienced, even within his own body, confused him. He wondered if having a family and growing older had changed him somehow.

"Okay, you're all done. You did great," the tech announced. "Doctor James will study the scans and talk to you through the speaker before you return to your room."

Silence was all that could be heard in the chamber.

"Mr. McLean?"

No sound came from the chamber.

"Arik? Did you hear me? Are you okay?" Panic was audible in the technician's voice.

The silence broke as the door to the imaging room was thrown open and emergency personnel rushed in, finding Arik passed out on the gurney.

Doctor James, after studying his patient's face, stats, and the MRI image shouted to his co-workers: "Prep him for surgery. Let's move!"

CHAPTER 6

"Why didn't you tell me you were having dreams about this place?" Julia demanded, frustrated with her daughter.

"This is *exactly* why," Neveah said, now wishing she had told everyone sooner. *Of course, even if I had, what difference would it have made?* "They were insane dreams, Mom. How was I supposed to know they were going to come true? I wasn't sure how everyone would react anyway; hell, I didn't even know how *I* was handling it."

"Your brother's going to lose it."

"It's not like they give me information; I don't even know how it all works."

"Okay, okay...I guess it changes nothing," Julia said in a defeated tone. "Let's just keep your dreams to ourselves for now."

"Okay. Thanks, Mom."

Neveah was still feeling like all the pressure was centered directly on her shoulders.

"But keep me updated on your dreams. I don't know what to believe anymore," she added, before hearing Liam's little voice.

Liam came running out of his mother's room with a stuffed horsey in his arms.

"Where's Mommy?" asked Liam, hugging his comforting animal.

Julia remained quiet, wondering what they could say to such an easy question, when looking at from his point of view. Liam was too young to understand anything that was going on, but they still needed to tell him something.

"Mommy is at a friend's house," Julia replied. "We will see her later."

"What about Daddy?" he asked.

Julia's heart sank, not even knowing if they would ever see Arik again...or the rest of the family.

Thankfully, Neveah saved her. "Daddy has a long work trip. It's going to be a while until we see him again," she said quickly.

"Okay," Liam said, pointing at his highchair. "Eat?"

Neveah and Julia looked at each other and broke out laughing. At least they'd finally gotten an easy question. Of course what they were going to feed him was a bit of a mystery. They couldn't use anything electric, but they still had water from the stream in the backyard that, thankfully, had come with them on this surreal journey. By utilizing the wood stove, they could fill buckets and boil it on top in order to have the supply necessary to drink and cook food with.

Neveah was placing Liam in his highchair, running around and gathering any snacks she could find, while Julia began cooking oatmeal and eggs in a pan on the wood stove.

"Juice. Please? Show?" Liam pointed to the television set, as Neveah placed the snacks in front of him.

They still had juice boxes from the last time they'd gone shopping, so getting him the drink request was simple; turning on the set was going to be a different answer.

"Buddy, I'm sorry. The TV's broken," Neveah said. "I could read you a book?"

"Yay." Clapping his small hands, the excitement for 'aunty' reading to him was easily seen.

Walking into Angela's bedroom, Neveah went directly to the white bookshelf located under the bedroom window. Scanning the fun reads until she found one about puppies—the perfect book for a little boy who definitely loved dogs—she then walked back to him with book in hand, pulled up a chair and sat down to begin.

Julia was spending her time setting up six plates and bowls with oatmeal and scrambled eggs. She decided to eat with the family, unsure of what they would ingest at some fantastical castle they'd never even seen.

"Neveah. It's time to wake up everybody," stated Julia.

Neveah stood up, set the book down on her chair and walked back to the bedroom, softly shaking Sylvia and Bella.

"Time to wake up, girls," she said.

Met with only grumbling, Neveah smiled. She knew the girls were still tired. After all that had happened, they'd been too excited to fall asleep. They'd been busy talking about what they were going to do today, and what other amazing sights they would see.

"Ugh. What time is it?" Bella asked, still groggy.

"Is it even daylight yet?" Sylvia asked, while Neveah turned to shake Zack's shoulder.

"Yes, it is. Wake up. I don't know what time it is, but Grandma's got breakfast ready," announced Neveah.

"Good. I'm starving," Zack said, holding his stomach.

The trio rose, dragging their feet to the kitchen table where they slumped down to eat the breakfast that smelled extremely good within the confines of the house. Neveah followed along, retaking her seat.

"So I figured, while we're all eating, I could tell you what those men said yesterday." Julia continued to speak, trying her best to inform the children as calmly as she could about how they were in a different realm; how the men promised Angela would be just fine; and how the entire family was going to be traveling today to a beautiful castle. By the time she was finished, all three children were as excited as could be.

"My mom's going to be okay, then," Bella said with a smile, now wearing a mask of relief.

"We're going to an *actual* castle? We have to pack," Sylvia bounced up from the chair, wanting nothing more than to do her make-up and get dressed right away.

"Will there be other kids to play with?" Zack asked. It was hard being the only boy his age around, always wanting to make friends, so a new realm was perhaps exactly where he'd find some.

"Yes...to all of your questions," laughed Julia. "We will start packing as soon as we are all done eating."

Even though the adults in the room were still utterly confused, and a bit awestruck that they were now speaking about castles and other realms as if the subject was an everyday occurrence in their lives, the children spent the last ten minutes of the meal positively giddy about the journey.

* * *

This odor is hideous...

As Angela woke up inside the horrible smelling dungeon, now also fragrant with the sickening odor of warm milk encrusted to the floor, she wanted nothing more than to brush her teeth, shower, and feel clean, freshly laundered clothes against her skin. Her own scent filled her nostrils and she crinkled her nose, wincing in disgust.

She jumped at the sudden clearing of a throat. Shutting

her eyes and feeling like she was going to die from embarrassment, knowing the supposed so-called Majesty was watching her, she felt the heat of her skin rise. Turning around slowly, her gaze fell upon him...seated in the chair just a few feet away from the bars.

Instantly getting mad, she gasped, "How long have you been here? You could at least let me know when you arrive. What kind of a pervert are you, anyway, who just sits and watches me sleep?"

"I was hoping you wouldn't wake up today. Then I wouldn't have to listen to you complain."

"You're incredibly mean," yelled Angela, rising from the bed and walking to the bars, glaring at him between the poles of steel. "I still have done *nothing* to deserve this!"

"Well...you are in my realm without permission, so I consider that doing something wrong," he bellowed back. Rising from his chair, he met her angry glare with his own furious eyes.

Angela had made the decision to not back down. She was not about to give him the satisfaction he so obviously craved by allowing him to scare her anymore. Standing her ground, she looked him up and down. Feeling the smile begin to form on her face at his ridiculous historical garb, she began to laugh her ass off, choosing to do what she did best—turn to humor in a stressful situation.

And this time, she knew, she'd scored. Her laughter was infuriating him. Listening to the small growl emanate from his throat, she laughed even harder as he turned around and quickly disappeared up the steps to get away from her.

What she didn't know is that he was about to lose control. However, picking up a weapon wasn't where his thoughts were leading him. In fact, a cold shower was now what His Majesty needed in order to cool himself off.

* * *

Izak awoke and stormed out of his room. Not happy, without saying a word he began to search for something to eat. A couple of minutes went by before Julia interrupted his mini tirade.

"There's more food on the stove."

"Yeah." Izak grabbed a plate from the cupboard above the sink, and loaded it before turning and stomping back into his bedroom.

"Did you pack?" Julia asked, just before the door closed behind his retreating form.

"Last night," he screamed back. Izak wasn't feeling at all well. Julia knew from the familiar symptoms that he'd obviously run out of the drugs that kept him level, and was becoming more agitated with each minute that ticked by.

"You could eat with us?" she urged, desperate to break through Izak's infernal stubbornness.

"I'm good," he barked, slamming the door.

Without commenting on the all-too-familiar sight, the children got up and brought their dirty dishes to the kitchen, setting them on the counter next to the sink.

"Bring Liam with you and go pack as much stuff as you can. If Leah wakes up, come get us. We're going to see to the cats," Julia told the group, as she and Neveah opened the door and walked out to the barn.

Looking around for the felines, who still seemed to be in hiding, Julia opened the door on the motor home that she stored in the barn, yelling their names. Not noticing the presence of Pearl, Pumpkin or Kali—nor recognizing the slightly eerie aura of a stranger within her midst—Julia gave up for the time being and headed back into the house.

* * *

Arianna remained crouched down, hiding inside the motor home. She had heard Neveah and Julia yelling outside for the cats, and listened to their footsteps enter the barn. Nervous the entire time they were there, her heart had jumped to her throat when Julia opened the door and peeked inside the motor home. Thankfully, Julia had gotten tired of the search quickly, allowing Arianna's pulse to calm as she finally took a breath.

She knew she would have to move. She could not risk being discovered; if she was, all her plans would be ruined.

* * *

Neveah and Julia walked back into the house to find Sylvia and Zack were packed, and Leah was awake.

Bella had already put Leah in her highchair and started feeding her snacks and dry cereal; she was now in the process of reading her a Dr. Seuss book.

"Bella. Outstanding job," said Julia.

"We packed for Leah and Liam, too." Zack was proud telling them the news.

"And set it all in the kitchen," Sylvia added, pointing to the big mound of bags in front of the microwave.

"You guys are amazing," said Neveah, taking off her coat and strolling to Angela's bedroom to load up her own belongings.

She had little to pack, seeing as that she'd only planned on staying at her mother's house for a couple of days over the Christmas holiday. Throwing her minor wardrobe items and make-up into a bag, she went to grab the bathing necessities to toss in as well, not knowing what would be found at this castle in their future.

Julia followed suit, packed her bags, got dressed, and brushed her teeth with some water grabbed from the stove. When she and Neveah had finished cramming their things into sacks, they set everything in the kitchen with the children's belongings.

Izak came out of his room in silence, joining the family as they heard the odd sounds of horses pulling a wagon down their drive. Minutes later, when the knock resounded on the door, they knew their escorts had arrived.

* * *

Angela sat on the back-breaking bed of the dungeon listening to the man walk down the wooden steps. Presenting himself in front of her, Angela felt her anger refire at seeing him clean, showered, and looking very refreshed. That was what she wanted more than anything. Another thing that made him even more evil in her eyes was the fact that, cleanly shaved and sporting a new shorter cut of hair, made him even more handsome than he'd ever been before.

His Majesty simply stared at her sitting on the bed. She knew he was feeling pompous at the fact that she remained absolutely disheveled; her hair was a mess, clothes dirty, eyes dark with circles from being haunted by her dreams.

"Are you hungry?" His voice was calm.

Angela, stuck inside the depths of her own angry mind, didn't hear a word he said over her own internal seething.

"Are you going to answer me?" Irritation at not being acknowledged the first time crept into his voice.

"What? I didn't hear you," replied Angela. "I was thinking about my babies."

"Are you hungry?" he asked, his gaze now cast with an unmistakable flame of sympathy.

"Yes. I'm hungry *and* filthy." She looked at him, holding her stomach. "I would *really* like to get cleaned up."

"I'll bring you some food when I make it," he said. "I don't happen to be famished as of yet, so you'll have to wait until then."

"A *majesty* with no servants?" Angela asked sarcastically, wondering how much of this man's information was really a lie.

"I live alone!"

"But what about the dragon? Doesn't it live here too?"

"He," bellowed the man. "There is no such thing as 'it' when it comes to the drakon. And there will be no more questions asked by you. I am the only one allowed to bring about inquiries here!"

"What do you want to know?" whispered Angela in defeat. Feeling weak, she chose to remain on the bed and not fight the next round.

He could sense her frailty and it was making him oddly guilty. She wasn't sick, but everything about her seemed fragile, and he could feel the sympathy well up inside his soul, knowing he was the reason behind her break.

"You can start with where you come from," he said, while he thought about what he would do next. *Maybe I will let her out to eat and clean up.*

"Earth. Of course."

"Start from the beginning. Your place of birth. Your parents. Your family." He began to wonder if he sought her information out of need or simply wanted to know more about this woman who made his pulse race.

"That is a long story," she said. "But...I guess I have nothing but time." Sadness filled her voice as she told her tale.

"I was born in 1989, in Judy, Alaska. I had two brothers and one sister, but my oldest brother died as a teenager from severe head trauma. My other siblings never really cared much for me when I was little, so I was always alone. My father passed when I was two years old in a bar fight, so our mother moved us to McCleary, Washington. I never left the town or lived anywhere else. I met my first husband when I was young, working at a fast-food restaurant."

"What is this, fast-food?" he asked, not hearing of any location she'd spoken of so far with the exception of Earth. "How can food be fast...it runs after you?"

Angela felt like rolling her eyes back into her skull. "You order a meal and you get it quickly, very quickly; it's pre-made," she replied, rubbing her own hungry stomach once again, trying to drive home the point.

He simply nodded, yet looked more confused than ever. "Continue."

She sighed. "I had my first daughter at twenty and my last two with my second husband, Arik." She smiled as the faces of her loved ones formed inside her mind.

The man could literally feel Angela's mood change from one of weakness and defeat to pure happiness while talking about her children. He couldn't help but feel the twinge of jealously inside of him when she mentioned her family, for he had no one. ...Not anymore.

"I want to know how you got here. Do you have a sorceress or witch in your family?" he asked.

"There are no such things. I don't believe in that kind of stuff," Angela shook her head. "Of course, I also didn't believe in dragons, but that didn't stop one from snatching me up and carrying me here," she snorted, looking over at him. "By the way, how do you know the dragon is male?"

Instead of rising up in anger, he simply sighed, coming to the decision that he would at least offer up a little data on his own realm. As little data as possible, of course.

"Because he is. He's an important leader and a personal friend," he responded. "He told me everything about grabbing you, that you screamed and refused to be silent, so he let go of you and you fainted."

"Personal friends? Well, it fits. You're both heartless assholes," Angela shot back.

Although only understanding a part of the title she'd placed upon his head, he knew 'heartless' was a perfect description of what he'd become. But it wasn't like that from the beginning. Having love and kindness in his heart had been the norm at one time, until said heart had been broken into a million pieces, bringing about the destruction of both his personality and attitude.

"Tell me how you got into my realm. Now!"

"I don't know! And I'm not saying another word until I get food, a shower, and clean clothes. Please...you have to let me out," screamed Angela, grabbing the bars and pulling hard, already knowing they wouldn't give an inch.

"You don't get to make demands. I tell you what to do or say and you do it," he ordered.

"How could you be so unfair? What I'm asking isn't unreasonable." After staring at him, Angela said in a calmer tone: "Someone must have really done a number on you, for you to treat me this way. However, I think you're all talk. And, again, my lips are sealed until I get clean clothes and food," Angela said, turning away.

"You don't have permission or the power to turn your back to me, little one." He didn't know why he'd addressed her as such; the words had just appeared. She was small, though, he'd observed. Yet even on the shorter frame, she was strong and curvy in all the right places. Having dark brown eyes that were more than mesmerizing, with her back to him now, he also admired the long hair ending at the start of her well-toned hips that led to perfectly shaped buttocks and legs.

Clearing his throat, he headed for the staircase without another word. Fleeing up the steps, he heard the sobs coming from behind him.

"It's just attraction," he whispered to himself. He knew there was no way in hell he could actually like her; certainly not while owning the bull-headed, stubborn, and undermining personality she claimed. *Could it be that I find her intriguing?* He had no answer. All he knew was that her strength still put him over the edge...every time she opened her unforgettable lips.

* * *

Taking a deep breath, Julia opened the door to see Atticus standing there looking as handsome as he had the last time they'd met.

"Hello, Atticus," she said with a slight bow of respect. "Come in."

Atticus, offering a bow in return, smiled as he slowly walked through the door. It was evident he was both confused and amazed by his surroundings, having never seen anything like Julia's home before. He looked around at the faces of the eager humans standing in the kitchen and offered a smile to them as well.

"You are lovely," said Atticus, offering a bow to Bella. "What is your name?"

"I'm Bella. These are my cousins, Zack and Sylvia." She pointed to the left and right of her, making her introductions.

"And this is my brother and sister, Liam and Leah." She walked to pick up her brother in her arms, and pointed to Leah sitting on the floor.

"Well, it is a true pleasure to meet you all," Atticus said. "I love the serenity of children. I have three of my own, in fact, and I know they would love to meet all of you."

"Cool," Zack said.

"Is everyone ready to go?" he asked, addressing the adults in the room.

"Yes, but we couldn't find our cats. They usually roam outside the house, but they are hiding, most likely from the trauma of the...event. Could someone bring them to us later?" asked Julia, worried they might starve if someone wasn't left behind to feed them.

"Of course. I will tend to it personally," Atticus vowed. "I will have my brothers grab your things and bring them to the carriage."

"Thank you," said Julia.

Izak, not offering a word, started grabbing the family bags and carrying them outside. Securing bags on the back of the carriage, Izak lifted himself inside the slightly fancy wagon, taking the far side where he could look out the window on their journey.

The rest of the family was escorted out of the house and into the carriage. Atticus offered his hand to Julia and Neveah, helping them into the large, elegant seating area where Julia settled beside Izak and Neveah took the seat across from her brother. Placing Leah on her lap and Liam beside her, they were followed by Bella, Zack, and Sylvia, who spread out across the soft cushions beside Julia. It was certainly the carriage of royals, considering that even with all of their forms taking up the space, room still remained for the canines to join them. Atticus picked up Maui and Duke, one in each arm like they were light as feathers, and set them down beside the children. Finally taking his own place, Atticus settled in so he could answer any questions the family had on the way to the castle.

Julia watched the brothers of Atticus walk into the house. After reappearing with the remaining luggage from the kitchen, they loaded the rest on top of the carriage and tied everything down securely, making sure nothing would be lost along the way.

"Are you all ready?" asked Atticus, before knocking on the wall to signal the carriage could begin its voyage.

"Yes," the kids yelled in unison; the choir of voices was filled with excitement.

"Seems we're ready," Julia laughed.

The signal was given and the carriage began moving forward, bringing about the smiles of humans and the nervous whines of dogs. As soon as Julia's home disappeared, the eager eyes looked at the swath of green grass spread out for miles before them. As the familiar birds flew above them, the carriage seemed to follow the one enormous eagle that they'd found yesterday perched on Julia's barn.

"Anything you see or wish to know more about, feel free

to ask," said Atticus, not knowing he'd opened the door to an outburst of questions.

"Have you heard from the dragon? Anything about my daughter?" Julia was the first to speak.

"No one has seen Alister since your arrival. He has not been reached yet," replied Atticus. "I'm sorry, but I assure you, he *will* release her soon."

"I believe you, Atticus. Thank you." Julia took a deep breath.

Atticus hoped with all his heart that what he preached was the truth. Although, he couldn't help but wonder why Alister would've taken her daughter in the first place, let alone do it and then choose to not offer a word of explanation for his actions. He certainly wasn't known to kidnap people. Criminal actions or not, Alister always sought counsel from his friends and peers, and always had others do any questioning for him when the need arose. If he handled anything by himself, Atticus knew that it *had* to be personal.

* * *

Opening the steel doors, he set the plate of food on her little table and walked back out, uttering not a word.

Angela wouldn't even look in his direction. Laying there, with her back to him, she was still very upset. Apparently, they'd both chosen to invoke the silent treatment. As frustrating as it was, it seemed they'd both decided that enough had been said and yelled for the day. They would continue their battle of wills tomorrow.

When he exited the cell, Angela sat up in her bed to look at the food he'd brought in; it smelled absolutely delicious. Picking up a spoonful of the thick stew and bringing it to her lips, Angela felt utter bliss as the marvelous taste flowed down her throat. Engulfing it, like a starving animal who'd finally found succulent prey, Angela raced through the small, warm loaf of bread, as well. She scanned the very interesting piece of fruit he'd added to the tray. Big and fuzzy, she bit into it, releasing an obscene amount of juice inside her mouth.

"Oh my god, this is so fantastic," she announced to her now peaceful stomach.

Belly full, Angela felt energized. *Figures he'd leave*, she thought. *Now that I'm ready to go another round.*

* * *

Passing through the active forest, Julia and the children were thrilled at the sights that met their eyes. Pointing, they watched with awe at the little wolf cubs wrestling in the grass. The sweet pups stopped only to inspect the carriage from a distance, as if wondering who or what was inside.

"Look. They're so cute." Julia always loved wolves. The respect they gave, the lifetime partnerships they made, and the family aspect of how they treated their cubs were just a few of the amazing qualities their species possessed.

Julia caught her breath upon seeing the large adult wolf come out from behind the tree. In a way, it seemed as if all the natural activity in the woods suddenly stopped. She could feel the strength emanating from the creature, as if he was the alpha male that ruled the territory all around. A strange thought ran through her head...a voice...a moment that made her truly believe that the wolf was paralyzed by her presence. If anyone asked her, Julia would vow that she could feel the beast's heart skip a beat, and that his thoughts were actually telling him to not chase after her down the road. The animal was actually forcing himself to keep his paws firmly on the ground.

Neveah, not noticing her mother's odd silence, took in the scenery and noted the familiar looking bird perched on a large tree branch they were passing by. Smiling at the eagle, it extended its wings and retook its place up above, soaring over the carriage and leading the people on.

As the carriage continued, the scenery began to transform before their very eyes. What had been nothing but green, turned into a world of blue ocean waters and golden sand.

Sylvia admired the waves, watching the seagulls circle the beach. Gazing at the water, she jumped in surprise as a pod of dolphins appeared, interacting with each other, their familiar smiles adorned to their precious faces. She watched them jump in the air and back into the water, doing flips, issuing the familiar 'clicking' sounds as they played. Suddenly, the glint of gold caught her eye. "What is that?" she whispered to no one in particular. *No*, she thought. *It can't be.* But the longer she looked, she knew her eyes told no lies. The sparkling gold fin did, indeed, appear at the end of the green, glossy tail.

"Oh, my god! Is that a mermaid?" Sylvia shouted, pointing to the ocean.

After spotting the mythical entity, the family turned to Atticus with disbelieving eyes.

He smiled, seeming a bit confused by their incredulous expressions. "Well...yes. They keep to themselves, though. There's no need to worry."

"What? Oh, my god," Sylvia squeaked.

"How many are there?" an excited Bella chimed in.

"Are they nice?" Zack asked, trying to spot one.

"Can we meet them?" Neveah asked, her eyes wide open. "I mean...right now? Can we stop the carriage and you... introduce us?"

"You look doubtful," Julia commented. "Are you sure they're not mean?"

Atticus put up his hand to halt the questions. "I don't know how many are here," Atticus replied honestly. "I don't know a great deal about their society, in fact. But I am well aware that they have families, just like you and me. I don't know if they would be willing to meet all of you, especially all at once, because they generally stay away from land creatures. They have their own culture and royal beings; a king rules the waters in this realm. The only one who could introduce them to you, however, is the king of our entire realm."

"There's one above all the rest?" Julia asked curiously.

"Yes, but he doesn't present himself often. He may, however, because he knows all of you are here." Atticus remained secretive about this particular ruler. He had no other choice, especially under the circumstances.

After Atticus had answered their questions to the best of his ability, they continued their study of this new world, seeing if they could spot anything else they deemed 'unique' or 'magical.'

As the sun moved in the sky above them, the ocean gave way to field after field of fruits and vegetables. Huge gardens could be seen, with large trees bearing some of the biggest, most colorful berries imaginable.

"Yummy." Zack's stomach grumbled. "I'm hungry, Mom."

"Vegetables are *so* good," Bella said, surprisingly. Julia laughed, knowing that this had to be the only child to ever make that statement.

"I just want a big apple," Sylvia said, as famished as the others.

Having been on the road for hours already, Atticus sensed the family's need for sustenance would increase. Knocking on the carriage wall, notifying them to stop, he then helped the family step down into the road.

"Let's take a break and stretch our legs." Atticus offered his hand to Sylvia and Bella. "We can also pick some fruits and vegetables while we are here and feed these hungry mouths."

Declan and Leo were on the other side of the wagon, offering their aid.

Atticus picked up Leah and handed her to Sylvia. Turning back around and retrieving Liam, he spun him in the air and held him in his arms, smiling.

"Hello, little one."

"You a horsey!" screamed Liam, pointing at Atticus.

Frozen in place, Atticus stared Liam down. Retaining his smile, not afraid of the large man at all, Liam gave him a big hug.

"Oh...how cute. He must really like you," Neveah said, taking Liam from Atticus and putting him on her shoulders.

Atticus, still a bit stunned by Liam's words, made a note to speak with the little man later.

"Are you sure this is okay?" Julia walked around the wagon to where Atticus was standing.

"Yes, of course. I was told specifically to stop here, in fact, so you can all enjoy Queen Tiana's gardens."

"This queen sounds quite nice," assumed Julia.

"That she is. I do not believe one could find a kinder moodamorph," replied Atticus, preparing the family for a very different species of human.

"What's a moodamorph?" Julia asked.

"They are...mood people. They actually wear the color of their mood," Atticus did his best to describe them until a little girl came running straight toward him. He was relieved to have one of the creatures now standing before him. This, a garden moodamorph, was very excited. She wore a bright orange body, like a sunset. And when she ran, her two thick, green braids that stuck out from the top of her head bounced around her face.

"Hi, Atticus." The little girl beamed, showing off her adorable dimples set in the center of her brown freckled cheeks.

Atticus laughed as the family watched, practically hypnotized by the sight.

"Well...hello there, Ziara. Where's your mom?" asked Atticus, glancing behind the girl, as if peering into the fields of corn.

"Not far behind." Ziara's look turned to one of visible annoyance. "She's never going to let me grow up, you know.

One, two, three."

"Ziara!" The party heard the definite yell of a concerned mother.

"See? Told you," Ziara said, rolling her eyes. "Over here, Mother."

Another mood person suddenly appeared from the cornfield. Tall, she boasted the same green braids as her daughter, but her color was a definite yellow. Atticus explained that the hue came from worry.

"Ziara, you cannot run off like that. There are strange beings that have come to our land who could be violent." She said the odd words without looking up to see the humans surrounding them.

"Look, Mom," she pointed out Atticus and the visitors.

Turning in their direction, her sickly color immediately transformed to a bright red that defined sheer embarrassment from head to toe.

"It's okay, Delphine. They are strange, but they are also kind; not violent at all. And *human*," laughed Atticus, in a slightly teasing voice.

"*Completely* human? Like, pure-bred?" Delphine had apparently never seen what Atticus explained was a 'complete' human before. They had chosen to only observe people from a distance.

"Yes," replied Atticus.

"Why do you call us pure-bred, like we're some kind of dog?" Julia asked, a bit uncomfortable with the term.

Atticus was quick to answer: "We have many species in our realm, Julia. Most of us are only half-human. I didn't want to scare or overwhelm you, but you see...there are no other pure-bred humans here. They became extinct during the wars fought long ago. You have no need to concern yourself with our history, though. I assure you."

Silence fell as the adults stood there thinking about all that'd been unveiled by Atticus and Delphine. They briefly wondered if they even wanted to return to Earth when there was a realm that was without their own kind.

The kids in the group were at the front of the carriage. Petting the horses, they looked at Ziara. Bella, Zack, and Sylvia wanted to talk to her but felt too shy to approach.

Bella, finally making the first move, waved at Ziara to come over and join them.

Walking away from her mother's side, Ziara went right to them, showing no shyness at all.

"Hi," she said in a bubbly tone to the new visitors.

"Hey," Bella and Sylvia replied. Zack stood there staring at her, smiling.

The girls laughed, snapping Zack out of his trance. "Hi," he finally said.

While the new group chatted away about both their realms, the adults remained at the end of the carriage, looking on.

"Do you want to pick fruits and berries with me?" asked Ziara. "We could head down to the grapevines. They're my favorite."

"Yes. We're starving," Zack said, rubbing his tummy.

The same as they did on Earth, the kids ditched the adults but announced where they were going in order to avoid punishment of any kind.

"Could we play with Ziara?" Bella, Zack, and Sylvia asked. "We'll pick food and won't go far. We promise."

"We don't mind, but it's up to Ziara's mother," responded Neveah and Julia, looking in Delphine's direction for her answer.

"Yes. This is okay with me, but do not go far from us. If we can no longer hear you, you have gone too far," Delphine said in a serious tone.

"I promise, Mother." Ziara smiled up at her annoyed mother and ran to the three strangers. Wrapping her long, orange fingers around Bella's arm, the quartet took off in a cloud of laughter.

* * *

Arianna, while crouching in the barn when Neveah and her family had been packed up and driven away, had been presented with her next steps as she'd listened to the tall, handsome men speak just a few feet away.

When the sound of the horses leading a carriage arrived in Julia's driveway, her heartbeat had immediately gone out of control. "Are they coming for me? Do they know I'm back?" Arianna whispered in panic to the empty barn, listening to the carriage stop in front of the house. Moving closer to the barn doors, she tried desperately to hear what was going on.

Quickly learning they were there for Neveah's family, Arianna had sighed. "Thank goodness they're not here for me." She had continued to eavesdrop on their conversation.

"Julia wants us to come back for the cats," Declan had declared. "I like them. Never had a problem with petting their soft fur."

"How many does she have?" Leo said with disgust in his voice. "You know I can't stand the creatures."

"Oh, please."

"I was attacked as a boy. You know this."

Declan sighed, as if annoyed by his brother's theatrical statement. "I don't know how many are here. I think we should just look until we can't find anymore."

"Great," Leo said in a tone that was absent of happiness.

And with that, Arianna knew it would be more than easy to hitch a ride to the castle. Smiling, she'd crouched down and continued her observation.

When Neveah and her family were packed, in the carriage, and heading on their way, once Arianna knew no one else was present, she'd snatched the closest thing to her and covered herself up with it. Trying to be careful, she ran from the barn into the house. Opening the door, she walked in and locked it behind her. Thankful for finally being out of that filthy area, she scanned the house for something to eat. She also kept an eye open in search of the crystals. Trying to use all of her heightened senses, she attempted to focus in on the mystical energy of the crystals that should be pulsing inside the abode. It didn't take long to figure out the power they held in them was nowhere to be found; it was clear they'd been taken away by the family.

Moving on to her other desire, a starving Arianna checked out the kitchen, opening and closing all cupboard doors in search of something to eat. Stopping on one holding beans, soup cans, homemade jam and peanut butter, she quickly went through the drawers in an attempt to find a can opener. Discovering the utensil, she lined up the cans on a counter and opened the soup and beans. For the peanut butter and jelly, she found a loaf of bread hidden in a cupboard above the coffee pot.

Arianna made the sandwich and, upon transporting all she'd found to the table, sat down and gobbled up the food. The feeling of a full stomach was one of pure bliss.

Utilizing the water of the stream and the stove to boil it, she proceeded to clean up and head into the bedrooms of the adults that dwelled inside them. Finding comfortable clothing, she dressed, brushed her hair, and admired herself in the mirror. Once she was pleased with her appearance, she walked back into Angela's room and climbed into her bed, falling into a calm, peaceful sleep. She would keep one ear alert in order to hear her escorts' return.

* * *

Keeping close to the children, Julia and the rest of the adults, along with Leah and Liam, walked through the cornfield to the far side where they discovered the trees laden with fruit.

Neveah handed Liam back to Atticus, seeing as that he seemed to adore the man, and turned her full attention on Leah.

When they got to the apple trees, there were already baskets awaiting them. Made of bright yellow straw and horsehair string, Neveah asked, "Can we use these?"

"There were more mood people here," replied Delphine. "I'm afraid they got frightened and departed quickly. But yes, please use them."

"I'm sorry if we frightened anyone. I hope we can meet them all one day...under easier circumstances." Neveah offered a smile with her heartfelt apology.

"I'm sure they would be happy with that, as well. It would be wonderful to make new friends." Delphine's color returned to normal as she finally broke into a welcoming smile.

Picking the apples, the adults moved on to the pears and then the peaches.

"Wow, these are all so ripe. They also look a bit...different from the ones we have back home." Julia picked up an apple and a pear, studying the interesting designs that seemed to be a part of the exterior.

"We grow all of these on Earth," Neveah agreed, "but they don't exactly look like this." Choosing a peach, she bit into it, not prepared for the succulent juice that spewed across her face.

"What do they look like in your realm?" Delphine asked.

Julia began telling Delphine about the characteristics of apples, peaches, and pears on Earth. The more descriptions she mentioned, the more confused Delphine's expression became.

"That is very strange. I don't think we have anything that looks like what you have described."

Done with their gathering, their baskets filled to the top, Atticus offered to take them back so they could pick vegetables and berries as well.

He seemed to have a bit of difficulty carrying all the baskets in his hands.

"I'll help you bring them back," Julia offered. She attempted to hide her knowing grin; it was easy to see Atticus was a proud man who did not ask for help often.

"That would be great. Thank you," Atticus replied, surprising her with his quick acceptance.

Atticus and Julia lifted all the baskets and headed to the carriage, leaving Neveah and Delphine alone by the peach trees.

Sitting down on the lush, green field, they talked about their daily lives and their children. With words and descriptions being 'new' phrases to Delphine, Neveah ended up explaining many things, especially the world of electronics that'd become the largest part of their lives. From phones to tablets to television, Neveah watched Delphine's eyes widen.

"That's marvelous," Delphine shouted, clapping her hands.

Her sudden reaction made Neveah laugh. "Yes...well, it's a nice change being here, actually." Neveah didn't miss their realm at all. The idea of never having to see her ex-husband again made her feel more like celebrating.

"I will go check on the kids. I'm sure they've wandered," Delphine said, the yellow hue returning slowly as she walked into the cornfield.

Neveah sat there alone with the younger children, noticing the loyal eagle soaring above her.

Leah had been picking up leaves and dropping them repeatedly, over and over again, while she and Delphine had sat talking. Liam, who had fallen asleep in Atticus' arms when they'd made it to the peaches, was lying on a bed of grass where they could all see him. Raising her head to witness Liam still napping, a sudden surge of panic rushed through her when she noted, in the blink of an eye, Leah had up and vanished.

"Leah," Neveah yelled at the top of her lungs, rushing toward the field. "Where are you, Leah?"

Beginning to hyperventilate, Neveah walked in circles. Struggling for breath, she screamed with all the strength she had left; her power was dwindling, quickly being replaced by absolute fear:

"Answer me, Leah! Where *are* you?"

CHAPTER 7

"CODE BLUE: Imaging Room. CODE BLUE: Imaging Room." The technician announced the emergency over the intercom.

Nurses and doctors came from all directions to help, joining with Arik's primary who'd already announced that surgery was immediate and their only step.

He clarified to all the new faces: "This man needs a surgical team STAT. Someone page the neurosurgeon and let's move him to the OR now," he ordered.

As the well-oiled crew they were, the group lifted Arik off the sliding bed and onto the gurney before rushing him down the hall into a prepped OR.

"One, two, three, lift." Placing Arik on the bed, the doctor remained in his professional, yet vocal, mindset. "Someone get me those MRI results."

"Right here, Doctor James," a resident said, handing the

scans to him. The doctor scanned the images of Arik's brain. "Looks to be a temporal hematoma."

"What's the problem?" The hospital's primary neurosurgeon, Dr. William Lars, asked as he walked into the room.

"This is Arik McLean, thirty-eight, fell into an unconscious state during the MRI; images show a hematoma on his left temporal lobe believed to be sustained from a car accident.

Dr. Lars took the scans from his peer, already walking his own brain through the operation. "Okay, get him ready," he instructed before exiting the room to get prepped for the surgery ahead.

The team went to work, placing his head in a three pinned device attached to the table in order to secure his head in place. Administering a brain relaxing drug into his system, they shaved his head and sanitized the area.

As Dr. Lars reappeared, the green surgical gloves and apron were placed on him by the nurse. When completed, he walked over to Arik and looked down at the young man's head.

He nodded to his constituents. "Let's do this. Ten-blade," the surgeon instructed the nurse, holding out his hand. Taking the ten-blade scalpel, he cut into Arik's flesh.

Continuing to work away, he handed the scalpel back, not taking his eyes off Arik for a single second in the process.

Tucking four fingers under the skin and muscle, he pulled it back slightly from the skull.

"Drill," he stated.

Taking the drill, he made a burr hole into his skull. His movements were delicate, making sure not to hit the brain.

When the step had been completed, the surgeon moved forward. "Craniotome saw."

Turning it on, he brought it slowly to the burr hole. Cutting an outline in the bone above the hematoma, he lifted the bone flap and set it aside.

Years of practice had created a familiar dance of cutting and retracting, exposing the hematoma, joined by the consistent process of suction and irrigation, allowing the hematoma to be successfully removed.

"Everyone breathe. It's like crickets in this room," Dr. Lars stated with a laugh, attempting to calm his team and let them know that everything had gone like clockwork. "Let's close him up." He turned to the surgical resident.

Registering his gaze, the resident spoke, "Yes, sir?"

"What's your name? Have you ever finished an open craniotomy?"

"Ethan, sir, and no."

"Well then, it's your lucky day. Walk me through it."

"Really? Thank you, sir," Ethan said, taking the exclusive spot of 'lead surgeon.' "First, I flip the dura back over the brain, suturing the aspects back together."

"Looks good. Now what?"

"I place the skull back on the dura and brain, then place the titanium plate and screws over the bone. I then pull the flap of skin and muscle over the titanium plate, suturing it together."

He heard members of the team offer their congratulations.

"Excellent job, Ethan. Okay. Let's get this man into recovery," instructed Dr. Lars. "You all did amazing."

Leaving the room, the team went about cleaning Arik up, disconnecting the now unnecessary wires, releasing his head from the pins, and wheeling him into the recovery unit.

After a few hours passed by, Arik struggled but succeeded in opening his eyes.

The doctor waited for a few more minutes in order for Arik to show signs of clarity. Finally, he spoke, "Sir, do you know who you are? Can you speak?"

"Yeah," Arik replied softly, his voice cracking.

"Can you tell me your name? Do you know where you are?"

"Um...I'm at Pluto General Hospital. My name is Arik... Arik McLean."

The doctor nodded. "That's perfect. Do you know how you

got here?"

"Uh...no," Arik said, his voice one of pure exhaustion.

"That's okay, sir. You get some sleep, feel better, and we'll try to get you home soon," Dr. Lars instructed.

Arik did very well as the days went by. Concentrating on eating well, his systems became regulated, and the time came for his parents to come check him out of the hospital. Arik was wheeled out to his mother and father who pulled up in a rental car.

"Hey, champ, how are you doin?" asked David, yelling across the passenger seat through the open window.

"Just great, Dad," replied Arik, as his mother and nurse joined forces to help him into the passenger seat, before his mother got in the back.

The drive home was quiet, allowing Arik to nap all the way there. Waking when they pulled into the driveway and opened the gate, they drove up to the house and parked.

Mary came running out the front door. "Hey, big brother. Are you okay? You look like crap."

"Mary," Kate scolded, helping Arik carefully up the front steps.

"It's okay. I know I look like crap," Arik issued a small laugh.

"Are you ready to go in?" asked David, coming up the steps behind them.

"Yeah, let's get it over with."

Mary led him through the door, as Arik stepped over the threshold and looked around the front hall that he still had no memory of. His eyes fell upon a coat rack to his left. Hanging there was a little pink coat beside a black camo one for the winter. Told they were Leah and Liam's garments, he put his face close to them and breathed. No familiar odor spiked his memory. Turning around and looking to the right, his eyes met with a shoe rack on the floor. A pair of female heels sat atop the small shelf. Bending down to pick one up, he stared at the glittery fabric before dropping it onto the floor.

"Did you guys stay here while I was in the hospital?"

"No, honey. We all stayed at a hotel. We thought it was...the right thing to do," Kate answered with sad eyes.

"Do you know where my room is? I would like to go to sleep in my own bed."

"Yeah, son. I do," David said, helping Arik to his bedroom door and opening it for him.

Walking in, Arik sat down on the bed.

"You got it, buddy?"

"Yes, Dad. Thanks."

"Have a...try to have a good sleep, son."

Arik took his shoes off, and got comfortable on the bed as his father walked out the door. Looking around the room, Arik could certainly see the "special touches" that the woman he loved had placed all around. He studied the family pictures on the wall with everyone wearing the same happy smile; he stared at the lovely paintings decorating the room, as well as the vanity in the corner, smiling at the clothing scattered on the floor. Closing his eyes, he allowed himself to drift off to sleep while trying to conjure any memory he could possibly find stored deep within his soul.

Waking up the next morning, Arik winced at the residual pain of the bruises and wounds that he'd been told came from his accident. Slowly and carefully getting out of bed, he walked to the open door of the bathroom to get cleaned up. Feeling much better than he had only a week ago, he finished a morning routine that he felt must still be floating around in his brain, and walked down to the living room. Observing everything he walked by, he stopped every once in a while to take in the plethora of pictures, paintings, and collectibles sitting on the bookshelves, struggling to unearth just the smallest memory.

"Hi, honey. Good morning," his mother said, walking out of the kitchen that seemed to be filled with succulent smells.

"Are you hungry?"

He smiled. "Starving."

"Well, come and sit down. Let's see if we can talk some more about the past, maybe even go to some of the places you and Angela visited on a daily basis; anything we can do to get those memories of yours back," she said with a strained smile.

Arik walked over to the tall, black table with matching chairs sporting black leather seats. Sitting down on one of the chairs, his mother set a delicious looking plate of biscuits and gravy down in front of him.

"Where's mine?" asked David.

"We're not married anymore. You can get it yourself."

Everyone let out a small laugh, trying to expel the nervous energy and tension that was apparent in the room.

Sitting down beside her son, David rose to get himself a plate before returning to the table.

"So...you guys know where Angela and I used to go?" asked Arik.

"You loved the beaches—rivers, too—and you both loved to hunt for agates. In fact, you have many of the stones on the bookshelf in the living room. There's also a specific beach the two of you used to go to every year because it was the best camping spot. They call it La Push Beach. It's a couple hours away, though," answered David.

"Let's go there today," Arik said, before diving into the most scrumptious plate of food he'd had in a long time.

After breakfast was done and his sisters arrived, they piled into the car and drove to La Push in Forks. Once they made it to the beach, getting a day pass, they drove up to the resort and walked to the sandy beach. From the jetty to the trees washed up on shore, to a cave and even more debris lying outside the dark and mysterious tunnel, Arik took in their surroundings.

"I came here with you and Angela one year on the Fourth of July. It was awesome," said David.

"Let's walk around. I don't want to stay too long, but it is beautiful...I can see why it's one of our favorite spots." The sadness evident in Arik's voice seemed to move across his face like a veil of mourning.

Walking, he instinctively looked down and began picking up rocks. Not even noticing he was doing it, Arik studied every one of them, as if they each had a secret encapsulated inside their stone bodies.

"You're looking at the rocks," Mary said with a smile, continuing to inform him of things that should be normal to him. "You never used to do that before you met Angela."

"Really? I guess I didn't even notice," Arik said.

Continuing to walk down the beach, his pockets now full of rocks, he made it to the jetty where his parents said Arik would fish every morning he and the family stayed at La Push. Listening to the waves, he closed his eyes. Feeling the mist on his face, he searched his brain. Receiving no memories of fishing, rock hunting, or even the location, itself, he became frustrated and started throwing rocks into the water.

"Don't overexert yourself, honey. Your leg is still healing, along with your head. And like Dr. James said, it's okay you can't remember yet. With all the trauma you experienced, it's bound to take some time." Being a nurse and working in the medical arena, Kate had seen many cases just like her son's.

"Plus, you're stubborn. So it may take longer," Jennifer teased, causing the rest of the family to laugh.

Continuing their walk down the beach, Arik continued to collect his rocks while heading for the cave. Sitting down with his sisters, they posed for a picture at the front of the cave's opening. Walking atop large rocks, they witnessed the purple and orange starfish decorating them. It was a truly awesome sight to see.

As the day slipped away, the family—somewhat depressed that nothing they'd seen had spurned even a flashback—gathered into the car for their drive back home.

Arriving exhausted from the day's adventures and failed goals, Arik convinced them to forego the hotel and stay with him. Everyone settled in comfortable beds for the night and quickly fell asleep.

For two days straight, Arik stayed inside and went through everything he found. Clothes, pictures, letters, scrapbooks Angela had made that included pictures of the children and everything about her pregnancies. Arik found himself thrilled at the fact that his beloved significant other hadn't missed a moment of their lives together, and as he read the stories Angela wrote, Arik's heart warmed at learning how in love they were. He somehow just knew that he'd never been that happy in his life before.

David popped his head in to say hello. "Wanna go fishing, son? It might help you get some memories back."

Arik looked up at his father. Seeing his desperate look, Arik knew that all this father really wanted to do was get out of the house and away from his ex-wife. Enjoying the fresh, clear winter skies was just an added benefit for the man who loved the Great Outdoors.

"Sounds good, Dad."

They walked out to the garage to choose from all the fishing poles hanging on the wall. Without thinking, Arik pulled down the ones needed along with the necessary accessories; the entire time he looked like an absolute outdoor pro.

"See what you're doing?" David said.

"What do you mean?" Arik looked down to where his father's gaze had landed to see all the tackle and equipment he'd chosen. "Wow...I guess I've done this recently."

"All it takes is a little time, son. Baby steps."

Feeling a bit calmer from witnessing his own "habits" come back, Arik prayed that the train of luck would continue.

As Arik climbed into the driver's seat, David paused. "Are you sure you want to do this? I can drive, you know."

Arik thought for a moment but shook his head. "No. I can do this, Dad. I want to."

David grinned. "Okay...but don't tell your mother."

With his dad in the passenger seat, Arik drove down the road, unsure of what direction he should go. For no particular reason, Arik picked a spot and parked on the side of the road beside a glistening river. Getting out, he stared down the bank and set his eyes immediately on the perfect place to fish.

David chuckled. "You always knew the best ones."

Arik was very pleased with himself. Happier than he had been in the last few weeks, he unloaded the tackle box and poles from the cab of his truck. Carefully walking down the bank of the river, he tried not to giggle like a boy as he watched his father—the slightly hefty, six-foot-seven frame behind him—struggle to make it down.

"*That* was not easy," David said, breathing heavily, attempting to wipe the wet soil off the back of his pants.

"Oh, you got it, Dad," Arik said, letting his laughter out.

Setting down the gear, they baited their hooks and cast the lines. Feeling an odd sensation that his chosen location was not right, Arik stepped off the dirt and onto one of the large, flat boulders sticking out of the water. *This is right,* he thought. Knowing he had stood there, in that exact spot many times, Arik finally felt a little of the peace that'd been eluding him.

After hours had gone by and they still hadn't caught anything, Arik still felt calm at being able to spend the entire day with his father. Attaining even the slightest feeling of normalcy was a blessing in itself.

Deciding to stay a while longer, watching the fish jump as the daylight changed brought the men even more hope for success. When Arik cast his line out yet again, he suddenly felt the jolt from the fish retrieving his offer of bait, and Arik quickly gave the line an intense pull. Struggling with his catch, he pulled the pole left and right, keeping up with the fighter as his feet remained firmly set on the boulder. "Dad, hand me the net."

An equally excited David moved forward and handed the net to his son. Taking it with his right hand, Arik pulled the pole hard with the other. Lifting the trophy salmon into it, Arik panted and laughed at the same time.

Calling the adventure a success, Arik and his father loaded up the gear and headed home. Ecstatic all the way, when they arrived home and showed off the fish, the men cleaned, cooked and enjoyed the hell out of the meal, the company, and what turned out to be a much-needed happy day.

* * *

As the week progressed, Arik began rediscovering his own habits, and the normalcy made him feel even more hopeful that one day soon all of his memories would return.

When the time came for his family to go back home, Arik drove them to the Seattle-Tacoma International Airport. Dropping them off, not wanting a long goodbye that would make him fall into tears, he simply waved. Although he despised the reason for it, Arik had truly loved the visit and being able to spend time with the people who made it all seem easier.

When he arrived home, he unlocked the front door and walked in, ready to settle in for the night. Lying in bed, he twisted and turned, completely unable to find the sleep he longed for. Turning on his back, Arik stared at the ceiling and thought about all they'd done during his family's visit. He conjured up the images of the exciting fishing trip, the beach of La Push, the waves crashing on the jetty...Finally successful, Arik drifted off to sleep. Unfortunately, it wasn't for long.

Waking up with a sudden jolt, Arik jumped out of bed in alarm. *Was that a memory or just an awful dream?* Sweating, he walked to the bathroom. Turning on a cool stream of water, he stepped into the shower and allowed the water to run over his head and down his back. He was so desperate to unlock the memories buried in his mind; he wanted so much to remember his baby girl and son. Most of all, he wanted to see his wife in his mind's eye and remember how it all began.

Turning off the water, he grabbed a towel from the back of the door. Wrapping it around his waist, he brushed his teeth and stepped back into the bedroom to get dressed for the day.

Hungry, he headed for the kitchen and made himself something to eat. Sitting at the dining room table, he concluded that today he was going to head back to the black pit now sitting where a loving home used to be, and face it head on. *I just have to remember!*

Leaving his now empty plate on the table, Arik grabbed his keys and raced to his truck.

Driving through Elmer, he passed the last gas station and proceeded to head out into the country. Eyeing little bridges, taking in the old mill on his left, Arik drove over the railroad tracks and finally made it to Julia's road. Stopping on the bridge, knowing from what his family had told him that it was the spot where he'd crashed his wife's van, Arik peered down at the water below. Trees were still crushed around the creek. As his head began to hurt, Arik decided to get back into the truck and drive around the corner.

His headache grew worse as he spotted the caution tape blocking off the road. Parking the truck, Arik sat there and rubbed his now throbbing head. Slowly opening the driver's side door, he left it open behind him as he walked to the tape, stepped over it, and stared down into the black pit that seemed to be the opening to Hell itself. Feeling absolutely stunned, Arik fell to his knees, completely paralyzed.

Like bullets from a machine gun, the snippets of memories began flooding back. The smiles, the pain, the good days and bad, the family vacations, the births of the children, the love of his life...then, as if switching gears, the bright light flashing as the ground trembled beneath his tires, sending him barreling into the ground with a feeling of pure fear rushing through his veins.

Arik's eyes filled with tears as he fought to catch his breath. Lifting his arms to the sky, he let out a scream so loud it would easily wake the dead.

"WHY?"

CHAPTER 8

Neveah's world was falling apart. Kneeling down on the ground crying, she held her hands over her face, as if the reality that Leah had gone missing while in her care would somehow become nothing but a nightmare if she closed her eyes to the real world.

Hearing a twig snap and feeling a sudden burst of cool wind moving the corn stalks all around, Neveah jumped up quickly and turned to see a tall man standing directly in front of her. Not only was he a surprise, he was an angel in her eyes, for he held the missing Leah in his muscular arms. Even though she'd been told 'humans' were not what she'd see in this realm, the man certainly looked like a male...a beautiful one at that. His hair was slightly long and full, and black as onyx. The forest green of his eyes made her melt, and his tan, well-shaped build on his six-foot-one frame belonged on the cover of magazines.

Not even recognizing the fact that her mouth was agape, Neveah watched in silence as a gorgeous, slightly teasing smile began to appear on his striking face.

"I heard you screaming and then saw this little one run right by me," the man said in a truly seductive tone. "Is she yours?"

Still staring like a teenage girl at a rock concert, Neveah literally became weak at the knees. Slowly coming out of the trance, she yelled at herself: *Say anything, don't just stare like an idiot with your mouth open.*

Finally, she remembered English. "No. Um...she's my sister's daughter," she stuttered.

"She's beautiful," he replied, handing her to Neveah. "Quick, too."

"Thank you...I mean, and...yes. Too quick." Neveah cleared her throat. "I'm new here, my family's new here, and I thought she was lost forever." Neveah turned to Leah as she both hugged her tight, thankful for her safety, and growled at her in fear. "Don't you *ever* run off like that again!"

Taking a deep breath, Neveah lifted her head up to thank the man again, but he was gone. Feeling the ache in her heart, she looked around, turning in circles with Leah in her arms who was giggling at the dance.

"Neveah, where *are* you?" Julia's voice entered her ears.

"I'm coming." Still stunned, she walked slowly out of the cornfield.

"What happened?" Julia said, her face a mask of worry. "We heard you screaming."

Neveah felt as if she was still trembling, yet she wasn't sure if it was from the anxiety or the stranger who'd disappeared. She turned her focus back on Julia. "Leah took off into the cornfield and scared me. I couldn't find her anywhere." Neveah felt the fear creep up inside her once again.

"It's okay. What happened? How did you find her? Did she come back on her own?"

"A man..." Neveah began, watching Julia's face change. "A man came out of nowhere and he was holding her in his arms. I was just talking with him, right before you called out, but he disappeared before I could ask him his name."

"Well, thank goodness. I wish I could thank him; talk about a guardian angel showing up at the right time. Let's all get back to the carriage and get out of here."

"I agree," said Atticus.

As they packed up and got ready to return, Delphine appeared, escorting the children. Baskets full, everyone was smiling.

Loading everything, saying their goodbyes to Delphine and her daughter, they munched away on the tasty treats they'd picked, as they took up their journey to the castle once again.

Upon entering the inner town of Diathesi, known as Mood Town by the citizens, they were met with many old shops. The stores were inundated with merchandise, even beautiful dresses hung in the windows of the clothing shops, and both the stores and sidewalks were 'decorated' with different creatures the family had never seen before.

"Wow! Look at how tall that one is," Sylvia said, pointing to the man that sported legs so long that he towered over their carriage. Skinny build, he had an abnormally wide nose with big nostrils, a short haircut, long facial hair, and skin with a hue that matched the trees on the outskirts of town.

"They are called Dentromen," Atticus explained. "Or Men of the Trees."

"What about those? They're so colorful," Bella asked, pointing to the tiny, multi-colored people who reminded her of leprechauns.

"They are called Toxomen, or Rainbow Men, but I don't recommend you ever address them that way," Atticus laughed. "They have a bit of a...complex."

Bella grinned.

"Those are *insanely* bright." Zack squinted as he stared at a woman whose skin seemed to be covered with a glossy sheen. He couldn't seem to turn away; the woman drew his gaze and he stared at her with a longing in his soul he couldn't describe.

"Stop!" Atticus' call made everyone in the carriage jump. "Her kind is not supposed to be in town when they're that bright. Stop the carriage!" Atticus knocked on the wagon. Before it had come to a complete halt, he jumped out and quickly walked toward the creature.

The family watched as the woman, looking suddenly afraid, began running in the opposite direction.

"Halt, bright one!"

"I'm sorry...I can't...I didn't mean to. I can't control it." She yelled over her shoulder at Atticus before racing off into the woods as fast as her little feet could take her.

Because of the sudden sounds, creatures began turning and swarming around the carriage. Terrifying the children, the dogs began to bark and growl at the group that was amassing.

Atticus, taking his focus off his original prey, turned and eyed the crowd. "Alogo!" Atticus released the one word and then repeated it, making it sound like a chant. Immediately transforming into an elegant black stallion, he seemed to race at the speed of light towards the carriage. Rearing up, he made the suddenly fearful crowd disperse in all directions.

"Andras," Atticus whispered, turning back into his original state. He found himself staring at a line of wide-eyed, open-mouthed humans.

"Horsey," Liam said in a truly excited voice as he pointed at Atticus.

Atticus shook his head in confusion. "How did you know, little man? No one has the power to see the truth. That is what makes all shifters safe."

Everyone joined in Liam's excitement as they smiled at Atticus, fascinated by what they'd just seen.

"What *are* you?" asked Julia, feeling strangely hurt that he hadn't told her.

Sighing, he explained, "I'm a shifter, like everyone else here. Although appearing human at all times, I own the ability to transform into a powerful steed. They call us Centremen."

"I think that's awesome," Izak said, breaking the silence.

"Damn, you *scared* me." Neveah practically jumped out of her skin when she heard her brother's voice come from out of nowhere. The rest of the family laughed.

"Let's go on to the castle; you can explain more on the way," Julia said, taking charge of the group once again.

Atticus stepped into the carriage and sat down next to the children. Answering all the questions that were being thrown at him, Atticus only avoided speaking about any other shifters that may be in their realm, explaining his hesitation by saying, "It's not proper to speak without first having the other's permission to do so."

Instead, he spoke about himself. Entertaining Liam, he told the family about how fast he could go. Not knowing what to compare his speed with from their country, he told them he was a part of the fastest land shifters in this, his own realm. In addition, he was so strong he could bring down the entire stone bridge they were about to stop at by simply running over it after his horse transformation had occurred.

"And yes," he said, laughing, "I can give you a ride anytime you want. I also can talk to you and you'll understand me no matter what form I happen to be in at the time."

"Cool," the children agreed, already excited about the future.

As they took a turn in the road, the beautiful blue ocean once again appeared out their window.

* * *

Julia kept an eye on Atticus' brothers, watching Declan and Leo stop at the gate. Talking to the gatekeepers to get permission to cross the bridge, the strangers asked to meet the visitors confined in the carriage.

Leo and Declan turned around and led them towards the wagon.

"I apologize. They just wanted to meet you," Declan said.

"Oh, that's fine," Neveah said, turning to the gatekeepers. "Hello, I'm Neveah."

The men looked at each other and then back at her as if mesmerized by her beauty and sweet voice. Their shared stare made her feel like she was a goddess. Her embarrassment rose as she thought back to the same silly expression she must've been wearing when gazing at Leah's savior in the cornfield.

Continuing to make the introductions, Atticus ended with Liam.

"Teddy bears," Liam smiled, pointing at the gatekeepers.

"What did you say?" Atticus was getting more and more concerned, wondering how many the little boy could unveil as shifters. He knew that gift would be dangerous for Liam, especially if their enemy found out.

"You, horsey. They are bears. Roar," Liam said shyly, not normally speaking to anyone he didn't know.

The bear shifters laughed, but then stopped, staring at the little man, wondering if it was possible Liam was a warlock. After all, not even witches could tell as quickly as he had what species were what.

The gatekeepers nodded at each other and turned back to Liam. Bending down, the one named Theodore smiled. "You are going to be a great deal of help to our realm. Liam. This, I know." He made his strange announcement and then the gatekeepers walked back to the bridge. Lifting the steel gate that stood in their path, they allowed the carriage to move across a bridge that Atticus informed them was made of brick, solid gold, and diamond-encrusted sand. The family remained silent. They were in awe as they stared at the most royal bridge possible. Gorgeous, it glittered in the waning sun, as it protected travelers from the ocean below.

The children looked out the windows and over the sides of the bridge, excited as they continued to a mystical castle they had not yet laid eyes upon. Yelling and waving at mermaids swimming along, the kids were rewarded by a couple of younger creatures who waved back. As the mermaids immediately got chastised by what looked like their elders for having the nerve to address humans, they disappeared to what the kids could only assume was the ocean's floor.

Arriving at the most exquisite castle that not even fairytales could do justice to, the entire family studied the amazing dwelling. A front staircase that looked to have been created with golden sand was offset by strands of ivy growing up the sides of the castle walls like blooming, green banners. With onyx on the turrets and rooftops, there seemed to be hundreds of windows decorating the place. Flowers, bushes, and small trees that looked to be sprouting ripened mushrooms, came in all colors and filled every inch of the expansive yard. Trees reached up into the sky, as if a lookout was at the very top where one could go to view every inch of the sparkling ocean.

Completely captivated by the castle, the family watched in awe as a shimmering golden woman came running down the ornate stairs; a little one ran close behind.

Julia and Neveah stared at the bowed heads all around, not sure what they should do or how to react. Bow? Curtsy? Fall to the ground before them? Coming to a joint decision, they tilted their heads in greeting as the gold-skinned moodamorph approached.

"Nonsense," she said with a smile, running directly into Julia's arms. Hugging her close and then repeating her actions with everyone else, the woman scooped up Liam and squeezed his happy, little cheeks. She then spun Leah around in a circle, making her laugh out loud.

"I'm sorry. I'm just *so* happy you all are here. At last."

Puzzled, the adults looked to Atticus for any explanation.

He cleared his throat. "Let me introduce Queen Tiana Chalkos and Princess Jaclyn." Atticus bowed and waved his hand towards them.

"Queen Tiana, this is Julia, Neveah, Izak, Sylvia, Zackary, Bella, Leah and Liam." He paused for a moment before adding in a low voice, "There was one more, but she was snatched...by Alister."

Understanding filled Queen Tiana's eyes. "Well, we shall take care of that as soon as possible," she replied in a serious tone. "In the meantime, please come in. You are very welcome here. Men," she turned, addressing the servants, "bring up the bags and personal belongings and put them in their rooms."

"Of course, My Queen."

Queen Tiana led the family into the Great Hall. Extraordinary in size, colorful lights seemed to be decorating the area. Yet upon further inspection, the adults noted that the many hues came from light filtering through lines of crystals hanging from the ceiling and embedded in the windows. Moving forward, the queen proceeded to give them a tour.

Leaving the Great Hall, the family walked through a dining room that could easily seat an army. Next came the kitchen that smelled of a delicious supper being created just for them. Room after room was shown, ending with a grand ballroom where the queen screeched, "We are going to have a ball in your honor. That way, everyone can get to know you."

"That's not necessary," replied Julia. "You don't have to go through such trouble."

"But it would be so much fun. *Please*," the children begged.

"Plus, you can't say no to something I already know you will love," the queen smiled while offering her stubborn tone of voice.

"Well then, since I can't say no..." Julia said, realizing in this realm she was not in control.

"Perfect. We will have it in twenty-one days' time," Queen Tiana replied ecstatically.

Not asking what the exact time was based on, Julia remained silent and followed the queen while she continued to lead them through her home.

Princess Jaclyn, who'd been watching Bella, reached out and tapped her on the shoulder.

"Hello. I'm Jacky," she introduced herself. "How many days are you?"

"I'm Bella. I'm twelve years old, but I'm not sure how many days that is," she replied, trying her best to add up the number in order to answer the question correctly.

"I'm four thousand, five hundred days old today."

"Wow...that's a lot when you put it in days," Bella said, her eyes wide. Doing the math in her head, she added, "So that would make you exactly twelve-and-a-half-years old today."

"We're the same then. Want to be my friend?" Jacky smiled.

"Best," Bella replied, accepting Jacky's warm hug as they turned and ran to catch up with the family, chatting all the way.

Once everyone had rejoined the group, Queen Tiana led them to their bed chambers. Showing them each their own lavatories, she went on to explain that a maid would be attending to their needs and would appear soon to help get them ready for supper. After once again offering hugs to everyone, the queen and her princess left each family member alone to admire the beautiful rooms.

The family was able to rest in their new beds for only a short while before each of their doors was knocked upon by pleasant women following Queen Tiana's orders.

Neveah rose from her oh-so-comfortable bed and walked over to open the door.

"Hello, Miss. I'm here to help you get ready for supper."

The young woman stood there holding buckets of steaming water.

"Of course, please...come in," Neveah said, moving over so the woman didn't have to break her back continuing to hold the heavy pails. "Let me help you."

"Oh, no! Please. I've got it."

Neveah watched in silence as more young women and mood skinned people rushed in and out of her room, each carrying their own buckets of hot water into the bath, until only one was left.

"May I help you undress and wash?"

"No, thank you. I've got that," Neveah replied. "I don't need any more assistance, really. But thank you."

"My lady, I need to come back in order to do your hair and tie the back of your dress laid out on the bed. You cannot do that yourself."

Neveah sighed. "Okay, I guess it wouldn't hurt to get a little dolled-up." She smiled. "I will call for you."

"I will wait outside your door. Just knock and I will come and assist you," she replied before stepping out into the hall to wait.

Not arguing, even though she felt a bit guilty that the woman would simply just stand there and be bored to death while waiting, Neveah undressed and climbed into the marble tub. Letting the hot water cover her sore, exhausted body, she soaked in the tub and thought about how amazing it felt to release some of the aches and anxieties she'd been carrying all this time. She thought about the images she'd seen of this new, mysterious realm, its plethora of unknown creatures, and was still amazed that she was setting her eyes on things her own dreams had shown her long ago.

Realizing that she never wanted to leave this realm, Neveah honestly felt that there was nothing on Earth she would miss.

* * *

As the rest of the family received the same pampered treatment as Neveah, they donned their elegant clothes, playing a game of dress-up for the dinner that lay ahead. Stretched out on their beds were classical gowns with tight bodices and long, flowing skirts for the ladies, and black pants, white dress shirts, and polished boots for the men. Seeing Izak in pants that fit perfectly was nice, and the clean, well-ironed shirt made him handsome to a fault. And if Angela had been there to see Leah and Liam dressed up, Julia knew she would beam with pride.

Walking down the staircase and into the brilliant dining room, all eyes were locked on the family as the double doors were opened by servants who then led them to the center table.

"You all look darling," the queen said, clapping. Rising from her golden chair, she walked over to them and brought Julia to sit beside her, as Princess Jacky settled by Bella at the end of the table, and the rest of the family took seats all around.

As soon as the queen sat down, the rest of the gathering gave slight bows and took their seats.

Izak looked around the room at the different species, basically viewing them as 'freaky.' Knowing the human looking figures were actually some species of animal or mystical being, he continued to scan the room until his eyes fell...on her.

Izak locked eyes with a gorgeous goddess who sported smokey, baby blue eyes surrounded by long, full eyelashes. Her honey-blonde hair was piled loosely on her head, with stray curls falling upon the smooth, peach-colored skin of her shoulders.

Not realizing he'd been under the woman's spell for so long, Izak practically jumped out of his skin when Neveah pinched his ear. "Ow! What the hell was that for?"

"I've been trying to get your attention," she teased. "If you're so intrigued by her, why don't you get up and go talk to her?"

He snapped, immediately looking down at his plate. "No...I don't feel so great. I'm going to eat and go to bed."

"Can't help you. I didn't spot any drugs here," she stated, already annoyed at his belligerent behavior.

"Shut the fuck up," he said. Standing up, he quickly walked away from her to take another seat.

People entered and immediately began serving succulent platters, followed by glasses filled with water, juices, fresh milk, and various wines.

"No, thank you. I don't drink wine anymore," said Neveah, handing the goblet back to the server.

"I apologize, Miss," he said, taking it away and bowing his head as he took a step backwards.

Sitting beside the queen, Julia wondered why her gold skin never altered like the others. She was adorned with the same long, green braids growing from the top of her skull as Delphine and Ziara. Her curvy form and bright blue eyes were also not unique. However, her golden skin—as well as her daughter's—never changed a bit with her mood.

"May I ask you a question, Queen Tiana?" Julia asked.

"Anything, my dear. And call me Tiana," she winked.

"We met a garden moodamorph on our way here. Her skin changed colors with her mood, and I was just wondering why yours never seems to?"

Queen Tiana gave a sudden loud laugh, getting everyone's attention. She'd briefly forgotten that Julia and her family had no knowledge of her realm.

"I'm sorry, my dear Julia. My tone is gold because I am royalty. With that distinction and honor comes the fact that I am never allowed to hide it...unfortunately," she added, snickering.

"Atticus told us there was also a king."

"Why, yes, of course. He is out with troops securing the lands, but you will meet him soon. In five days' time," Tiana replied, yet again giving an exact time as if she'd planned everyone's schedule weeks ago.

* * *

Finishing up the dinner, making small talk and learning of the realm, they were just calling it an evening when a server walked to little Liam and began pouring him another glass of juice. Out of the blue, with no warning, Liam began pointing and yelling at the top of his lungs.

"Monster!" Crying out, Liam attempted to get up, but instead fell out of his chair and began crawling backwards to get away from the server.

The man's eyes widened as he stared at the young one. Walking towards him, he looked Liam straight in the face.

"Guards," yelled the queen. "Arrest that man!"

Before their eyes, the human figure transformed into a black, cloaked creature. Emitting the strong odor of vinegar, a tar-like substance seemed to drip from a silver weapon that the creature looked ready to throw at Liam's frightened body.

In the blink of an eye, others within the room's walls shifted into their own incredible forms and covered Liam with their own bodies. The guards, not fully shifting into their huge bear bodies, extended their claws to take down the evil creature.

As the would-be murderer was taken away, and the others shifted back, a group of finely dressed people just stood there, completely astonished by the scene that'd just played out before their eyes.

With a myriad of questions running through their heads, a loud 'thump' echoed throughout the room. Focusing on the area where the sudden noise had come from, the family saw

Izak's body lying prone on the elegant marble floor.
He'd fainted dead away.

CHAPTER 9

Arik was sitting down in the middle of the road with the black pit looming large beside him. His face was cradled in his hands, as he went over in his head the plan for what he was going to do today. Above everything else, he needed to find answers.

What could possibly have happened to my family? The explanation he'd received in the hospital from Dan was nothing in comparison to how the reality of it all actually felt. All the memories that surfaced in his mind, coming in bits and pieces as he sat with his eyes closed, were a jumble of emotions and colorful images. Past memories of La Push Beach had come back strong, reminding him of all the wonderful vacations they'd enjoyed with the kids, and the amazing spot where his wife had gone every 4th of July since she was a teenager. Going fishing with his wife and laughing at her amazement and struggle when she caught her first fish. Each and every memory made him smile, yet brought on a horrible new feeling of absolute sadness and despair. He even felt an incredible disappointment in himself for not being able to remember his own babies for a time. Looking at the pictures in the house as if they were strangers. All those lost days where he could've been searching for his family.

Getting up and wiping his tear-stained face with the sleeve of his coat, he took one last look at the empty hole his wife's childhood home once sat upon—a hole that mirrored the dark void in his own heart—and walked back to his truck. Getting in to return to his own depressingly empty home, made Arik even angrier. The place that was once full of laughter, and his kids running around, chasing after each other with their toys...the beautiful chaos that should *not* be missing.

Pulling into his driveway, a wave of guilt came over him; he wished he had been with them when the horrible event had occurred. Needing to know more, he picked his phone up from the center console of his truck and called Dan.

"Hey, Arik. Everything okay?" Dan asked him right away.

Arik found the question insane. "No, Dan. Nothing is okay."

Dan remained silent, as if realizing the ridiculousness of his question. Just from the tone of his voice, Dan could also probably tell Arik's memory had returned.

"After the investigation, did they find *anything* on Julia's property?"

Dan's voice was calm. "Nothing. They really had no ideas, except for an asteroid of some kind hitting the place. That's why all the news people showed up so fast. They say only something of that magnitude could have crashed and left nothing behind. There *was* some proof to back up the theory, though; four crystals were actually found in the pit. Scientists from some lab reported they were crystals created from the intense heat and impact of the asteroid."

"This sounds like some out-there sci-fi flick."

"I'm so sorry, Arik."

Arik listened to the words coming out of Dan's mouth but found no way to believe the load of shit that was being said. He was absolutely baffled. All he could think of when the word "crystals" was mentioned were the stones Neveah obsessed over. They had to be part of the large set she had for making jewelry. He realized he was not going to get any real answers from Dan; he could tell that anyone foolish enough to believe there wasn't more to the story would be useless.

"I'll call the police station and see if they found anything else. I need to know more."

"I get it. I really do. I wish there was more. Let me know what you find out."

"Okay."

"Bye," Dan said, hanging up the phone.

Setting his phone down, Arik felt his body begin to boil from the inside out. Angry as all hell, he was ready to put his fists through a wall. Thinking of the crystals they found kept his focus. The government, the police, *someone* had to be covering something up. It could have been a huge accident from a missile, or something related to them. Not to mention, with all the technology that existed in the world now, *someone* would have known an asteroid was headed into Earth's atmosphere and released immediate warnings. Either way, someone fucked up, and his family were the victims.

Getting out of the truck and heading inside the house, he sat down in front of his own technology to research information on crystals. How could they, of all things, survive an asteroid? What kind of crystals are created from an asteroid? There was nothing that provided any real information; all he could track down were sites that spoke about crazy gypsy stuff. Maybe if he was in a book that would be helpful, but whatever this was had nothing remotely in common with a fairytale...not even one classified as 'grim.'

Setting the phone down and taking a deep breath, he laid his head back on the couch and proceeded to drift off into an uneasy sleep. He'd slept on the couch every night since his family had gone back home. And now it broke his heart to sleep in the bed he shared with his beloved wife without her. Before this horror had occurred, Arik had actually gotten quite used to the couch. His five-year-old daughter had been having dreams and had come to sleep with Mommy for safety. After that, he'd soon found himself on the couch when Angela kicked him out of their own bed for snoring like a train.

The nap didn't last long before his phone rang. Waking up with a jolt, Arik reached for it and read the words 'McCleary PD' on the screen. Shocked, he answered it quickly. "Hello."

"Hello. This is the McCleary Police Department. Am I speaking with Arik McLean?"

"Yes, you are."

"Could you come down to the station today?"

"I can be there in fifteen minutes. What's this about?"

"It's just a follow-up on the...situation regarding your family. We have some questions we would like to ask you."

"I'll leave right now."

"Thank you, sir." As if the gods had heard him state that the police station would be his next stop to get some real answers, Arik instantly jumped from the couch, grabbed his keys and headed directly to what he hoped would be an explanation. Was it possible they *had* found new clues? *Was* there someone to blame for this tragedy? Not sure what to expect, Arik drove as fast as possible.

Pulling into the police station, he parked his truck, walked through the large glass doors, and went up to the front desk. "I'm Arik McLean."

"Yes. Just take a seat and the chief will be out for you in a few minutes."

Arik sat down on a hard chair. Only five minutes passed before a man walked up to him and introduced himself. "Mr.

McLean, I'm Robert Henderson, Chief of Police," he said, extending his hand.

Arik stood up, a bit taller than the lawman, and shook his hand.

"Come with me, please."

Robert Henderson walked towards the back of the station to his office. Opening the door, he pointed to a chair. "Please. Have a seat."

Arik followed orders and waited for the man to begin.

Closing the door, the chief walked around his desk and sat down. Looking at the worried face, Arik could see that the Chief Henderson was genuinely concerned.

As the lawman sat back, he ran his hand down his black beard. "How are you doing today, Arik?"

A bit sick of being asked the same silly question, Arik tried to keep his tone as level as possible. "I'm actually a bit confused. I literally just got my memory back two hours ago."

"Thank goodness. I was informed that had happened. It must have been awful for you." He cleared his throat. "I need to ask you just a couple of basic questions. Please know, you're not under any obligation to answer them and you're not being accused of anything. We just want to know if you remember why you weren't with your family when this happened."

"I don't know anything more than you do, sir. I can tell you, however, that I was out getting coffee for my family. They'd made a list and sent me out to bring it back. I remember coming back in my wife's van and...a flash of really bright light suddenly blinded me. That's when I lost control and went off the bridge."

Chief Henderson nodded. "Yes, we have multiple people confirming seeing the same bright light."

"Sir, I have many questions, but I don't think I'm going to get any real answers," Arik said, trying to be as calm as possible. "I've been led to believe that you found some crystals, or something, in the pit?"

"Yes. Actually, the investigators have done all they can with those," Robert said, completely understanding Arik's anger. "Would you like to take them with you? They didn't, unfortunately, give us any answers, but the scientists at the lab believe they are something called astro-crystals which are formed by impact and heat." Robert handed Arik the crystals in a Ziploc bag.

Arik stood up, clearly done with the interview.

Chief Henderson stood as well, apparently not knowing what more to ask. It was as if he, too, was as confused by the strange situation as Arik. "I'm sorry for your loss, Mr. McLean. Please feel free to call if you need anything, or remember anything that might be useful." Robert lifted his hand and shook Arik's once again.

Not knowing what to say, Arik nodded and left the police department behind as he walked back to his truck.

Looking closely at the crystals, Arik saw that each one was tagged with numbers and the type of crystals they were. Scanning them, he tried to find anything that might spawn a memory. Odd in shape, the stones were smooth, beautifully colored and, unlike the ones he found online, they were in perfect condition—there wasn't a scratch on them. Putting them in his pocket, he drove home as fast as possible to do more research.

When he arrived, he sat down on the couch and went back online. Pulling them out of his pocket, he looked them up one by one. He found nothing out of the ordinary until he researched one that looked remarkably like something called The Dragon's Heart.

All kinds of odd things were written about the particular crystal. Having mystical powers, it was said to open new realms when a powerful witch or warlock holds it in their hand. When combined with other crystals, it was said to build a protective barrier around the people and area of its possessor. Other articles talked about destruction and mayhem, showing incidents where The Dragon's Heart was somehow "responsible" for slowly destroying everything in its path.

Highly skeptical, thinking all the research was a load of crap, Arik slammed the laptop shut. The only thought that filled his mind was the fact that the crystals were the only surviving thing from his family, and he would *always* keep them close.

* * *

As a month passed by, the day of the family memorial came about.

Dan was having it at his home, which was unusual for him. Even birthday parties used to drive him insane. Stressed to the max, he was always worried that both kids and pets would scratch his precious floors. Not at all social, he was quiet and distant around everyone at gatherings—an attitude that made him seem pompous.

No funeral had been had for the family, being that there were no bodies to bury. The remaining family members of Julia's all pitched in and had created huge posters from the family pictures they'd had. They were hanging from the rafters of Dan's mansion made of logs. Within Julia's family were some of the best cooks in the state, and the potluck they provided was absolutely scrumptious. Stories were told, and family members chose to celebrate the lives lost instead of mourning the tragedy, itself.

Arik entered the house with his parents, already feeling horrible as the looks of pity and sympathy accosted him from all sides. The hugs were also abundant as he tried to walk through the crowd. Appeasing everyone to the best of his ability by returning hugs and giving his thanks, Arik finally walked up to Dan in the kitchen. Dan looked like he was trying with all his might to not be overwhelmed by all that was going on.

"Lots of people here. How are you handling it?" asked Arik.

Dan shrugged. "It's for the family. Time to be calm. I've been seeing a counselor who helps a bit, too."

"Really?"

"Yeah. You should think about it; might be good for you."

"Maybe." Arik paused. "Have you seen Bella or Zack's dad?"

"No," he said. "They couldn't make it. Honestly, I don't blame them."

"I'm going to go say hello to Paula. I'll see you around."

Leaving Dan with his parents who had come up to join them, Arik walked around looking for Paula. Finding her in the corner, she held a handkerchief in her hand and was sobbing into it. His heart hurt. Poor Paula had lost her favorite sister, and so much of the family. Walking up to her, he put his hand on her shoulder to try and give some sort of comfort.

"Hi, Paula," said Arik kneeling down in front of her.

"Oh, my gosh! Arik." Paula practically dove into his arms, sobbing even louder than before. "I'm so sorry, honey."

"Me too," said Arik sincerely, letting tears escape down his own face.

Arik and Paula began reminiscing over good times. From Arik and Angela's wedding to the birth of the babies, they were all happy memories, yet sadness seemed to take hold inside his heart.

As if feeling his pain, Paula changed the subject to her memories with Julia. She started to speak as if she was in a confessional and Arik was the pastor who would grant her forgiveness. She truly felt awful about things that'd happened a very long time ago when she and her sister had been basically children. Paula looked back on bringing Julia to a neighbor's house and setting her on top of a horse that took off running, causing Julia to tumble off as the beast then kicked her in her back, leaving a perfect black and blue hoofprint on her skin. Paula also brought up the time she forgot to put sunscreen on her sister when they were at a lake, and how Julia got severely burned and blistered by the hot sun. She stated that it wasn't until they were in their fifties that they were able to build a sisterly bond.

A couple more hours went by, as family members would take the floor and toast to all the people lost, and talk about how much they'd miss them.

Having had more than enough, Arik and his family made the decision to leave. Saying all the appropriate 'goodbyes' and how they would definitely 'stay in touch' with one and all, they drove away from Dan's and dropped Arik back home.

After the memorial, Arik unlocked the cabinet and began to drink. The alcohol kept running until the lights dimmed and he passed out cold on his couch.

Waking up with one of the strongest hangovers he'd ever experienced, Arik went to the jeweler in town to have the crystals made into rings. Wearing them consistently once he had them all back in his possession, Arik went on to spend the next year drinking. His days seemed to mesh together as he searched for psychics, trying to figure out if the crystals were indeed magical. Coming across a great deal of fakes who only wanted the money for the 'reading' appointment, Arik spent the rest of his time going to bars and getting hammered.

He even went so far as to get in touch with Izak's old drug dealers. Partying at their houses, he would set down lines of coke across tabletops and snort them, trying each and every hour to keep numb. By doing this, he succeeded at his goal to stay completely disconnected from everyone and everything around him.

Parking in back of the local, run-down hotel one late morning, too drunk and too high to drive, Arik checked in with the cute lady at the front desk. Arik retrieved his key and proceeded to pass out hard on the bed, not waking up until three o'clock the next morning. Hearing a sweet, young woman's voice outside his door, obviously showing a guest to a room, Arik listened.

"This is one of our best rooms. Will you be having anyone with you?"

"No. Just me," said a man's voice.

Hearing the door open to the room beside his, Arik then heard the woman again.

"What are you doing? Let go of me!" The woman's scream was followed by a loud 'thud' and the door slammed shut.

Instantly pulling Arik out of his frozen state, he heard the violent sounds intensify.

"Shut up. Don't make a sound," the man demanded.

"Why are you doing this?" she cried.

"What did I say? Shut the fuck up and get on the bed."

Standing, Arik quietly opened his own door and raced to the abandoned front desk. Grabbing the manager's key, easily spotted because it hung from the hook behind the counter, Arik ran back to the door where the screams of distress were coming from.

"If you bite me, I will fucking kill you!"

"Please, stop. I'm scared," she pleaded through her sobs.

Arik had enough. Opening the door as slowly and quietly as possible with the manager's key, he witnessed a tall, skinny man standing above the crying lady on the bed. With his trench coat wide open, the man gripped the back of the lady's head, forcing her to bring him release.

Anger and adrenalin radiated from Arik's body. Furious, he was more than ready to kill the sick son-of-a-bitch. Running to the man, he grasped his coat collar and threw him on the bed with his left hand, before bringing his right fist down hard, connecting with his nose. Pulling his body up to meet the next blow, Arik felt a sense of pride when he heard the crunching sound of the nose breaking. He moved on to connect with the slime's right eye, repeating this process again and again.

Completely ignoring the woman calling 9-1-1 and telling the officer she was sexually assaulted and a man was now beating her assailant to death, Arik continued hitting the now unconscious creep. Finally feeling human hands pulling on his arms, he stopped for just a second before two officers grabbed Arik from behind. Cuffing his wrists, Arik stared at his own reflection in the mirror on the wall of the hotel room.

Blood was splattered all over him; both his face and clothes were drenched with it. Feeling it drip from his face, the officers led him to the back seat of their police car, taking him to jail.

* * *

The following days clumped together like a mish-mosh of insane images, some that Arik couldn't believe himself.

The man he'd beaten had been taken to the hospital where he fought for his life. Constantly monitored, he died three days later from a blood clot in his brain.

Arik was thrust into court, eventually being found guilty and given a sentence of eighteen months in prison for involuntary manslaughter. He avoided the murder charge due to the woman's testimony and the overabundance of proof that showed Arik was under the influence when the incident had occurred.

Spending only a year in prison and being released for good behavior, Arik's journey had him turning over a new leaf. Staying away from drugs and alcohol, he vowed to get his life back on track.

Finding a job came first, seeing as that Arik had spent every dime he'd had on meaningless call girls, bar tabs, and drug dealers. Getting hired by the same construction company he'd worked with once before; Arik followed the boss's orders and kept his nose clean. Contacting his parents, he planned to pay them back everything they'd spent for the upkeep of the house, but the people they'd rented it to had paid everything and left the house open for the last three months.

As a new year of his life began, he threw himself into work as much as he possibly could. Getting back to a healthy lifestyle, he worked out every day, beginning improvements on the house in his spare time. Moving forward, the crystal rings also returned to his fingers, reminding him of the man he used to be...and the woman and children who'd loved him. He would stop at nothing to make them proud.

A day came when he was building furniture in his shop. Sanding the lovely cherry wood, the lights suddenly started blinking. Looking up, watching them go out one by one, Arik's heart began to beat fast in his chest as the floor of the shop began trembling under his feet. When the unmistakable flash of lightning released from the sky, it came through the window and then...everything stopped.

The trembling ceased.

Walking slowly to the door of the shop, Arik put his hand on the knob, turned it, and was met with sunlight so bright he could barely see. Regaining his focus, he stared out at the strangest sight imaginable.

"What the hell...?" Arik looked around. Feeling the excitement grow, he knew that a journey was about to commence that may just lead him back to his lost family.

CHAPTER 10

His Majesty was already sitting in his chair outside the steel bars of the dungeon, watching her face as she slept. It was an odd viewing. One moment, her lips pursed and her brows fell in sadness; the next moment, the corners of her mouth would rise as she broke into a warm smile and released a small laugh in her sleep. Feeling emotions roiling inside him, he chastised himself for finding her so inviting. Standing up quickly, he hit the bars with his fist.

"Wake up! I'm here. My presence should be acknowledged, correct?"

"Whatever. But now I feel like I haven't had much sleep. Which means I can be grumpy, too," Angela snorted before sitting up in the bed. Yawning, she reached for the sky in a stretch, trying to move the muscles that ached from being stuck in this small place for so long. Pulling her hair back from her face, she winced, apparently still smelling the personal odor that was getting worse by the day.

He tried not to feel guilt. Setting it aside, he told himself that the only reason leniency would be given was because *he* could no longer deal with the scent either. "I've decided to let you out today. You do *me* a great disservice by smelling this badly."

"Oh, my gosh...thank you. I am so grateful," she said, walking toward the bars. Ready to get the stink off, she offered him her biggest smile.

More emotion flooded his soul. Shaking his head, he pulled the key out of his pocket and unlocked the steel—looking straight in her eyes at all times.

"Am I going to need these?" he asked, holding up the heavy manacles for her wrists and ankles.

Her eyes widened at the chains and then she moved her focus to the man's eyes, speaking with utter sincerity. "No. Definitely not. I promise."

"Good," he said. Pulling her from the cell, he walked her up the staircase, standing behind her with his hand upon her shoulder as if reminding her at all times that she was his prisoner. Upon entering his lovely home, he rushed her past everything, pushed her up yet another staircase, and brought her into an enormous bedroom.

"You will wait here. I strongly suggest you don't even try to go anywhere. This will be your room from now on. I will get someone to prepare the water for your bath." His voice was a growl, as he watched her face turn from pleasant to absolutely beaming with joy and appreciation.

"You have no idea how grateful I am. Thank you so much."

His Majesty left the room, leaving Angela alone to look around. She was amazed at her surroundings. In minutes she'd been taken from an odorous, dark, frightening, cold cell and was placed in a literal haven that looked like one made for a princess. Everything she set her eyes on looked handmade, even the curtains and bed linens looked to be handwoven silk and satin, but she didn't want to pick anything up. The last thing she wanted to do was transfer her grit and grime onto the beautiful items. Walking to the large window, she stared out at the divine scenery. Desperate to walk in the colorful gardens that spread out below, she was suddenly startled by the loud sound echoing behind her. Walking into the bathroom, expecting to see a servant girl, it came as a complete surprise when she set her eyes on her own kidnapper filling the tub and testing the temperature.

He stood up quickly. "It should be perfect. I don't really understand what it is you're wearing, but it doesn't look like you need help getting out of it. Look around, grab anything you need. Clothes will be laid out on your bed while you're bathing. Simply call for me if you need any help." His Majesty's polite words came out as orders.

When she smiled, he turned around without another word and left the room.

Undressing quickly, desperate to get the horrible, dirty cloth away from her skin, Angela stepped into the hot water, sat down, and let it consume every inch of her body. Closing her eyes, loving the steam entering her nose, she released a sigh that'd been building inside her for quite some time.

When she looked around the room, she spied the bars of soap and hair products in her midst. The soap smelled like roses, and the milky bottle that she assumed was shampoo gave off the lovely scent of lavender. Scrubbing herself with all her strength, Angela found that she never wanted to leave the glorious tub.

Knowing there was no choice, she eventually rose and grabbed the long, wide towel sitting on a marble countertop. Wrapping herself in the soft, warm cloth, she found a horsehair brush and removed the snarls and snags from her own long mane. Looking for something that could help her oral hygiene, Angela opened a drawer and found a small, slender brush sitting beside a bar of paste; it gave off a minty smell. Assuming this was the treasure she'd been searching for Angela tested it and then scraped the brush against the bar of mint to clean her teeth. If there'd been a clock to judge it by, Angela knew that she'd done the process for so long that her teeth had to be as clean as they'd ever been.

Stepping out of the fancy lavatory into the bed chamber, she was once again in awe to see the gorgeous dress awaiting her. The shade of dark maroon was lovely, and the 'V' shaped design of the bodice placed it into the sultry category. Picking it up, she rubbed the elegant fabric along her cheek, reveling in the silky touch.

The undergarments, however, were a far different story. Picking things up and examining them, Angela studied a contraption that closely resembled a straitjacket, with ties going around the back. From the look of it, she knew it was meant to go under the dress in order to cover both her breasts and stomach. "How the hell am I supposed to get this thing on?" she whispered to herself, already feeling the pain that the thing could create. Going slowly, Angela first put on the leggings. When she tried the straitjacket, she pulled the dress over it and looked in the mirror, quickly realizing she needed someone's help. Just when she felt completely helpless, Angela heard a knock on the door.

"Are you alright in there?"

Already feeling the heat of embarrassment, she knew there was no way to avoid asking for her captor's aid.

"Yes...I do need help, though."

Taking a deep breath, he opened the chamber door slowly and set his eyes on the woman. Emotions raced through him as she saw her donning his wife's dress; although he was attempting to fight the feelings, he was stunned at how beautiful she looked in the garment.

"I can't reach," she explained, turning around and exposing her back.

Instantly running to her aid, trying not to view the clean, lovely smelling skin, he quickly tied the knots on the corset without difficulty, having done it for his wife in the past. He smiled as he remembered her face...and how much they'd loved each other.

Angela looked at him in the mirror. It was almost like he was struggling internally. Watching his gaze move quickly away as he finished with the last knot; he pulled the strings hard, making her gasp for air.

"Jeez...you cut off my oxygen."

"Sorry," he mumbled. "It always seemed to be the way women wear these corsets."

Angela rolled her eyes, finally remembering the name of the garment. "Well...not me; at least, not in my day and age. I can barely breathe."

Wearing a slight grin, he loosened the knots a bit, giving her room. His smile was almost teasing, making Angela wonder if her "tough" accuser actually possessed a playful side.

"Thank you," she said, turning around and looking up into his face. She tried to avoid the lightning bolt of passion that raced through her when his eyes sparkled.

"You're welcome," he replied, staring down into her eyes for far too long. "Come along. It's time to eat." Grasping her hand, he tugged her down the ornate staircase into the grand dining room below.

What sat before her had to have been the largest table she had ever seen. The walls were decorated with the most gorgeous paintings imaginable, allowing a visitor to enjoy everything from sunsets over an ocean to the lush greens and browns of a forest, where fox hunters rode grand steeds amongst the trees. Whoever the artists were who'd painted them were extremely talented.

Sitting down to eat, Angela found herself lost in a painting of the dragon that'd taken her from her family. The colors were exact; the spikes had been drawn so well that it looked like, if she touched the canvas, they would tear into her flesh.

"Where is the dragon right now?"

"He's called a 'drakon' in my realm."

"A drakon...is that part of your specific language?"

"Yes," he replied simply, pouring wine into Angela's glass.

"Who painted that?"

He paused for a moment. Angela noticed the sad look that appeared in his eyes as he stared at the wall. "My wife painted them all." Taking a drink, he slammed his goblet hard on the table. "She's dead. The horrible woman who wears your face is responsible."

Angela looked down at her lap. "I am terribly sorry for your loss. That explains so much," she added in a quiet voice.

She cleared her throat. "You take care of the drakon, then? You and your wife did? Where is he?"

"The drakon is securing the lands, why?"

"Because I would like to meet him," she said, not sure how His Majesty would react. Out of the blue, he began laughing.

"You want to *meet* him?" He was amused. "After everything that happened?"

Angela shrugged. "Yes. I would very much like to clear up this misunderstanding. Plus, I have to say the drakon is one the most beautiful creatures I have ever seen. Scary but gorgeous," she said.

"Okay, then after you eat I will call for him."

"Really?" Angela clapped her hands. "That would be so cool."

Shaking his head, befuddled by both her request for a meeting and her odd words, he completed the delicious meal on the plate before him. Finishing, he watched the woman take her last bite, sigh in complete happiness, and finish off her wine.

Standing, he shook his head as if once again clearing unwanted thoughts from his mind. "Come outside after you wash up. The drakon will be in the front of the castle."

Angela walked into the kitchen, searching for a place to wash her hands. She thought about the man's wife being somehow killed by the woman with her face. *Who could she be?* Angela thought.

Washing her hands with warm water found atop the large, metal stove, Angela walked out the front doors of the castle. She stopped at the base of the stairs, observing everything around her and the beauty of it all. Turning her head away from the gardens, she instantly set eyes on the drakon. This time, however, he exuded a different energy than when she'd first run from him. Walking forward, her eyes remained on his face until she was near the claws of his front feet. He laid out on the ground before her.

"Hello." Was all she could think to say.

"Hello...human," he replied. Even though he was in a relaxed stance, he peered down at Angela—his figure still towering above hers.

Smiling, Angela scanned his scaly body as she walked around him; she fought the desire to touch him, to prove to her incredulous mind that what she was seeing was truly real.

"May I touch your skin?" Feeling suddenly embarrassed, Angela felt herself blush at the words she'd just spoken.

Watching her, the drakon looked confused, as if wondering why the human wasn't afraid. He had taken her from her family, after all, and dropped her to the ground. Did she own some kind of invisible strength that allowed her to just brush their first meeting off so easily?

"Yes, you may. You're not at all afraid of me," he stated.

"No. I'm fascinated by you," she replied, running her hand across the side of his shoulder, moving along to the fearsome spiked tail.

"Be careful," the heavy voice spoke. "That is incredibly sharp. I don't want to hurt you." His eyes grew wide, as if he'd surprised himself with his declaration. He knew his thoughts would actually scare her more than any defense mechanism he had at his disposal. In fact, he longed to be touched. As the tips of her fingers moved around and over his scales, the drakon closed his eyes, as if lost in some sort of sensual feeling. When he reopened them, Angela was directly in front of him.

"Could you bring your face down here?"

"Why?"

"I can't see it."

Lowering his head, she put her hand on his cheek, feeling the heat radiating from his nostrils. Reaching up as high as she could, Angela touched the lush purple hair the drakon sported.

"Wow, this is really soft," she let out a small giggle. "For a dragon, of course. In fact, your entire body is like satin. I expected it to be...different."

"Would you like to fly?" The offer seemed to come from out of nowhere.

"Really? You would let me fly with you?" she said, unable to hide her excitement.

Looking surprised yet again by her reaction, the drakon spoke in his deep voice, "I believe your first experience wasn't a good one. I can assure you; this time would be different." He paused before lowering his shoulder as far as he possibly could. "Are you able to get on my back?"

"I'll try."

Standing on his left knee and placing her hand on his shoulder, Angela hoisted herself up and onto his back. She seated herself comfortably and securely by grabbing on to the mane of hair. "Now what?"

As the enormous wings spread out in the air, they lifted off the ground, causing her to lean forward and grab his neck.

Closing her eyes, she felt the air on her face as they rose higher and higher into the sky.

"You can't see anything with your eyes closed," the drakon announced, following with a small laugh and a blast of fire from his nostrils.

Raising her eyelids, Angela's breath caught in her throat as she took in the clouds that looked like soft, white pillows floating beside her. The view was absolutely breathtaking. Reaching her right hand out, attempting to catch a cloud, she laughed at her own silliness. As they flew closer toward the water, Angela gasped as she took in the beautiful turquoise layer that protected the ocean's creatures. Quickly realizing he was slowly going down, Angela let out a yell, "Oh my god!"

With a large splash, the drakon slammed into the water. Slipping from his back, she let go and kicked her body back to the surface. Being the horrible swimmer she was, Angela caught water in her nose and mouth. When she finally reached the top, she jumped from the ocean, coughing and spitting out the salt water...looking for her flying partner.

"Help! I can't swim," she began to panic. Suddenly, the drakon appeared beneath her and they both came out of the water, flying back into the sky. Angela hugged him tighter than before.

"I'm sorry. I was just being playful," he said. "I didn't know you weren't a good swimmer."

"It's okay," Angela said, trying to calm her heart. "How could you have known? You don't know anything about me."

Silence met her ears. Securing herself, she wrapped her arms around him even tighter as they flew toward the mountains in the distance. Landing calmy and softly on a cliff, Angela watched the last bit of sunlight set into the ocean, causing a rainbow of color to spark in the sky just before it disappeared. Proceeding to talk and laugh for hours, the drakon and Angela shared backstories until she let loose her first yawn.

"I should get you back. Wouldn't want His Majesty getting mad. Keeping you out so late."

"Hah. What could he do? You're a huge, powerful dragon. Sorry...*drakon*."

The creature issued a deep laugh. "You would be surprised."

Taking her place atop his back, they headed to the grandiose castle where he let her down safely. She hugged him tight.

"That was the most fun I have had in my entire life. Thank you." Turning to walk away, she suddenly turned back with a smile. "I never even asked. What's your name?"

"Alister. I have had fun, too. It has been a long time."

"Could we go flying tomorrow?"

"We will see. His Majesty says he plans to return you to your family soon."

"I hope they can meet you."

"I imagine they hate me very much."

"No. They just don't understand you. You would be surprised at what my family can handle."

"Goodnight, Angela." Bowing his head, his wings released and Alister took off into the now jet-black sky.

She slowly climbed the steps, feeling her adrenaline begin to wane as she made her way back to the bedroom and fell asleep in all her clothes. Briefly she wondered why the king would have allowed her to go off with the dragon, completely unsupervised, seeing as that escape could have been a huge possibility.

Waking up to a knock on her door, she walked over and opened it, revealing a very different kind of man.

"Good morning," the king said enthusiastically.

"Good morning," she replied, wiping the remaining sleep from her eyes.

"Is there anything you would like to do today? I have beautiful gardens, a duck pond, a warm river...a great deal is at your disposal. I also have horses in the stalls, if you wish to go for a ride and enjoy the land." He was looking at her expectantly, grinning from ear to ear.

His kindness and absolute giddiness shocked her. *Who is*

this man?

"Yes...yes, I would love to do all of that."

He clapped his hands together. "Great. I'll bring you some proper riding clothes to change into. Oh, and breakfast will be ready soon. We should eat before we go."

"Oh. Okay. Uh...thank you."

He rushed down the stairs, leaving Angela standing at the doorway completely bewildered.

Quickly reappearing once again, the king handed her new clothes made up of leggings, a woman's blouse and black boots. She noted her original undergarments had also been washed and sat on top of the stack.

"Come down for breakfast when you're ready."

Changing her clothes, Angela braided her hair. Looking into the mirror, she felt like a silly teenager for wanting to look nice. She was married, after all...but would she ever even see her husband again?

Walking down the steps and into the dining hall, Angela and the king began talking pleasantly as they ate their delicious breakfast. Sweet to a fault, Angela was surprised that the king had done a complete turnaround; not only was he more than tolerable, he also wanted to talk a great deal about Earth.

"So, what were you doing when the earthquake hit?" he asked.

"My sister and I were looking at some crystals she got from a lady at a fair." Angela's hand stopped in midair as she dropped her fork onto the plate. "Oh my god...*her* name was Arianna."

The king's face immediately turned to stone. "What kind of crystals were they?"

Angela's thoughts were locked on what her sister had said. She thought out loud: "But if that woman had looked just like me, my sister certainly would have pointed that out. And she didn't."

"No! She has the power to appear differently," he bellowed. "What were the crystals called?"

Angela closed her eyes and recalled the conversation. "Um...agate, Tiger's eye, amethyst, and...a Dragon's Heart." Opening her eyes, Angela started to shake. She'd never seeing the king this angry before. His voice...his face...his hands balled into fists at his sides; he exuded no emotion other than rage and looked like a block of ice.

Standing up, he threw his plate against the wall, shattering it into a thousand pieces. Turning directly at her, his eyes flared, like the flames of Hell were burning inside them.

"You lied to me, Angela. You said you don't have a witch in your family. Yet you would need a witch to activate those crystals and enter my realm. Arianna set your sister up...which means I can guarantee she has returned to this realm." His voice was more frightening as he accused her in a sharp, level tone. He reached down, grabbed her arm and ripped her from the chair.

Marching her back to the dungeon, he threw her into the cell and locked the door behind her.

"Please, Your Majesty. I promise you...I had no idea. There's no way my sister is a witch. She's as normal as I am. We're just humans. *Please* believe me."

She reached her hands through the bars trying to grasp his coat and pull him towards her. She wanted his attention; she needed him to see and understand that she was telling nothing but the truth.

"I will get the facts. I will go and meet your family. They're at...another place in this realm. I will confirm your tale, or disprove it and make sure you no longer see the light of day for the rest of time," he seethed. "In the meantime, you will stay locked away."

"*What?* What other place?"

He remained silent; his eyes remained distant.

"Please...none of this is necessary." A thought jumped into

her mind. "Please...get Alister. I can always spend the day with him; he certainly would never allow me to escape."

"You will stay *here*!" He yelled in her face, turning around and leaving her in his angry wake.

Joining his fury, the tears fell from her eyes. She would not forgive him this time. There would be no 'nice' girl; Angela now wanted nothing more than for him to be gone...out of her life for good.

The worry and fear she had for what the king would do when he met her family filled her thoughts. How she wished Alister would appear and keep her company. Talk to her until she was all better. He had a way of making her feel better.

* * *

The whole day had gone by. Her stomach growled as she laid on the bed and began to fall asleep, completely sickened by the hideous, stale odor she'd left behind when she'd finally been freed from the cold cell. Waking up in the middle of the night, Angela briefly saw a form, the king's form, set a platter of food and a glass of water by the freezing cot. Hearing him mumble what she thought was an apology, he left the room. Waiting to hear his footsteps disappear, Angela then sat up and gobbled down everything he'd brought, washing it down with the water before going back to sleep.

When the next morning came round, Angela woke up to the sound of the steel door creaking open. The king was there, holding a cloth in his hands. Oddly, he wore a look of regret.

"I'm taking you to the castle where your family now rests. What you said is correct. Your family and sister had no idea Arianna was a witch, and no one in your family showed any signs that they practice her evil ways." He paused, then cleared his throat as he looked her in the eyes. "Your children are precious, Angela. Your family is truly missing you."

Listening to him talk made her insides boil. Jumping from

the cot, she slammed her fists into his chest. Catching him off-guard, he fell to the stone floor.

"I told you, you son-of-a-bitch! You've kept me from my family...my *babies*, for nothing!" Sitting on top of him, still hitting him with her fists, Angela continued to curse at the egotistical bastard who'd refused to believe her words.

Grabbing her wrists with one hand, the king brought the cloth up to cover her face with his other hand.

As if time suddenly stopped, Angela's movements began to slow and the stone walls began to move in front of her eyes. Angela suddenly realized that he'd drugged her somehow with the cloth, most likely pre-arming himself with it because he expected some form of retaliation for what he'd done. Her eyelids grew as heavy as bricks, and the darkness came swiftly.

When she awoke, all Angela could hear was a small chorus of children's voices. Sitting up quickly, Angela felt the warmth flood her heart—she'd been reunited with her beloved babies.

CHAPTER II

Arianna had been waiting for three days when she finally heard the unmistakable sound of carriage wheels being pulled by horses' hooves 'clicking' on the gravel in the driveway. Waiting inside the house until she heard the carriage come to a halt, she peeked through the window as the two large men got out of the carriage and walked around the property; they called out for cats.

"Here, kitty, kitty."

As they shouted, she gripped her sapphire in her hand. "Metamorfónomai ailouroeidís!"

Turning into a feline once again, Arianna bolted through the kitchen and out the doggy door. Jumping on the side railing of the porch, she let out the familiar cat call and made herself as cute and cuddly as she possibly could. Purring, she walked back and forth upon the wood. Her 'meows' grabbed the attention of the youngest brother.

Leo turned at the cat calls and walked around the side of the porch, looking up at the railing, seeing the animal's black sheen offset by a collar with a glistening blue stone hanging from it.

"Hello, little kitten," he said, picking her up. He moved slowly and carefully so as not to frighten the animal; he definitely did not want a repeat of the attack he remembered as a child. Walking back to the carriage to take his seat, he mumbled, "Be good, you evil creature."

Arianna heard the insult and laughed internally, deciding then and there that she would get him back for it later. Curling up on his lap, she pretended to sleep, waiting for the perfect time to make her escape and race back to her father's castle. It was a homecoming she was definitely looking forward to.

Declan came walking out of the barn with three other mousers in hand. Settling in his seat, Declan commanded the driver to head back to the castle.

Not long after they hit the road, Arianna felt her own power begin to drain; transformation always took far more energy than anything else in her witch's bag of tricks. She needed to cut her plans short. Jumping into the air, she hissed and dove at Leo's face, scratching him across the cheek before he threw her out the window. Landing on her paws, she ran as fast as her little legs could take her. While crisscrossing the ground through the tall trees, Arianna transformed back into her human state as she sped across the brush-laden turf. Stopping, she immediately crawled into a nearby cave. All she could do now was sleep, and hope to recover faster than the last time.

Upon waking, Arianna was a bit foggy; she wasn't sure how long she'd been healing while hibernating, but by the look of the sun's position in the sky, she knew that at least a few hours had passed. Crawling out, disgusted by being covered in dirt, and angry at her legs hurting from being thrown out a window, she slowly walked the Forbidden Lands in the Drakous Realm.

"Home at last," she snorted in derision. "They know not what they have done."

As she walked further, the surroundings became more and more familiar. Soon, she came across the small castle that her father had abandoned long ago. Although he referred to it as a castle, with the exception of a turret, it more closely resembled a falling down mansion in her eyes. But it's all she needed. Here she would fully rejuvenate her magic and make the old home into tip-top shape once again.

Walking through the large, heavy doors—with one creaking so badly, it sounded like it was going to fall off its hinges— she proceeded up the once lavish staircase, now in disrepair. Coming to the threshold leading to her father's old room, she pulled with all her might; it'd been years since anyone had been in the place and the door was more than difficult to open. Finally giving way, Arianna entered the room to stare at the layers of dust and mighty cobwebs that'd formed in all the corners. Remembering her father's stories about how he and her mother had met, she almost felt as if they were once again standing beside her.

* * *

Mother of Arianna, the high-spirited Elizabeth Butler was born in Drakous Realm. A true sorceress, she used her crystals to hop into different realms as a game, loving the fact that she could explore various locations, learn everything about them, and return home unharmed. One day, however, when her father attempted to marry her off to a royal she most definitely did not love, Elizabeth had jumped to a location that she knew no one would follow her to because of the legends that surrounded it.

"Earth" had been her chosen leap. Here, she was unique.

After all, Earth could boast no real magic; all they'd ever had throughout history was a rare bloodline of witches that had disappeared hundreds of years ago. She'd settled there, taking a job as a nurse where she used her exceptional talents to provide care for the sick and dying.

One person whose bedside she'd sat at was a woman named Miranda; she was the mother of a gentleman named Isaiah. Too far gone for Elizabeth to save, the kind woman's dying wish was for her to marry her son. Which they did. But, oddly enough, not because Miranda had requested this happen, but because they had already fallen head-over-heels in love. After joining in wedlock, a baby girl was granted to the couple and they named her Iris. Afterward, Elizabeth did finally reveal her one secret and told her beloved husband of her magical powers; a secret she'd always regretted not telling him sooner. Thankfully, because of their love, Isaiah had understood and accepted her. Of course, he'd never even believed in magic, but he'd chosen to believe in his wife.

Two years later, Elizabeth died while giving birth to Arianna.

* * *

Lost in thought, standing in the middle of her father's room, Arianna finally snapped out of her mental flashback and went in search of a knife from her father's collection.

Walking over to the cabinet next to his bedside table, she opened the top drawer; there they were, sitting side-by-side in a perfect row. Still in mint condition. Choosing one, she left the room behind and went back to the hall where she took yet another staircase leading to her old bedroom situated in the turret. This had not been a place she'd been "sent" to because she'd been bad, she'd chosen it herself, wanting complete privacy when she was young. The door was still sealed with her blood magic and childhood password. Holding the knife in her right hand, she poked her finger and created a perfect bubble of blood on her skin. Reaching out, she touched the center of the door and said, "Anoixe sousámi," causing the lock to release and the door to move inward.

Entering, she opened the drawer of the table and withdrew the box holding her most important crystals. Sitting upon the dusty bed, she scanned the treasures inside the box and located the clear quartz responsible for healing. Holding the crystal in her hands, she felt the healing energy the crystal possessed enter her body, repairing her aches and wounds and rejuvenating the weary muscles inside.

Now that Arianna was completely healed from the transformations, and her power had been fully restored, she could now use her perfect skills to open a small door. A door that would lead directly into the Destructor's Realm.

Setting the clear quartz back in its box, she walked over to the loose floorboard under her bedroom window. Bending down, she wiggled the plank of wood back and forth until it popped out. Reaching her right hand in the hole, she pulled out a small object wrapped in a beautiful, violet-colored cloth. Releasing the item, she stared down at her mother's realm-hopping crystal: The Dragon's Heart.

Much larger than the one she'd sold to Neveah, she walked back to the box of crystals while holding The Dragon's Heart in her hand. She was careful not to get the crystal too close to the others, seeing as that when they were all together the power they exuded was beyond strong and could not be reined in by any witch. She searched for the Pietersite. This was the crystal of control. Ironic, in fact, because its swirling colors resembled a storm that made some refer to Pietersite as a tempest, the exact opposite of control. She would need this in order to control whatever demons came through the portal of the Destructor's Realm. Also necessary was the rose quartz; with this, she would 'scratch' the opening into her bedroom wall that would allow the demons to come through.

After attaining the correct crystals to start the process, she stared out at the full moon now glistening through her bedroom window. She was all set to open the portal.

Taking the rose quartz and scratching an "O" shape next to the window, Arianna held The Dragon's Heart in her right hand and the Pietersite in her left. Standing in the moonlight, she held the two crystals over her head until they each shot out a beam of light that meshed into one and burst open the door she'd drawn into the wood. She chanted: "Anoíxte tis pórtes ton katastroféon." The door was now open.

Quickly, Arianna watched seven men and seven women walk through the opening. Although they stepped through as beasts, their transformation into humans was fast. Bringing down the crystals, she looked towards the figures now standing before her. Still holding the Pietersite in her left hand, she aimed it at them. "I am your leader now. You will obey me," she stated, not allowing the demons a moment to get out of control.

Watching as the group fell to their knees and bowed at her feet, they spoke in unison: "What do you wish of us, Our Queen?"

"You will go to the castle of the mood people and take positions there. You will pose as normal servants while you spy on the new creatures that have arrived. You will be my eyes when I cannot be present, and report back to me whatever you find out regarding the Earth people." Further explaining the appearance of the family to the demons so they'd know who to look for, she also directed them to the town and the castle therein.

"Yes, Our Queen," they responded, getting back on their feet.

"Now, go. And do not disappoint me," she demanded.

As the demon pack left her room and headed in the direction of the map she'd drawn out for them, Arianna took a deep breath. She tried not to address the small fear that they would not obey her commands.

Resealing the door to the Destructor's Realm, she walked out of her bedroom, relocked the door, and trekked down the steps. On the second floor, she hesitated outside the first room. Even though she screamed at herself to continue walking and not look inside, the emotions that'd been called up since she'd arrived inside the castle won out.

Without any difficulty, the door opened. Arianna walked in and observed the décor that called out to guests that this was a nursery for a newborn baby girl. *Her* baby girl.

Walking over to the dusty, lacy bassinet, she peered down at the lovely lavender and yellow colors of the satin sheets. Bending down, she picked up the royal purple baby blanket that she had crocheted herself, and sat down in the wood rocking chair on the side of the bassinette. Holding the blanket in her hands, Arianna buried her face in it. The tragic memories remained fresh and at the forefront of her mind. The horrible memories of losing her beloved father, devoted husband, and exquisite infant came...one right after the other.

CHAPTER 12

Marrying a Centreman, who was gorgeous both inside and out, was the happiest day of Arianna's life. She felt blessed, and became even more so after finding out that she had conceived a child on their wedding night. Four months into the pregnancy, both her husband and father were called to fight the war against an evil army that'd come to their land: the army was made up of Destructors—demons that came from the blackest of all realms.

Her father and husband were among the many obliterated by these demons, causing Arianna to fall into a deep depression. Only the precious baby girl growing in her tummy gave her the will to continue living. When she was nine months pregnant, setting up her baby girl's nursery gave Arianna her only path to happiness. One day, as she was doing just this, her water broke.

Unfortunately, Arianna had been in the castle completely alone. Lying on her large bed that she'd placed next to the bassinet, she screamed in pain, making the entire realm shake and tremble. As dark clouds formed over the castle, Arianna finished labor by passing out. Waking up, Arianna heard the ungodly sounds coming out of her sister Iris' mouth. Looking around, she witnessed the once lavender quilt covered in an obscene amount of blood. As the realization hit, her adrenalin rose tenfold at her sister's cries.

"Arianna...oh, my God. Oh, my God," Iris repeated, sobbing. She rocked in the rocking chair and held something in her arms...wrapped in a sheet.

Arianna stared at the shape, seeing the spots of blood that seemed to be coming from within the fabric. "What...?"

"I am so sorry, sister." Tears ran like a waterfall down Iris' rose-colored cheeks.

"Iris, hand her to me now," Arianna screamed, causing the castle walls to shake with the amount of emotion exuding from her voice.

Iris had stared down at her dead niece before handing the infant to a furious Arianna.

Frozen, Arianna had felt oddly possessed as she took her child and set her on the pillow beside her own body. Then came the darkness. Everything had gone blank. There was no memory, no explanation as to what happened next. All Arianna's brain allowed her to see was the clear shot of her dead infant...and then the memory of waking up in a dark, cold dungeon.

"Where am I?" She had yelled out, hearing the echo of her own voice in her ears. "Iris...are you there?"

Iris had appeared at the call; her face had been a mask of fear, sadness and absolute pain. "I know you didn't mean to," Iris sobbed uncontrollably. "It wasn't your fault."

"What are you talking about, sister? What did I do?" Arianna had panicked. "Where is my baby?"

Before Iris could reply, guards came rushing into the dungeon. Throwing open her cell, they'd proceeded to shackle Arianna's wrists with thick, steel chains.

Bringing her to the king's castle, she'd been forced to her knees. Staring up at the monarch's angry face, she said. "What's going on? Why am I here?"

"Silence! You have killed my wife and unborn child," the royal man roared from the depths of his soul.

"What? I did no such thing," Arianna exclaimed. "It is my child who died, Your Majesty. I have no recollection of what happened after I held her...watching her cold, lifeless body."

"I'm sorry, sister," Iris whispered once again, still shedding her tears.

Arianna didn't even glance in her direction; the pain was still too great. "I don't know what happened. I swear, Your Majesty."

The king of the realm glared at her; the flames in his eyes burned so bright, it looked as if they would somehow shoot out and set her very flesh on fire. "I cannot read your emotions, but it doesn't matter. Nothing matters now. Your jealousy and uncontrollable power caused these unbearable outcomes. It is time to face what you have done and go straight to Hell."

"No...please, no," Arianna pleaded.

"I sentence you to death!" His Majesty ordered, throwing down the gauntlet.

"No...please...she didn't mean to. She has no idea what happened. Please reconsider," Iris scrambled to change the verdict. "Send her back to our birthplace. It is a non-magical realm, and I will cast the spell myself. She will not be able to use any magic as long as she's there."

The now weak voice of a woman who'd seen what life would be like without her loved ones took over the hall. "No," Arianna choked. "Kill me. I can't go back there. I'll be trapped in my own mind. Just kill me."

"Silence," the king ordered once again. "What is this realm you speak of?" he asked, turning to Iris.

"Earth, Your Majesty."

Knowing the horrible legends of this particular world gave the king a sense of evil enjoyment. Perhaps it would be far better to make the horrible murderess suffer a long, drawn-out, brutal life than give her what she wanted and end it in seconds. "Very well. Cast your spell and be done with this." The king turned away.

"Please, sister. Just let him kill me," Arianna now begged.

Without a word, Iris began to conjure her spell. But seconds before banishing Arianna to Earth, she threw their mother's sapphire around her sister's neck and shoved an item wrapped in paper into her sister's hand.

"I love you, Arianna," was the last thing she heard Iris say before being thrown into the unknown abyss of Earth.

* * *

With the last of the memories of that horrible time waning, Arianna stood from the rocking chair and set the royal blanket back down in the yellow and lavender bassinette. Anger had taken the place of her pain and sadness.

Exiting the nursery, Arianna easily transformed her wardrobe; she went from dirty cave-clothes to a long, royal purple dress with black lace. The dark colors provided a checkerboard pattern on the sleeves that now ran down her arms, the full skirt of the dress was adorned with a black lace train, and the front boasted a "V" shape. The perfect garment for a black-hearted witch.

Casting her magic everywhere, without losing a breath, Arianna turned the old, dusty castle into a clean, glittering, renovated home. Tossing the purple and black colors in all directions, she made the walls, ceilings, and opulent staircases match her in every way. Walking outside, she simply touched a finger to the ground in front of the castle. In seconds, she watched the heavy green vines bloom with dark purple clematis flowers covering the entire exterior of the castle. Joining with them were strands of climbing roses in ivory and black; their sharp thorns were like well-honed blades, guaranteed to slice unwanted visitors who were too stupid to understand their innate power.

Walking even further, Arianna pointed her hands to the sky and cast a spell that surrounded her section of the Forbidden Lands, making an invisible barrier that only she and those loyal to her could pass through without permission. Others would face complete unconsciousness as soon as they attempted to cross the shield's invisible line.

Everything was sheer perfection as the enormous powers came from the years of anger and revenge that she'd held bottled up inside her; the more anger she felt, the stronger the barrier became. Upon completion, feeling her weakness at the tirade of energy she'd utilized to make sure her own realm was brutally mean and as secure as possible, Arianna went back inside to restore and refresh with the family crystals.

After going through the process, Arianna sat on the bed and retrieved her sister's letter. She'd carried it with her since Iris had thrust it in her hands with the small, wrapped package. Unfolding it carefully, she read it for the millionth time.

Dearest Arianna,

Please understand, sister, I don't want to lose you. I want more than anything to see you again someday. Thus, I have attached instructions on how to return, along with these stones mother kept for us. She got them from a rare tribe in Juneau, Alaska.

Arianna, there is a witch on Earth from that first and only bloodline. The stones will work perfectly in her possession, and she won't even know it. All I can pass on to you is her family's last name of Michelson, and that she comes from the joining of a Tlingit and Haida tribe. Find the woman and give her the stones. Then, make sure to keep a close eye on her. You will find your way home if you are close to her when she activates the stones, so be sure you remain as close as possible. I'm not sure who or what will come with her when she's transported to our realm, but I know this will be the only way to get you back. Also, make sure you wear Mother's sapphire at all times. It will provide you a little mystical energy in the non-magical world.

I love you, dear sister. And please remember, I did not want any of this to happen to you. I will always regret it.

I will miss you always, and every day I will look to the gods and pray for your safe return.

All my love,
Iris

Arianna finished consuming the words she already knew by heart. She was still amazed by the feelings of love expressed by the sister she'd once cared for, yet now despised to her very core. Iris had not told her what happened in the letter...what she'd supposedly done. She had not even allowed the king to take her life when Arianna had so desperately wanted to die. It was all unforgivable. She had not even been allowed the chance to hold her beloved daughter one last time.

She would make Iris pay for all of it, along with the ridiculous king. Luckily, Arianna had stumbled across the witch who'd harnessed hundreds of generations of witches that'd come before. Neveah would soon see how powerful she really was, and Arianna would harness all of that power when the time to use it came around. She would drain it out of Neveah until she stole her very last breath.

Then...Arianna would unleash the almighty Destructors

into the Drakous Realm, and a new bloodthirsty war would begin.

CHAPTER 13

Izak was incredibly ill. After Liam had cried "monster" in the dining hall, Izak—along with everyone else—had stood from their chairs. When the server dressed in an odd cloak had transformed into a horrible creature, it had emitted an odor so strong that it'd literally knocked Izak out. On his way to the floor, he'd hit his shoulder on a chair. Queen Tiana had then requested her guards to place Izak carefully in his chamber.

The intoxicating woman he'd been mesmerized by in the dining hall had taken it upon herself to care for him. Now, as he laid in bed, he watched her mix mullein leaves and sage in warm water that sported little, round, opal pebbles swimming in it. She placed a cloth in the mixture and then set it on Izak's forehead.

"This will help your fever subside as the strong aroma of the herbs works to get rid of the smell released from the

Tarman."

Izak was amazed that her voice was just as beautiful as her face. He felt the relaxation take him over. Finally coming more into focus, he continued to stare. "Who *are* you?"

"I am Iris Vickens," she replied. "My role is castle witch." Smiling, she set her left hand upon his chest. "You must rest. You are very sick."

Taking in her words, he also realized that his system had been without drugs of any kind for more than a few days, meaning the fever, shaking, and pains he was experiencing came from that, as well. As he grasped the truth, his mind went into overdrive. The more he thought about it, the more he felt the intense pain in his stomach and kidneys; it felt like someone was stabbing a knife into him and twisting with great force.

"Ah!" He yelled out in pain. Holding his stomach with his arms, Izak rolled up into a ball.

"Ypóloipo," Iris whispered as she blew a small cloud of dust into the air above his head, making him instantly fall back into a calm, peaceful sleep.

Iris set the selenite crystal down that she'd used to create the dust, and stayed by his side until his eyes opened once more.

When he came to hours later, she was setting a bowl of chicken bone broth with chamomile on the table in his room. She added the necessary magic to ignite the healing properties of the herbs, doing all she could to relieve any pain and discomfort he may feel.

"You shouldn't be here," Izak said, trying to sit up. "This is embarrassing."

"Oh, hush," she replied, adjusting the pillows so he could sit more comfortably. She handed him the bowl. "This will help. Please drink."

Unable to make his own decisions, due to her bewitching tone, Izak could only do what she told him. Tilting his head back, he let her pour the soup down his throat, swallowing every last, delicious drop.

"Very good. You will get better quickly."

"Why are you helping me?"

"Because I can and I want to. That is an unusual question," she paused, while pouring what looked like lotion into her hand from an obsidian crystal container. By combining the lotion with her magical hands, she made the strongest healing concoction alive. "Lift your shirt, please."

"What?" he gasped.

She put the container down and grabbed the hem of his shirt, lifting it up.

"Hey, what are you doing?" he said, grabbing her hand, a bit embarrassed by the protruding ribcage he'd gotten from his constant drug use.

"I have to rub this on your stomach and kidneys. Your pain will subside, and you won't get inflammation in your kidneys. Unless you'd rather be in unimaginable pain and end up lying here curled into a ball." She spoke sternly this time.

"Why can't I just do it myself?"

"Can you conjure healing magic with your hands?"

"No. You're a *witch*?"

"Yes," she sighed. "The longer we sit here doing nothing, the longer you have to suffer. So it's up to you."

Without saying another word, he assessed the situation. Knowing he didn't want to be in pain, he rolled over onto his stomach and let her start on his back first. Feeling the warmth and then the coolness spreading out across his upper and lower back, he also felt the pain in his kidneys subside while she massaged the lotion onto what little muscles he had left.

"Now, roll over."

Izak rolled over onto his back exposing his pale, sunken stomach. It wasn't at all difficult; even though his stomach still hurt terribly, his kidneys and back were magically without any pain or even the slightest discomfort.

Iris looked at his appearance and her face dropped in sadness from the damage done to the handsome man's body. Turning to the table, she added more lotion in her hands before returning to Izak's stomach. She then ran her hands softly across his skin, from the ribcage down to his belly button.

As she was administering the lotion, she daydreamed about her sister and wondered if she had returned with this family. She ignored the man shifting under her hands, stopping only when he grabbed her wrists. Looking down, she noticed his...excitement and pulled her hands away as quickly as possible.

"Okay...I think you fixed me. I officially can't feel any more pain. But if you continue, I promise that we'll have another issue." He laughed, staring at her now embarrassed expression.

Iris brought her hand up to her mouth before she let out the giggle of a teenage girl. "Yes, that would be a problem," she winked, causing them both to burst out in a fit of laughter.

Iris stayed with Izak, asking him endless questions about his life. She'd begun with how he'd made such a mess of himself in the first place.

He explained how he started smoking marijuana with his own father when his older brother and sister went to visit him in Alaska, when he was just a middle-school boy. Returning home, he continued to use drugs, which made him fall in with the wrong crowd.

Getting the attention of a girl he had a crush on for a long time, she introduced him to pills that could give him a more intense high, and he ended up using the worst kind of drugs—meth and heroin. Never able to truly escape from the drugs' grasp, he lost himself and his family, who were unable to help him when he wasn't ready or willing to help himself. Feeling sorry and miserable, he was sent to an island in Alaska where his family hoped and prayed there was no such kind of drugs.

Unfortunately, they had been wrong.

Falling in love and marrying a woman who helped him continue his torturous lifestyle, it was ten years later that he returned home wanting nothing more than to have a sober new beginning. Wanting to meet his nieces and nephews and reconnect with his family, Izak left his wife to her own destruction.

Unfortunately, his wife had followed him back to Washington, only to poison his life all over again. Even though he had relapsed a couple of times, he still woke up every day to try again. She made it more difficult, waving the drugs in his face on a daily basis until he caved once more. This led to his family disowning him. Due to the children and his aggressive verbal outbursts, he and his wife were kicked out of the house, along with their four dogs.

He'd tried to continue to get help; he even forced his own wife to seek counsel, not realizing you can't help someone who doesn't first want to help themselves.

Officially leaving his wife with a signed divorce document in hand, Izak's mother accepted him back into her home. All the while he reassured her he was better, but at times, the unbearable side effects from not using hit him hard. He'd convinced himself he could use "just enough" to keep himself from feeling the pain and agony. Until Christmas...when everything else had occurred, which he continued to share with her.

Not believing his whole tale, Iris replied to it by saying, "Well, you definitely have no other choice than to live here. We don't have those drugs in our realm. The most we have is wine and tobacco. I have seen drugs in action on Earth, as a young girl. It's awful watching people go through that."

"You have been to Earth?"

"Oh, yes. I was born there," she replied.

"You don't have a way to send us back, do you?"

"No, I don't. Not without the crystals that got you here. My magic alone is not enough. I need to harness my sister's power, along with the stones, in order to cast the spell needed to send you all back."

"Where is your sister?"

"She was banished to Earth from a curse that was cast. I will explain more with the rest of your family present, for they are asking questions, too."

"That's a good idea. My mother would appreciate it," Izak said in all honesty.

* * *

The king had left Angela in the dungeon and headed to Mood Castle, needing some proof.

Arriving at the castle early that morning, the guards announced his presence as he walked into the Throne Room. The king, queen, and princess all got up from their royal chairs and walked towards him. Bowing their heads to His Majesty, he watched the king and queen of the two-legged creatures who'd been appointed to their stations by him, because they had royalty in their blood already. He was pleased he'd chosen the couple to play the roles.

"Queen Tiana, you look lovely as always." His Majesty smiled, greeting the royals and kissing her on the cheek before turning to the princess. "Hello, little one," he pat Jacklyn on the head.

"Hey," she grumbled, pulling her head away from his infantile greeting. "I'm not that little anymore."

"That is true," he chuckled.

"King Dustin, you're back early. How are the troops? We may need them. Arianna may be back."

"Yes, Your Majesty. I am back because my wife wished me to meet the visitors. The troops are on high alert; they have also been informed of Arianna's return. A black Tarman, in fact, interrupted my wife's dinner the other day."

"Is that so?" his eyes flamed at the news.

"Yes, the youngest son of the woman named Angela identified him as a demon while he was still in human form."

"That's not possible. No one and nothing can identify a shifter in their human form." His Majesty was dumbfounded by King Dustin's words.

"I assure you the boy has this power. I saw it with my own eyes," Queen Tiana chimed in.

"Where is this boy now?"

"In the day care with the other young children," Tiana replied.

"Good. I wish to speak to the adults in the family before I return Angela to them."

"Yes, of course, right this way. Dustin has yet to meet them himself."

"Has Iris met them yet?" His Majesty asked.

"Not all of them. The man who arrived in their company fell ill at the odor of the black Tarman. Iris hasn't left his side since," King Dustin explained while they all walked up the staircase to Julia's bedroom.

Queen Tiana lifted her hand to knock on the door lightly. Just after the third knock, Julia opened her door.

"Good morning," she smiled.

"Good morning, Julia. Did you sleep well?" Tiana returned her warm smile.

"Very well. Thank you," she answered, then looked at the man who appeared human. Just by looking at his posture, she could tell he sat 'high upon his horse.'

"This is the ruler of the entire realm. Would you mind bringing the rest of your adult family down to the Throne Room? Don't worry, there is no trouble," Tiana said quickly.

He cleared his throat. "I just want to officially meet you all. There are some things I understand you wish to discuss about your daughter who was taken. I wish to know more, too," he said.

"Of course we will come down. Just give me a moment to gather everyone up." Julia kept her smile in place, wondering if this man was anything like the shifters she'd seen in the realm thus far.

"I look forward to it," His Majesty said before turning and walking back down the steps.

Julia informed the rest of the family that the ruler of the realm was at the castle and wanted to speak to them, leaving the kids to play.

* * *

Iris and Izak found out His Majesty was at the castle after everyone had already been informed.

"Can you walk?" Iris asked.

"Yes, I can. I want to see if my sister is okay," Izak replied, lifting the blanket off himself and slowly moving his legs, he set his feet on the floor. His shoulder hurt from bruising it on his way to the floor at dinner. Iris reached out and slowly helped him stand.

"I feel fine," he said, attempting to show her he could do it on his own.

"Are you sure you're not just trying to be a tough guy showing off in front of a pretty lady?" Iris asked, teasing him.

"That's a given. First of all, you're gorgeous. Secondly, yes. Any chance I get to show off for you, I will," he laughed as she helped him.

"Good, because you're taking me to the ball in a month. You can't say no either, especially considering all that I have done for you."

Letting out a huge sigh, he said, "Okay."

* * *

All the adults entered the Throne Room at the same time.

Walking up to the chairs that the royalties sat in, His Majesty got up from his seat to walk towards the family. First, he spoke to Julia. He extended his hand, just as Angela had done with him.

"My name is Julia Michelson. Your name?" she asked, looking rather confused.

"Not at this time. It's nothing personal, I just need to trust you before I go giving my name out," he said, trying to force a smile.

"Have you heard from my daughter? She was taken by a huge dragon."

"Yes, in fact, I have. She is in good health; that I can tell you. She is happy to be coming back to her family tomorrow morning." He tried to hide the sound of his gritting teeth from all the questions. Moving down the line, he stood in front of Neveah.

"You must be the beautiful witch that brought your family here," he said, waiting to catch her in a lie.

"I'm Neveah. I'm no witch, though." She blushed at his comment and extended her hand.

He didn't take her offering. "Iris!" he yelled instead.

Leaving Izak's side, she walked up to him. "Yes, Your Majesty?"

"Is she not a witch?" he asked, pointing at Neveah.

"Actually, she speaks the truth. She doesn't know that she is a witch; she has not ever experienced any surges of power. This entire family is from the same non-magical realm of Earth where my sister was sent. The woman is an incredibly powerful witch, however," Iris explained, looking in Neveah's direction.

"That's silly. There is no way I am what you say," Neveah said, completely doubting them.

Iris' questions were delivered one after the other: "Are you a non-believer or, deep down, do you believe it is possible? Have too many unexplained things happened in your life? Did you ever experience a feeling of emptiness? An unusual connection to crystals or stones?"

"Yes...to all of that, but I never would have thought in a million years that witchcraft had anything to do with it."

"Do not worry. I will teach you and the little girl. She is actually more powerful than you and I combined."

"Who?" His Majesty asked.

"Little Leah. You probably know her as Angela's daughter."

"That's impossible. Leah is autistic," Julia argued.

"No, she's not. That's what the doctors used as an excuse for her personality and her inability to vocalize her needs. She has strange repetitive actions and is antisocial, but incredibly smart. Have you ever seen her head produce oddities out of nowhere? Does she have seizures that last unbelievably long?"

"Yes, she does," Neveah answered.

Iris continued, "Well, Leah is trapped in her own brain by magic that she's unable to release. When she does, there's no telling what her magic will be like." Iris went on to tell them about her own sister and their upbringing.

"My sister was incredibly shy as a young child. She wouldn't speak for years and then was diagnosed by the doctors as having 'nonverbal autism.' Our father didn't believe the doctors. He wanted to go to the realm our mother had always spoken about and was able to convince me to study our mother's spell books. When my sister turned five, I completed the spell only because I was holding on to her hand. Bringing us all to Drakous Realm, my sister began to lose control of the power that had been trapped by Earth's boundaries. They had been bottled up for five years and she possessed an unbelievable amount of strong, uncontrollable power for one little girl. I had to teach her relaxation techniques with chants to help tame her magic. Working, for the most part, she then started speaking just thirty days after being here."

She turned to His Majesty. "So, you see, Leah has the same

misdiagnosis. The son of Angela's is also of magic blood. He is an Identifier."

His Majesty looked at her with wide eyes. "That's amazing. I have never seen one in my entire life." Looking back at the family, he studied their expressions of disbelief; they were not able to wrap their minds around anything Iris had revealed. They remained silent, waiting for more to come.

"You are from a line of witches who lived hundreds of years ago. Your line went dry until you were born," Iris now spoke directly to Neveah. "The crystals worked for you simply because they are your family crystals handed down from your Alaskan Native tribes."

"So...I unlocked the magic not only in myself, but also in my sister's children? That's insane."

"Well, something like that," Iris replied. She glanced at Julia and they locked eyes, as if knowing they shared a mutual secret.

"So. It's true. None of you were ever aware of magic or believed in it until you got here?" His Majesty felt incredibly guilty over not believing his own prisoner. "I must go. Expect Angela here before morning."

His Majesty walked away from the still confused family, completely angry with himself. Regretting all that he had done and said to Angela, he hated himself for leaving an innocent woman who'd told him repeatedly that she and the rest of her clan was innocent. He had felt her truth but he'd been consumed in the hate he possessed, refusing to believe the woman who wore the same face of the witch who'd killed his wife.

Stopping on his way out of the castle to get a look at Angela's children in the day care area, he remained quiet as he watched the little, blonde-haired girl run around after a little, blond boy. Making him smile, he was a bit confused because neither one of the children resembled their mother in any way. Wondering what his own child would have looked like, he daydreamed until the little boy locked eyes on him and froze.

The child halted as his sister following close behind ran right into him and fell. Now knowing the child an Identifier, and not sure if the boy would scream or not, His Majesty left them alone before he could find out.

CHAPTER 14

King Dustin and Queen Tiana excused themselves after His Majesty's exit, and left the newcomers behind because they were holding a meeting in their forum within the castle.

Among the attendees were the King of the Skies and the King of the Shapeshifters. The King of the Waters had refused his invite because the King of the Realm wasn't going to be present. Atticus and his brothers were included, as well as some of the townspeople and guards who were curious as to what the meeting would bring to light.

"Everyone ready to begin?" the queen asked.

"Yes," the group answered in unison.

"Good. First we are going to discuss any concerns there might be regarding the newcomers, as well as who would like to know more about them."

"I would like to meet them tomorrow," the King of the

Shapeshifters said, expressing his interest. "I'm not opposed to them being here, by the way. I believe we could learn a lot from their kind."

"I second that. I have been watching them since their arrival, and they seem to be a wonderful and loving family," the King of the Skies agreed.

"I have had the pleasure of meeting all of them," Atticus chimed in. "They could make this kingdom untouchable by any dark force, which makes them a great asset to our realm."

"We don't need any strangers here," a few of the townspeople shouted out.

"We know nothing about them except what has spread through town." More complaints echoed off the walls of the chamber.

As questions and concerns kept being thrown in Tiana's direction, she began to worry about the overall acceptance by the township. How could she convince her people...her followers...that the new family posed no threat?

"What does the King of the Realm say?"

"We want to meet them." Different voices chimed in showing definite interest.

The queen raised her hand in the air. "Everyone, please calm down. We are planning a ball here at the castle where everyone can set their eyes on the family, as well as receive introductions. This will be the perfect event, allowing one and all a chance to get to know each other."

"What do they want?" a deep voice asked from the crowd.

"They wish for nothing from us. They simply want to live in peace, as we do. They find themselves unable to return home," the queen informed them.

"Where do they come from? What exactly are they?" the voice once again shouted.

"They are purebred human; their realm is Earth," Atticus stepped in and answered for the queen.

"They wish to walk through town tomorrow which will

give some of you a chance to meet them," Tiana stated, leaving the room in complete silence. No more questions or concerns were voiced.

"Next, I would like to inform all of you that these purebreds are like all of us. They have children; this family has a total of five they need to provide for. Who is willing to help make them feel welcome? What can we do to make this drastic change in their lives more tolerable? Their entire home, all of their land, was thrown into our realm. My personal desire is to rebuild their home to where it fits in with our realm."

"We will do all the labor," Atticus and the guards volunteered.

"We will provide food for the cellar," Delphine spoke.

The queen grew warm, beaming at her people who decided to give their talents and friendship to the family. "Thank you all."

"We could make up a wardrobe for all of the family members, once we gather their measurements," tailors and seamstresses offered.

Tiana remained silent as she listened to her people volunteer left and right to help the strangers. She had done an incredible job running her kingdom, because even the original naysayers remained loyal to her.

"Now that we have that settled, I wish to talk about the ball. Is there a decorator present?" the queen asked, looking around the room.

"Over here, My Queen." A rainbow-colored woman stepped forward with a pen and paper gripped in her hands.

"Excellent," Queen Tiana said, before explaining her plans to the woman. Her desires included having formal invites made and delivered to every house; she wished for fancy dresses to be made, and everyone to attend in formal attire. There was to be a feast prepared of all the different foods in the realm, as well as all the drink choices. Music and dancing would also be offered to one and all.

After the queen had finished explaining her requirements for the event, sounds of excitement invaded the room, spreading throughout the castle as her people left to get started.

* * *

His Majesty had dealt with the situation as best as he could when Angela swung her fists and attempted to beat him into the ground when he'd returned.

Mentally, he was already beating himself up for the way he had treated the woman. While she slept in his arms—made motionless by the liquid-based selenite on the cloth he'd put to her face—he kicked himself. It was supposed to give her a peaceful, calm sleep, but it had caused her to choke and then knocked her out cold.

This was the last thing he would regret doing. Making a vow to be the perfect gentleman going forward, he maintained that he would do whatever it took to get Angela to forgive him for his actions. He hoped one day she would understand the pain he had endured in the past, the huge impact it had on his life, and how horrible it was to see the face from his nightmares once again pasted on Angela. He hoped she'd give him a chance to show her the loving, caring, compassionate man he so wanted to be again.

They arrived back at Mood Castle and were welcomed by Queen Tiana, who showed him to Angela's room.

"Understand, she is not Arianna. I already made that mistake," he explained to her.

"I know, Your Majesty, but convincing others Arianna hurt in the past will be a different story. Angela's life will be in danger everywhere she goes. I want to avoid that."

"As do I. We agree on that point." He looked down at Angela with admiration written on his face. Setting her on the bed, he kissed her forehead before leaving the room with

Queen Tiana.

"You care for the woman."

"Yes. More than I would have ever expected," he admitted, with sadness and regret in his heart. "The only reason I tell you is because I know your special power."

"Is that so?" she laughed.

"I know you can read my mood. That you see others in color. That's why you like this family so much."

"Yes, well...all of that is true. Angela has the purest of all colors, by the way. She is truly a rare soul with a heart of acceptance, but she feels hurt and betrayed by you. It will take a long time for you to achieve her forgiveness."

"Well then, I will spend the rest of my life making it up to her," he replied, determined to make his words come true.

A moment of silence filled the hall before Tiana asked him a very important question. "Have you told her what you are?"

"No."

"You need to tell her. Certainly before she finds out from someone else."

"I know. I don't want to lie to her anymore. She was just so happy with me in my drakon form. It will break her heart. She even asked for him when I left her in the dungeon."

"Your attempts at gaining her forgiveness will be all lies unless she knows who you really are. It will break her heart even more if the news comes from someone else," Tiana added, yet knowing either way the results would probably be the same. "How you have been able to keep yourself in human form so many hours while around her is incredible. With all the anger balled up inside you."

"I haven't been in human form since my wife was killed."

"No one will ever forget Alison. She was an honest ruler and a dear friend," Tiana said sadly.

"It hasn't been easy being in my human form. My anger has been getting the best of me. Angela, in fact, is as stubborn as a mule; all the gold in this realm couldn't tame that woman," he said, looking back at the closed door with a smile.

"You don't say? Well, I'm sure you had nothing to do with her stubbornness at all," she said sarcastically, teasing and laughing along with him. "In all sincerity, I'm so happy for you. I never thought you would feel this way ever again."

"I will never forget my wife."

"Neither will I."

Sharing a hug, they went their separate ways.

* * *

Angela had woken up, grateful to hear the sound of her son's voice in the distance. When she'd looked around the room, she instantly realized she was not familiar with her surroundings. Wherever she was, it was a huge bedroom. All the furniture looked handmade, just as it had in the king's castle. *The king....* Remembering their battle in the dungeon and being forced into a blackout after being smothered with something, she winced.

"Mommy's in here?" She heard Liam's sweet voice.

"Yes, but she's sleeping, bubbas," Neveah replied.

Angela jumped out of bed and raced towards the door. Praying that it wasn't a dream this time, she put her hand on the knob and turned it. Her heart was full as she set eyes on her children's safe and smiling faces; it felt like an eternity had passed without them. Bella held tight to Leah and little Liam jumped at Angela's legs.

"It's really you?" she said, as she bent down and pulled her babies into a tight embrace, letting the tears trickle down her cheeks. "I thought I was dreaming again." Smothering them in hugs and kisses, Angela couldn't loosen her grip. Actually, she didn't want to. "Oh my gosh...I never want to let you go. I've missed you all so much."

Hugging Neveah once she had finally let go of her children, Angela spoke, "Where is Mom and Izak?"

"A lot has happened since you were taken. You won't believe any of it. I think it would be better if everyone explained together. Izak is sick and in his room, but I'll go get Mom," Neveah explained.

"I'll wait here with the kids."

"Okay. I'll be right back," Neveah said, quickly disappearing down the hall.

Angela walked back into the room with her three children. The two younger ones instantly ran over to the bed, jumping up and down on it; even Leah joined in the fun, which was out of the norm for her. They seemed happy about this new realm they'd found.

"So, what have you been doing while I've been gone?" Angela asked Bella.

"I made a best friend. She is so awesome, Mom. She's a Moodamorph and a princess; she's the same age as me, too. You have to meet her." Bella said, her speech so fast that it was hard to keep up.

Just when Angela went to ask Bella what a Moodamorph was, Julia burst through the door with an expression on her face that Angela had never seen before. She was crying as she walked straight to her, embracing her tightly.

"I'd thought I lost you," Julia said. "Tell us everything. Are you okay? Did it hurt you?"

Angela was so happy to be back with her entire family. She told them all about her experience with the king. She explained the dungeon, how rude and mean His Majesty had been to her, and then spoke highly about her second encounter with the dragon and how exciting it was. She passed on the fact that he was a truly incredible creature and that the first meeting was simply a misunderstanding.

"We actually met this king yesterday. He never said he was the one who had you, however. That explains why he looked so guilty," said Julia.

"He is really handsome, too," Neveah added her input.

"I don't care. I hope I never see his face again. He kept me from my children...he was awful to me because he was thinking I was someone else. And just when I thought everything was good, he got angry with me again, saying my sister was a witch...or helped a witch...whatever. He's crazy."

Julia and Neveah shared a look, making Angela question what was going on.

"Actually, I am a witch, sis," Neveah said, looking guilty for something she had no control over.

Angela's eyes widened in surprise. "How could that be possible? Why would you just be finding out now? You need to explain *everything* to me."

Julia explained all that had happened from the very beginning. The brothers who arrived at their door. The carriage ride. The creatures they saw, and the gardens where they'd stopped and gathered food.

Not wanting to lie and shoulder more guilt, Neveah stepped in and added the horrible event where she'd lost Leah in the cornfield.

"Are you kidding me? You lost my daughter and some guy had her? You're lucky she was brought back."

"Neveah was distraught, Angela," Julia said. "She was frightened. So frightened, in fact, that she hasn't taken her eyes off Leah since."

Angela was still upset with her sister after hearing all that had happened, but she certainly knew it was a mistake. She could tell her sister felt horrible just thinking about it. Not only that, but Angela also knew that she, herself, was guilty of losing Leah in the past. Leah was a clever little girl and knew just how to sneak away, and fast.

Completing the tale of their journey to the castle, Julia spoke about Izak and what'd happened with him, mentioning the castle sorceress named Iris and her sister, Arianna.

Angela was shocked. "That's the woman His Majesty believed *me* to be. Why would he think we were the same person? We couldn't possibly be related," Angela stated, staring at her sister and mother.

"We should let you get dressed and bathed. There is so much more to talk about. We should wait until you meet Iris before getting into the rest." Julia still couldn't believe she was in a place that boasted magic and that her own daughter was a member of some mystical community that supposedly died out hundreds of years ago.

Angela's mother and sister stood up from the bed. As they were about to take their leave with the kids, so Angela had time to get ready, there was a knock on the door that caught them off-guard. Julia opened it to view a young mood person carrying buckets of steaming hot water.

"I'm sorry. I didn't know you were all here together," the young woman said, turning yellow with worry as she stared at Angela.

"That's okay. My family was just leaving so I could get prepared," Angela stated while getting up from the bed.

It was obvious to Angela, Julia, and Neveah that the mood girl somehow knew of Arianna, because when she set eyes on Angela, she noticeably stiffened and a mask of fear appeared on her face as she turned gray.

"I'm Angela McLean. What's your name?" she said with a smile, fascinated by the woman's appearance.

"I'm...I'm Rose Efthymos," she replied in a somewhat shaky voice.

"Well, it's wonderful to meet you. Can I help with your buckets?"

"Nice to meet you, too," Rose replied, as the sheen of her skin changed slightly to blue. "But no, thank you, I'm fine with the buckets."

Rose headed into the lavatory while Angela's family said their goodbyes and hugged once again.

More mood people entered Angela's room with buckets, bathing necessities, and a fresh set of clothes.

Rose informed Angela she would be right outside when she was ready to get dressed and have her hair done before heading to town.

"Thank you so much. You are very kind," Angela spoke.

"You're welcome." Rose issued a far more comfortable smile before exiting the room.

Left alone once again, Angela observed her surroundings. Everything about the room was glistening in various gold tones. Inside, even strands of ivy grew along the walls sporting little, colorful flowers. Pictures of flowers and colorful mushrooms hung on the wall. Each painting was adorned with a signature in the bottom right corner that matched the one found in the king's castle: Alison Cirillo. These, too, were creations by the Queen of the Realm.

Stepping into the bath before the water got cold, Angela cleaned her sore, aching limbs. Closing her eyes, all she could see was the image of her hitting His Majesty. And all she could feel was the anger that'd exploded out of her because of how long it'd taken him to get over himself and bring her back to her family.

When she was done in the bath, she went to retrieve the clothing laid out on the bed. Angela let out a sigh of displeasure at the straitjacket. Putting everything on she possibly could, she then walked to the door to ask for Rose's help.

"Can you come in now?" she said, poking her head into the hallway.

"Of course." Rose entered the room, shutting the door behind her. "Walk to the bed and brace yourself."

"Not too tight, please." The first experience she'd had with the unwanted corset made her feel suffocated.

"As you wish."

Rose tightened and knotted the strings as Angela held onto the bed post. Taking her mind off the annoyance, Angela decided to learn more about Rose and the realm she was now in.

"Have you worked here a long time?" asked Angela.

"Yes. I have served, what you would say, twenty years. We go by days, but your oldest daughter says it's easier for you to go by years."

"Sounds like my daughter," Angela laughed.

"She's a born leader. Maybe she will marry into royalty someday."

"We are not staying in this realm. I want to go home, but I appreciate the comment."

Finishing with Angela's dress, Rose sat her in front of the vanity so she could do her hair.

"Are you married?" asked Angela.

"No, Ma'am."

"Please call me Angela. I would love to be friends."

"Me too." Rose beamed; her skin tone now completely matched her name. "Are you married?"

"Yes, but he is back in our realm. I fear that no one wants to leave this place. I know we're all unsure if we can even *get* home."

"I am so sorry. I heard that you and your family were staying, and that there was no way to return."

This news caused Angela to choke on a wave of new tears. She wanted to be strong in front of this woman; showing her vulnerability was always difficult for her. But everything that'd happened in this realm had, thus far, been miserable for her. She wondered why she'd ever longed for more, seeing as that now all she wanted was to return to her boring home.

"Oh, it's okay. I'll be here for you." Rose hugged her, trying to offer comfort.

Angela took a deep breath, getting her emotions back under control. Before she knew it, she was smiling and laughing with Rose. They were on their way to building a bond that, Angela hoped, would end up convincing one and all that she was *not* Arianna.

"All done." Rose was happy with her work.

Once she was prettied up, Angela was led downstairs to see her family, meet this woman named Iris, and check on her brother. The castle she was now walking through sported amazing differences from the one she'd been trapped in. Every corner of this one was beautiful, full of personality and warmth.

Rose guided her, as they walked down the exquisite staircase and down a long hall that stopped at a set of huge doors.

"This is the forum."

"Thank you so much, Rose. I hope to see you again soon."

"As I do." She bowed, leaving Angela to walk through the doors alone.

Stepping in, Angela watched heads turn in her direction, and she smiled. Walking up to the woman who Neveah whispered in her ear was Iris, Angela extended her hand. "Hello, I'm Angela McLean."

"I know who you are," the tearful woman replied, quickly reaching out and wrapping her arms around Angela's neck.

Angela felt her heart skip a beat as Iris took a step back, smiled wide, and said, "We are back together at last, dear sister."

CHAPTER 15

Angela was glad to receive the comforting hug the woman offered, even though she was more than a bit confused by her words.

She shook her head. "I'm sorry, you have me confused with someone else. But you're not the only one. Apparently I wear the same face as this other woman named Arianna.

Iris put her hands on Angela's shoulders and stared down into her eyes. "Actually, I understand completely. You are Arianna's twin sister, and my little sister." She beamed; the tone in her voice made it seem like she was stating facts that Angela should already know.

Angela slowly looked around the room. She scanned each one, stopping only when her eyes lit upon her mother's guilt-ridden face. "What is she talking about, Mom?"

Looking desolate, as if she knew this day was going to

come, Julia answered, "What she says is the truth."

"I'm *adopted*?" Angela suddenly felt ill. Her entire world was crashing down around her from just this one admission. Perhaps it shouldn't have hit her so hard, being that she'd always felt oddly different from her siblings. Angela now knew the emptiness that she'd felt came from knowing something was missing.

"Why didn't you ever tell me? How did this happen?"

Julia sighed. "You always asked. You always said you felt different and always claimed that I treated you differently because I held some hidden bias or hated of you. But, Angela, I have *always* loved you the same as your siblings. Please honey, you must understand that if I had told you, you would've believed for the rest of time that a hatred truly existed because you were adopted. Even though from the moment you became mine, you *were* my *natural* daughter."

Remaining where she was, Julia begged Angela for forgiveness, and then went on to tell her tale...

* * *

On May 29th*, 1989, Julia was in the hospital giving birth to her little baby girl. There were complications during labor; every time she would follow the doctor's directions and push, the heart rate of the baby would drop into critical low levels. Going back and forth, switching positions, the doctor's tried their best to rotate the baby...but eventually it became too late. With the last push, the baby was delivered—a beautiful infant whose chest did not move up and down. The only thing that Julia remembered seeing was the fearsome snake...the umbilical cord wrapped around her daughter's neck that allowed no oxygen to get to her brain.*

Laying in the hospital bed in a fetal position, Julia held her stomach, screaming and crying as she felt the blood clots and excrement exit her body. Slowly walking to the bathroom, Julia sat on the toilet with her face in her hands as tears of despair fell. She paused only when she heard the outer door of her hospital room open.

"Just a second," she said, before getting up and washing her hands. Exiting the restroom, she looked up at the doctor who was now in her presence.

"Julia, my name is Dr. Albin Peterson, and I have a proposition for you." The doctor waited for more than a heartbeat as if to let his odd words sink in.

Julia went to sit on the foot of the bed; warning signals seemed to blast inside her head.

The doctor sat in the chair across from Julia, and continued, "A female infant was born just a couple of hours ago in this hospital, but we lost her mother during the traumatic birth. I can do two things in this situation: I can call the State and put the baby up for adoption; or...you could take her home and raise her as your own. There will be no red tape. The mother was single, living on the streets. She had no family, no kin whatsoever. I'll give you time to think about what I've just said." Dr. Peterson offered a smile of kindness before standing and exiting the room.

"Wait," Julia cried out, stopping him in his tracks. "I don't need to think about it. Please bring her to me. Now. My family will be here soon, and they don't need to know about this...at all."

The doctor nodded. "I will have her brought right away." He hesitated for a moment, giving her a serious, sincere look. "Julia, it's true that no one can ever know she isn't the daughter you gave birth to. I will lose my license and go to jail if that's ever found out. The nurse and doctor here will not say a thing."

She nodded. "I won't either. Never. Please...just bring her to me."

Appearing to be pleased with the outcome of the devastating situation, the doctor smiled and left the room.

* * *

Julia walked across the elegant floor to Angela. "When the nurse returned and set you in my arms, I swore to never let anything happen to you. I made a vow to always keep you safe. Maybe that's why I was always harder on you...because you always talked about leaving and wanting to go out into the world. I had made a vow, Angela. My...annoyances with you were never because I didn't love you, and I kept my promise. Until now." Without another word, Julia wrapped her arms around Angela and held her close, wishing that she could somehow erase her daughter's stunned expression.

As things started to make sense, and what she thought were strange moments in time started to come together, Angela suddenly felt a warmth for her mother she'd never felt before. No matter how it had occurred, her mother had meant well and had given her a good life.

Angela hugged her back. "I forgive you, Mom. Don't cry. I love you. This changes nothing, Mom." Angela took a step back so she could look Julia in the eyes and express her honesty. "I'm not a child anymore; I understand. If anything, I want to know more."

"I can give you answers, if you're truly ready to receive them," Iris said, stepping into the conversation.

"I'm ready," Angela stated.

"What would you like to know?"

"Everything. Why was I left by you and Arianna...and my father? My mother who died was obviously not a street person; I obviously did have kin. So, was I just unlovable? If you're my sister and Arianna is my twin, where is she now? What happened to her?"

Iris took a deep breath. "First, we had no choice but to give you up; you would have died, otherwise. Second, you were loved and wanted from the day you were conceived. By the look on your face, I can tell you are incredibly confused, so I will start from the beginning."

* * *

As Julia had done, Iris began by offering the explanation of how their parents met; she related in detail how their father was human and their mother was a witch masquerading as a nurse on Earth. She spoke of how their mother died during the birth of the twins. Shortly after the trauma, Iris had been standing in front of the window and staring through it at her new sisters. Immediately, Iris noticed the intense pain that one of the infants was going through.

"Daddy? Dying," a two-year-old Iris pointed to one of her baby sisters as she made the announcement.

Isaiah had rushed into the care unit and picked up baby Angela, noticing she was far weaker than the other.

"Daddy? One is a witch. She's killing the other." Iris tried to explain to her father what she could see, being of mystical blood, that he by being human could not see at all.

Believing his daughter, Isaiah sat down and wrote a note. Upon finishing, he folded it and called out for the doctor. He explained that he wanted to put his daughter up for adoption immediately. He said he'd remain silent about the entire transaction, but he knew that Angela could not be taken home. He told the doctor a lie, although he and Iris knew that the real reason was she and Arianna had to be split up in order for Angela to survive.

"Are you sure?" the doctor had asked. "A woman just down the hall had a baby who, unfortunately, was born deceased."

"Yes, I'm sure. Please give the woman my daughter...and this note. It will explain everything." As the doctor turned to walk out, Isaiah added, "Sir...please tell this woman that the child's mother was a girl living on the street and had no kin. I know this goes against your oath, but you have to understand me when I say that this is the only way for both children to *remain safe."*

After convincing the kind doctor he was right, with a little help from his daughter's magical abilities, the man left for a short time and came back only a few minutes later. He nodded at Isaiah and took Angela in his arms. Dr. Peterson left Iris, Arianna, and their father heartbroken as they watched her disappear from sight.

* * *

After the retelling of her birth had ended, Iris stood in the hall and continued her attempt at solving Angela's confusion. "Arianna was incredibly shy as she got older, Angela. She wouldn't speak for years. She was even diagnosed by the doctors as being 'nonverbal autistic.' Our father, not accepting this diagnosis, wanted to go to the realm my mother was from in order to see if there was some kind of magic that could help our sister. And I began going over our mother's book of spells."

Iris looked briefly out one of the large windows of the room, as if looking back into the past to recite every moment that'd happened. "When Arianna was five, I completed the spell and transported the family back here. It was a miracle, perhaps, but Arianna started speaking only thirty days after being here. She had magic within her soul from our mother, of course, but on Earth the power had jumbled inside her brain and overwhelmed it, leaving no room for communication. The power she held was making her lose control; it was waiting for a chance to break free which it couldn't in the non-magical world of Earth. Once here, there was no stopping it."

"And it was finally easy for her?"

"Not at first," Iris stated. "I taught her relaxation tech-niques, chants, and how to transfer her magic into something else when it got too much for her to handle. I stayed with her through the years and held her hand in order for her to gain the ability to tame the magic. By the time she was nineteen,

Arianna was able to keep it under control."

Angela shook her head, wondering why His Majesty and Rose, people she'd met in the realm, hated Arianna so much if she had learned to control her magic.

Hearing the thoughts swirling in her mind, Iris answered the silent questions. "When Arianna became a young adult, she married a Centreman."

"A what?"

"They are shifters; human forms that can change into valiant steeds in the blink of an eye."

Angela continued, "Did this...shifter harm her and change her into something evil?"

Iris shook her head. "No. He was one of the kindest, most sincere men you could ever meet." Iris paused again, as if saying some kind of silent prayer in her own head. "After their wedding night, it took less than a week to sense she was with child. They embarked on the most wonderful days of their entire life together. Unfortunately, the excitement didn't last long when both he and our father were called upon to serve in the Dark War."

"They were successful at first because the demons fighting were unable to sense the presence of a human, which is why my father was accepted here and asked to fight. His power was the fact that, by being human, he was invisible to them. Once they found out what our father was, they killed him. But it was because of Arianna's husband that we won the war; he'd been able to infiltrate the demons, with my father's help, and kill their leader...before his life was taken, too. Suffice to say, Arianna wasn't the same after her beloved husband sacrificed himself for the greater cause. She then fell into a deep depression."

"Then...the day came." Iris was able to tell the tale by projecting mystical images into the hall from her mind's eye; images that showed her rushing back to their father's castle. "I wanted to be by my sister's side when she heard the news,"

she said.

The images being seen on the walls grew dark while the avid crowd watched the picture of threatening clouds roll in and take their place above the castle. Entering the castle and running up the staircase to the room Arianna had made into a nursery, Iris shot the pictures from her mind, drawing gasps from Angela, Julia, and all that stood there.

The strong scent of blood from the past filled their nostrils, as they watched Iris run into the room and straight at her sister's prone form. She felt for a pulse, she set her hands on her sister's chest, sending a jolt of light into Arianna's body, causing her to move.

The infant...what would have been her beloved niece, had no pulse. No life force could be found within the child whatsoever. Looking around the room for anything sharp to cut the umbilical cord, Iris found scissors in the top drawer of the dresser, sanitized them with her magic, and cut the only line left between infant and mother.

Holding her niece in her arms, observing the child's gorgeous facial features, Iris suddenly let out a scream of terror, letting the river of tears flow from her eyes.

"Arianna...oh, my God. Oh my God...."

A fully awake and panicked Arianna demanded her sister hand over the infant, as they exchanged words and Iris apologized for the loss.

Not taking her eyes off the image, Angela not only saw but felt Arianna's anger erase all the other emotions a person could feel. As her twin stared at the motionless form, she said her goodbyes and a bright red light emanated around Arianna's body. She looked like she'd been possessed by some unnatural, dark force.

Floating above the bed, the dark clouds surrounded her as Arianna cast the worst spell imaginable. Iris did not allow the words to be heard, she just explained the inevitable outcome. "Our sister cursed all the women in the realm who were pregnant. They and their infants would lose their lives while giving birth. Then, Arianna fell back onto the bed and fainted from the enormous amount of energy it'd taken her to complete the spell."

Iris's own body began to tremble as she continued to project the past. The final images showed Iris on her knees, begging the guards to not hurt her beloved sister. Their time together in the dungeon...the words passed between them and Arianna's words to His Majesty that she had no recollection of what he was talking about. And, finally, Arianna's shoulders dropping, begging for death instead of having to return to Earth and live out a horrible life as nothing more than a human being.

The memory dimmed, as Iris spoke, "Seconds before I cast the spell, I wrapped the family sapphire around her neck, and placed the letter and the crystals in her hand. I told her I loved her."

"Did you ever see her once she came to Earth?" Angela asked.

Iris nodded. "I looked for my sister using blood magic; I checked to see how she was doing shortly after I sent her to Earth. That's when you, Angela, came into focus. I knew then and there that you were my other sister. I simply could not believe it when I found out that the woman who adopted you had actually married into the line of witches from Alaska. Although power skipped her generation, Neveah received it ten-fold. It is fate that brought us all together."

Angela's brain was overloaded with information. Not knowing what else to do besides accept what she had seen and heard, she addressed Iris: "I'm glad to have another sister. And...I'm sorry to hear about what happened to our parents... as well as Arianna."

Angela couldn't help but feel envious of these mysterious sisters who got to know her own wonderful parents.

* * *

The odd family reunion was suddenly interrupted by Atticus's brothers. The strong duo entered the room without warning, informing the family they had returned with the felines Julia had wanted. Without noticing the odd energy in the room, they explained that they would have returned sooner if the black one with the gem around its neck hadn't scratched up Leo's face and escaped, causing them to waste time looking for it.

"We don't have a black cat," replied Julia. She just stared at them as if they'd said something completely ridiculous, then shrugged. "I suppose it could have been the neighbors'."

"Well, that's a relief. It didn't seem to be very nice, but we have three others," Leo explained.

"Thank you so much," Julia expressed her gratitude.

"We will put them in the pet nursery where they will be fed and pampered."

Atticus spoke up, still a little flummoxed by the revelations Iris had shown. "Is everyone ready to go to town?"

"Yes, I think we're ready."

"Iris and I will stay here. I don't feel like going," Izak stated quickly.

"That's a wonderful idea. I would love to spend more time with my niece and nephew. If you don't mind of course, Angela," Iris said.

"No. I have no problem with that. I would love to have them get to know you," Angela said with a smile.

As the rest of the family got into the carriage with Atticus, they set out to town. Upon parking the carriage in the center of the square, people stopped walking to look at the newcomers as they exited the wagon, one by one. They did not hastily approach this time; instead, they looked at Atticus for some kind of permission.

"Where would you all like to start?" Atticus asked.

"Mom, I want to go shopping," Sylvia stated.

"Could I go with them, Mom?" Bella asked.

"Look! It's Ziara." Zackery pointed. "Can I go say hello?"

After admiring the well-organized town, noting the clothing shops along one side of the street that faced the food stores and bakeries on the other, the adults conceded it would be very difficult to get lost.

"I would like to browse if you don't mind, Atticus," Julia stated.

"Me, too," Angela agreed excitedly.

Neveah turned to Zack. "Yes, you can go say hi to Ziara. Tell Delphine I would love to visit with her after I take the girls shopping."

"Here." Atticus handed Neveah a bag full of coins. "This should get you everything you wish."

"Thank you, Atticus." Neveah smiled wide.

"I will follow you and Angela," Atticus told Julia.

Angela caught the statement and felt the bond that this particular man seemed to have made with her mother.

The family spread out on their own particular adventures, while Angela and Julia observed the windows of the beautifully designed shops, and smelled the divine scents that wafted from the bakeries.

Stopping at a lovely flower shop, Julia was fascinated by the unique flowers, some of which she'd never seen before. Suddenly, she felt a pair of eyes on her and quickly turned around. She spotted a man walking in her direction wearing a huge, warm smile on his face. Listening to her own heart skip many beats, simply looking at the man sent a shiver down her spine. She was suddenly lost in his high cheekbones, tanned skin, and thick, black hair. As he continued to get closer, she could tell from his proud and honorable stance that he was a muscular man—an alpha male if she'd ever seen one.

When he stopped before her, she looked up into eyes that were as black as night; his eyebrows were drawn together as he smiled, making it seem like his happiness was also held within those midnight eyes. Julia felt like he had Indian or perhaps Asian in his background. What she did know for certain was that the longer they stared at each other, the stronger their connection grew.

Atticus coughed, as if trying to break the silent spell and get Julia's attention.

"Are you okay, Mom?" Angela asked, tugging on her shoulder. "Who are you?" she shot the question at the stranger who was now standing only a few feet away from her mother's face.

"Your Majesty," Atticus spoke up, quickly taking a knee in front of the King of the Shapeshifters.

"Hello, Atticus," the man replied, taking his eyes off Julia for the first time to address one of his own subjects.

"I'm sorry. I'm confused. Your *majesty*?" Julia asked, feeling like she already was introduced to the kings and queens of the realm.

"Let me explain." His smile grew wider, as he bowed at the waist. "My name is Jenesis Alphious, my ladies. I'm King of the Shapeshifters and Alpha of my pack."

Words couldn't describe the emotions that suddenly shot through Julia as the memory of her staring at the gorgeous wolf on their journey to this realm emerged within her mind's eye. Suddenly, as with the books she'd read and the movies she'd seen, Julia knew she was standing before her destined mate that fate, itself, had sent.

CHAPTER 16

"Why do I have to wear a dress?" Bella groaned.

"Bella, it's a formal ball. You can't wear a suit," Sylvia answered, annoyed.

"Well then...could I customize mine, please?" Bella asked the mood man at the counter.

"Of course, young lady. What would you like?"

Bella explained exactly what she wanted her dress to look like and what material it was to be made from. The man told her he would have it delivered to the castle as soon as it was finished.

"Thanks," Bella said, offering him a huge smile.

Neveah was bringing her daughters' dresses and accessories to the counter to pay for them, while the girls looked out the window.

"Could we go with Zack and Ziara while you pick out your

own dress, Mom?" Sylvia asked.

"Yeah, I'll catch up with you guys later. Stay together."

The girls ran out the door to meet up with the other kids while Neveah exited the shop and walked down the line of clothing stores to the formal shop for adults. Viewing the beautiful selection, she came across a dress that was her favorite color green. Made of silk, the stunner had lace shoulder straps, an open back and a beautiful brooch to top it off located in the center of the bodice. The dress swayed gracefully, barely touching the floor, when she tried it on.

"You look lovely," a woman told her while Neveah was admiring herself in the mirror.

"Thank you." Neveah blushed at the kind compliment.

The two ladies continued to talk for a good ten minutes, getting to know one another.

"My name is Lilian Lefko," the woman introduced herself. "I own this shop."

"My name is Neveah Michelson. It's nice to meet you. I hope it's not impolite to ask, but would you mind telling me what kind of shifter you are?"

"Not at all. I'm a tiger. Fast and strong." Lilian held her arms out, pretending to flex her muscles before bursting into laughter.

"Oh, wow. I bet that's fun. I would love to see you shift." Neveah grinned. "But now, I have to get out of here and locate my kids."

"How many children do you have?" she asked, waiting for Neveah to get done changing back into her regular clothes in the dressing room.

"I have a son and a daughter. My son is ten and my daughter is fourteen. Do you have children?" Neveah asked, walking out of the dressing room. She joined Lilian as they walked toward the counter to pay.

"Yes, I do! A daughter. She is...eleven. Sorry for the pause, I had to think in 'year' form."

"That's okay. We would love to meet her."

"I'm sure she would love to play with your children, too."

Neveah paid for her dress and Lilian nicely folded it in the basket. Saying their goodbyes, Neveah walked out the door.

Standing just to the left outside the store's door she turned around when she heard a squawk from above. There, perched on the roof, was her loyal eagle.

"Oh goodness, you scared me. It's easy to get scared here. Especially after seeing that awful creature at dinner. Want to know a secret? I was scared out of my mind when I saw it," Neveah told the eagle while it just sat there tilting its head, studying her.

"I got a beautiful dress for the ball. It's one of my favorite colors; army green. I know that sounds weird, but I've been told it looks really good on me," she said.

"Mom? Why are you talking to a bird?" Zack said, coming up behind her.

"Oh, I was just taking a minute, thinking about what to do next, and then it joined me. So, I just started talking to it."

"Wait until you start talking to yourself. Then you'll *really* have something to worry about," Delphine laughed. She glanced up at the eagle before it took flight and soared away.

The kids and the ladies stood there chatting away about what had been going on since the last time they had seen each other, when a little girl suddenly walked out of the same dress shop Neveah had exited.

* * *

Izak and Iris were in the daycare with Leah and Liam. They sat at a table entertaining the babies while Liam colored with turquoise, forest green, and royal purple crayons.

"That's really good, Liam. What are you drawing?" Izak asked.

"A dragon. He had sad eyes," Liam replied.

Izak looked at the colors Liam was using and suddenly noticed a distinct resemblance between the dragon that had taken his sister and the colors he'd chosen to create his own. *Liam never saw the dragon; how could he be drawing it?*

"Have you seen this before?" Izak asked in a concerned tone.

"Yes, he was here before Mommy came. He was watching us. He was standing over there." Liam pointed to a nearby tree.

Liam was about to continue when Iris stepped in and whispered to Izak that there were many paintings of the drakon in the castle. "He must have seen one," she said.

"Leah, watch this." Iris picked up one of the crayons and used her pointer finger to suck the color out of the crayon and then use her finger to transfer the color onto the paper.

Leah watched the whole thing. He eyes widening, she started clapping joyfully before one word escaped her lips. "Cool!" she intentionally spoke for the first time in five years. Jumping up and down, she added, "Again!"

Iris and Izak looked at each other in complete amazement.

"You can talk?" Izak asked with a big smile on his face.

"Yes," Leah replied, looking down at her feet.

Scooping her up in his arms, Izak twirled her around in the air, making her laugh and giggle.

"Down," she ordered.

"Okay Leah, I'm sorry," he chuckled, setting her on the floor.

Iris watched Izak with his niece. She hadn't seen him smile like that before. Even when he teased her, his smile wasn't as big as it was at this very instant. "Do you want children someday?" the question released through her lips before she had a chance to stop it.

"No. Not really. I had dogs instead. I never wanted to bring a child into the awful world we lived in and risk exposing them to all the possible dangers of drugs, disease, and other people."

He was looking at the ceiling, still thinking about what he had said. "I don't think I would be a very good father anyway. I never had good examples of one growing up."

"You will find living in this realm, those kinds of dangers, are literally absent here. You have had experiences that most of us couldn't even imagine. I can see you have a kind and genuine heart, however, without the temptations of those drugs that alter you," she said, smiling at him.

"Uncle Izak!" Liam cut through both their thoughts, pointing at Leah.

Leah was trying to do the same thing Iris had shown her. Sucking the colors into her fingers so she could draw with them, she went too far with her newfound magic. Her fingers were now the same colors of the crayons she had sucked dry. In addition, her small fingers had literally turned into the shape of the crayons.

"We have to get Angela," Iris gasped.

* * *

Julia, Angela, Jenisis, and Atticus were walking along the street, looking into the bakery windows. Julia and Jenisis chatted away like they had been long time friends. When they were about to walk past the tobacco shop, Angela stopped.

"Atticus, could I have some money, please? I would like to stop at this store," Angela said.

"Of course. I have your share here," he said, handing her a velvet bag, much like the one he'd handed Neveah.

"Thank you." Angela entered, leaving Julia to continue forward with Atticus and his king.

Angela walked into the store and browsed at all the different types of tobacco held in exquisite wooden boxes like the ones that held fancy cigars. The only difference was that brownish, cigarette-shaped objects were in the boxes.

"Can I help you?" a rainbow-colored man asked.

"Yes, please. Everything in here looks so different from what I'm used to," she replied. Looking at the colorful little man smiling, she felt a bit taller in his presence.

"What flavors do you like?" He returned her smile and escorted her around the store.

"A strong, stress-relieving flavor," she replied.

"I have just the thing. They are bark flavored. Personally, I like them, too." He handed Angela the box as he walked her up to the counter so she could pay. Observing a unique looking coin, she pulled it out of the bag and turned it over; strange markings decorated one side, while the head of a mighty drakon was carved on the other.

"I don't know how many to give you." Angela looked up at the man behind the counter, obviously now standing on a stool of some sort.

"One of the silver ones will do just fine." He smiled once again at her concerned face.

Angela looked through her bag, discovering a silver one. Still holding a gold one in her hand, she held it up and asked: "How much is this worth?"

"That is way too much for your purchase, Miss. It's worth fifty," he replied. "The silver is worth only one."

Angela thought about what the man said and then handed him the gold one. "Please take it. I have many more in my bag like this. You have been very helpful and kind," she smiled.

"Ma'am...this will feed my entire family for thirty days."

"You deserve it."

He sighed before taking the coin. "You're really overpaying."

"I'm glad to contribute...to your family and your store. Have a wonderful day, sir." Still smiling, Angela waved and walked out.

Looking around, Angela did not notice any smokers on the streets. She didn't want to feel even more judged, so she walked around to the side of the shop to try out this unique, hopefully relaxing cigarette. The box contained something that looked like matches so she held the cigarette up to her mouth and lit it. Taking a drag, the sudden strong flavor made her cough, like she hadn't ever inhaled smoke before. It was certainly something she never expected. A nutty type of flavor came from it. Standing there, trying to relieve stress, she thought about her mother's strange behavior. Suddenly she spotted a man and a woman walking slowly towards her, coming in-between the two buildings.

"Can I help you?" Angela asked, looking in their direction.

"Our Queen, you shouldn't be here," the man stated.

"Someone will certainly recognize you in your normal transformation," the woman added.

All Angela could think was that these people had her mixed up with Arianna and were among her followers. Not wanting to fight, she decided to play along. "I suppose you are correct, but I'm all the way back here. Surely no one will notice me." Angela felt her heart start to speed up as they continued to walk towards her.

"I can't sense her magic, Vodka. Can you?" he spoke to the woman beside him.

"I can sense nothing, which can only mean one thing, Whisky."

"She's human...and not Arianna," he added, before turning around to see more people gathering and beginning to yell at their little group.

"That's the witch that killed our wives and our babies!" A person from the street yelled. Angela abandoned her original thought of playing the part to keep herself safe. As they all came closer to her, she started walking backwards until she no longer could. Being surrounded and unable to escape, she slid down the wall to a sitting position, tucking her knees to her chest and wrapping her arms around them to bury her head. She hoped they would just leave her alone if she showed fear.

"Stop! That's not Arianna, it's Angela. One of the new-comers!"

Angela heard the familiar voice; it was Rose, her mood-skinned friend. She peeked over her knees for just a second to watch some of the crowd stop, as only the first two that had begun it all continued forward. As they got closer, she started to smell an awful odor before covering her face in her knees once again. The smell was getting stronger and stronger. Then came a loud 'thump' and a new voice joined the mob.

"Did you not *hear* the mood girl?" The dominant tone that was one she never wanted to hear again was now bellowing at the people.

As he stood there, angry, showing his sharp teeth, he aimed his glowing eyes at the two people who continued their progression. Suddenly, however, they dropped to their knees and bowed at his feet, along with everyone else present.

"We apologize, Your Majesty. We had her confused with another," the man and woman said with their faces to the ground.

"Get away from her," he yelled once again. "All of you get out of here. Now!"

Watching the crowd get up quickly and scurry like mice out of the alleyway, he transformed his sharp teeth back into normal looking ones and calmed his eyes, allowing them to go back to their natural color.

He had not missed seeing the woman he now deeply cared for in her scared, balled-up position against the wall. Wishing to see the smile he missed very much, he hoped she was okay.

Bending down to cover her hand with his, he felt her body jump as she looked up at him.

He was looking at her with so much feeling and such intense worry for her that it warmed Angela's heart.

"Are you okay?" he finally spoke.

"Yes. Thank you for saving my life," she replied, her hands still trembling from fear.

"Can you stand?" he asked, extending his hand to help her up.

Remembering how he hadn't taken her hand when she'd offered hers once before, Angela instead used the wall to push off of in order to stand upright. Her defiance of his help seemed to make him smile, as he stood shaking his head.

"What?" she asked in a stubborn tone.

"Nothing," he replied, still smiling. "How have you been? Have you been okay?"

"Yes, now that I'm out of your grasp," she replied, watching his face fall. Remembering the story Iris had told her about his wife and child, the guilt started to run through her. "I'm sorry. I have been...great."

Going further, she told His Majesty about everything that'd occurred since she'd been brought here. Getting excited, she described all the people she'd met. Feeling like a teenager herself, she jumped up and down inside as she told him about how crazy it was that there were new family members added to her life, and that Arianna *was* her actual identical twin.

"Iris hadn't mentioned any of that to me. I know she's been mad at me for all these years." He appeared guilt-ridden. "I shouldn't have sent Arianna away without knowing the whole story. I didn't know she was possessed by her own magic. Had to have been caused from the pain of losing her child. I remember what it was like for me."

"Well...promise me something?"

"Anything," he replied.

"Don't go around kidnapping random women until you know who they really are first."

"I promise," he said, letting out a chuckle of his own. Watching her smile and laugh made his heart brighten; the lovely sound matched the lilting music that the birds sang outside his window every morning. A sound that made him think there was no better time to tell her his secret than right now.

"How's Alister?" Her face lit up happily, like she was asking about an old, long-lost pal.

He took a deep breath. "I need to tell you something, Angela. Something I'm sure you're not going to like. But...I don't want to lie to you anymore." He paused. "But I don't want to break your heart either."

"What is it?" her smile faded.

"I'm—" His Majesty got cut off by the sound of Angela's mother, who was most definitely concerned.

"Angela, come quick! We need to hurry back to the castle. Something's going on with Leah."

Unable to finish telling her his secret, she fled. Her back was to him now, running towards her mother. *What could be wrong with Leah?* Jumping into the air and taking flight, he flew at top speed to Mood Castle to see what all the commotion was about.

CHAPTER 17

The family arrived at the castle, running through the doors to the day care.

"Iris!" Angela yelled.

"We're in the art room," she hollered back.

Angela and the rest hurried to the art room and threw open the door. Walking over to Leah, they calmed down as they saw her simply sitting there at the table, coloring. They were beyond confused about what the 'big hurry' was all about.

"Leah has been talking," Izak announced.

"What? Really?" Angela said excitedly.

Getting ready to sit on the floor beside Leah's chair, Angela looked at what she was coloring. When she bent down on one knee...she saw it. Leah had five fingers in different colors; they were actual crayons.

"Oh my God...what happened?" Angela gasped, picking up her daughter's hand to examine her fingers. She shot Iris an angry look.

"Look, Mommy. Magic," Leah said, like absolutely nothing was wrong at all.

"Uh...yes. Yes it is, honey." Angela was stuttering, experiencing shock at the beautiful sound of Leah's voice, while tears of thankfulness trickled down her face. "Did everyone hear that?"

"Oh, yes," the family replied in unison.

Iris tried to explain. "What happened though, Angela, is that Leah copied me. I sucked the color from a crayon into my pointer finger and released it onto the piece of paper. She tried to do it while Izak and I were talking. I'm very sorry...I didn't expect her to copy me."

Angela shook her head. "I don't understand. How *could* she copy you?"

"Um..." Iris looked over at Julia and Neveah, then continued, "Leah is a witch. She can do magic. Didn't they tell you?"

"No. They didn't. Must have slipped their minds," Angela said, staring at her family with complete irritation.

"Don't worry, Mommy. I was just having a little bit of fun." Leah placed both of her hands on her mother's cheeks. Looking down at her fingers, she wiggled them and giggled before sliding her left hand over her new, colorful one. With that one swipe, the crayon fingers immediately disappeared, reforming into her regular appendages. "See? All gone."

Angela gasped, along with the rest of the adults in the room.

"Leah, how did you do that? It took me years of practice to even color with my fingers, let alone learn the much more complicated magic to return them back to normal," Iris asked.

"The friendly voice tells me how to do it," Leah replied.

"What friendly voice?" Angela asked.

"The voice in my head."

"I know what she's talking about," Iris said, smiling. "She has guidance magic. It is magic that's passed down from generations to guide you. It already knows how to do all the magic, until it learns something new. It's amazing. If I can touch Leah, I could read where it came from and if it's light or dark magic."

"Please do. I don't want her to have it if it's bad."

Iris lifted her left hand and wrapped it around Leah's wrist. Closing her eyes, she mouthed something they couldn't make out. A bright white glow suddenly appeared where her hand was resting. With a smile, she looked at Angela. "It's mother's light magic," she said, now shedding her own tears of joy and happiness before hugging Leah.

"Can she feel our mother? Like...her presence?" Angela wanted to know more.

"Yes. It's incredible."

* * *

As the day went on, everyone wanted a piece of the action with Leah. They wanted to hear and converse with the child who'd never been able to talk before. And now that she was talking in full sentences, she expressed her desire to play with the older kids and Liam.

Angela wanted to see Leah progress, but something deep down concerned her with Leah suddenly not being autistic. It felt like a prayer had been answered, yet it also felt like she'd just been given a greater thing to be worried about—her daughter being magic. Not knowing how to teach her any of it, she felt completely useless once again. She thought she had felt helpless before, trying to teach her child to progress through her disability, and then finally accepting the fact that she may never speak or grow up to have children and a genuine love of her own. Now that all that was possible,

Angela was even more frightened. She thought of poor Leah having to go through the pain and heartbreak that men brought, and having to live through all the fears of becoming a mom and having other little people to be responsible for. Nothing can ever truly prepare you for motherhood, no matter how old you are.

"Mom. Come on. Let's go," a very excited Bella was pulling Angela around the castle.

"Where are we off to?" Angela laughed.

"To meet Jacky and her mother in the decorator's room."

"Lead the way, I guess." Angela let Bella take over.

She was now pulling her mother down the hall into the Throne Room, and out another door on the left side. Angela had never been through these specific doors before. There was another hall with three doors on the right. Bella brought her to the one in the middle, opened it and rushed in, letting go of Angela's hand.

"My mom came," Bella said with excitement.

"Well, she basically dragged me. I clearly had no idea where I was going," Angela laughed, looking at Bella showing off her young, innocent self—jumping up and down like she was five-year-old Leah.

A gold-skinned girl got up and ran to Bella, hugging her. Shortly after, a curvy, beautiful, gold woman turned away from her personal project and walked right up to her.

"Hello, I'm Queen Tiana. It's so nice to finally meet you," she said before wrapping her arms around Angela.

"I have heard wonderful things about you," Angela stated, hugging the woman back.

Stepping away, Tiana winked, as if keeping some sort of secret. "Likewise."

* * *

Neveah was out in the flower gardens where she could write

in peace and quiet. She loved to keep a journal, even back in their realm. Sitting on the lovely bench looking at the butterflies, she began writing about the day she had and the new people she'd met. How her son had looked like he had a crush when a little girl walked out of the store. The image made her laugh while she wrote. Looking up from her writing she spotted a friend who had come to rest on the bottom branch of the large tree in front of her.

"It's you again. Are you following me?" she said, looking up at the beautiful eagle.

"Of course you're not going to answer me. You're a bird. Well then, I don't mind the company," she spoke again.

Deciding she would just talk to the bird, even though it had nothing to say, she told it everything about her life—from her first love to her ex-husband. Then about her parents and siblings. She dove into her personal feelings of fear, happiness, doubt, and anxiety, and told him everything she would never tell another person in her entire life. Of course, she was talking to a bird, so it couldn't hurt.

"Wow, I feel a lot better. Getting all of that out feels like an enormous weight has been lifted off my shoulders. Thank you, Mr. Eagle." She smiled. Watching the bird tilt its head down, it took flight and landed right beside her on the bench.

Standing quickly, she told herself not to touch the bird because it would most likely bite. Her brain was giving her these instructions, yet her hand was still reaching out to touch the feathers of the gigantic eagle perched atop the seat.

"Neveah, I need your help," her mother yelled out the window.

Snapping her out of the odd trance, she pulled her hand away and shook her head. *What was I thinking? It could have bitten my hand off.* Walking away, she went to help her mother with whatever new emergency she happened to be having now.

* * *

Tiana could see the colors of sadness, confusion, fear, and unsettlement in Angela's eyes; complete exhaustion was also apparent. Smiling, she walked over to the table and poured two glasses of peach wine, bringing it back to her.

"You look like you could use this."

"Oh. I could use many," Angela laughed, taking a large drink. "Thank you."

"Are we going to make vases?" Bella asked.

"Yes, we are. Jacky, will you set up the other two stands?"

"Yes, Mother. Come on, Bella, I'll teach you."

"I heard you had quite the day. You saw His Majesty?" Tiana asked, already knowing she had when he'd rushed to the castle to check on Leah, wanting to see her to make sure she was okay. Acting very protective of the little girl, Tiana had to hold him back from rushing in, frightening Liam, and confusing everybody else. Making him go home, she'd told him to come back another time. He had offered a grunt, but in the end, had listened.

"Yes, I did. He rescued me from the townspeople who thought I was Arianna. He's really something, isn't he? Quite the character. I don't know what to make of him," Angela spoke.

"He is. Back when we were kids, he was always the protector and had to make sure everyone was happy and smiling. Constantly doing the decent and right thing. He *is* trying to go back to what he was before."

"Before his wife and child were killed by my sister's magic? I have learned magic can be light and dark. Can it control you, too?" Angela asked with concern.

"I'm not sure. That would be a question to ask Iris."

Angela paused. "I think my twin is here. I almost got the information from those two people that called me their queen. It was odd; they smelled of a strong vinegar odor."

"She is here; she also has followers that appear human but are actually demons. You were lucky."

"My family told me about dinner and what could have happened to Liam." Angela's eyes watered, and she guzzled the rest of her wine.

"Another?" Tiana asked.

"Yes. I hope no one wants anything else from me today," Angela laughed through her tears.

"Come on, everything is set up." Jacky ran up to them excitedly.

The four of them walked to the art stations and took their seats to make vases. All were soon laughing and having a wonderful time getting clay all over their hands as they attempted to make anything they could. Bella and her mother wiped clay on each other's faces, beginning what eventually became a clay throwing fight.

Getting everyone involved, they laughed constantly until they were all covered from head to toe.

* * *

"What do you need help with Mom?" Neveah asked.

Julia was incredibly excited running around her bedroom looking at all the clothes provided by the castle. Looking at dresses, riding clothes, and the apparel she'd brought with her from the house, Julia was completely unsure of what her date had planned for the evening.

"I'm going on a date but I don't know what to wear. Do you know how long it's been since I dated?" Julia was almost ready to give up until she remembered how amazing she'd felt in his presence.

"Who is it?" Neveah asked, showing the same excitement as her mother.

"A shapeshifter I met in town. He's a wolf and King of all the Shapeshifters," Julia said in a romantic tone, as if daydreaming about a regal hero.

"Like in the fairytales? Could he be like...your destiny?" Neveah asked with an extremely interested look on her face.

Julia paused for only a second. "I think so. I feel very connected, safe, and oddly bonded to him. Instantly, when I first saw him, all those emotions happened. I still feel the same away from him but also guarded and full of questions. You know my track record."

"You and I both, Mom. I would just play it safe. Show him the real you. Don't spoil him and attend to his every need."

"Neveah, it's a first date, what could possibly happen? It's not like he's going to confess his love for me." Julia laughed, yet in the back of her mind she truly felt like, if that were to happen, she wouldn't mind a bit. She was getting older, after all, and she would actually enjoy spending the rest of her life with a proper partner. Like everyone else, she wanted her happy ending. She was just afraid of running into more frogs that got the kiss but never turned into the prince that was promised.

"You never know with this place. I think anything is possible."

"Okay, honey. Will you please help me get ready? I don't know what we're doing or where we're going."

"Well, I'm sure he will have you out late, so dress warmly but nice. Maybe something from our realm." Picking out a simple but sexy black dress with long sleeves, she paired it with black leggings and boots without heels from Julia's large closet.

Julia changed her clothes and sat in front of the vanity to have Neveah apply light make-up and do her hair. Just when she was finishing up, there was a knock on the door.

"Is he meeting you at your bedroom door, Mom?"

"I don't know. Maybe."

"I'll get it," Neveah said, extremely curious.

Opening the door, Neveah looked up into the older

gentleman's eyes and smiled. He was dressed nicely, but also casually, holding a handful of yellow roses in a beautiful vase.

"Hello. I'm Jenisis. I'm here to escort Julia." He smiled, showing his pearly white teeth.

"I'm Neveah. Julia is my mother. Please come in."

Jenisis walked in the room and looked up at Julia. Paralyzed by her beauty, he seemed unable to find his words. It felt like his heart was suddenly in his throat. Observing her silky hair and captivating hazel eyes with specks of green surrounding her pupils, he also took in her stunning body clothed in black material that enhanced her lovely skin.

Walking towards her, he handed her the flowers he had picked himself.

"You look breathtaking," he finally said. He mentally kicked himself for being unable to say it when he first entered the room.

Hearing both Julia and Neveah laughing once he finally spoke, Jenesis realized he had been staring for far longer than he originally thought. This made him add his embarrassed laughter to the mix.

"Thank you, Jenesis," Julia said, offering a smile. "Ready to go?"

"Yes, of course," he replied, offering his arm. "It was a pleasure to meet you, Miss Neveah."

"You as well."

Walking down the steps and out to the carriage. Jenesis gave his hand to Julia before stepping into the carriage himself.

"Where are we off to?" Julia asked.

"We are going to go to my lands. Start with dinner." He could hear her stomach grumbling from hunger.

"Wonderful. I'm actually starving," she admitted.

"Then, I would like you to meet the pack. I mean my pack." *Slow down, Jenisis. Don't get carried away yet and end up scaring her.*

"Will any of them be in their wolf form?"

"Would you like to see them in their shifted form?"

"Yes! I really love wolves. They are such beautiful creatures."

"I'm so glad you feel that way," he said, happy that his destiny at least loved the essence and appearance of his chosen form.

* * *

Talking the rest of the way to his lands, they stopped at a lovely outdoor seating area in front of a huge den; chairs and a table had been set, adding a romantic note to the image. With a fire pit cooking rotisserie, something that smelled absolutely delicious was being prepared.

"Oh, wow. This place looks amazing, and whatever that is smells incredible," Julia said excitedly as the smell of the cooking pork hit her nose, making her stomach grumble even louder.

He reached up and lifted her from the carriage, making her feel light as a feather as he set her down directly in front of him. Standing close, she blushed like a schoolgirl.

"Let's eat. Shall we?" He spoke, offering his arm and walking her to the table, pulling the chair out for her to sit.

She now thought him to be a true gentleman. After all, she knew he could have his servants do all of this stuff for her, but he chose to do it himself.

A server did finally arrive at the table to pour them both glasses of wine and attend to the first course.

"Hello, Ashkii. How is your training going?" he addressed the boy by name.

"Not very good, Your Majesty. I'm on work duty today for losing the deer we were chasing earlier." The boy hung his head, ashamed.

"I lost many shapes and sizes of game when I was your

age. Don't worry, son, you will find a way that works best for you," he reassured the young lad.

Julia couldn't help but admire how he handled this simple server, treating him like family instead of his servant.

"What?" he asked Julia.

"Oh nothing, just impressed at how you treated the boy."

"He is part of my pack. The entire pack and the rest of my shapeshifting followers are my family. They deserve the same respect. We are all connected," he replied.

After they ate their courses, completely stuffed by all the delicious food, Julia still ate the dessert that was offered. The night, between the food and the conversation, was completely satisfying.

"Walk with me?" he asked, reaching out his hand.

Taking it, Julia walked beside him feeling like she never wanted the night to end. He had showed his character as a leader; he also didn't receive any strange looks from anyone that she met as if the man was somehow acting outside his normal character for her benefit.

As they walked under the bright stars and full moon, they asked each other the 'getting to know you' questions, eventually getting to family.

"Were you ever married?" Julia asked.

"Yes. She died several years ago before she could have the next alpha; my son," he explained with a sad expression on his face. "She was part of Arianna's curse."

"Oh, no. I'm so sorry. But isn't it a bit late to be having children at our age?" The sudden personal question made him explode in a deep laughing fit, causing her complete confusion.

"Sorry," he said. "I'm a wolf. For us, it is never too late. Plus, I have had the pleasure of having many children. Six to be exact."

"Six children?" She was open-mouthed, shocked at the number. Now thinking he had many lovers she was determined not to be another notch on his proverbial belt.

"Yes, usually wolves find their true mate when they go through puberty, but I have never found mine. So, being king, I was used for those from different packs until they found their mate. Ever since my wife died, I have been just used as a stud to increase security in other packs." He paused, as if knowing how bad this would sound to a woman. "I will never lie to you, Julia, even if it gave me a better chance at earning your affections. From the moment I saw you in the carriage riding to Mood Castle, I knew I was in the presence of my destiny. And from that day on, no one else measures up to how I feel about you." He gave his speech with absolute sincerity.

She could tell he was trying to tame his affections towards her. Most of it matched with the strange feelings she already had for him. Understanding all that he was saying, however, was in part making her question her own sanity. *How can any of this seem normal?* That was what got her the most—this sudden natural ability to accept and believe everything he was telling her. She would never in normal situations trust and believe anything a man said or did, always assuming it was for his personal gain, making her seem like nothing but a judgmental woman. But she had every right with men in her past, after having to experience two failed, physically abusive marriages. She had learned to not let her guard down and always be aware of what a man was capable of doing.

She spoke, "I understand. I've had my fair share of experiences with the opposite sex. Not from a realm where people are fated or destined to be together, however. In my world, that's all considered to be fantasy. I also have had little luck in love and partnerships."

He smiled. "Well, I'm determined to change all that. I will work to prove to you the loyalty, respect, admiration, and love you deserve, and the fact that you will never be without them for the rest of our lives together."

Julia quit walking. *He didn't just say what I think he just said...did he?*

"What...what do you mean by that?" she was slow at asking the question.

He turned around to face her again. Bending down on one knee, he took her hand in his. Muttering words she could never imagine being said on a first date, a voice deep down inside her soul screamed at her to accept his proposal. Yet, her controlling personality and skepticism of men was trying to drown that command out.

Opening her mouth to reply, Julia listened while the two voices fought a battle inside her head.

CHAPTER 18

The entire town was gossiping about the ball that was to be held that very evening. Caterers and wine deliverers were bustling around the castle. Rushing left and right were Rainbow people and Tree people decorating the ballroom, making it look absolutely perfect per the queen's instructions. Iris was volunteering with her magic as well to make the ceiling of the castle look like there was no ceiling at all. Adding her light magic, she taught Neveah and Leah how to float large crystals up in the air in order to create twinkling strings of lights that looked like stars above. Going into the gardens, they made it look even more romantic with their twinkling lights and floating lanterns that highlighted the cascade of flowers, making them gleam.

Queen Tiana was around the caterers making sure they had all of her mushroom specialties prepared. Her love of mushrooms showed in every dinner party she ever had, and she made sure that all the flavors of all the mushrooms were present for this particular feast. Some even tasted like cotton candy, which was perfect for desserts.

* * *

While Julia listened to the huge commotion downstairs, she laid in bed feeling pain and agony in her heart...all because of the still unanswered question the King of the Shapeshifters had asked on their date. It's not like she had said no; she'd simply stated that she needed time to think about his proposal and that she would have the answer for him when he showed up to escort her to the ball. She hadn't realized at the time that being away from him was going to be so much harder than she would have ever imagined. Every part of her body, heart, and mind missed him. Still struggling with the answer in her mind made her physically and mentally distraught, and all she wanted to do was see him right now.

Julia turned and hugged Maui to her like she was begging for any affection from him she could get in order to make her longing less painful.

* * *

Angela stood there watching Leah, Neveah, and Iris laugh over this new connection they had built through magic. Usually she never got jealous about anything, so it was odd that suddenly she felt unable to shake the envy that'd crept up on her over the past couple of days. Unable to do magic, because her twin had stolen it from her long ago, made her feel weak and useless in this realm. *What part am I to play?* she wondered.

"Angela, how are you this bright, beautiful morning?" Queen Tiana asked with a smile of satisfaction on her face.

"I am just thrilled. Never better," Angela replied, knowing

she was not telling the complete truth.

"Liar," the queen teased as if she knew exactly what Angela's thoughts were.

"One of these days I'm going to find out how you seem to always know what I'm feeling. Mark my words," Angela said, focusing and squinting her eyes, trying to figure out what Tiana's secret was.

"I don't know what you're talking about," she said, putting her hands halfway up in the air, clearly pretending to know nothing.

They both just laughed and gave each other a hug before walking around the room, where everyone waved at Angela and bowed to Tiana as they passed.

"Everyone loves you, Angela. You and Bella. She has made a tremendous impact on my kingdom. Teaching everyone customs from your realm. They listen to her with great respect, I must say. You both have the aura of leadership."

"Oh, goodness no. I just love people of all shapes and sizes and want to listen to them tell me everything, not the other way around," Angela laughed.

"Nonsense. You help everyone left and right. Everyone feels like royalty around you, Angela," Tiana urged her to believe what she stated.

Angela *was* listening, but when it sounded like boosting her up and putting her on a pedestal, she had a harder time believing the words. Tiana made her strong and believe that she could be so much more than a housewife and mother of three; that there was more to her life than just cooking and cleaning and maintaining her own sanity while stuck inside four walls that always seemed to be closing in on her each and every day that passed. Now, in this realm, she had no walls and could do so much more. What would come of it, though?

"I hear the king accepted his invitation," Queen Tiana said, breaking through Angela's thoughts.

"Is that so?" she asked, acting like she didn't care.

"Don't you dare pretend like you are not interested to know if he's coming alone?" Queen Tiana stated.

Angela turned bright red. She hadn't even thought about that. But now that she had said something regarding dates, the thought of him coming with someone was the only thing pressing on her mind. "Oh, great. Thanks. Now I am," Angela laughed, feeling her face grow even hotter.

"Don't worry, he doesn't have a date."

"Oh, great. Now I can exhale and feel better that he's not dating someone...even though it's none of my business seeing as that I am married," Angela said sarcastically, rolling her eyes at her own ridiculous thoughts.

"Honey, you told me yourself that he was boring and when he wasn't around anyone else, he wasn't as pleasing and generous as everyone thought him to be. You said it had taken years to get him to be how he was before you left your realm," Tiana reminded her, clearly trying to help Angela move on.

"I also had way too much wine and talked too much."

"What you mean is that you were honest with yourself and me. Men only appear to change over time; in reality, we as women just learn to expect less and less from them. I would know. My king is the same 'macho man' type. They always go back to the way they were once they're out of the doghouse, as you say," Tiana laughed.

"Yeah. Well. I can't argue with you there," Angela agreed, still embarrassed about confessing to Tiana during their clay fight what her husband was really like. It was hard to get him to help with much of anything. Always telling her she'd *chosen* to be a mother and, as the father, he was actually the one that made all the money and went to work every day. So her *duties* as a mother were to pick up the slack on everything else. The house cleaning, the children, groceries, and being a twenty-four-seven babysitter. What more could she ask for when she did get a couple of hour breaks here and there?

They continued to walk around as Tiana barked orders at

everyone left and right. Angela added 'please' and 'thank you' to everyone her friend was showering with stress and anxiety. She also noticed that the queen looked a little overwhelmed as it got closer and closer to showtime.

* * *

Izak was watching Iris throw her magic around the room, making everything as bright and beautiful as she was. He was all better and had no more cravings or withdrawals regarding his bad habit. In fact, he had found it to be too hard being around Iris with that feeling in the pit of his stomach, so he was determined to make this day the best she ever had.

Catching his eye, she waved him over. He playfully danced towards them from the lessons she had been making him take when he had said he couldn't dance. Leah, Neveah, and Iris started clapping when he reached them. Taking a bow, he laughed.

"Bravo, Uncle Izak," Leah acknowledged him, making him pick her up.

"Thank you very much, Leah. Don't tell Aunty Iris that it's the only dance I know." He felt a bit strange that he was her uncle, and she was her aunty.

"It will be our little secret," Leah whispered in his ear.

"What do you think?" Iris asked, pointing at all the lights and decorations.

"It's amazing. Very bright."

"Typical thing for a man to say," Neveah said, rolling her eyes.

"*What?* It takes my breath away, and the lights are mesmerizing as my eyes lock onto their bright, glistening..." He couldn't finish his sarcastic description as he burst out laughing. "What the hell do you want me to say?"

"Hey, stop that language. There are children present," Iris said, covering Leah's ears.

"That's nothing compared to the things I would hear come out of my mother's mouth when she would fight with Daddy," Leah giggled, removing Iris's hands from her ears.

"Doesn't make it any better, missy. Us adults need to learn a little more self-control," Neveah said.

"Is your suit ready?" Iris asked Izak, avoiding any sibling fight that could rear its ugly head.

"Of course. Is your dress ready?"

"Is that even a question?" Neveah asked.

"Guess not," Izak grumbled, trying to make simple conversation.

"I wanna go," Leah whined.

"We will have a ball just for you little ones soon," Iris told her.

"Okay." Leah hunched down, kicking the floor.

"Well, I'll see you guys later. Where's little man?"

"He's outside playing catch with his new buddy. Says he's a wolf. You know how he has always loved dogs," Neveah explained.

"Well, I'll go play with them. Later guys." Izak waved goodbye and headed to Liam.

* * *

While the others buzzed around the castle, Sylvia, Bella, Zack, Ziara, and Princess Jacky were all jumping off the docks into the sea, splashing and laughing.

Sylvia decided to stop and sit on her towel away from the rest so her journal wouldn't get wet. She, like her mother, loved to write in her journal. Right now she was writing about her brother flirting and doing it all wrong. She wished there were more boys she could hang out with that were her own age. Laying on her belly, she wrote these feelings and more. Taking in the hot sun on her back, she suddenly noticed a couple of drops of water on her paper.

"Hey, guys! You're getting my paper wet; the ink is going to spread," she yelled at the frolicking teens.

"Sorry," they all said in unison.

She started writing again when another splash of water hit her paper. This time her ink had mixed with the water, causing her to have to rip out the page and start over. When she looked up to yell at them, however, they were all out of the water. Confused as to where the water came from, she gave up and continued to copy what she'd already written. Going back and forth from the loose page to her book, she looked at the wet one for the third time and was shocked. It was completely dry...and the ink was not smeared at all.

"What the heck?" she got up and looked around. Nothing was there but the others, and none of them had magic. It had to be the sun, she thought to herself. Laying back down on the towel, she was about to reach for her journal when she ended up being drenched in a cascade of water. Not by her friends and family, it'd come from the other side of the dock. Getting up, she walked to the edge to peek over the wood and look down into the water, only to receive a face full of it. Then she heard the unmistakable sound of a boy's laughter. Wiping her face and opening her eyes, she saw him in the water. Highly visible, he had bright, white hair and black freckles on his cheeks. When he smiled, it showed off his dimples.

"Hello, prosopon gis," he spoke.

"What? What is that?" Sylvia asked.

"It means land person," the boy said.

"I have a name, you know. What are *you*, exactly, if you're not a land person?" she said in a snooty tone.

"I'm a Merman, of course," he said, lifting his tail and bringing it down fast on top of the water.

Sylvia had no words to express how excited she was to meet a real Merman. She forced herself to be cool as her eyes gazed upon his silver tail.

"That's...that's awesome," she said.

An amused grin appeared on the boy's face. "So, what is this name of yours?"

"You first," she said stubbornly.

"I am Prince Simon Pontos of the Waters," he told her, looking extremely proud.

"I'm Sylvia Michelson."

"Beautiful name," he said quickly before diving under the water and then swimming back up to the surface.

Sylvia blushed at his words, becoming more polite with the boy. Sitting with her feet dangling off the edge of the dock, she smiled, allowing her braces to shine in the sunlight.

"What's that in your mouth?"

"They're called braces. They'll make my teeth straight." She could tell he was confused, so she explained further, "They're something from our realm."

"Earth?"

"Yes," Sylvia said, a bit surprised he had heard of it.

"Want to come swim with me under the water?"

"I...I can't breathe under the water. I'm just human," she said, looking bummed.

"You can if I'm with you." He reached his hand up to her.

Ignoring the offer, she stood up and did a cannonball into the water. Before she came up for air, the boy grabbed her hand. In the blink of an eye, Sylvia saw her own tail appear and felt gills growing behind her ears. She was still holding her breath; afraid she would drown if she let go.

"It's okay. You can breathe now. I've got you. Trust me, Sylvia."

She let out the air she was holding and took in a small breath. She was amazed that it was so easy. "This is outstanding!" she screeched.

"Come on. Let's go deeper down. I have friends I want you to meet," he laughed, pulling her further under the sea.

She was excited about everything she saw: little fish that swam by her as she waved at them; seahorses of all different colors; and jellyfish that glowed so brightly, they almost blinded her.

"Don't look at them too long. They are Bright Ones; some will literally take your eyes out if you stare too long. The younger ones have no control," he informed her.

"Wait, I have heard of those, but the creature they'd been talking about then was a girl on land."

"They do go on land but they're not supposed to shine brightly enough where they draw in eyes. My father's waters are very strict. No one is allowed to go on land without his permission. He hates land people, though. I've never known why," he said, looking rather down.

Sylvia squeezed his hand and smiled at him when he looked back up at her. Making his frown turn upside down, she felt his hand squeeze back.

"We are almost there."

* * *

He was rushing her to his hangout to meet his buddies. Excited that he had gotten this far with the girl, Simon hoped he could find a way to just get her around the corner.

Right in front of his tunnel entry stood two of the king's guards. They stopped him and Sylvia instantly, placing their two swords in the shape of an 'X' in order to bar entry.

"Hey guys, how's it going? Looking good," he said, trying to act casual. "Can you let us by, please?"

One stepped forward. "Your father wishes to speak to you."

"Come on, guys. You're embarrassing me in front of my new friend. Can't you just tell him I'm taking a nap?" he asked, winking at the men. He noticed that their faces exhibited no emotion whatsoever. "Really? You never been a teenager before? Or did you just forget? Please, don't let me down."

The men stared at each other and drew closer, whispering

so that the prince and Sylvia couldn't hear them. He looked hopeful that they would let them pass so he could show off his pad to the pretty girl, but their faces faded into frowns after turning to him once again. The fear that suddenly appeared in their eyes could only mean one thing.

"Hello, Father," Simon said, turning around, still holding Sylvia's hand.

"Son. Who's your friend?" his father asked, pretending to be friendly.

Like he does around new, potential slaves, Simon thought to himself.

"This is Olivia, Dad. You don't remember her?" he lied.

"Is that right? Well, hello Olivia," he said, moving closer to her.

"Stay away from her, Dad. Don't touch her!" Simon's voice rose and he jerked Sylvia backwards.

"You bring a prosopon gis in my waters and you think you can bark orders at me, boy?" his father roared before bringing his right hand up and connecting it against Simon's cheek with so much force he almost let go of Sylvia.

"Please stop! I'm sorry. This was all my fault, Your Majesty," Sylvia interrupted, bowing her head to the King of the Waters. "Please don't get mad at Simon. I love the ocean and I begged him to bring me down here."

"What is your actual name?" he demanded.

"It's Sylvia Michelson, Your Majesty."

"You brought a human land girl in my ocean? Let go of her now," he yelled at Simon, expressing even more frustration than before.

"I would rather die than let go of her," Simon yelled back.

"We can arrange that." His father moved swiftly to grab the guard's sword and spun in a circle, looking like he was ready to strike his own blood.

Seconds later Simon put his hand up and blew his father across the ocean floor, sending him backwards where he hit a coral reef.

"Stop it," a woman suddenly screamed.

"Mom, go away," Simon yelled at the lady.

It was too late. The king swam towards her and grabbed her, pulling the sword up to her throat.

"Your mother or the girl, boy?" he said in all seriousness. "Pick one."

Simon looked from Sylvia to his now weeping mother. Could he count on the fact that this was nothing but a bluff, or would his father actually kill the girl holding on to him for dear life. Observing his father's face, he hoped he wouldn't do it. "Father, please. Don't hurt anyone. Why are you doing this?"

His father didn't have the chance to reply as an enormous figure suddenly entered the water; swirling around, it felt like a tornado had touched down on the ocean floor. Trying hard to hold on to Sylvia, Simon embraced her in an enormous bear hug.

Feeling the waters calm, Simon looked up to see that the figure had not been a sea creature at all. They were now in the presence of His Majesty.

"What is the meaning of this?" he bellowed. "How *dare* you do this, Tarence!"

"Your Majesty," King Tarence bowed, dropping the sword and releasing Simon's mother. "The boy needed to be taught a lesson."

"You make me sick, Tarence. You are to exit these waters immediately. I have waited a long time to deal with you. Now you will meet the consequences for your actions." He turned around to stare at the boy. "Simon?"

"Yes, Your Majesty?"

"You are the new King of the Waters. I have had enough of your father."

"Your Majesty, look out!" Simon yelled.

King Tarence had re-grabbed the sword from the ocean floor. Angry as all hell that he'd been relieved of his title, he was ready to kill His Majesty. Coming forward, he aimed the point of the huge weapon directly at his chest.

Everything was happening too fast. Simon covered Sylvia like he was protecting her from the mere sight of what was about to occur. Closing his own eyes, it took only a moment to smell the blood releasing into the water all around him. Opening his eyes, he witnessed red everywhere. He was unable to make out what had happened in the incident until the waters cleared...and the sound of his mother's screams pierced his ears.

CHAPTER 19

His Majesty was looking over at the older children, laughing to himself as Prince Simon playfully messed with Sylvia. Overhearing Simon's plan to take her into the ocean, His Majesty had suddenly become highly concerned. *What is the boy thinking? His father will have his head.*

Getting down from the tree and walking to the other children, he felt somber as they looked up at him with fear on their faces. Wishing he didn't have that effect on them, he frowned.

"Your parents need you to go back to the castle," he lied; he needed to make sure that whatever was happening in the waters below was not going to be seen by them.

"Okay, Your Majesty." All of the children got out and ran with their belongings back to Mood Castle. The hasty congregation made him chuckle a bit before bending down and listening to the water...searching for Simon's voice. Upon locating it, he laughed at what the boy was saying to the guards.

As time went by, he could hear the situation escalate, knowing there was about to be a dangerous stand-off. Alister dove down into the waters at full speed causing a whirlwind to form around his body. His natural ability to breathe while under the sea made it possible to intervene and destroy King Tarence's plans to kill his own queen. Knowing he would have to sentence him to death made him uneasy, but Alister was strong in his decision.

Landing on the ocean floor between Prince Simon and King Tarence he yelled at the royal father. Turning to the boy to announce him King of the Waters, he was blindsided.

"Your Majesty, look out!"

Turning around and seeing the sword coming at him, Alister swung his own tail around, connecting with the center of Tarence's body. Quickly, he felt the slice of Tarence's skin and saw the blood fill their surroundings. Hearing Queen Maria's screams of horror, Alister watched as Tarence's body separated into two parts.

"No...No...No...Tarence," she cried, trying to put his figure back together. "What did you do?"

"I'm sorry, Maria, I had no other choice."

"Mom, it's okay. We're free now," Simon said, trying to reassure his mother.

"None of you understand.... You will pay for this!" she screamed, swimming away with the parts of her king.

"I'm sorry, boy," he said, now looking guilty.

"I understand, Your Majesty. He would have killed my mother. There was no feeling in his eyes. My father was evil and jealous."

"You are now king, son. I hope you run the waters better than he ever did."

"You can count on it," he replied.

"Come to the ball tonight. Take the pretty girl to the dance," His Majesty suggested.

"I suppose...if she ever wakes up," the boy replied, looking down at her.

"She has seen a lot today. I certainly hope you like her as much as your face shows. If you ever do her wrong, I can assure you that you'll meet the same fate as your father," Alister threatened.

"I would rather die than bring harm to her."

"I know. I heard." Alister smiled. "Let's get out of here."

The new King of the Waters looked over at the guards, still standing dumbfounded, unable to go against the ruler of the entire realm in order to save their own king. "I am in charge now," Simon said. "It will all be better...I promise you that."

As they bowed to the newly crowned ruler, Simon nodded, took Sylvia's still unconscious body in his arms, and swam up to the surface.

* * *

When Sylvia woke up, she was dry and in her bedroom. Sitting up too quickly, she held her hand to her aching head, feeling like she'd just witnessed the most traumatic nightmare of her entire life. Looking to her left, she saw the boy named Simon sitting in the chair beside her bed. Grunting and laying her head back down on the pillow, she covered her face with her blanket and screamed into it.

"It wasn't a dream at all. Was it?" she said, still under-cover.

"I'm afraid not," he replied.

"What happened?" Pulling the blanket from her face, she sat up. "What happened to the dragon?"

"He's fine," Simon replied.

"But the blood. Oh my gosh...it was everywhere," Sylvia said, feeling sick all over again.

"It was my father's blood. Alister was simply faster. He deserved it," Simon said, looking angry at all the man had done.

"He was your father, Simon," Sylvia said gently. She was sad for Simon; after all, she had lost her own father just a few years ago, so she knew what loss felt like even though she'd barely known him.

"He was no father. He was evil and let the power go to his head."

"Yes, but he still died. Don't you feel anything?" she asked, looking at him.

Just when she thought Simon was cold hearted and closed off, he hung his head low and tears fell down his cheeks and dropped to the floor. He did care...and now the reality was hitting him hard.

"Come here," she demanded. As he walked toward her, she wrapped her arms around him and wiped his tears. "Now I know you have a heart after all. I was worried. I hated my stepfather. He was always mean to me, but I still cried knowing he was gone forever."

Simon looked up into Sylvia's eyes. She felt like he could tell how much she cared for him. Holding his head in her hands, she smiled at him as he moved slowly forward and placed a soft kiss on her lips.

"Sylvia, are you okay?" Neveah asked as she entered her daughter's room.

Both kids jumped and the boy removed himself from the bed quickly, rubbing his eyes and attempting to straighten his posture.

"What's going on in here?" Neveah said, turning her head slightly. She smiled as she looked at her daughter's flushed face.

"Um...I'm sorry, Ma'am. I kissed her. I was sad, she was kind...it happened so fast..." Simon put his head down towards the floor.

"Oh my gosh, Simon!" Sylvia covered her head with the blanket. "Why would you tell my *mother* that?"

Neveah smiled at Sylvia's absolute embarrassment. "Who are you?" Neveah asked the boy.

"I'm Prince Simon Pontos, Ma'am, of the Waters."

"A Prince, you say?"

"He just became king. He's a Merman," came Sylvia's muffled voice from under the blanket.

"Yes. That still needs to be announced officially, however, before I am actually seen as a king. For now, I'm just a prince. Technically, I can't fully be king for two more years."

"You're a Merman?" Neveah had a hard time being anything more than excited for her daughter. Knowing nothing about the boy made her a little unsure, of course. He did just tell her he kissed her daughter.

"Yes, and I would like to court your daughter. Please," he asked, standing tall.

"This is so embarrassing. Can you tell him, Mother, that he doesn't have to ask you? That he could ask me himself," Sylvia said, pulling the blanket away.

"I like that he asked, Sylvia," Neveah said. *I do like him,* she thought.

"How about you tell me exactly what 'court' means to you?"

"Well, I would spend the next two years getting to know her and your family, and then simply ask you if I can marry her," he said calmly, like it was the customary thing to do in their realm.

Sylvia jumped from the bed and stomped from the room, as if sickened by the fact that Simon and her own mother were discussing and deciding *her* future.

Neveah let out a loud laugh at the disgruntled form. She also realized he may have just scared her daughter away by announcing all of that information so soon. The realm was definitely different from their world. It was never as simple as what the boy had expressed. Everything to do with family, love and marriage on Earth always had to be so ridiculously dramatic.

"Well, you should probably follow her. I'm sure she is just dying to take this out on you." She stared him straight in the eyes and added in a stern tone, "I also expect the door to be open in any room where you two are alone from now on."

"Absolutely, Ma'am," Simon said, bowing his head to her.

"Call me Neveah. I'm not that old," she said, rolling her eyes and leaving the door open behind her.

"Yes!" He jumped, fist-pumping the air.

He had gotten the mother of the girl he liked to accept him. Now he just needed to find Sylvia and apologize. Thankfully, walking around on two legs wasn't as difficult as he had imagined.

He tried to dodge all the different people rushing left and right in Mood Castle as they counted down to the main event. He was positively fascinated by everyone, smiling and waving at them, yet receiving no acknowledgment back.

"Excuse me, sir," he said, stopping one of the party planners by tapping him on the shoulder.

"What?" he turned around to face Simon.

He was immediately taken aback by the sickly-looking man with dark circles under his eyes and sporting a smoky grey appearance. Not to mention, the awful smell coming from him made him hold his nose as he asked, "Do you know where the older human kids are?"

"Garden," he said, pointing outside the large open doors.

"Thank you, sir." Simon ran in the direction the man was pointing and could hear Sylvia's voice as he got closer. She was complaining about him. It was making him smile before he jumped out of the bushes.

"Boo!" he yelled, making everyone scream.

"Simon," Sylvia yelled at him, "you scared us half to death."

"What are you guys doing?" he asked.

"I was just telling them how much you embarrassed me in front of my mother."

"Oh. That again. I had to say something. Adult women make me nervous. Then I start blabbering," he admitted.

"I'm still mad," she said, crossing her arms and turning her back to him.

"That I kissed you, or that I told your mother I plan to marry you?" he said, whispering in her ear.

Sylvia made a gasping sound before turning around to smack him. Before she could connect, he lifted his hand to grab hers. "Please don't ever hit me," he said quietly.

"I...I was just...teasing. I'm so sorry," she said calmy, realizing she was speaking with someone who had seen abuse and been abused for most of his life.

"It's okay. Just don't. Please." He pulled her close in front of her cousins and friends and hugged her. Feeling her relax, she hugged him back.

"I never will. I promise. I forgive you," she whispered in his ear.

"Hah! That tickles," he said, tickling her back and listening to her laugh.

"Yuck." The chant of the younger kids filled his ears.

They continued, "Simon and Sylvia sitting in a tree, K-I-S-S-I-N-G." They all started to laugh.

"It's time," Julia poked her head around the side of the castle and hollered into the garden.

"I'll see you on the dance floor," Simon said, twirling Sylvia in a circle before waving at everyone and leaving to get ready for, what he hoped, would be the first memorable night of the rest of his life.

* * *

All the men and woman were getting ready for the ball. It was to be the biggest event the realm had ever thrown.

Arianna was getting ready in front of her vanity mirror. Wearing a blood red dress, she was satisfied with her appearance. Happily, she made her way with some of her demons to Mood Castle.

Upon changing her appearance to the same red-headed woman she was when last she'd met Neveah, she handed the guards her invitation, getting through the gates without any issues.

Watching the sky as the drakon landed on the castle, entering from a different direction, she was grateful that she wouldn't have to encounter his presence anytime soon while being perfectly transformed into a mystery woman.

"Bastard," she mumbled to herself, watching him.

"Are you ready?" one of her demons asked, offering his hand.

"Of course. You know the plan?" she asked in a stern, reprimanding voice.

"We do, My Queen."

"Good. Then get on with it," she said, marching through the castle doors.

* * *

"Is Jenisis going to be escorting you to the ball?" Neveah teased her mother as she was piling her luxurious curls on top of her head.

"Of course he is," Julia said. Smiling, she thought of seeing Jenisis again and her heartrate immediately sped up.

"What about you, Sylvia? Will the young Simon be waiting on you?" Neveah taunted her.

"He said he would," Sylvia replied, unable to stop the blush from appearing.

"He and my beloved daughter got busted kissing, Mom," Neveah announced.

Julia choked on the water she was sipping; hearing Neveah's words shocked her. "What? You kissed a boy?" Julia shot a look at Sylvia.

"He kissed me, and I didn't really have time to think about it."

"How well do you even know him?"

"How well do you know Jenisis, Grandma?" she shot back.

Everyone, including Julia, burst out into laughter as the servants of the castle came in to finish styling hair, add make-up to their faces, and apply a hint of gold powder on their cheeks.

"I'll let that one slide, but just this time," Julia replied. "You're right though. I don't understand a thing going on in my head. These two voices are just constantly bickering in there...throwing thoughts back and forth."

"Mom, just be happy. That's all we want for you," Angela added.

"We want *all* to be happy," Iris smiled.

"Speaking of...what's going on with you and Izak?" Angela asked.

Everyone turned to look at Iris and hear her reply. Julia was just as curious to know. They had been spending a lot of time together, and she would be thrilled to see her son with such a wonderful person.

"Well, I really enjoy being around him. He can be pretty stubborn, though, and it seems lately he has been more distant. I don't know why."

"Maybe it has something to do with him finding out you're Angela's sister and the other one..." Neveah's comments faded out.

"Sure, but it's not like we're blood related and he should understand that." Angela also had her input.

"I don't know how he feels. He doesn't tell me much."

"That's strange for him. He usually is quite expressive with his...emotions," Neveah said.

"Yeah, but this is different. These are matters of the heart, honey. It's not as easy as throwing temper tantrums," Julia informed them, always thinking about Izak's go-to dramatic move.

* * *

Izak and Zack were getting ready in a separate room. Izak was informed to wear a royal blue collared shirt to match his date's wardrobe that she'd chosen for the evening. He would do anything for Iris that she asked, and he was determined to make tonight all about her and enjoy himself in the process.

"How's it going, buddy?" Izak asked Zack.

"Fine. Nervous. I have two girls expecting my attention and dancing tonight," he said with a thoughtful expression.

"Player. Player," Izak said, teasing him.

"I don't know what to do," Zack said, slumping down on a bench as if defeated.

"Do you know which one you like more? You're young, buddy. I wouldn't worry about it."

"No. I don't know. I enjoy being around them both. Never even noticed girls until now. So confusing."

"Well, you got your head out of your computer and hands off those silly controllers. Makes sense that now you're noticing things you haven't before. Just have fun tonight. Okay?"

"Okay, Uncle. How did you know when you started caring for Iris?"

He wasn't sure how to reply. He had no idea if he could pursue anything with Iris, not after finding out she and Angela were blood sisters. Everything was confusing for him. It shouldn't really even be an issue. Maybe, in reality, it was just the fact that Izak felt Iris was far too good for him. He had felt like a failure his entire life, and certainly knew he wasn't worthy of such an incredible woman.

"Who says I have any feelings for her?" Izak asked.

"Dude, it's obvious. You smile every time you're near her; your face lights up. I have never seen you look like that before, Uncle Izak."

"There's your answer then. If one of those girls makes you feel that way tonight, I would go that route. Get to know them both. They might surprise you with the more time you take to get to know them. Just be kind to both. Whatever you decide," he said, turning the conversation away from his own issues.

"Thanks. I feel better," Zack told him, standing in his underwear and shirt. "I'm ready."

"I'd suggest you get some pants on first, stud," Izak laughed.

"Oh yeah," Zack said, running into the bathroom and leaving Izak to think further about the mystery that was Iris.

* * *

Landing on the castle, he was careful not to get scuffed up. This was a big night for him to finally tell her the truth. He was determined to make good with the woman that he found himself caring deeply for more and more each day. Walking down the steps from the rooftop, he entered the castle. His Majesty of the Realm opened the door. Dressed in his turquoise shirt, under a formal black tuxedo, he was freshly shaven and his hair was styled to perfection.

Entering the ballroom, a hush fell over the gathered crowd as everyone turned to bow to His Majesty. Nodding his head to everyone, he made it through the crowd. He hoped that he hadn't missed the announcements of the humans and seeing Angela walk down the glorious steps toward him.

He wasn't late, thank goodness. He made it just in time. The announcements of the ladies had just begun. First, was Julia Carrier escorted by the King of the Shapeshifters, Jenisis. *What a lovely match*, he thought. Next came Neveah descending the stairs with no escort awaiting her. That was fine,

Alister already knew someone had their eye on her from the very beginning. Iris was announced next and Izak was waiting for her at the bottom step to take her hand. Knowing Angela would be next, he felt the excitement shoot through his body at the thought of how beautiful she must look this very night.

Feeling like her entrance was taking far too long, he walked over to the announcer to see Queen Tiana making a special request.

Suddenly, the deep voice of the announcer pierced the room. "Miss *Angela* McLean and dear friend of Queen Tiana." He was apparently reminding one and all that their next guest was most definitely not Arianna, even though her face would perhaps make some of them gasp. "So, everyone, be on your best behavior."

The entire crowd let out a laugh at the announcement. Everyone was waiting for her to appear; His Majesty had to stop himself from running up the stairs to make sure she was safe and okay. But not a second later, everyone heard her voice.

"I'm coming! Sorry! My damn shoes are hurting my feet!"

Again, an uproar let loose in the room and spread throughout the castle.

Alister took a deep breath. Finally he would be able to set eyes once again on the beautiful woman he'd been waiting for.

CHAPTER 20

They were ready to join the crowd of people, and Izak was anxiously awaiting his chance to escort Miss Iris. Listening to his mother being announced, he also heard the name of her escort who, by all accounts, he'd heard was a wolf and had already asked for his mother's hand in marriage. Izak was positive she was going to say yes. Then came his very own sister with no escort, but by the 'oohs' and 'aahs' that filled the room, he was sure that fact wouldn't last long. Then came the gorgeous Iris in her royal blue gown, matching his shirt perfectly.

The dress fell past her feet, causing a train to accumulate behind her. The satin material draped her hips and created a mermaid-like tail. The sweetheart shaped bodice was decorated with pearl beads embroidered over her chest and stomach, allowing viewers to see a hint of the rounded, lovely breasts beneath.

Looking at Iris, her face grew a smile as he extended his hand.

"You are breathtaking," he said, kissing her on the cheek.

"You clean up quite nice yourself."

Angela was waiting upstairs with Sylvia and Bella, fidgeting with her heels. "Oh my gosh, these are so uncomfortable. Who could *wear* these?"

"Should have worn tennis shoes," Bella chastised her mother lifting up her own dress to show off a pair of black and white, comfortable looking shoes.

"Bella!"

"What? They're comfortable. Unlike yours."

"Screw this," Angela said, removing her shoes and running back to her room to grab a pair of flats.

Hearing her name being announced as she was putting the new shoes on, she came racing back to the stairs, hopping up and down.

"I'm coming! Sorry! My damn shoes are hurting my feet." Blushing by the time she was presented, she heard everyone laugh even louder.

Looking at all the people and smiling down at them, she felt a little proud as they clapped when she started walking down the steps, waving at friends she had made. Locking eyes with His Majesty, a smile she couldn't control appeared on her face as she noticed he was wearing the same turquoise color that perfectly matched her dress.

She had chosen the color because of the transitions her friend, the drakon, made when it came to his skin tone. The strapless, heart-shaped dress embroidered with silver along the breasts reached to her ankles, and the chiffon fabric of the skirt made it wave as she walked.

Once she made it to the floor, she walked straight to Tiana.

"How much did I embarrass myself?"

"Oh, believe me, everyone will talk about your announcement and entry until the end of time."

They both broke out in laughter.

* * *

Sylvia took a deep breath, wanting to make a fabulous entrance. She turned around to look down at Bella's face; she was pale and nervous, weaving her dress between her fingers.

"It's okay. You look beautiful. Don't worry."

"I hate dresses," Bella groaned.

"Get used to it," she replied, hearing her name being called. "See ya later."

Sylvia walked down the steps expecting to see the handsome Simon waiting for her below. But when she made it down and looked from left to right, no one was there except her brother. He smiled and took her hand.

"You look great, sis."

"Where is Simon?"

"I guess he's running late."

Sylvia stomped her foot in annoyance. Turning, she listened to Bella be announced as she appeared at the top of the staircase.

Bella took deep breaths as they said her name. Walking to the top of the steps, she could hear a variety of 'oohs' and 'aahs' emanate throughout the room. Heading down the staircase, adults and children were waving and saying things about how lovely she was in her unique dress.

Bella was wearing a garment that was absolutely special. The mesh embroidered sleeves reached the palms of her hands, ending in a 'v' shape above her fingers. The silvery-light blue fabric produced a 'V'-neck bodice, and as the skirt fell to the floor, each layer turned a deeper shade of blue, giving it the look of a beautiful waterfall.

Once she reached the bottom of the steps, Princess Jacky pulled her by the hand through the crowd of people to a group made up of her own friends.

"Thank you so much," Bella expressed, thankful to Jacky for saving her from all the uncomfortable compliments being tossed her way.

"I have to say, you walked down those steps very calm; totally straight spine for someone who was worried," Jacky remarked.

Smiling, she lifted her skirt and showed off her tennis shoes, making the group laugh.

Various shop owners from town walked over to her to ask about her fashionable clothing, causing even more chuckles.

"First off, you all need to learn how to make jeans and jumpers. Dresses all the time are overrated and outdated," she voiced her opinion.

"Do you have any drawings of your fashion ideas?"

"No, but I could. I can show you some if you give me a couple of days."

"Wonderful. Thank you, Bella. You look amazing," they acknowledged before moving on and continuing to mingle.

"Thanks." She'd blushed every time someone had complimented her; so much so that she started to feel like her gown would end up catching fire or melting into a puddle on the floor.

Turning back to her friends, she was welcomed by all the mood children, along with Sylvia and Zack.

* * *

Angela was standing by the long tables piled with delicious food. Taking in the sweets made with mushrooms that Tiana had recommended, she picked one up and threw it in her mouth before turning around to catch His Majesty walking towards her. Everyone he passed chose to either bow their head or bow at the waist in respect. *They must think if they bow with half of their body, they'll get in his good graces quicker.* Giving him a critical stare as he reached her, he simply stood beside her and said nothing.

"I certainly hope you don't think *I* will be bowing to you anytime soon," she said, raising her eyebrows.

Instead of replying, he simply bowed at the waist, extended his right hand to her and covered his stomach with his left. Listening to the entire crowd whisper and gasp in what she could only assume was amazement at the respect he was showing to her, Angela's eyes grew wide. By the looks all around them and the reverent silence that had settled, she could only assume his gesture was a big deal. All she could do was let out a slightly nervous laugh, making him smile and close the gap between them, making her heart race.

"Dance with me?" he asked, offering his hand.

"Nope."

"What do you mean by 'nope'?" He looked confused.

"It means no." She clarified so he wouldn't take it personally, "I can't dance."

He didn't seem offended by her rejection, so she just shrugged it off and listened to his feeble attempt at small talk.

"Anything new in your life?" he asked, not realizing what doors he'd opened by asking that question.

She stared at him. "Lots of new things, actually. First off, I have stayed safe from any kidnapper. My daughter's a witch, my son's an Identifier, my niece is dating a Merman, and my mother's going to marry a wolf. Not just any wolf, of course, but the king of the entire shapeshifting species."

"Well...guess I've missed some stuff," he teased.

"Will you ever allow my sister to see Iris and me?" Angela asked, desperately wanting to know her and try to understand how 'evil' she actually was. "If we could convince her that we mean her no harm, maybe she'll come out of hiding."

"I never knew she was possessed; I didn't even give Iris the chance to explain anything. Watching my wife die, never getting to hold my unborn child...sent an explosion into my heart, shattering it into many pieces," he explained. "Angela, if you wish to meet your sister, I would be willing to listen to her...but she is dangerous. I would have to request that she not have her magic anymore."

His Majesty had never expressed anything so emotional to her before. This was the first time he had shared even an ounce of what he'd experienced during that tragic event. Angela also noted that he did say he'd let her see Arianna with only one stipulation. Without thinking, she pulled him into a long, sympathetic hug. Getting more attention from the simple embrace than expected, she let go and looked straight at his shirt, determined to change the subject.

"How did you know I would wear the same color?" she asked, looking at it.

"It's my favorite color," he admitted. "Well, this and royal purple."

"I chose mine because it has also become my favorite color. Alister actually inspired me to pick it. His skin produces a gorgeous sequence of colors," she said, still missing the wonderful adventure they had that day.

His face fell as he tried to come up with the words to tell her his secret for the second time. Wanting a quieter area to talk, he offered her his arm. "Join me in the garden?"

By taking his arm, Miss Independent surprised him. He'd expected her to just lead the way and go on and on about how Leah, Iris, and Neveah all used magic to decorate the garden, but she remained silent.

Working their way through the crowd and out the garden doors, they headed to the bench to sit and talk. Before they could reach it, however, a familiar couple crossed their path and chose the bench, quickly throwing themselves into a deep conversation followed by a wealth of passionate kisses.

The situation had turned a bit awkward.

* * *

After Jenesis had taken Julia's hand, he'd asked her to dance and headed straight for the center of the ballroom. Her heart fluttered as he walked her to the dance floor and stopped. Looking into his eyes and feeling the sensual touch of his right arm wrap around her waist and pull her close, he entangled his left hand in hers. Dancing perfectly, they swayed romantically around the room, never taking their eyes off each other.

"I have missed you." He was the first to speak.

"I have...missed you as well," she admitted.

He bent down and kissed her warm cheek, making her turn even redder. Dancing until the song had come to an end, Jenesis held her tight as he dipped her with the last note and then brought her back up to his chest. Everyone clapped at the beautiful voice and amazing musicians who'd graced them with their song.

"Would you like to eat a little something or take a stroll through the garden?" he asked.

"I would love to see the garden. My daughter and granddaughter helped to decorate it," she spoke proudly.

Entering the garden and looking at the shimmering lights, Jenesis led her to a bench. They sat by each other's side, turned in order to face one another.

"Have you thought about my proposal? You don't have to answer now but—"

"Yes," she responded, cutting him off quickly.

"What? *Really?* Oh, we are going to live a long and happy life, I assure you," he said, taking her hands in his and kissing them multiple times.

She laughed as he picked her up and spun her in the air. Setting her back down on the bench, he looked into Julia's eyes. Lifting his right hand, he ran it along her check and tucked the stray curls behind her ear.

Julia looked up at him as he lifted her face to his and kissed her with so much passion it took her breath away.

Releasing from the hot, wet kiss, he looked up. Smiling, he grabbed Julia by the hand. "Come with me," he twirled her around. "I wish to tell the King of the Realm. He's a dear friend of mine."

"Okay."

"Alister! She said yes," Jenesis yelled as he rushed to the silent, fidgeting couple who had stopped very close to the garden bench.

* * *

Neveah was smiling and drinking lemon water, chatting with her friend Lilian from the dress store. Lilian had introduced her to many more of her friends – some of whom were most definitely eligible men. Standing there, entertaining the men's sweet and overly pleasing attempts to catch her attention, she looked around the room in order to find a possible escape route. Suddenly, she spotted a familiar-looking face; a face that had been entering her dreams and thoughts since the first time she'd seen his forest green eyes.

With the same entertaining smile, he approached her with his hands behind his back. "Hello again, Neveah," he spoke.

"Hello. I'm sorry...I don't know your name," she said, remembering he'd never offered it back in the cornfield.

"It is Nicolas Aero. It's a pleasure to meet you. Would you like to dance?" he asked.

"Uh...sure." She set her drink down on the table and walked with him to the dance floor.

They slow-danced together while making small talk.

"I was wondering if I would ever see you again. You took off so quickly that day, I was starting to wonder if I'd just imagined you. Did I say something wrong?" she asked.

"Not at all. I just wasn't prepared to meet everyone. I'm a very cautious person; one who likes to find out more about strangers before introductions occur," he said, twirling her in a circle before bringing her back close.

"We seem to have that effect on many of the species here. Trust needs to be earned for others to feel safe presenting themselves," she said.

"Yes. Showing our true identity is like standing naked in a crowd. Everyone can see every part of you...making you vulnerable," he said, looking down into her eyes.

"Being vulnerable isn't always bad, though," she said, smiling. "But I'm guessing you won't be telling me what you shift into anytime soon."

"Not quite yet. I would like to know you well enough one day to do so, though," he smiled back, twirling her around the floor.

Just when the music stopped, with Neveah and Nicolas still in each other's arms, an angry screeching sound filled the room. Making a huge scene, Angela ran through the crowd and up the steps with her hands covering her face.

"Please don't react that way when I present myself to you in my shifting form," he whispered in her ear.

Turning around fast to face him, her heart broke to see that he was already walking away, disappearing from her sight yet again.

* * *

Frozen in place, reality had just struck her across the face at hearing Jenesis' words. He had not announced 'His Majesty' nor did he address him as 'Ruler of the Realm.' No...the happy man who was thrilled that his proposal had been accepted had shouted 'Alister.' As in her own dear, caring friend, the drakon. Feeling the sudden betrayal and dishonesty consume her mind, body, and soul, Angela stood staring straight ahead, as if in a trance.

Hearing her mother's voice but unable to exit the trance, she turned slowly and looked up into Alister's eyes. As if suddenly noting the familiar color, her own eyes filled with tears projecting all the hurt and pain she was feeling.

Loosening her grip from his arm, she heard his voice.

"Angela...I tried to tell you twice, which is why I asked to take you to this garden. In town I tried to tell you, too," his voice held a pleading note, begging for her to understand and listen to his tale. But she couldn't speak. All she could do was close her eyes and shake her head.

"Liar...Liar...Liar!" Each time she said the words, her voice grew louder, ending in a scream. All the strange moments were coming together. Why he had never said his name. Why he was never present when the dragon was. His odd eye color and the glow that they would emit, added to the heat that would radiate from his body when he would be furiously mad at her in the dungeon. All of it made sense now.

Putting her hand in his face, she walked away, not getting far before he grabbed her arm to attempt to reason with her.

"Please forgive me, Angela. I *didn't* want to lie to you. That's why I'm here. Please."

She stopped, slapping him as hard as she could across the face. The violent action produced the loudest sound she'd ever heard; it rang in her own ears.

Her voice was strong. "Never touch me. Never talk to me again. I don't ever want to see your face for as long as I live. I don't believe a word you say...you are nothing more than a liar."

Without another word, she ran through the doors, smashed through the crowd in the ballroom and covered her face as she ran up the steps to her bedroom door. Stumbling over a woman in the hallway, she fell to the floor, sobbing in sadness, choking on her tears. "Oh gosh. I'm sorry. This is so embarrassing," Angela said, standing up and facing a woman who'd stopped beside her.

She had red hair and freckles along her cheeks; she displayed perfect white teeth when she smiled. Wearing a lovely blood red dress, the woman remained silent.

"I'm sorry," Angela spoke. "I just...I hate him. The King of the Realm is a liar."

"That is a fact," the lady agreed, reaching her hand out to rub Angela's shoulder. Pulling her hand back quickly, an odd look of shock came over her face.

"What's your name?" Angela asked, feeling a strange connection from the woman's touch.

"Honey, life's a bitch. But it will get better, I promise," she replied in an almost casual tone. Continuing down the hallway, she disappeared down the staircase and out of Angela's sight.

The woman had never even bothered to tell Angela her name. Not only that, she'd used a term from her own realm. She'd learned that no one from this world cursed whatsoever, at least...not in English. Angela was completely and utterly confused. "Wait. Please! You don't have to fear me," Angela yelled for the woman to come back. She even attempted to follow her until another realization hit her square between the eyes.

That was my sister in disguise.

* * *

Arianna was racing far away from Angela. Distracted and a little disoriented, she stumbled on some loose gravel outside the castle as she tried to wrap her head around the fact that she'd just stood in front of a mirror. A myriad of thoughts ran through her head. *But that's not possible. There were only two of us...me and Iris. Who the hell was that?*

"My Queen. Are we to continue with the plan?" one of her demons inquired.

"Yes," she shook her head, trying to dispel the thoughts. "Why wouldn't we?"

He paused. "Well...you don't look...like yourself."

"Nonsense, you idiot! I'm going this instant and all of you better be ready." Stepping into the carriage, she left her demons behind to walk.

Driving to the gates to exit Mood Castle territory, she met three very familiar faces. As they approached the carriage to wish her farewell, Arianna blew a white powdery substance in all three faces, making the trio drop to the ground immediately.

* * *

Atticus, Declan, and Leo all had to leave the ball to take the night shift on guard duty, which was already proving to be more than slightly difficult. Leo had drank too much, Atticus was tired already, and Declan just simply had no desire to be there at all.

"Why couldn't the owls take guard duty tonight?" Leo complained.

"Because they need strength this evening, not flight shifters," Declan stated, clearly annoyed because he really wanted to party.

"Arianna is back in this realm; they need nothing but the best," Atticus pointed out.

They sat there in stone silence, perking up only when they heard a carriage going over the bridge to exit the castle. Reaching up to raise the gate, they donned their fake smiles as they stuck their heads in the windows to tell the people inside to have a wonderful night.

Each receiving a sudden blast of powder in their faces, the trio of men dropped their gear and passed out cold before their bodies even hit the ground.

CHAPTER 21

Arianna's demons had kidnapped the three men at her request. Bringing them to her castle, each was stowed in their own individual cell in her large dungeon.

Before heading upstairs to her room, Arianna gave further instructions to her minions. "When they wake up, I need you to interrogate them. I need answers about who the land people are that the witch, Neveah, brought to this realm. Do they have special powers? Who the hell is this woman who looks like me? I need all the information you can get from them about the family. And whatever you do," her voice grew sinister, "do *not* disappoint me."

When she arrived in her room nestled in the turret at the highest point of the castle, she pulled the cloth still embedded with Leah and Liam's blood out of her bag. She had gone to Mood Castle to retrieve their blood in order to know who they were and see if there was any connection between them and herself. She was wishing now that she'd gathered more blood from the rest of the strangers.

Giving each a little pinprick on their toe while they slept, she immediately kissed the wounds and healed them immediately. She didn't want them to wake, nor did she want to hurt them or cause them any pain. They were absolutely adorable to Arianna; even now just thinking about them made her smile as she set up the crystals in order to see who they were. The same routine she'd used when first meeting Neveah.

Working with Leah's blood, she found out that the young girl harnessed Arianna's own mother's power, making Arianna happy to feel the smallest hint of her beloved mother's presence. Working up to Liam, she unveiled his ability to identify shifters in either form. Impressed by both their talents, and having them at such a young age, she knew they would both be indestructible in this realm and likely protect everyone around them.

Next, she worked on the connection to see how they were related. Adding her own trickle of blood to the mix, she had found that the two children were made of her own flesh and blood. *They are my niece and nephew*, she clapped with glee, fascinated by the fact both children sported golden hair but had her eyes. Realizing now that the woman who wore an identical face to her own *was* another sister, she was shocked to discover that she actually had a twin. Unsure why Iris had kept the information from her all these years, she was even more surprised that their father hadn't mentioned her other half either. There was no way to answer her questions unless she spoke to Iris, and she was not prepared to face her just yet. Arianna knew she needed more power to make herself shatterproof to the drakon when he came for her head...which was exactly what he would do.

Wondering who the other half was to these children, she continued her search in order to find their father.

Coming into focus on her crystal was the image of a familiar looking gentleman. She remembered him as being the attractive man who pulled up in a van behind her as she received her coffee from the local shop in McCleary on Christmas morning.

"Oh, my God...it's him," she was astonished at her sister's taste in appealing men, seeing as that she'd felt the same attraction.

He was not looking as well as before in the projection her crystal was giving off. In this new image, he looked ill and pale. Nothing like the strong, cheerful man with gorgeous dimples she had seen before.

Watching him getting high and sleeping with countless woman made her feel more than uncomfortable. She attempted to close the images as quickly as possible, but just before they faded she looked down at his hand and saw the stones, now set in rings, wrapped around his fingers. Her excitement exploded now that she knew who had them...and how she could get them back.

* * *

Following Queen Arianna's demands, the demons prepared themselves to interrogate the strong men. Not needing to do anything but shift into their natural demonic appearance, they began with Atticus. As they transformed into their hideous true identity, they watched Atticus squirm in his chains as he, too, tried to shift in order to break the iron that held him...but was unsuccessful.

Watching as they slowly approached, Atticus was unable to identify any of their features. And the closer they got, the more difficult he found it to breathe—the horrible odor they gave off was already burning his throat and nostrils. One of them wiggled a sharp, needle-shaped finger in his face; black tar seeped out of the tip as the demon scratched him across his cheek. Breaking the skin with ease, Atticus' own blood mixed with the black, sickly substance and it felt like the gel was literally boiling on top of his skin. Showing his strength and not giving them the satisfaction of seeing him in pain, Atticus stood taller and heard only what he could assume was a laugh exiting the open space carved into the demon's face.

"Who is the family you brought to this realm? What do they want?" The thing spoke in an odd screeching tone.

"I'm not telling you anything. You're wasting your time on me," he stated before spitting in its face. Hearing his saliva connect, sizzling filled his ears. It was as if he had spat into a fire as the demon ejected smoke before laughing once again. Tensing, Atticus prepared his body for more pain he would surely receive.

"Oh, no, this is our pleasure. We are getting to the best part," two of the demons said, looking at one another.

Walking forward, a new demon brought its finger to the inner part of his elbow. Atticus just stared at the ceiling, showing his pride until the demon put pressure on Atticus' skin and pressed straight through; its finger reached a vein where he injected a shot of black poison into his body.

The once tough man couldn't keep his stance for long as the burning and uncontrollable desire to scratch his own fingernails into his arm and rip out that particular vein took over his mind, draining him of the fight he had left. Letting out a high-pitched scream, his arm began to boil and turn black, dripping hot tar. Squirming, he ripped and pulled on the chains until he could hear his own wrist bones crack and break.

"We ask you again. Who are the newcomers and what do they want?"

He refused to answer the question. His body seemed to be going through a natural numbing stage, fighting against the poison, making the traumatic pain slightly subside as the shock arrived.

The demon injected his inner knees and his other inner elbow. This one felt like intense cuts were being made all the way down his arms and legs. Screaming again at the unimaginable pain, Atticus released a sound from his very soul that would make any decent person cringe...and run for their lives.

Getting frustrated that the man still remained silent even though they'd injected enough poison to break any other creature, they sent the third demon forward. A female, she walked slowly towards Atticus, visibly excited to do her part. She covered his mouth and nose with her wretched black hands and blew her toxic smoke into his lungs. Smiling wickedly, she stepped back to watch the man suffer.

The effects were supposed to make his lungs feel like he was drowning repeatedly, only allowing him a minor, satisfying breath when it got to the point of passing out. The breath, however, would make his lungs feel like they were sucking up needles as he desperately tried to inhale and exhale.

Watching all the man's senses go dark, she was thrilled to see the black blood emerge as he coughed continuously, struggling for every breath.

The demons stood looking at him with satisfaction before she walked back, covered his mouth and sucked out some of the toxic acid within him. Slowing his death to a crawl.

"You're willing to *die* to protect that family?" she asked him.

He nodded.

"What a shame. You would have been an incredible addition to our army. Your heart is pure. It sickens me," she said with pure disgust as she walked back to join her demon brothers. "We will get nothing from him. Just let him suffer and die."

Leaving him, they exited his cell and went to work on the next brother. They used the same process of interrogation on both Declan and Leo, yet the youngest passed out cold before the female got a chance to do her happy work. Making Leo the most boring out of the three.

The middle brother was difficult as well, though he wanted to strike a deal. He wanted something in return for the information he would give.

"I want to go with you when you return to your realm. I will tell you anything you want to know," he begged them. "But I need to never set eyes on this world again."

Not liking how he tried to negotiate, the demons proceeded to torture him just for the fun of it, making him faint as well.

The Tarmen became bored...

* * *

After the two men woke, it was the Destructors' turn to use their torture tactics. Just as harsh, they attacked the same areas as the Black Tarmen had.

Appearing to have crystalized bodies, these creatures were surrounded with microscopic bugs that they used, beginning on the youngest of the men.

Forcing his eyes to remain open, they pushed the strange bugs into his eyes, where they then ran in all directions throughout his body. They infected him as they burrowed under the skin where they then injected him with their own brand of electric shocks and poisonous substances.

Removing the chains that held him up, he began scratching his own face uncontrollably. Screaming in terror, his face began to bleed from his own fingernails gouging at the crawlers under his skin, now working on his arms and legs.

They watched as he ran into the concrete wall of the cell, bashing his head repeatedly until he fell to the floor where he took his last breath. His body went stiff.

"What a shame. That didn't last long." They laughed,

exiting the dead boy's cell to enter the next.

Giving them no reason to move on to the oldest of the brothers, they got what they needed from the middle one. All it took was one look at the demons and Declan caved, spilling everything, answering all the questions they asked. Seeing the black in his heart, they offered him a chance to join them when they travelled back to their own realm.

Not having the strength to even look at Atticus, he kept his gaze on his attackers. "Yes. Thank you," Declan said. He bowed at their feet.

* * *

Arianna finished up what she was doing and stored all of her ingredients, making sure to keep some of her concoction in order to bring the stones and the man back to this realm. Feeling a sense of relaxation and happiness enter her body, she suddenly remembered her prisoners down below. It was time to let them go home. After all, she had found out everything she could ever hope for just by utilizing the blood of her niece and nephew. There was no reason for more pain or anguish now.

Walking down the dungeon steps to inform the demons she no longer needed their services; Arianna was shocked when she opened the door to the cell holding Atticus. Rushing over to his limp body, covered in tar, hanging from the chains, she checked to see if he was breathing. He was, barely, but she could hear him slowly suffocating in the fluid. Listening to his heart rate she heard his last breath and, without thinking, placed her hands on his chest and restarted his heart.

Pulling the quartz out of her pocket, she held it in her hands and healed everything inside him. Taking away his pain and agony, she healed his brain of the side effects the poison would give to him, restoring his strength.

Opening his eyes, he stared at his rescuer.

"Are you okay?" she asked, panicked. Releasing him from his chains, she further showed her concern by wrapping her arms around the large man as he fell to his knees.

"What happened? What did they do to you?" she cried out.

He opened his mouth but shut it again. She could see from his condition that they had gone way too far with their interrogation. Apparently they had done things even she could never imagine doing.

"I didn't want any of this. They were just supposed to question you and rough you up a little to get the answers. I am so sorry," she expressed her very pure, very *real* concern as tears fell from her eyes.

"My brothers," he grunted, struggling to get up on his feet.

"Of course. You all can go home. I'm so sorry," she said again.

Helping him out of his cell, she walked with him to the next one. The demons had already released Declan from his chains. He was sitting on the cot drinking a glass of water looking rather...refreshed. He was munching on some food that they'd obviously brought to him.

Seeing her minion in the corner, she marched into the cell and lifted her hand, striking the first one with magical strength and knocking him to the ground. With the word, "aposynthéto," she closed her fist and watched the demon turn into nothing more than a black puddle of its own self on the cell floor.

"Who made the decision to go so far as to kill these men? I said to question them, not kill them," she bellowed in outrage, as she spotted the other two now trying to hide in a darkened corner of the dungeon. As she marched toward them, they spoke quickly.

"Our Queen. That one cooperated and told us everything," they explained.

Bringing her hand up to her mouth, she gasped at the information that seemed to be coming forth from the minds of the demons. She suddenly knew...she saw the image of how she'd cast the curse once upon a time that killed all those mothers to be.

She turned to Atticus and began to cry, "I really didn't know."

Atticus could tell by the release that her emotions for everything that had happened in the past were genuine. Killing was not her intention at all, now or then. Watching tears fall from her eyes and listening to the endless chant of apologies, he suddenly thought of Leo.

"Wait, my youngest brother," he said, worried and concerned about Leo's poor strength.

"Yes, go. Tend to him and I will heal any injuries he has sustained," she reassured him before turning to the others. "As for you demons, you will all go back to Hell where you came from."

Atticus thanked her as he ran to the next cell, only to let out a blood curdling scream. He heard Arianna run into the room behind him to witness what Atticus couldn't take his eyes from.

Leo was surrounded by his own blood; it'd created a black pool covering the floor. As Atticus looked down at his face, he was unable to recognize his baby brother. Bending down to hold him in his arms, he sat on the floor and let himself sob as he held onto his now lifeless brother.

"I can fix it," she said. Arianna rushed to Leo and began healing his body and face as Atticus watched in awe. Unfortunately, no matter how hard she tried and how much power she used, she could not revive Leo's heart.

Running out of the cell, she grabbed the female demon and returned. Holding on to her wrist and placing her other hand on Leo's chest, Arianna siphoned the life out of the demon and transferred it into the young boy. The demon immediately dropped to the floor, turning into a pile of white ashes right before their eyes, As the time ticked by, they waited in silence as Leo finally opened his eyes and looked up at Atticus.

"Brother," Leo cried. Reaching up to feel his own face, he sighed in relief.

Looking over at Arianna, she looked weak; she was on her knees in total exhaustion. Lifting her chin slowly, she met the eyes of Atticus.

"It was worth it," she said. Noticing the blatant concern for her in his face, she was surprised.

"Thank you. Everyone will know the good you have done by saving my brother's life," he informed her.

"I appreciate that," she said. Putting her hand against the wall to steady herself, Arianna stood up slowly. "Now...I must answer to the rest of my sins."

"I'm going with them," Declan interrupted their moment of silence.

"No, you 're not. You're coming home with us," Atticus yelled at the preposterous thing his brother had just said.

"No, I'm not. There is nothing here for me. I want to go with the Destructors, brother. And I *will* kill anyone who stands in my way. Mark my words, just try to stop me," Declan stated, glaring at both of his brothers.

"Very well. You made your grave, now you can rot in it," Atticus said calmly. He would not give Declan the satisfaction of seeing how hurt he was by his complete betrayal.

"Take my carriage and return home safely," Arianna told Atticus before heading back upstairs to send the demons and the traitor Declan back to the evil realm.

Entering the dungeon, all of them stood before her as if waiting for her next instruction.

"Now go!" She demanded. As her powers opened the door to the realm, she watched the demons leave, except for the ones she'd rightfully killed. Waiting until Declan was the only one left to walk through the door, she changed her mind. Closing up the path, she did not allow him to exit.

"*What?* No!" He yelled, banging his fists on the now solid

wall of stone.

"*You* need to pull your head out of your ass and go back to the family that loves you. What is wrong with you, anyway? Nobody actually *wants* to go to Hell," she yelled at his back.

Minutes had gone by and he hadn't turned around. Arianna couldn't help but wonder what was going on inside the man that could possibly make him see Hell as some kind of escape route. Not understanding why anyone who had people to love them would ever turn to the evil side, she walked toward him with concern in her voice, "Are you okay, Declan?"

"I'm not going anywhere without you," he stated. Turning around, he slammed his fist into the side of Arianna's head before she could react.

Delivering his strange words and sudden punch, Declan succeeded in knocking her out cold.

CHAPTER 22

"Simon, get out here this instant!" Sylvia shouted, still fuming. She couldn't believe that he had stood her up at the ball a month ago when she was so looking forward to spending the evening getting to know him better.

Stomping her feet on the deck, she kept screaming into the sea, yelling his name. Suddenly, she saw his white hair slowly come out of the water to reveal his regretful, apologetic face.

"Where have you *been*? I have come here countless times," she asked, with her hands on her hips.

"I have no excuse...I was just not...not ready to face all the people that would look at me. The son of the *evil* king that His Majesty had to kill," he sighed. "I went to see if my mother was okay after I left Mood Castle, and she was acting crazy. She said she wished I had died instead of her beloved king. Then she said that I was *lucky* they took me in when I was just a

Merbabe, and I should have been grateful...no matter what the SOB did to me. I have been searching for answers," he explained, pausing only to look up at her face.

"What is that supposed to mean?" Sylvia couldn't believe what he was telling her. She was beyond shocked. But she had to give him credit; it was definitely the best excuse she had ever heard. She sat on the edge of the deck to be closer to him as he continued telling her what his mother had related to him.

"I asked her the same thing. She wouldn't tell me anything. She just said that I wasn't her babe and that the king wasn't my father. I couldn't believe it. I loved her like she was my mother and protected her when Father would harm her, allowing him to beat me instead. How could she?" He got so mad the water looked like it was boiling underneath him.

"Um...Simon, maybe you should calm down. I think you're doing something to the ocean." She was suddenly worried his anger was going to cook all the innocent creatures below.

"I have no family left. I have to tell His Majesty that he's got the wrong Merman for the job of King of the Waters," he stated.

"You know as well as I do, he won't accept that. He made you king because of you, not because of your father. If anything, he wouldn't have chosen you because of who your father was," she reassured him, trying to make him see how the rest of the world would look at his situation.

"You're right," he sighed again.

"What do you plan to do now?" she asked.

"I want to know who my parents are. If they're alive. If I have siblings," he told her, looking hopeful now.

"I want to come with you," she said with a smile. "It could be our own adventure. I'm sure my mother will allow me to come every day."

"You would do that for me? Spend all your time with me and search for my family?" he asked, slowly lifting himself out of the water until he was face-to-face with her.

"Of course, silly. But I'd be doing it for me, too. I want to spend time with you," she added with a wink.

He was looking right into her soul; he was so close to her face she could feel the heat of his breath on her skin. And he just stayed there, still, just smiling, making her feel like the most beautiful girl in the world.

"Can I kiss you?"

His words made her heart jump and butterflies arrive in her stomach. It impressed her that he was so close, but had taken a moment to ask this time. Just smiling, taking a couple seconds longer with her reply, she built up the anticipation.

"Yes," she finally muttered, before he closed the small gap between their lips, softly kissing her like it was the first time.

He lifted his head away from hers—but this time, not because her mother had burst through the door. Looking at her rosy cheeks, brushing his fingers over them as he smiled, he moved his right hand along her cheek to the back of her neck to pull her into a longer, more passionate kiss.

She had never kissed a boy like this before. Feeling unusual sensations come over her body, Simon lowered her onto the deck. Never releasing the kiss, she wrapped her arms around his neck.

Coming up for air, he smiled at her again, before running his lips down her cheek to her ear, making her giggle until he reached her neck.

"Simon? Simon...stop," she demanded, suddenly feeling uncomfortable and confused, pulling herself up to a sitting position.

"Of course, no problem," he said quickly, looking rather flushed himself. "I'm sorry. I never want you to feel uncomfortable."

"I just don't have any experience, like you must have," she said, feeling a tad bit annoyed that he would think she did.

"What do you mean? I have little experience, let me assure

you. I'm in *no* hurry. I promise you, Sylvia," he said. Laying on his side, he propped himself up on his elbow.

"Really? I just know, well...you're older and I just assumed..." She couldn't finish. She was embarrassed by her assumption.

"I'm not much older than you, and my father never let me get close to anyone," he said. "Or...whoever he was."

"How old are you?" she asked, just being curious.

"I'm seventeen. Why? How old are you?" he asked her.

"Wow. I'm fifteen. Time has gone by so fast," she said, thinking about her own age.

"See, told ya. So, want to go into my waters and ask around with me?"

"Yes, I do," she replied. *Anything to get out of this awkward conversation.*

* * *

His Majesty was still very upset over what happened at the ball. It had been a month, but he was hoping he could fix it somehow. He had been driving himself crazy thinking about Angela and the pain he had caused her. Why couldn't she understand? He had tried to tell her. Walking around in circles, he suddenly heard a carriage outside.

Looking out the window, he laid eyes on Atticus and his youngest brother, Leo. He was a bit amazed; it had seemed so long since anyone had seen him or his brothers because of their long camping trip.

Running outside and down the steps, Alister offered his help to Atticus getting Leo out of the carriage and ushering them both inside his castle.

"What happened?" His Majesty asked.

"Demons. Tortured us for information. You won't believe what I'm about to tell you," Atticus stated. He then told the entire tale to Alister, from their time in the cells to his other brother's treachery. He regaled him with how Arianna, the horrible one, had brought Leo back to life and how she promised to send his brother and the demons back to their realm.

Just when His Majesty was about to reply, a stallion raced up to his castle carrying an unconscious woman on its back. The stallion shifted after dropping Arianna to the ground.

"Your Majesty. I have Arianna the Witch for you. I have broken the spell she had cast upon me." Declan transformed before their eyes and bowed.

Alister was walking over to Arianna and bent down to see a large bruise on her face. He was appalled at the shape of a fist made upon her cheek.

"What did you do to her?" Alister asked with anger.

"I had to do something. She would have killed me," Declan shouted.

"I don't think so. I think you're lying. I can smell it on you and it reeks. Your brother told me everything already." Alister was now glowing in anger. "Atticus!"

"Yes, Your Majesty." Atticus heard him from inside the castle and came running out. His eyes widened as he looked upon the traitor.

"Bring your brother and follow me," Alister said, picking up Arianna and walking toward his dungeon.

Approaching the first cell, he carefully set Arianna on the bed and locked the door behind him. He was still amazed at the identical face she had with the woman he could not stop thinking about.

"Why am I here?" Declan asked.

Not answering his question, Alister opened the next cell door and grabbed Declan, throwing him in and slamming and locking the door in his face.

"If I had anywhere else to put you, I would. You're a liar. I will wait for Arianna to wake up and tell me exactly what happened. You sit there and think about what you have done.

Hitting any woman is against my laws. No matter what the situation. I don't believe you anyway," he stated. Hoping to teach the man a lesson, he left the dungeon, transformed, and flew away from his castle.

* * *

Angela, along with the rest of the women, were having a girls' day. She was still very upset about Alister and the King of the Realm being the same creature. But she knew she would have to get over it, at least for today. It was her mom's day. As they all 'day' drank, Neveah sipped on her fruity water. Julia had been beyond excited to tell everyone about her acceptance of Jenisis' proposal of marriage.

"Sorry, honey," she was talking to Angela.

"Oh, don't worry about me, Mom. I'm fine. Today is about you." She smiled, wobbling a little already towards her mother to hug her. "I'm so happy for you."

"Me, too," she said, beaming at her engagement. "Did I tell you the best part? He's hunting for the perfect stone. He said it can take a while to find it and then he is supposed to bring it to—" Julia was explaining until Iris chimed in.

"Me! To have it magically set, blessing it." She smiled crookedly, just as sloshed as Angela.

"Yes," Julia continued. "Blessing it."

Listening to her going on and on about not even being on a first date in over eighteen years, Angela smiled at her exhilarated mother as she finished yet another glass of wine.

Neveah had enough of all the drinking. She had been doing well with sobriety for far too long to mess it up today. Getting up and giving her congratulations to her mother, she waved at everyone as she left the party, wanting to get out of the castle for a walk.

She decided to head to the forest because she'd heard Bella's endless tales of spending her time climbing the tall trees, with her journal in hand.

Taking a seat in a bed of grass in the middle of the trees, surrounded by shade flowers, she grabbed her pen and started writing down more of what had happened at the ball. Now that she had a name to put to the face she had seen in her dreams and mental flashbacks, she could write it.

As she was writing how she felt about the mysterious Nicolas, she heard the creak of a branch from the tree that grew before her. Looking up, she attempted to cover her eyes with her hand to block out the sun shining brightly, only to see her beloved eagle resting above.

Like she had been waiting for him to show up at any minute, she stood and walked closer to the tree.

"I wondered when you were going to arrive," she said, smiling. "I bet you didn't know that I'm from an Alaskan native tribe and my animal is an eagle. My father is an eagle in the tribe, so that makes me one," she related to her friend. "Seems I haven't seen you lately. Not getting bored with me, are you?"

Like she thought he would answer, she finally laughed at the silence and went back to sitting in her spot and writing. She spoke her words out loud as she wrote.

"I met a very handsome man at the ball. As he walked up to me, I could feel my heart flutter, getting lost in his forest green eyes of freedom. Then we danced like our bodies were one and I could feel myself falling."

"Stop!"

She heard the sound come from where the bird was perched. *Did I just hear 'stop', or just a squawk?* Thinking she must be going crazy, she watched the eagle lift off the branch, landing right down in front of her on the grass. She just wanted to touch its feathers. Her fear at touching a wild creature was calmed. After all, would it really follow her around so much if its only intention was to bite her hand off?

She put her journal down and slowly reached out as it remained still and watched her.

Yet again, though, she didn't get to connect. In the blink of an eye, the bird that'd perched before her feet transformed into a man now squatting in a froglike position. Lifting his head and the rest of his body, he slowly rose up, standing straight and proud and staring down into her eyes.

Her mouth gaping in surprise, she jumped up and made her own squawking sound of sudden fright. Going over everything she had told the bird, she thought about her dreams of the creature and now...so much more. Feeling a lot like how Sylvia had felt when the boy had confessed to kissing her daughter, she suddenly felt humiliated because she had nothing left to hide.

Instead of a normal response, she burst into laughter and started acting crazy, pacing and talking to herself.

"Of course, he's a man. Not any man. *The* man." She mentally beat herself up for not realizing the truth sooner.

* * *

He still had said nothing; he just watched her pace and let it all out. He figured she would have a reaction. The information she told him throughout their meetings was very personal. He knew he could trust her, at least with his secret. After what had happened with his ex-fiancé, trusting another woman was going to be difficult for him, at least in the romantic sense. He was still trying to deal with the fact that after ten years of being with the 'right' woman, she took off with his younger brother when their father had passed. And he still had no idea how long the affair had been going on.

"Are you done?" he asked, after the sounds had stopped coming from the woman's mouth.

"I think so," she answered.

"Good,"

"Oh my God," she screamed. "Okay...now I'm done."

"Are you sure?"

"Yes."

"I'm sorry it took so long to show myself. After all this time, you make me nervous, Neveah," he said, swallowing his words.

"How do *I* make *you* nervous?" she asked, looking confused.

He had to be honest with her about not being ready to give himself to another; he wanted her to get to know him and see if she could help pick up the broken pieces of his heart. If there was anything left of it.

"Remember the dance, how we were talking about being vulnerable? Well, you make me vulnerable. Watching you for the time you have been here has made me build a...softness towards you," he tried to explain and give her the most he could at this time. She had told him so many feelings she had to deal with that he should have learned a thing or two about explaining his own.

"Well. Who says we have to start courting or whatever? Why can't we be friends and get to know each other?"

Feeling an enormous weight lift from his shoulders at her suggestion, he smiled with joy and let out a sigh of relief. Afterwards, the silence was overpowering, making the situation escalate from thoughtful to awkward yet again.

"Can I touch your damn feathers now?" she asked, commencing in laughter at the very thought.

* * *

His Majesty burst through the door that held the sounds of multiple laughing women coming from within. Looking throughout the room, his eyes landed on Iris.

"Oh, wow. Look who it is. Everyone get up and bow," Angela taunted, attempting to get up only to stumble over her own two feet and fall to the floor.

Running to her aid and help her up, she clung on to his

arm. Turning his face away, he was surprised she reeked of wine. "What happened? Why is she...drunk?" he asked the women who were watching.

"You." Their answer came as a chorus.

Feeling guilty as he held drunk Angela up on her own legs, he looked down into her face.

"Hey, hot stuff. Oh, my gosh, why do you have to smell so good?" she said, before laughing hysterically.

"Servants," he yelled until someone came to their aid. "Cold ice bath. Now."

"Right away, Your Majesty," Rose replied, running to do as he asked.

Setting Angela back in her seat, he got up and grabbed a piece of toast off a tray nearby.

"Eat this," he requested, placing it in Angela's hand. "I came here for you and Iris. I have Arianna in my dungeon."

Reality struck Angela like a ton of bricks when he mentioned her name. Wanting to see her sister, she started eating the toast he handed her. In seconds, it was gone.

"I'm fine, Your Majesty," Iris told him.

"So am I." Angela attempted to stand again, only to end up back on her butt.

"Not yet, you aren't. Iris, make her an elixir that's fast. I'll take her to her room; meet me in there," he ordered. Lifting Angela up, he held her like she was a baby that couldn't move their neck.

As he walked with her in his arms, she couldn't help but play with his whiskers by brushing her fingers along the spiky beard.

"So pokey," she spoke, feeling an unusual urge.

She knew they'd entered her room, seeing as how messy it was because she never allowed anyone else to clean up after her. Watching his eyes look just as stressed as she had been, she reached up and wrapped her arms around his neck, hugging him. Lifting her head off of his shoulder, she pulled herself up higher and kissed him on the lips.

What the hell was she thinking? That's the problem, she wasn't. Unable to pull herself from the kiss, she found she was enjoying it. Enjoyment that increased when she felt him kiss her shoulder for just a split second before he exited from the move. He looked away from her eyes that were now wide open and alert.

"I hate you. I hope you know that." She stated, right before she was dropped and landed in freezing bath water up to her neck. She inhaled a deep, gasping breath as the water hit her like an explosion of pins and needles.

Normally, one would tiptoe into the winter lake or river water inch by inch, but now she was being completely consumed in ice and it was shocking and torturous. As she screamed angrily, she smacked the water with her hands.

"Sober up and come downstairs or I will leave you here," he said sharply and walked out of her bathroom.

Iris had arrived as His Majesty was leaving the room, setting the elixir potion on the sink.

"Take this and you will feel better quickly. You must keep it down," she said, before leaving her in the bathroom as well.

Angela jumped out of the water as quickly as possible, grabbing the drink Iris had made for her and downing it in one gulp. Attempting to run and change her clothes, Angela covered her mouth before it could come back up. Seconds later, the feeling subsided as she went back into the bedroom and changed into a casual pair of her jeans and a sweatshirt.

Rushing as fast as she could down the stairs and outside the castle walls, Angela stopped as she saw Iris standing next to the most marvelous creature she'd ever set eyes on.

Smiling at her friend as if she'd forgotten his originations, she walked up to the drakon, buried her face in its neck, and sobbed, "Oh, I missed you. Don't ever lie to me, please," she expressed.

"It's still me, Angela," Alister replied to her sudden odd

behavior.

"I know...but I missed this side of you," she said in all honesty, apparently able to deal with the creature and not the man himself. Hoisting herself up from his leg to his back, Iris joined her, sitting comfortably with her arms wrapped around Angela's waist.

"We finally get to see our sister," she cried softly in Angela's ear.

"I know." She patted her sister's arm, hoping the experience would be filled with enjoyment and not pain. "I know."

* * *

Angela dismounted from Alister's shoulders as he shifted back into his human form to lead the way to where Arianna was being held.

Opening the main door to the dungeon, they walked down the steps into a space Angela knew all too well, although being on the outside of it this time was a pleasant feeling. The trio stopped and stared.

The door was wide open and the bed was empty. Arianna was nowhere in sight. The cell was completely vacant. Looking to the right, their eyes landed on Declan. Hogtied and gagged, he was wiggling in the center of his cell like a worm.

"Serves you right," His Majesty chuckled.

CHAPTER 23

The chuckling faded fast. *What was I thinking?* His Majesty chastised himself for choosing his moves completely wrong. *Locking a witch up when I knew she could escape? Without the chains on her, she could still use her damn magic...*

* * *

Arianna ran as fast as she could away from Drakous Castle, using her magic to speed herself up until she could get safely back to her own domain.

As she entered her barrier, she finally could breathe...and walk. She knew what she needed to do to keep herself safe from what His Majesty could do to her. It had been too close waking up in that awful dungeon cell. What could have happened made her cringe. She did, however, get to enjoy taking her revenge out on Declan for hitting her and knocking her out. After hogtying him and gagging him with magical bonds, he had to prove himself to be honest in order to get out of them. Which would be an impossible task, seeing as that she had bound him to the evil that lay within his heart.

Running up the steps to her bedroom—her body surging with power—Arianna entered through the door and walked over to the desk to get her mother's grimoire. She needed to locate something in the Book of Spells that would make her indestructible against the mighty drakon. Flipping through the pages, she landed on a picture of a Foinix, known to be the most powerful creature in all the realms. Its regenerating talents and power enhancing qualities were exactly what she would need to survive against the drakon. Her own magic was useless against Alister, being that she was just a mere human casting frivolous spells upon him.

Reading over the incantation to open up the Foinix Realm, Arianna learned how she could walk through and harness the power of the king that resided there. Known to be a trusting, caring, very naïve ruler in the presence of a pretty face, she thought it should be quite easy to get close to him and steal his power, leaving *him* to be the powerless human after all was said and done.

Closing the book, she picked up The Dragon's Heart and a fire agate crystal in one hand, the fluorite in the other. Walking to the wall and making a drawing in the shape of a door, she stood back from it and held the crystals in her hands up to the sunlight, projecting the bright ray towards the door she had drawn.

"Anoíxte tis pórtes ston megálo kósmo tou Phoenix," she chanted until the door opened and she could see inside.

Walking up to the door, about to take a step into the realm, Arianna halted when she saw an enormous bird covered in fire flying towards her.

"Wow, what luck," she whispered. Smiling, she was

hopeful that she didn't have to go through the journey at all; it was coming to her instead.

As it got closer, she noticed it was still coming in hot.

Reality struck. "Oh, shit!" she yelled when it transformed into a distraught boy who landed right on top of her, knocking her to the ground.

"Close it! Close the door! My father's trying to kill me," he screeched.

She looked at the door to see what looked like a ball of ice with iron in its center coming directly at them. *Holy shit, he is trying to kill his own son.* She shouted the word, 'Kleise' and closed the door just in time.

"My father's gone crazy! He's killing everyone in our realm that he thinks is planning something against him, or if they do anything wrong at all. He was trying to kill me just because I dropped a sword during training...saying I made too much noise!" The boy was hyperventilating; his last flaming feather disappeared as he transitioned fully to human form.

Watching him switch, Arianna noticed the pain it was causing him in his eyes. Afraid he would hurt himself, or her, she blew dust on him, effectively putting him to sleep.

The child was adorable as he peacefully slept on her floor. There was no way she would use the boy; he looked to be no older than thirteen. She would never risk his life to make herself more powerful. She knew that.

Arianna would just have to think of some other way to protect herself.

She was also completely unsure of what to do next. She couldn't send him back where his father would kill him, and she was in no condition to care for the boy herself. Deciding she needed to take him to Mood Castle to have Iris and the others take care of him was the best solution.

Elevating his body, she walked him down the stairs and outside her castle past the magic barrier. Walking through the dark woods to the extensive field that lay beyond, she readied herself to run and find cover once again. Before she stepped into the light, Arianna looked up in the sky, seeing the drakon flying above.

Putting the boy down, she knew she had to abandon him and run back to safety. The drakon must be coming back for her head; or worse, to banish her back to Earth. She was not about to have either of those things happen.

As she ran away, she wondered if the drakon had seen her or caught a whiff of her scent. Because if he had, he would've picked up the boy, which meant she was now in even bigger trouble.

* * *

Alister was flying to Arianna's castle, certain that she would take him up on his offer of freedom. She should have known once she woke up without the chains on that he wasn't trying to keep her captive. Giving her the opportunity to notice and think about it was wrong. Maybe he should have left her a note.

Flying above the grassy fields right before the dark forest of the Forbidden Lands began, he noticed a bright red figure being laid on the ground below by a black figure now running away from it.

He stopped in midair to turn around and land beside it. Looking down at the boy, he knew right away what he was. *But how did he get here?* His Majesty thought. *Arianna must have brought him here...but, why?*

Picking him up carefully in his grip, Alister flew back to his castle. When he arrived, the boy still hadn't woken. Alister carried him up the steps and through his castle doors. He continued up the ornate staircase to what was supposed to have been his own child's room and laid him on the bed.

"You look just like your father, Basil," Alister spoke, already knowing the young man.

He got up and walked out of the room to let him sleep. Hoping he would wake up soon so he could ask him what on earth had happened.

* * *

One year later...

"Why can't I go outside, Uncle Alister? I've been good. I have been stuck in here for an entire year. Please, can I go play with kids my own age?" Basil begged.

"It's too dangerous, son. I don't know if the witch wants you for something or *what* she has been doing all year," Alister told the boy, trying to look out for his safety.

Basil slumped down in defeat on the bench seat next to his bedroom window.

"I also have to leave now for a bit. I'm attending a wedding tonight and need you to stay put. I have a lot to do. I haven't seen anyone in a year either," Alister told him, watching him roll his eyes.

"Can you at least come back for me and let me go with you to the wedding?" he asked with hope in his voice.

"I'll think about it," Alister said before leaving his room.

"It's not fair. Stuck in this immense place. I feel like a prisoner," Basil said, talking to himself.

Looking out the window, he watched as Alister's drakon form flew off. Getting up, he ran to the door and turned the handle only to find it locked.

"Really?" he chuckled sarcastically, before calling up his wings, jumping out the window and taking flight.

He landed on the ground in-between a grove of trees and put a black hat and cape on to cover his bright red feathers. He then stood there wondering what he would do next.

Hearing a branch snap right above him, he looked up.

"Watch out!" yelled a young female voice.

Basil was shocked as he watched the girl, donning some type of wings but clearly with the inability to fly, fall on top of him. Knocking him over, she landed right on his head.

He fell to the ground with his arms wrapped around her and grunted.

"Sorry. I tried to warn you," Bella spoke, trying to get up but not before staring into the boy's brown eyes that held flecks of gorgeous red fire.

Jumping up and off of him quickly, she brushed the dirt from her knees and checked her wings. One was broken. "Dang it," she groaned. "It took me months to make these."

The boy was just standing there staring at her, looking confused. Bella smiled at his sunset orange face and fascinating eyes.

"Are you some kind of...bird?" he asked.

"Oh, he does speak. I was beginning to think you were mute. No, I'm human. I'm Bella. What's your name?" she asked.

"I'm Basil. I have heard about you. You're Angela's daughter, right?"

Bella paused. "Yes. How do you know us?"

"My uncle told me about you. He's the drakon."

"Alister's your uncle? Does that mean you're a dragon, too?"

"No. I'm—"

"Leaving!" Alister's stern voice broke through before Basil could introduce himself properly.

Shocking the teens, Bella and Basil jumped at the sudden loud voice in their conversation.

"Hi Uncle, I was just talking to Bella. It's okay, right? Since you're all in love with her mother, right?"

"Basil Sebastian the Third, it's time to go home. Now!"

"No way. You can't make me. *Please*, I finally made a new friend," Basil spoke, looking desperate.

Bella just stood there watching and listening to the guys'

bickering, trying not to burst into laughter at what they were speaking about. Did he really love her mom? If he did, why hadn't they seen him in a year? Before she could stop what was about to come out of her mouth, she spoke.

"Are you really going to keep secrets again, Alister? How well did that work out for you last time?" Bella's words were nothing less than true.

"It's dangerous for him, Bella. With the witch out there, and not knowing what she's planning...I have been keeping him safe."

"By keeping him prisoner?" she said, standing up to what he was saying.

Watching him smile and shake his head at her, Alister looked from Basil to her before sighing and nodding his head.

"Okay, you two can hang out for a *little* while. I should've known; like mother, like daughter. Strong, stubborn, and beautiful," he commented.

"Don't worry, I won't tell her anything. I'll wait for you to tell her yourself. Might want to hurry up with it, though," she told him, watching his face go on alert.

Without finishing her thought, Bella and Basil went running off into the woods away from the boring Alister before he could change his mind. Bella looked at Basil, really wanting to know what he was. Wondering what color his hair was, she ran up behind him and stole his hat right off his head, racing past him. Looking back, she teased, "Come and get it, if you want it back." She stopped dead in her tracks when she glimpsed his hair.

Surprised, her eyes almost popped right out of their sockets when she saw this particular feature; she gazed at the feathers that went from orange to red sticking out of the top of his head.

"Wow, that's amazing. You *have* to tell me what you are now!" She was jumping up and down.

"What do you think I am?" he asked.

"Um...well, a bird of some sort, that's obvious. Oh my God, are you a phoenix?" she squeaked.

"Foinix," he corrected. "And yes, I am."

"I'm so excited. I don't even know what to say. That is *so* awesome," she beamed at his species. "You are one of my favorite mythical creatures."

"Thank you. I like you, too." He smiled at her. "In fact, I think you're awesome, brave and beautiful too, just like my uncle said."

Pacing back and forth, she put her pointer finger up to stop him. About to say something but unable to form the words, she put her finger down. Feeling embarrassed, Bella continued to pace.

"That's nice. So, you want to climb a tree?" she asked, intentionally changing the subject.

"I could just fly you up there," he suggested.

"No thanks, I like to climb. Come on, let's go," she said, waving her hand to have him follow her.

Never having to climb a tree in his entire life, Basil was concerned that he might not actually be able to succeed. Watching how easy it was for her, however, like a monkey swinging from branch to branch, he grabbed the closest one he could find, lifted himself up and over it, and looked around for the next one.

When he went to grab it his foot slipped, causing him to hang from the higher limb. Hearing a high-pitched laugh, he looked up at Bella who was already high up in the tree.

"It would have been easier if you went up the right side; it has more branches than the left. Do you want some help?"

"No...I got it," he replied, trying hard not to embarrass himself further.

Swinging his legs to the branch resting to the right, like she had suggested, Basil tried to call up his male ego and show her that he could climb, no problem. If the move would just work and he could hang upside-down before he hoisted himself up on the branch, he would surely get her attention.

Once he got his legs around the branch and let go of the other, it was all downhill from there. Swinging too fast, his legs uncurled around the branch, making him fall and land on his butt on the ground.

"Okay, I can't climb trees," he said, struggling for the breath that the fall had knocked out of him.

Bella was laughing so hard as she climbed down from the tree, she ended up landing right next to his body, flat on the ground.

"Are you okay?" she said, still giggling. Extending her hand, he took it as she helped him to his feet. "It's okay, I have to get back to work anyway, but this was fun."

"You have a job? Can I come with you?" he asked.

She knew he didn't want to go back to Alister's castle and be stuck inside, and she was sure that her mother would want to meet him.

"Sure. I own a designing store with my mother—clothing and accessories and whatnot, but you can come along," she said, waving him to follow her again.

They walked from the forest into Mood Town where she and her mother had their store, talking all the way.

* * *

Arianna had been lying low ever since she'd left the boy at the edge of the dark forest. Knowing that Alister picked him up had made her paranoid.

She wanted to get the stones back that her niece and nephew's father had in his possession, but she couldn't do it without harnessing a rare moon; the Blue Moon, to be exact. Only coming once a year, she knew that finally her chance had arrived. The wedding of Julia and Jenesis was scheduled to be blessed by the moon, itself. So it would be the perfect distraction for everyone while she cast the spell to bring the

'Family Crystals' of Neveah back to this realm.

The process was fairly easy, actually. She would open a door near the man who had the crystals on his fingers. She would then use the moon's projection through The Dragon Heart stone and aim it at the man's hand; this would ignite them and cause an earthquake like before, transporting both him and his surroundings to the realm inside Arianna's borders.

She was overjoyed that finally her plans were going to be put into motion after months of waiting in fear. Never able to sleep well, she still remained completely surprised, paranoid, and confused that no one had tried to cross over her barriers in all this time.

* * *

Angela was working at the store the morning of her mother's wedding. Thankfully, this new endeavor had kept her busy for almost a year. She knew beyond a shadow of a doubt that without the store, she'd have gone crazy from not seeing or hearing a word from His Majesty in all this time.

Today was stressful, making her remember her own wedding to Arik. But it was also an exceptional day that took her mind off everything as she worked diligently to finish up the tuxedo orders for all the groomsmen and dresses for the bridesmaids.

Her own daughter had designed the dresses herself. Since the wedding was going to be decorated in red roses, garlands and bushes, all the bridesmaid dresses were an emerald green, like the leaves of a rose. Even the skirts were accented in leaf-shaped mesh over the shiny green silk. To top the outfits off, hallows would be placed on top of their heads made of red rose petals and thornless stems. Leah had cast a spell on them to make sure they would be lively for the ceremony and not wilted or discolored at all.

Angela looked down at her watch, suddenly wondering where her oldest daughter had gone off to since she was supposed to be helping her with the rest of Julia's wedding dress. Leah would enchant the dress as she had done with the flowers so nothing would wilt on it, even after her mother had taken it off and packed it away.

Angela was going over all the men's tuxes for the wedding, making sure none of them were missing and all were ready for the big day. It was still hours before showtime, but she wanted to make sure that everything was entirely perfect for her mother's big day.

Picking up the one meant to be worn by her son—the little black tux with a green bow tie—made her smile, imagining him wearing it. He was becoming a big boy, five years old already and so strong with his Identifier powers. He could now tell you the full name of who he had identified during their shift before they had become human.

Looking at Leah's dress and thinking about when they had just arrived here almost two years ago, Angela thought of how quickly it had gone by for everyone. How easy it had become to adjust to the customs, creatures, and people of this realm. Her baby girl, now seven years old, made her wish she had more children so she could go through the baby stage just one more time.

Hearing the bell ring out in front of the store, she put the little dress back in its place until it was time and yelled "Coming!" from the back where she kept all the wedding clothes tucked safely away.

Walking up to the front counter to see who had entered, she made it halfway to the cash register before she looked up into a pair of glowing eyes. He was happy, smiling from ear-to-ear, looking gorgeous in a pair of designer jeans and dark turquoise t-shirt.

"Hi Angela. How have you been?" he asked.

She felt the cheerful smile spread across her own face,

realizing just how much she had missed him. Forcing her feet to remain firmly on the ground, she suddenly thought, *Fuck it.* Racing the rest of the way to the counter, she stopped in front of him and pulled him into a long embrace.

Hearing the bell on the door ring once again, she heard the slight growl of annoyance from Alister when she pulled out of his hug.

"There you are. I have been wondering when you were going to show up." Angela smiled as she watched her boyfriend walk through the door.

Alister became stiff as a board, not knowing how to react. He watched the woman he loved walk right up to the visitor and try to kiss him, only to have the man refuse the show of emotion out of respect for His Majesty. He not only wanted to hit the man upside his head for turning down such a magnificent gift, he also wanted to set him aflame as Alister felt the pain running through his heart.

CHAPTER 24

Bella and Basil were headed to the shop when they saw him enter the store. They ducked down behind a trash can across the street and watched Bella's mother race up to him and pull him into a big hug.

"Oh no," she said, as she watched the new boyfriend walk into the store shortly after His Majesty.

"Who's that?" Basil asked.

"Colton. He's from the wolf pack my grandmother's marrying into. He's also my mother's new boyfriend," she sighed, not liking the man very much.

"Oh, that's not going to sit well with Uncle Alister. He hasn't stopped talking about your mother from day one when I entered this realm."

"Well, hopefully he can convince my mother he still cares about her. I heard her say they kissed a year ago and then nothing came of it. Maybe he is just confused. I'm sure she would choose him instead of the wolf if she knew." It was clear that Bella was one hundred percent on Alister's side.

* * *

Angela was taken aback by Colton's icy reaction to her attempt at kissing him. He kept looking from her to His Majesty like he was waiting for an introduction. She sighed deeply before walking him up to Alister.

"Majesty, this is my—."

"Colton, Your Majesty. Colton Kasmiri from the Blue Moon Pack," he said, cutting Angela off and choosing to introduce himself.

Royally pissing Angela off, she left the men to step outside for a smoke. Standing there she thought about why Colton had acted that way. *Alister must intimidate him like everyone else*, she thought.

As she smoked her cigarette, she saw the tops of two heads poking out from behind the trash can. Smiling, she walked across the street.

"What are you two up to?" She peeked behind it, scaring them both.

Angela was surprised to see a rather orange-colored boy with freckles and unique looking eyes staring up at her. Just to see a boy in her daughter's presence was fascinating all on its own, but the hat he was wearing made him seem even more strange.

"Mom, you scared us," Bella said, holding her hand over her heart.

"Well, she was scared, but *I* wasn't," Basil spoke.

"Were you eavesdropping again?" Angela asked with a hint of teasing in her voice.

"Okay, you caught me. What's going on in there?" Bella asked, pointing at the men now talking inside the store.

"I don't know; manly stuff, I guess. But let's not take the attention off you. Who's your new friend?"

"I'm Basil. My Uncle Alister has been taking care of me this last year," he informed her.

"*Uncle* Alister?" Angela burst into laughter. "He has been caring for you for a year. Well, that at least is a reason why he disappeared. What makes him your uncle?"

"He told me my father had requested that if anything ever happened to him that Alister was the one he wanted to care of me. I just call him uncle," Basil explained.

"Where do you come from?" Angela asked.

"Foinix Realm. I'm a foinix, or phoenix, which is what I'm told humans call it."

"Of course Bella would bring home a phoenix. The most powerful mythical creature ever," she laughed. "Well, it's a pleasure to meet you, Basil. Let's say we go break up this man-talk going on in my store," Angela suggested, leading the way.

* * *

Neveah was waiting on Nicolas. Something she seemed to do quite a bit over the last year as she waited for him to decide what he wanted in life. She was ready to move on and meet someone that she could share her life with, seeing as that she had put her life on hold once again to see where things would go with yet another man.

"What do you think of this one?" he asked, looking at his tux in the mirror.

"Same as the last one. It looks great," she answered with a sigh.

She looked away from his handsome figure and down at her own feet, thinking of the adorable shoes she would wear as she walked down the aisle. She was getting irritated with herself that she had wasted so much time on this particular handsome man who she had been sure was going to make some type of move. Feeling like she had already told him everything in her life, including her deepest, darkest secrets, she knew that there was no longer a mystery about her. Yet after all this time, his continued silence—with the exception of being vain and talking about his looks—had kept him the most mysterious man she had ever met.

"Well, I have got to go get ready for *my* mother's wedding. See you later." She got up to walk to the door.

"Wait, aren't we going together?" he asked her.

"Um...no. Carson asked me to go with him to the wedding. He's Jenesis' right-hand man and already walking me down the aisle," she explained, feeling awkward.

She hadn't thought Nicolas would ask to escort her, yet the now depressed look on his face signaled that he had planned to. *It's his own fault for making me wait on him.*

"Carson Mavros? Oh...okay. I'll see you later then?"

"Yep. See you later." She left the store as he was trying on the next tux and headed to her sister's shop.

She felt just a wee bit of guilt for causing the look of sadness to cross Nick's face, but she was determined to find a love of her own. She was done waiting for him...for any man. Walking into her sister's store, she was greeted with cold, delicious orange juice and led to the back to join the rest of the bridesmaids and her amazingly happy mother.

* * *

Sylvia was climbing out of the ocean with Simon close by her side. Day after day, for a year, they'd been searching for his actual family, only to receive silence or meet up with creatures too afraid to say anything. Each and every time Simon would become annoyed, making the water do crazy things: underwater tornados, boiling water, freezing it and creating icebergs that he'd eventually melt. He needed to get it under control.

There was literally not enough kissing or kindness she could give in order to make all his troubles go away. Frankly, her lips had become sore from it all. Still not wanting to move forward from the kissing, even though she was older now, it seemed his only happiness came from being physical in order to get rid of his frustrations. At times this made Sylvia nervous; her emotions and thoughts seemed to twist and turn like a hula hoop, bringing up sensations she'd never experienced before. She wanted to be with him, but not because he was upset or simply wanted to release stress. All Sylvia wanted was romance and, above all, wanted Simon to show her that he actually loved her.

Happy to be out of the water, she ran with Simon's hand in hers to get to her cousin and Aunty Angela's shop on time. Thank goodness she didn't have to carry anything with her.

Simon appeared to be just as excited to be on dry land as she was. He was smiling and couldn't wait to get into town. She had asked why he was so excited; the wedding was from her side of the family, after all. He, however, had stayed mysterious, telling her he was just excited to see her all dressed up and that seeing her in a bikini top all the time was driving him crazy. A speech that made Sylvia laugh.

They had made it just in time to watch Neveah enter the store.

"I'll see you as you walk down the aisle. I love you," Simon told her, making her light up like the brightest star in the night sky.

"I love you, too." She answered with a kiss and then pushed away, not wanting to get lost in the passion for too long. Entering the shop, she was offered a glass of orange juice, because she was still too young to have champagne, and led to her family congregating at the back of the store.

* * *

Julia looked around. She was so proud of Angela and Bella for opening a clothing store for all of Bella's designs. Her heart warmed as she listened to everyone laugh and talk about everything under the sun.

Neveah was going on about Nick. Julia liked Nick, but she knew Neveah needed someone without damage and to just enjoy life right now. Julia's daughters were in the prime of their lives, and she knew they shouldn't waste that time on men who didn't understand the gifts that were right in front of them.

Angela was going on about being mad at her boyfriend. Julia cared little for the man. She knew that Angela had a pattern of dating those who were lazy and never gave her the respect she absolutely deserved. Therefore, she was worried, knowing that her daughter usually ended up getting hurt by every one of them.

Izak, on the other hand, was different. Julia didn't see him often; ever since he and Iris parted ways over a year ago he'd been hanging out with multiple girls, wallowing in self-pity, beating himself up that he'd been dumb enough to let go of Iris. Whining that she had never fought to keep him in her life. After they'd parted, Julia had given him a hard time, telling him he was making a mistake and that a strong woman like Iris would never grovel at his feet, no matter how much she cared for him. It wasn't *her* job to keep him by her side, it was *his* job to get over all the crap and enjoy the beautiful woman he had. Iris already told him how she felt a year ago, but he had just backed away and took residence in Julia's newly built home to stay clear from her.

Julia's mind switched back to happier thoughts. She had put many plans in motion for today. One being that none of the ladies knew who they would walk with. What a shock it was going to be for all of them. Letting out a silent giggle, she was certain someone was going to fall in love tonight.

She continued sipping her champagne and orange juice

while Rose worked on her hair. The mood girl was definitely very rosy, her color rarely changed. Julia watched her as she placed the crown covered in rose gold with emerald stones securely on her head. A beautiful gift from her husband-to-be.

"It's time for the dress, Julia," Rose informed her.

Smiling at the crown, she thought back to when Jenisis had returned from his hunt with the perfect stone, only to then hide it. She still, to this day, had not been able to see it. That was just one of their 'wolf customs' Julia hadn't liked. The one where she had to refrain from sex with Jenisis until their wedding night commenced, was the one she hated the most.

She didn't understand. It's not like she was a virgin or anything. He had told her if they waited, there would be an even better surprise in store for her. It wasn't just custom, he'd said, it was the beginning of their destiny.

She stepped into her gown as Rose tied up the back and waited for Iris, Neveah, and Leah to add all the magical touches to the gown.

"Are you ready, Mom?" Neveah asked.

"You have no idea," she laughed.

They all walked out of the store and straight into the grand carriages that would take them to Jenisis' land where he would marry his beloved Julia.

Julia was excited to see the ceremony grounds all set up. Everyone had pitched in to plan nothing but the best for her. She still couldn't believe she was getting married for the third time, but she was sincerely hoping that the old saying 'third time's a charm' would definitely be truth.

As the carriage pulled into the lands, she could see a clearing in the woods. Getting a little sneak-peek at the setup, she watched shifters and creatures take their seats on benches carved out of trees sitting on both sides of the aisle.

Pulling up to the large cabin she was to walk out from, all the ladies piled out of the carriages and ran into the building in order to not be seen. There, they waited patiently until everyone heard the sound of the lovely violins begin to play.

"You're first, Angela," Julia said, giving her a friendly push to walk forward.

"What? Really? Okay," Angela replied, a tad confused. As she entered the walkway, Alister joined her. Once again surprised, Angela took his arm as they walked slowly down the aisle.

"You look absolutely gorgeous, Angela," he whispered in her ear, sending goosebumps down her arms.

"So do you. I mean...handsome. You look very handsome." Blushing, she veered off to the left side of the altar to wait on her sister who would be coming down next.

Watching Neveah walk down the aisle with Carson, she smiled as the man leaned in and said something in her ear, kissing her cheek before sending her to stand next to Angela.

Iris came next, walking with Izak, who looked to have tears in his eyes and a wounded dog expression on his face. He was clearly upset at having to walk with Iris. Not because he was disgusted by her, but because he was clearly still madly in love with her. It was plastered all over his face.

Next was Sylvia, and then Bella and Zack soon after. Sylvia looked around for someone and Angela knew it must be Simon. Finding him on the left side, she waved and blew him a kiss. He caught it and blew her a fresh one. *They're so adorable and young*, Angela thought.

Next was Liam, so handsome in his black tux and green bow tie. Such a grown-up little man. Leah followed close behind. Blowing pieces of paper, she shredded them in the air, then turned the streamers into bubbles that went to the left and right above the heads of the crowd. Everyone clapped at the beautiful display.

As the violins stopped and the familiar melody resounded, everyone stood up from their benches and turned. It was time for the bride to appear.

* * *

Jenisis excitedly awaited his bride, wanting to set eyes on the lovely woman he was soon going to spend the rest of his life with. Standing there in his special tux, even he admired the vest accented with a red rose pattern.

Finally, after a year of waiting, he got to set his eyes on his breathtaking bride walking down the actual aisle. Forcing himself not to cry as she walked under each arch decorated with red roses, he ached to hold her in his arms.

Dressed in a gorgeous satin sweetheart gown with rose stem beading along the bodice and placed randomly along the skirt and train, rose petals ran along the waist and the trim; it looked to the naked eye as if magic was the only thing holding them in place.

She'd taken his breath away by the time she made it to the steps of the octagonal wooden gazebo, fully decorated in twinkling lights, thanks to the family witches. He couldn't hold the tears back any longer, allowing them to fall down his cheeks.

Atticus stopped at the end of the steps, kissed Julia's cheek, and told her she looked lovely before handing her to Jenisis and taking his seat.

Finally able to hold his bride's hand, Jenisis walked her up the steps to the center of the dais to be married by the castle witch, Iris.

"You may take your seats," she told the audience.

Jenisis wasn't paying much attention to Iris, unable to take his focus off of Julia for a second.

"Rings and stone?" she asked Jenisis.

Jenisis pulled out the large chocolate diamond from his pocket and handed it to Iris, along with the rose gold setting.

"I bless this stone and this setting with the power of the Blue Moon, thus blessing this wedding and marriage to be a long and happy adventure. This union will be filled with love, trust, happiness and equality. The two of you will need to remember that you're equal to each other, no matter what happens in your days to come." Iris finished up her blessing and handed the rings back to Jenisis.

The Blue Moon shone directly above the bride and groom, letting out its glowing rays upon their heads. Looking into his bride's eyes, Jenisis watched the rays change the shape of the pupils and irises, causing the latter to turn a shiny bronze color.

"What was that?" whispered Julia.

"I'll tell you later," he whispered back.

Just when they were ready to say the necessary 'I do's,' a tremble occurred in the depths of the ground. Shaking it to its core. Jenisis pulled Julia close, wrapping his arms around her until the tremendous flash of light came, and it was over.

Everyone in their seats stood up and clapped at the Blue Moon's blessing. Iris informed them that it was time for Jenisis and Julia to exchange rings.

"By the love, magical blessing, and power and acceptance of the Blue Moon, I pronounce you husband and wife. You may kiss your bride, Jenisis," Iris cried.

Jenisis pulled Julia close. Dipping her backwards, he brought his lips down on hers, kissing her softly and passionately. As he lifted his wife upright, they listened to the whistles and applause from the crowd.

"Mr. and Mrs. Jenisis Alphious," Iris announced, holding up their united hands.

Scampering under the arches, flower petal fireworks went off above their heads as the happy couple ran to the cabin.

* * *

Iris was sitting at a table surrounded by eligible men, laughing at everything they were saying. When they told her how beautiful she was, it hurt Izak.

He got up from his own table, completely irritated, and walked towards the scene.

"Can I speak to you in private, please?" he asked, lightly grabbing her arm as he looked her in the eyes and projected the sadness he had been feeling for what seemed like forever.

"Of course. Please excuse me, gentlemen," she said, taking her leave with Izak.

Rushing her past everyone and everything in their path. Rushing away from the den and tables where his mother had gone on about how she and Jenisis had their first date in this very spot, he led her into the grove of trees.

"Izak, what is it? My arm is starting to hurt," she said.

Swinging her around in a half-circle, he leaned her against a tree and kissed her firmly.

She pushed him away instantly. Her look was one of confusion, as tears formed in her eyes. "What are you doing?" she cried.

Izak took a step back and put his hands in his pockets. The last thing he wanted to do was cause pain or fear. "I'm sorry, Iris. But you need to know; there is no way I can go on without you. I'm in love with you, Iris. You were so mad when I told you it was too 'odd' to have feelings for you when I felt like you were my sister. But the truth is...I *never* felt that way. I *never* felt like you were my sister; I just used that as a cover. I thought you deserved better than what I could ever give you. Being a junky all my life, I felt like a loser, unworthy of a love like yours. But I swear, I'll do whatever it takes to be with you." Izak stopped, hoping beyond hope that she knew he was expressing his undying love.

Iris stood there in silence. The sincerity in his voice rang in her ears as he told her exactly what she'd wanted to hear long ago, after they'd enjoyed the most beautiful night of dancing and laughing.

Not one to hold a grudge, after thinking it through and standing there silently with her back against the tree, Iris reached out and pulled him close. Bringing her hands up, she wrapped her arms around his neck and pulled him back into a deep, loving, passionate kiss. She could feel the warmth and passion radiating from his body as Izak kissed and nibbled along her jawbone to her earlobe. Sliding his lips to her neck, he proceeded to run his mouth softly along collarbone until she felt shivers run down her back, releasing a soft moan through her lips.

"We should get back. Everyone is going to wonder where we are," Iris stated while still in his embrace.

"Okay, even though I could stay like this forever with you," he said. Kissing her hand, he wrapped his arm happily around her shoulder as they walked back to the reception.

They only stopped when they heard a couple arguing in the darkness.

CHAPTER 25

Arianna was prepared to use the Blue Moon to bring the man and the crystals into her realm. Opening up the doors to Earth using the blood magic of his children, and with The Dragon's Heart stone in hand, she was able to set her eyes on Arik.

Holding up the crystal in her hands and shining the power of the moon through the stones, she activated the rings he wore on his fingers causing Earth and her realm to shake and tremble in unison. Keeping her feet firmly on the ground, she held the crystal tightly in her hand until the flash she was waiting for came, making her shut her eyes tightly. When the tremble ceased, Arianna knew she had brought the man near her own home.

Closing the window to Earth, she ran out of her power room with sleeping powder in her bag to meet this new guest.

Running down the steps and out the front doors of her

castle, it surprised her to see his home and garage were *so* close to her front doors. *This is perfect,* she thought. Running to the front window of the earthly home, she peeked in at the same time Arik was looking out. She heard him say, "What the fuck?" before she ducked her head back down.

He came running out of his home straight at her. Picking her up in his arms, he twirled her in circles. Realizing that he thought she was his wife, she tried to tell him. But before she could speak, he lowered her to the ground and kissed her, holding her tighter in his arms.

Forcibly trying to escape the man's very strong muscles as he almost squeezed the daylights out of her, Arianna let out a screech from the depths of her lungs: "Stop! I'm not Angela."

Quickly releasing her, Arik backed up. "Oh...jeez. Oh... God...I'm sorry," he spoke fast, as if noting for the first time that although the face was a carbon copy, the voice was definitely not.

She started coughing, trying to catch her breath. Arianna looked back up into his bewildered, wide eyes. "You look very confused, sir. I'm your wife's twin. I brought you here because I need those stones you wear on your fingers," she spoke, pointing at them.

"You look just like Angela," he said, pointing out the obvious.

"I know. I told you. I'm her twin. They separated us."

The man looked sad now as he fell down in the grass of his earthly lawn and covered his face.

Something inside her couldn't stand to see his handsome face cry. "It's okay, sir. She's here, too. But I have to be honest with you," she added, taking out a handful of powder, "I don't plan on reuniting the two of you just yet. I need you as collateral, you see."

"What did you say?" he asked with a hopeful expression.

"Do I really have to spell it out for you? Do you have ears on the sides of that thick head of yours, or are you just all muscle and no brains?"

"Hey, that's enough. I'm in shock, okay? I thought my entire family was dead. Can you give me a second to register what the hell is going on?" he said, sighing and covering his face with his hands once again.

She waited until he showed signs of what she had just told him registering in his brain. The second he came at her, she would knock him on his ass, putting him to sleep.

"Wait, did you just say you're going to use me as collateral?" he laughed "How could a little princess like you hold me?"

"Oh, there are many things I could do to you. I'm a powerful witch," she added, trying not to sound seductive.

"A witch? Well, where's your magic wand, fairy god-mother?" he mocked.

"I don't have a wand. I just use crystals," she replied calmly.

"Great. My wife has lost her mind and turned into a whack job with a weird voice. Angela, what have you done with the kids?" His eyes showed concern and worry now.

"I am Arianna." She grabbed him by the wrist with her power and aimed his gaze at the building looming behind them. "See that? That's my castle."

Staring up at the black and purple monstrosity, he fell silent again. She wondered if he would just simply walk with her into the castle; he seemed dumb enough. A personality trait that made him less attractive in her eyes at this point.

Like his instincts had finally kicked in, he finally came around to making sense.

"I want to see Angela and my children. What do you need from me? What do I need to do?"

"First, I want you to come into my castle with me. Second, I need the crystals you wear. They're incredibly important."

"I'll give you the stones if you show me Angela," he tried to strike a bargain.

"In my castle, I can show you. I can't physically bring you to her because she's in a wedding at this very minute."

"What?" he yelled.

She could tell he was going to make a run for it. Before he got the chance, she blew the dust in his face and watched him immediately go to sleep.

Elevating him like she did the boy from the Foinix Realm, she carried Arik into her castle and up the stairs. Calling out an enchantment, she created a light chain and wrapped it around his ankle, locking the other end to a wall of rock so the man could bring no harm to her or try to escape when she woke him up.

Removing the crystals from the man's fingers, she separated them into little boxes.

Looking down at Arik, she set a quartz crystal on his forehead and chanted, "Xýpnios." With this one word, the quartz began to glow and the man woke from his slumber.

* * *

Arik opened his eyes, instantly sitting up and sliding back against the wall to get away from the woman. He immediately noticed his surroundings were different.

Watching the woman doing something at the small table, he stood up to run to the door while her back was turned, only to get slammed back into the rock wall behind him.

"I wouldn't do that again, if I were you." She turned around holding a large crystal in her hands. "Take a look."

He slowly walked closer to the crystal; when he looked into it, he saw Angela. She looked radiant...in another man's arms. His frustration mounted as he watched the dance come to an end and Angela walk up to her mother to hug her; Julia was wearing a red and white wedding dress. The image then faded into nothing.

"Thank you," he said, relieved to have seen Angela wasn't

the one who had been donning the gown. "What is it you plan to do, so I can finally see my wife and kids?"

"Well, now that I have Neveah's Family Crystals, I feel safer. I'm going to go into town and see my sisters in a few weeks, then I'm going to get answers. If I can trust them, I will let you go. I promise. If I can't, I'll trade you for my freedom. If that doesn't work, I'll unleash Hell by opening the realm of Katistrofia and freeing the Destructors to take care of all those in power. I will then be left as the leader of the realm, whether anyone likes it or not."

"You're crazy. You're like the evil witch in all the stories."

"I'm not evil. I have done what I have to in order to survive; you don't know what it's like to be in survival mode at all times. Can't sleep. Can't eat. Always scared someone is going to kill you or rip you from the only people that have ever loved you," she said, looking down.

His tone calm, he tried to reason with her, "I can tell you're in a lot of pain, and I'm sorry for whatever happened to you. But keeping me from those *I* love and who love *me* is just as bad."

"You call sleeping with random women, doing drugs, and going to jail for murder, *loving* your family? Do you really think my goody-two-shoes sister is going to ever take you back after she knows all that? Plus, I don't think her boyfriend would like that very much."

Arik could feel the adrenaline rising inside of him, ready to explode at any second. While she was talking, he felt murderous all over again, ready to choke the life out of this woman. Getting up and running at her, he could tell she wasn't scared at all. As he drew closer to her, enraged, he was suddenly knocked back against the wall, proving why fear was not something that plagued his captor.

"You can't hurt me and you know I'm right," she whispered in his ear as he lay on the floor. "I'm going to go now. When you get hungry, yell. You're pretty good at that. Ciao."

* * *

"You're such a coward. Fine. Go. Leave. I don't want to be with you either," Angela yelled at her now ex-boyfriend. He proved he was too much of a coward to stay by her side. Asking to talk to her in private, he told her he thought His Majesty didn't like him dating her, so he needed to end it.

"I'm sorry, Angela. I just think it's for the best that we don't complicate anything more. I want us to be friends. Your mother is married to my alpha after all," he said, without a bit of sadness on his face that he was letting her go.

"You know what? Go straight to Hell," she said, flipping him off even though she knew he had no idea what it meant, and walked away from his dumb face.

She bumped into her sister and brother on the way back to the reception.

"Oh, hey guys," Angela said, wiping her eyes with the back of her hands.

"Are you okay, Angela?" Iris asked.

"Yeah, fine. Colton just broke up with me. I don't even know why I'm crying. I'm kind of relieved, actually."

"Oh, thank God," Iris and Izak said at the same time.

"He was all wrong for you. I'm sorry," Izak added quickly.

"How do you know that? At least I tried to find someone. Unlike you. You've been in love with Iris for how long? Running from her like a—" she stopped herself, noticing their entangled fingers as Izak picked up Iris' hand and kissed the back of it.

"You were saying?" he said in a teasing tone. "Besides, the man you already know you want is coming this way right now."

"What?" she asked, looking around in a circle.

Alister was walking right up to her from the dance floor, still wearing the smile that made her go weak in the knees.

"Will you please do me the honor of this dance? Don't say

'nope' this time, I know you can dance." He winked, offering his hand.

"Okay, I supposed I won't say nope," she giggled, taking his hand and letting him lead her to the dance floor.

The music stopped and the announcer spoke: "It's time for the bride to throw the bouquet, so all you unmarried ladies gather round and be ready to catch it."

Angela parted from Alister with a promise to dance after the silly ceremony was over. Standing beside Neveah, she watched Julia turn around with the rose bouquet in her hands.

"One, two, three," she said, tossing it over her shoulder.

It landed directly in Iris's hands, making everyone laugh and applaud. Walking away from everyone, she marched right up to Izak and kissed him in front of the crowd—a move that caused a total uproar of clapping and whistles.

"You may continue the dance," the announcer spoke again, leaving the stage.

"Shall we try this again?" Alister asked, taking Angela's hand and walking to the center of the floor.

He closed the distance between them immediately. He didn't even need to be that close; he was just messing with her, she decided. Setting her head just below his chest, she felt him run his right hand up and down her back and listened to his heart rate speed up as they moved around the floor. It wasn't like they were dancing fast, but she sensed that he was going to say something...so she decided to beat him to it.

"So you've spent the last year raising a phoenix, and you said nothing?"

He chuckled. "I was keeping him hidden for his own safety, but he's a teenager now and they can be very stubborn. I remember being that way myself."

"I'm just glad Bella has a friend. She told me he's pretty forward, though. He's already told her he likes her, but maybe he will help bring her out of her shell," she laughed.

They continued to dance. It was amazing to feel comforted

in his arms instead of sad or angry. Angela finally looked up into his eyes and was surprised to see the angst deep within them. She could tell he'd missed her just as much as she had him.

"I remember the last time we saw each other. You kissed me. Care to try that again?" he whispered.

Angela wanted to. In fact, there was nothing she wanted more. But as she stood there, watching his face come closer to hers, a sudden feeling of fear shot through her. Backing up slowly, not wanting the crowd to take note of her refusal, a tear escaped her eye as she shook her head.

"No, Alister. I don't know if I can ever truly trust you. You broke my heart...and all my life I have allowed men to just stomp all over it," she spoke softly.

"I promise you, Angela, I will never lie to you again. I just want to be with you," he stated, taking a step forward.

Seeing the sincerity in his eyes, she said, "Then give me time. Be in my life and prove to me who you *really* are. If friendship is all I can offer, would you just be that?" she asked, testing.

"Yes. But if that is all we can ever be, I still want to be the best at it," he said, offering her a reassuring smile.

"Ladies and gentlemen, the bride and groom are about to embark on their honeymoon," the announcer broke through the music.

"Wait! You can't leave yet," young Simon said, running to the stage and standing in front of the microphone. "Sylvia, could you come up here?"

Blushing, Sylvia walked up on the stage and stood in front of Simon. Suddenly, he knelt down on his knee and presented an open clam shell that held a brilliant pearl in a white gold setting, surrounded by diamonds.

"Sylvia, I know I have been a bit difficult to deal with while looking for my family. I was too blind to notice my future and family was standing right in front of me this entire time. I promise that the next adventure we go on will be our own adventure for the rest of our lives. Sylvia, I love you. Will you do me the honor of becoming my queen?"

Sylvia listened to his perfect proposal, letting the tears fall from her eyes. She knelt down in front of him and wrapped her hands around his neck, looking him longingly in the eyes. "Yes!" She and the crowd both screamed with joy, as he put the ring on her finger, stood up, pulled her into a hug and twirled her in the air.

"You just had to do it. Build up the anticipation, you little brat," he laughed, covering her face and head in a dozen kisses.

Everyone laughed and congratulated them as they walked together towards Neveah and Julia. Smiling and still flushed, Sylvia looked at them as if searching for their approval.

"I still think sixteen is too young, but this is a new world with different customs. It won't be easy, but I'm so happy for you, sweetheart," Neveah said, hugging Sylvia close.

"You did great, Simon," Julia told him as Jenisis pulled her close, whispering something in her ear.

"You guys *knew*?" Sylvia asked, putting her hands on her hips.

"Of course we knew. He asked us for our permission first," Neveah added.

Sylvia spent the next ten minutes beaming with joy as she showed her cousins and friends her glorious ring.

"Does that mean we get to live together?" she asked her mother.

"Have you had sex yet?" Neveah asked.

"No, Mother!" Sylvia screamed. "I'm...I'm not ready."

"Best to wait. If I could go back, I would wait," Neveah agreed.

* * *

Everyone was hugging and saying their goodbyes to Julia and Jenisis as they sent them on their way. Finally, the newly married couple were escaping to their secret honeymoon spot to enjoy their very-much-needed alone time.

After leaving the crowd and the castle behind, Jenisis handed Julia a mirror.

"Why do I need this?" Julia asked.

"Just look. You will understand," Jenisis kissed her. "Happy Birthday, my love."

Completely confused by his words, Julia grabbed the mirror and stared into it. In the dark appeared a reflection that made her gasp. A pair of glowing bronze eyes stared back at her. Her mouth hung open as Julia realized that this new set of eyes were now her own.

Today *was* her birthday...her first day as a wolf.

CHAPTER 26

Arianna was finally going to do it; she was going to head into town and see her sisters. She felt far more secure now that she had the family crystals within reach, and the man her twin would surely want back, unharmed.

Arik had been driving her nuts, so she'd be grateful to hand him over. There was something definitely wrong with the man. Constantly pacing, she had to punish him like a child in order to make him stop touching her things. He also seemed to transform from a child into a man at times who had to fix everything in sight. He had even fixed the loose board in the floor where she kept her most prized possession: The Dragon's Heart.

"Please, at least let me outside," he begged day after day. "Or bring me something so I can work out. I'm going crazy in this room. It's been over a month and you haven't let me out of here once."

"Fine. I will extend your chain's length to allow you to go outside, but only within my borders. You'll find them when you get knocked back on your ass," she laughed, reaching down and adjusting the magical distance on his ankle chain.

"Thank you. Do you need anything fixed around here?" he asked.

She had been spending most of her time in her daughter's nursery and the kitchen. She thought the man could do a lot of laboring in rooms she cared little for.

"I'm sure there are lots of areas that could use a man's touch. Just browse around if you wish. I'm heading into town," she told him.

"When are you going to be back?" Arik asked, acting like he was a boyfriend that wanted to know what she was doing at all times.

"Why do you care? Are you going to miss me?" she teased, raising her eyebrows at him.

"No, I guess it's just habit. Will you bring me something cool back? Or some weights I can lift?" he asked with a thoughtful expression on his face.

"Maybe. If I'm not caught and sent to a dungeon of my own," she stated.

"Well then, be careful," he said, obviously not thinking before he spoke.

"I always am," she replied, happy that at least her prisoner cared enough about her to tell her to be safe.

Leaving the room, she headed for town.

* * *

Zackery was hanging out with Ziara and Zinnia, as always. Feeling like he should make a move after a year, he was still not sure which one he liked more. The only way he could really tell who he felt more about is if he tried to make a move.

The girls were picking berries in the fields where he had first met the lovely Ziara. At that time, he'd been certain that she was the one he wanted to have as his girlfriend.

"Try this," Ziara said, plopping a small berry into his mouth as he lay on his back in the grassy area with his mouth open.

"That's the best. Yummy," he said, munching on it before pulling on her arm to lie down next to him.

"What are you looking at?" she asked.

"Just the shapes the clouds are making," he said, as his palms began to sweat. Turning his head, he stared at Ziara, waiting for her to look at him.

She was pointing at a large, star-shaped cloud but he hadn't taken his eyes off her face. When she finally looked at him, she smiled, and he made his move. Leaning over, he kissed her on the lips.

"Yuck," she coughed, wiping her mouth. "Zack, you're my best friend, more like a brother. Boys are gross."

She surprised him with her response and he put his head down, completely embarrassed. He was sure she wouldn't act that way. The least she could do was say she simply wasn't interested and not be so dramatic about it. And why did she say boys were gross? Didn't she like *any* boys? She had lots of guy friends.

"I'm sorry, Ziara. I just never kissed a girl before. I felt like we were headed in a different direction. I'm sorry."

"No," she sighed. "I'm sorry. I never should have reacted that way."

"What way?" Zinnia asked, coming out of the bushes.

"Zack kissed me. I said yuck. I shouldn't have," Ziara explained.

Zack noticed the look on Zinnia's face. Instead of feeling gross, she was definitely mad; actually, upon further study, she was pissed. She started yelling at Ziara about liking him and how she knew it was true.

Zack stood. He didn't really care about her that way. Bossy, snooty and spoiled, picking on bunnies and prey when she transformed into her almighty tiger. She *was* pretty hot, though. Maybe if he tried with Zinnia, she would be nicer to everyone else.

"Okay, okay, girls. That's enough fighting. We're all friends. Like you said Ziara, you don't like me like that. I'm cool with it," he said, spreading his arms out and separating them.

Just when he thought things couldn't get any sillier, Zinnia pounced on him, knocking him over while still in her human form. Pinning him on his back, she leaned down and kissed him on the mouth. Turning red, he swallowed the drool that was trying to form in the corner of his mouth.

"*That* should have been your first kiss. You had to wait so long, didn't you?" Zinnia pinched his arm.

Grabbing her, he rolled her onto her back. Coming down on her mouth, he gave her another kiss. He laughed as the teasing bitchiness ceased and her face turned completely red.

"Maybe if you weren't so spoiled and rude, you would have been my first choice. You have got to change your attitude," he stated. Standing, he helped her to her feet.

"I will. I promise," she replied, staring at him like she had a crush.

"You both make me sick." Ziara acted like she was puking.

"Come on, time to head home," Zack suggested, putting his arm around Zinnia's shoulder.

* * *

Bella was playing inside Mood Castle, talking to her best friend Jacky about Basil. She told the princess how silly he was, that he was getting better at climbing trees, and how Bella still couldn't get over his fire-filled eyes and his soft, feathery hair. She had gotten brave enough to touch the feathers on his skull before flicking him in the forehead. Remembering the moment, she laughed to herself.

"Basil again?" Jacky sighed, now completely bored every time Bella brought him up.

"You never enjoy talking about boys. Don't you like *anyone*?" Bella asked.

Bella watched Jacky look down at her feet after the question. Mumbling something she couldn't quite hear, Bella told her to speak up.

"I *said*, I don't like boys at all. I don't know what's wrong with me," Jacky whispered.

"Do you like girls?" Bella asked.

"I don't know. I think so," she replied, looking ashamed.

"Don't be embarrassed. It's totally normal where I'm from. It just means you're a lesbian. I can't believe I didn't realize it before," Bella said, mentally smacking herself. Jacky was her best friend and she hadn't even noticed the confusion she was going through.

"I thought *you* liked girls until you met that Basil boy. Now I know you're not like me." Jacky looked bummed.

"Really? Why did you think that?" Bella asked her, still stunned by her friend's observation.

"Because you're not like your cousin. She talks about a lot of stuff. Way too much for my ears. You never talk about Basil like she does about Simon." Jacky seemed to be fishing for information.

"I'm shy. If I even think about kissing Basil, I blush and my face feels like it's on fire," Bella tried to explain, already feeling her cheeks getting hot at the subject. "It doesn't mean I don't want to...be there with him someday. I've just never kissed a boy before; in fact, I never even met one I liked enough to kiss before."

"You're going to be an old lady before you ever get kissed," Jacky laughed.

"No, I'm not, you weirdo." She laughed along with her best

friend.

"How long do you think he will wait for you?"

Bella thought about how it would make her feel if he up and decided he didn't actually like her anymore. It made her sad to think about it. But she suddenly remembered her mother's words about how "if a boy can't respect you and your boundaries, he's not worth your time."

"He will or he will not be in my life," Bella said, standing tall. "It's his choice."

"Go, Bella!" Jacky shouted her support.

* * *

Neveah and Carson had been a couple ever since the wedding. He had been kind, expressive, and giving—anything she had asked him, he had been open about giving her the answers, telling her everything she wanted to know. She was enjoying getting to know the man and seeing him in his wolf form. As far as she was concerned, both sides of him were the same.

She still hadn't been able to shake her thoughts about Nick, though. She still found herself wondering what he had been up to since her mother's wedding. He had left without saying goodbye or even hello.

"You ready to go?" Carson asked, breaking through her thoughts.

"Yeah," she replied. They were off to hike up a mountain.

He had mentioned seeing an extraordinary looking door at the top of Blue Moon Mountain made out of rock. He was sure it was a door because it had some strange writing on it that referred to opening it, words that sat beside the indent of a person's hand.

"How was training?" she asked. She'd missed it because Neveah was no longer interested in seeing him dominated by his fighting partner again.

"I lost again," he kicked the ground in frustration. "I need to learn his technique, but he said he would teach it to me next time. He really is amazing and super-fast," Carson said, as his tone turned to one of admiration again.

"Have you heard from your alpha or my mom?" Neveah asked, wondering how long their honeymoon was going to last.

He stopped walking beside her and stood completely still, looking like he had just seen a ghost. Picking up her hand, he continued to walk. *Did he get another message from Jenisis?* She wondered. He always acted like that when he said his alpha was speaking to him from afar.

"They're not coming back for a while still. They were going on a long adventure and meeting new packs. I really can't give a date. Things are different in our pack; that's all I can really say until they figure out what's going on. I mean...I literally can't talk without permission. They will explain everything when they get back, though," he sighed, as they walked in silence up the mountain.

* * *

Angela and Iris were in the store. Angela had let Bella have the day off to catch up with Jacky, so she had asked Iris to join her because she was swamped with making costumes for Halloween coming up.

Bella had asked about Halloween the year before and no one had known what it was. Of course, Bella quickly spread the story of all Earth's holidays throughout the realm and everyone was excited this year to dress up and enjoy their first trick-o'-treating event.

Angela loved doing all the costumes. She was also thrilled to be attending the first adult Halloween party to be held in this realm. Alister had promised to dress up as whatever she wanted...as if his drakon form wouldn't work well enough. She went with dressing him up as a pirate, providing the patch and a hat with a feather to round out the fun look.

"Have you seen Alister lately?" Iris asked.

"Yeah, just a couple days ago. Why?"

"You wrote his name down and put 'pirate' next to it," she said, pointing at the paper on the desk.

"Oh, wow, I didn't even know I was writing anything," Angela said, picking up the pen to look at it.

"When are you going to stop punishing him and finally give in? Hasn't it been long enough?" she asked.

"Well, I could be like you. It took you a whole two seconds to forgive Izak before you jumped his bones." Angela laughed, throwing the pen at her smiling face.

"Oh, my gosh, Angela. I told you that as a sister's secret, not to tease me about it," she fussed.

"Oh, sorry sis...it's only sex. It's not like it's all that rewarding, anyway. Unless you have children, then it's worth it," Angela stated her opinion.

"Then you have never experienced anything like Izak and I did," she beamed.

"Gross, that's my brother. I'm not listening, I'm not listening," Angela repeated, covering her ears like a five-year-old.

"What are you not listening to?" the voice that always got her heart racing spoke.

Watching Iris get up and walk towards the back of the store, Angela dropped her hands and turned to face Alister. "Hey, you."

"Hey," he replied, leaning on the counter and looking up into her eyes. "So did you choose my costume thing?"

"Um...I was thinking of making you a pirate," Angela whispered in case Iris was listening. It didn't make any difference because Iris squealed with laughter at what she said.

"What are you and Izak going as?" Angela shouted at her.

"Witch and warlock," she said, putting her nose in the air.

"You're already a witch, brat. Have an imagination."

"I have plenty of time to change my mind," Iris said, walking into the storeroom and shutting the door behind her.

* * *

Arianna was on the rooftop of the bakery across the street from Bella's Boutique, spying on Angela and Alister. Watching them flirt was making her sick. She definitely did not have the same attraction to that man as Angela did. Maybe it had something to do with hating him so much. Once upon a time she may have thought he had nice hair. Of course, so did Arik, only his was a glorious shade of blond.

Why is the hunk of muscles with no brain popping into my head at this moment?

She shook the image away and enhanced her hearing in order to not miss a word spoken inside the shop. There had been no mention of her, so Arianna didn't really care much. She was about to give up and go back home when she watched Alister exit the store, bid hello to some of his admirers, transform and take flight, going in the other direction.

Climbing down the ladder on the side of the shop, she jumped down into the alley and instantly put on her cloak.

Walking from the alley to the shop, Arianna opened the door of Bella's Boutique and could hear her sisters' laughing—a sound that truly pulled at her own heartstrings. Her twin came out from around the corner of a divider that sat between accessories and clothes, and gasped as she stared at Arianna.

The look of complete shock was all she wore, as Iris came out from the back of the store carrying a glass jar full of buttons. Iris looked up and immediately stopped moving, as if suddenly falling into a paralyzed state. Dropping the jar, the glass shattered and released the buttons across the entire floor.

So many journeys are happening right now, Arianna

thought to herself. *It will be interesting to see where we all meet up next.*

Removing the cloak entirely, Arianna reached back and locked the door, turning the sign to 'CLOSED.' She offered them a cautious smile. "Hello, my sisters. We have *lots* to talk about."

ACKNOWLEDGMENTS

It's not a leap that the title of this book refers to "Family," seeing as that my wealth of thanks goes to the ones I love. To begin, I would like to express my sincere appreciation to my oldest daughter, Izzabella. If it weren't for you, I wouldn't have started writing in the first place. You are my muse and my biggest supporter, and I thank you so much for never getting bored as I read out each and every chapter of this story for your thoughts and feedback.

I wish to thank the rest of my family for backing me up. We have had so many hardships throughout time, and I adore you for wanting me to create new, exciting, and adventurous realms to "play" in. You gave me the inspiration to write these characters, and I also thank you for listening to my endless chatter when it came to this book's creation.

Thank you to Talitha Cooper, my best friend and a truly hard-working mom who looks like a queen in my eyes. Thank you for being the first of my loved ones to read my manuscript; your feedback couldn't have made me more excited, proud, and determined to continue.

Lastly, my deepest gratitude goes out to Amy Lignor. I don't even know how or where to begin; saying she's an incredible editor doesn't do justice for what she has done in helping my book come to life. Something that started as a professional author and editor contract turned into someone who makes me brave and confident in my writing. When I didn't think it was good enough for the world, Amy gave me courage to continue writing and showed me that I was actually made for it. Thank you, Amy, for not only being my editor but someone I consider to be a sincere friend, and a colleague I will share the series with for a very long time.

ABOUT
ATMOSPHERE PRESS

Atmosphere Press is an independent, full-service publisher for excellent books in all genres and for all audiences. Learn more about what we do at atmospherepress.com.

We encourage you to check out some of Atmosphere's latest releases, which are available at Amazon.com and via order from your local bookstore:

Twisted Silver Spoons, a novel by Karen M. Wicks

Queen of Crows, a novel by S.L. Wilton

The Summer Festival is Murder, a novel by Jill M. Lyon

The Past We Step Into, stories by Richard Scharine

The Museum of an Extinct Race, a novel by Jonathan Hale Rosen

Swimming with the Angels, a novel by Colin Kersey

Island of Dead Gods, a novel by Verena Mahlow

Cloakers, a novel by Alexandra Lapointe

Twins Daze, a novel by Jerry Petersen

Embargo on Hope, a novel by Justin Doyle

Abaddon Illusion, a novel by Lindsey Bakken

Blackland: A Utopian Novel, by Richard A. Jones

The Jesus Nut, a novel by John Prather

The Embers of Tradition, a novel by Chukwudum Okeke

ABOUT THE AUTHOR

Born in one of the most stunning landscapes America has to offer – Juneau, Alaska – Amber Vonda was then raised in the small, quiet town of McCleary, Washington, with her two older brothers and one sister. Tragically losing her oldest brother at a very young age, Amber and family faced the hardship together. Moving forward in life, Amber was blessed with three amazing children who are the core of her world. When one of her beloveds was diagnosed with non-verbal autism, Amber's wealth of strength, courage, and huge heart took on the challenge, becoming a motivated stay-at-home mom. When she's not entertaining and finding fun things for her kids to do, she jogs with her two heeler pups or gets her hands dirty in the vegetable and flower gardens around her home. It was not a leap for Amber to enter into the literary realm, being that her own mind is constantly set on the "creative" channel. Inspired by her oldest daughter on a daily basis, a young girl who wished to write a book and loved brainstorming ideas with her mother, she asked Amber if she wished to write one, too. With that being said, Amber opened her laptop, released the ideas that were brewing, and typed until she had her first book written. "Family Crystals" is a fantasy that offers a tribe of unforgettable characters in action-packed realms that draw readers in from the first page to the last. It is also the start of a thrilling new series that will delight one and all for many books to come.

Made in the USA
Columbia, SC
25 September 2021